THE SILENT HAND

MICHAEL MERSAULT

T0007901

BAEN

THE SILENT HAND

A Baen Books Original

Baen Publishing Enterprises
P.O. Box 1403
Riverdale, NY 10471
www.baen.com

ISBN: 978-1-9821-9295-2

Cover art by Kurt Miller

First printing, October 2023

Distributed by Simon & Schuster
1230 Avenue of the Americas
New York, NY 10020

Library of Congress Cataloging-in-Publication Data

Names: Mersault, Michael, author.
Title: The silent hand / Michael Mersault.
Description: Riverdale, NY : Baen Books, 2023. | Series: The Deep Man trilogy ; 2 |
Identifiers: LCCN 2023028282 (print) | LCCN 2023028283 (ebook) | ISBN 9781982192952 (trade paperback) | ISBN 9781625799357 (ebook)
Subjects: LCGFT: Science fiction. | Space operas (Fiction) | Novels.
Classification: LCC PS3613.E7768 S55 2023 (print) | LCC PS3613.E7768 (ebook) | DDC 813/.6—dc23/eng/20230706
LC record available at https://lccn.loc.gov/2023028282
LC ebook record available at https://lccn.loc.gov/2023028283

Printed in the United States of America
10 9 8 7 6 5 4 3 2 1

To Jean Ann:

Though our shared childhood was no urchins' hell,

I was your Karl,

You were my Inga,

Tap Code and all . . .

THE SILENT HAND

Chapter 1

"The study of the Sinclair-Maru Family is a difficult thing, shrouded in secrecy and obfuscation, but much may be learned from the qualities of their tools...."

—Everest Compline, *Reflections*

DESPITE HER FEW YEARS, INGA MARU POSSESSED THE WISDOM born of hard necessity, a hyper-vigilance that utterly extinguished the innocence of childhood. On this special, terrible day, she sensed the eager excitement of her father seated across from her, his eyes shining as he picked at the tiny sores dotting his hands. His ebullience sickened Inga and prompted her to release her grip on Flops, resting the tattered little form upon her lap as she reached out to touch her siblings: dear Karl on her left, poor Mitzi on her right.

Inga's father, Lee, tried once again to engage the other occupants of the large, posh skimcar in what he viewed as conversation.

"Spaceport? Hah! Not so far now, but farther than you'd think. Am I right, Cousins? Yeah?"

Inga knew the six other occupants of the skimcar were not really her cousins despite sharing half a surname with them. In a rare moment of coherence, Father had once tried explaining how the powerful Sinclair-Maru Family owed their greatness to his great-great-grandaunt, Mia Maru. His pathetic exaggerations had prompted Inga's own research, and she now understood the

1

hopscotch of generations between the famous progenitors of the Sinclair-Maru House and her own humble birth.

A less perceptive child than Inga might not readily detect the distaste, the revulsion even, emanating from some of these high-class non-cousins as they shrank away from her father. Inga could not suppress the burn of shame, and could not blame them. Her hands felt the quivering in Mitzi and Karl; Mitzi sucking a finger and squeezing herself behind Inga's bony shoulder, while Karl just stared, hollow-eyed. Inga laid a hand upon each sibling, surreptitiously tapping her fingers on them, and they stilled, becoming attentive. She tapped again in unison a brief pattern in the secret code she had invented. Karl's sweaty hand grasped Inga's and he tapped his reply, while Mitzi merely nodded her head where it rested against Inga's shoulder. They blindly accepted their big sister's assurance: *Safe now.* Why wouldn't they? In their eyes Inga loomed: their protector, their provider, rather than a bruised and underfed ten-year old.

Inga looked across the skimcar at one of her strong-looking non-cousins in particular. She had noted him when they arrived to collect Inga and her family, his kindly expression the sympathetic conjunction of his brows, perhaps only a few years her senior. *Saef,* his classmates—his real cousins—had called him, and his gaze now held a question as it traveled from her hand up to her eyes. Inga inclined her head, hiding behind the disordered blond hedge of her hair until she felt him look away.

At that moment the skimcar passed through the tall double gates of the Battersea spaceport, a place Inga had never been, even sufficiently exotic to attract the interest of the five Sinclair-Maru youths. Their adult escort, Eldridge, did not even glance, his face a fixed mask of amiability.

"Spaceport?" Inga's father said, slapping his thighs repeatedly, his slack mouth wet. "Hah, spaceport. We—"

"Sarah?" Eldridge interrupted without turning his head.

"Yes, my lord?" one of the Sinclair-Maru youths replied.

"Name and class of every vessel you see, if you please."

Inga saw all five of her young non-cousins turn their focus outward to the collection of ships dotting the tarmac; four silent observers as Sarah began identifying and classifying each vessel.

This, Inga noted, effectively silenced her father, who muttered something inaudible, shrugging, no trace of his usual streetwise front remaining. She craned to see their path ahead weaving through a variety of craft, terminating at three large hangar doors sunk into a sort of hillside, a familiar crest over the arch. Any resident of Battersea's Port City knew the Sinclair-Maru crest on sight. Though they no longer stood among the greatest Families of the Imperium, on the planet of Battersea the Sinclair-Maru retained the fading brilliance of their former glory.

Inga eased back on her seat as they swept on through the cavernous hangar mouth, the girl, Sarah, breaking off in her recitation of ship names. The vehicle eased to a halt beside a pair of more human-scaled doors.

"Excellent, Sarah," their leader, Eldridge, said, looking at his students. "Debark and assemble, please."

The five youths stood nearly in unison, each clipping their training sword in place as the vehicle door sighed open, their neat uniforms adding to the martial air that clung to them. Like them, Inga and her siblings bore the right to the sword, Vested Citizens all, but Lee's cheap blade was the only survivor of their penury, Lee's dissolution. Instead, Inga, Mitzi, and Karl wore the black wristband of Citizenship, the outward sign of their *proud* right. Thus far in Inga's life that constituted a right to poverty and abuse, at times causing Inga to look with envy upon the lowly demi-cit residents in their comfortable domicile pods.

"If you please, sir," Eldridge said, beckoning to Lee as he stepped into the open expanse of the hangar beside his five young pupils. Lee stood, self-consciously straightening the rattling sword at his waist and running a hand across his garish shirt.

"Come on," Lee ordered without looking at Inga or her siblings. Inga lifted Flops from her lap, carefully holding its tattered, smelly form to her chest, its beaded eyes and long, cloth ears facing outward. She shouldered the satchel holding Mitzi's and Karl's meager belongings, and stood. Before Inga could lift her own bag, Mitzi seized her hand and buried her face in Inga's hip. Mitzi's fingers tapped out, *scared*, on Inga's hand. "Hold on to my shirt, Button," Inga whispered. "I've got to grab my kit."

Karl shrank back beside Inga, as the kind-eyed youngster, Saef, appeared at hand. "If I may, Mistress Maru," Saef said, lifting Inga's bag.

Inga eyed him carefully but said, "Thank you," as she nodded. Saef stepped back out into the hangar, Inga's mangy bag in hand, and Inga saw one of his classmates smirking to his fellows. Saef caught the exchanged look, too.

"Good manners amuse you, Omi?" Saef demanded of his *real* cousin.

Inga paused. She well knew a challenge when she heard one, and the Omi fellow seemed a trifle older and larger than Saef. In her experience, such a scenario generally resulted in a thrashing, at least in the dismal slum where failed Citizens like Inga's family lived.

Inga looked over at Eldridge standing beside her father, seemingly deaf and blind for the moment.

Omi opened his mouth, closed it, and then said, "No, Saef."

"Thought not," Saef said, motioning to Inga as Omi flushed.

Inga stepped into the hangar, Karl gripping her shirt on one side, Mitzi clenching her hand on the other, Flops bobbling against her bony chest.

"This way, please," Eldridge said, moving through the cavernous space toward a nearby door. Inga spared a look around the hangar, observing the spacecraft caged by gantries at one end. Even to her untrained eye the vessel seemed dated and worn; however, the peeled skin panels and half-assembled subsystems aided in that impression. Inga peered through the small door ahead as Eldridge led the way.

The room inside seemed elegant to Inga, with comfortable-looking couches on two walls below framed artwork, everything as clean as a storefront holo image. A low table in the center of the room held trays of food. Inga tore her eyes from the table, her mouth suddenly salivating.

Mitzi's thin face peeked around Inga's flank, finger still planted in her mouth, her nostrils quivering, scenting the air like some timid forest creature. *Hungry,* she tapped on Inga's hand. At almost the same moment Karl tapped the same word on Inga's other hand. Inga tapped back on both children: *Wait.* All three of them last ate the previous day at the Foundling Citizen's school, and many hours had passed since the provided juice and crackers.

"Please, sit," Eldridge said, and moved to an ornate door on the far side of the room.

"Hey now—" Lee began saying to Eldridge's retreating back, but the ornate door closed on his words. The Sinclair-Maru youths settled on one couch, closely packed, and Lee stood in place, swaying and rubbing his hands together, still staring at the closed door.

Inga led her siblings to the open couch, cautiously settling upon its soft, clean cushions. Mitzi and Karl stared fixedly at the food as they sat, pressing Inga from either side. Instead of sitting with his cousins, Saef stood at ease, his gaze still fixed upon Inga, Mitzi and Karl. After hesitating just a moment, Saef moved to the low table, loading two small plates, his every motion tracked by Mitzi and Karl's laser focus. Saef brought the plates and stood before Inga.

"A morsel for the youngsters, Mistress Maru?"

Karl and Mitzi stared at the pastries and cheese but made no move to accept the offered delicacies. In Inga's world gifts represented rather transparent tools of manipulation. She stared up into Saef's eyes for a long moment, seeing his confidence fade somewhat as uncertainty colored his cheeks. Mitzi and Karl seemed frozen, hardly breathing, while Lee did not shift from his place staring at the ornate door, lost in his own world.

"Thank you," Inga said at last, and Mitzi's finger popped from her mouth, her little hands receiving the plate as Karl followed suit. Saef seemed relieved at Inga's acceptance, while out of sight of his too-keen gaze, Inga tapped on Karl and Mitzi: *Slowly.*

As Saef stepped back, the ornate door opened and a young man strode into the room, clearly another of the Sinclair-Maru clan, perhaps a few years the senior of Saef, the lethal sword at his hip indicating his majority.

"Hugh!" Saef greeted, clearly surprised even as Saef's classmates called similar greetings, standing to their feet. "Didn't know you were planetside, Hugh."

Inga observed Hugh's unaffected smile as he greeted his younger cousins, but she did not miss the glance at Lee, or that longer look straight at her.

"Here now—" Lee began.

Hugh turned to Lee, his smile leaving. "If you please, sir, help yourself to some refreshments. They will see you shortly."

Lee frowned down at Hugh, a head taller and decades older. "If I please? *If I please?*"

Hugh seemed utterly unmoved by Lee's tone, only gesturing to the spread of food with an open hand.

Lee's gaze traveled to the food without much interest, and

Hugh directed his focus on Inga. "Mistress Maru? They will see you now."

Lee's head swiveled back to Hugh, his pale face suddenly suffused. "What? What? *Her?* No."

Hugh looked up without expression. "Please accept our hospitality, sir. They will see Mistress Maru now."

Lee's hands clenched and unclenched, and Inga cringed as she felt Mitzi and Karl shivering beside her, frozen in mid-chew. They knew the signs all too well.

"That so?" Lee snarled. "See *her* now? See her? What's she to say?" Lee pressed up to Hugh. "See *me* now, or take your—your highhanded ways to hell with you!"

Hugh remained devoid of expression, his shoulders relaxed, his face neutral "The door stands behind you, sir," Hugh said. "Consider your business with our Family concluded." Lee's instant transformation from rage to supplication twisted Inga's stomach.

"Well, now... well, hah-hah," Lee said, a sickly grin flickering upon his lips. "Just a—just a little... See her? Why not? Check the merchandise, right?"

Hugh barely took his eyes from Lee to gesture for Inga. "Mistress Maru?"

Inga began to stand, feeling Mitzi and Karl clenching onto her from both sides, when Saef appeared at hand again. "Perhaps your brother, sister, and I shall eat all the food while you take a stroll," he said in an even voice. He looked at Mitzi then Karl. "Or shall we save her just a little?" Saef settled on the couch, and Inga felt her siblings easing their grip. She tapped a brief message to both and then stood, Flops clenched to her chest.

As she walked through the ornate door, she cast one rearward look. The poisonous glare Lee aimed at her set her purpose in stone.

The door closed behind Inga as she sized up the three adults that all stared at her, waiting. Eldridge and the older woman she recognized, while the third man she had never seen, and he seemed to frown as he lowered his gaze to Flops in her arms.

"You remember me, right?" the woman said without preamble.

Inga nodded. "You're Bess Sinclair-Maru. Saw you at the school."

"A silly question, I suppose," Bess said, "considering your memory."

Inga said nothing, squeezing Flops tight.

The unknown third man, a bald fellow, thinner and taller than

Eldridge, cleared his throat. "It is a pleasure to meet you, child," he said in a rather whispery voice. "I am Kai, yet a member of the Sinclair-Maru Family...unless I am disowned after today's activities."

Bess and Kai sat, while Eldridge stood, his hands behind his back, his poise erect. Eldridge gestured to a chair. "Please, rest your feet."

Inga sat, studying Bess and Kai through the screen of her anarchic bangs. Bess seemed unchanged since Inga last saw her: quite old, but striking, serious, with the corded neck and thick wrists of a retired athlete. Kai's face betrayed some hint of disapproval or skepticism.

"You know why you're here?" Bess asked, resting her hands upon the sheathed sword across her knees.

Inga looked from Bess to Kai and back. "You are buying me."

Kai's eyebrows shot upward, his bald skull wrinkling. Bess offered only a faint smile. "One cannot be bought or sold in the Imperium, child. Slavery is not permitted within the Myriad Worlds."

Inga's gaze traveled to the painting upon the wall above Bess. "The Manumission Accord," Inga said as she tried to make out the signature scrawled at the painting's lower edge, ever curious.

"What?" Kai asked.

Inga looked back down, at Kai, then lower, at Kai's odd boots. "The Manumission Accord of 5049," she said, wondering if these three upper-crust Citizens actually believed what they said. People were bought and sold all the time where Inga grew up, with or without the Manumission Accord.

"That is correct," Bess said, glancing sidelong at Kai before turning her focus back on Inga. "So we cannot buy you. I can offer you a place, a position, and that is all."

"And Mitzi and Karl?"

"As we discussed some time ago," Bess said, "your siblings do not possess the qualities that interest us. But I will find a situation for them if you require it."

"I do," Inga said.

Kai frowned. "While we are making demands, what else do you want, Mistress Maru?"

"She knows what I want," Inga said, pulling Flops up to her chin and nodding toward Bess.

"It will be very challenging for you," Bess said, "with no time for fun and games."

Inga stared, wondering if they had any idea what comprised her nightmarish days and nights. "I don't care."

"There will be pain. You will come to hate me."

Inga shook her head, looking down. "No. Make me strong, like you, make a—a place for Mitzi and Karl . . . and I will die for you."

Kai smiled. "Strong words, child. I've seen your test scores, but Bess runs ahead of me. I am not entirely persuaded that you are what we seek."

Bess turned toward Kai with obvious displeasure. "She is perfect."

Inga felt her heart skip a beat. *Perfect.*

"She's clutching a doll, Bess, or had you overlooked that? Where does that fit with the psych makeup we are so enamored with?"

Bess turned back to Inga. "Why do you carry that toy, child?"

"*Why?*" Kai demanded of Bess. "It's obviously a self-soothing fixation for—"

Kai broke off and all three adults locked onto Inga, staring at the rough blade she had materialized. It fit her small hand perfectly, the hours she had invested honing the blade's rough length to a razor's edge apparent. Before anyone said a word, Inga stabbed the crude weapon into Flops, slicing through layers of fabric, pulling a wire free from the jagged wound. A sharp tug popped the beady eyes from its misshapen skull and a battered device from its fluff-filled torso.

Inga held the device up by the wires, the beads of Flop's eyes terminating each fork. She cast the eviscerated husk aside and hid her crude dagger away once again.

"What is that?" Eldridge said, staring at the battered case and patchwork of rough electronic repairs.

Inga said nothing for a moment and Bess filled the silence. "A very old vidcapture device, if I'm not mistaken." She looked from the tangle of wires to Inga's face. "Where did you get that?"

"The rubbish," Inga said, leaning slowly forward until Bess reached out to grasp the device. "I mended it."

"Concealed it within your toy and wired the input through the eyes," Kai's thin voice said. "Most enterprising, but why?"

Inga stared at Bess for a long moment before looking down at her dirty little shoes dangling above the floor. Inga shrugged.

Bess moved slowly, actuating the replay function. Inga looked up, seeing the glimmer of light reflecting from the older woman's dark eyes, knowing precisely what she saw: a vidstream journal of abuse, desecration.

Bess passed the device to Kai, her jaw clenched, and Eldridge leaned near to see. They only watched the images for a moment when Eldridge straightened, transforming as Inga watched, all hints of his former urbane ease vanishing, his hand dropping to the well-worn pommel of his sword.

"No," Bess said. "Let Hugh do it."

Eldridge frowned. "Hugh is a child."

"It will be a duel, not an execution," Bess said. "This...man possesses the advantage of height, weight, and reach over Hugh. No stain will attach to the Family, even without the formality of seconds and deliberation."

Eldridge reluctantly nodded, his hand slipping from his sword. His eyes flickered, Inga recognizing that he sent a message via his implanted User Interface to someone, likely Hugh.

Bess spoke: "Do you understand what is happening?" Inga nodded, and Bess steadily regarded her, meeting Inga's eyes. "If you...intervene, I will see your father spared."

Inga did not hesitate, shaking her head. Bess slowly nodded.

A moment later, the door opened and Inga turned to see Lee and Hugh entering the room. Behind them, Inga caught a glimpse of Mitzi and Karl, still chewing as Saef entertained them, a napkin folded into a bird.

Lee gave Inga's face one searching look as Hugh closed the door, his expression transforming in an instant. "She is a liar!" Lee shouted.

Inga jerked in her seat, steeling herself, but Hugh struck out, slapping Lee hard across the mouth. Lee staggered and Hugh followed, his young face pale but composed. He slapped Lee again, a ringing blow that spun Lee's head.

"Say it," Hugh said, slapping again, his voice strangely level. Lee's right hand fell to the pommel of his cheap sword, and seeing this, Hugh said, "Have you forgotten the words?"

Lee staggered back, wiping blood from his lips, rage and defiance battling fear. "No," Lee said. "She lies."

Hugh raised his hand, staring up at the taller man, and Lee's clouded eyes seemed to clear as he looked down at the youth who challenged him. "My—my honor is taken," he growled.

Hugh's hand dropped and he straightened. "Regain what you may. I will meet you...Citizen. Here...now."

Kai stepped near to Inga as she watched Hugh draw his sword, pacing away from Lee and swinging his arm, his face paler still. Lee's lips mumbled an endless angry chain of syllables as he faced his smaller, younger opponent.

"Come with me, Mistress Maru," Kai murmured, leading her to the door. Bess remained seated, her arms folded, her lips pursed. Flops yet lay, eviscerated and cast off, prostrate upon the floor.

The door closed behind Inga and Kai, her past suddenly sealed within its ornate wood, seemingly wiped away at last.

Mitzi and Karl still chewed and stared owl-eyed at Inga, the faint smile of greeting fading from Saef's boyish mouth, and Kai spoke, addressing the Sinclair-Maru youths, "Thank you, Cousins. You may return to Lykeios Manor now."

The youths stood uncertainly from the couch, darting puzzled looks at the ornate door, detecting an unfolding drama. Saef did not lift his gaze from Inga. No sound penetrated from the adjoining room, though Inga strained to hear as she returned Saef's measuring regard.

"Eldridge will rejoin you later," Kai continued in his thin voice. "Your investment of time today is appreciated."

Saef's companions filed toward the door. "Do you stay, Mistress Maru?" Saef asked. "Or do you return home too?"

Inga's straining ears detected a sound beyond the door. Was it a clash of blades? She shook her head. "I have no home now," she said, but her attention remained locked upon the invisible conflict. Could that young Hugh *really* best her father? Despite Lee's dissolution she knew he possessed a savagery that had surprised more than one rival.

She felt and heard a solid thump, muted though it was. Someone had fallen. Could it truly be over? A subtle quivering seemed to fill Inga's chest and she felt Mitzi and Karl shifting beside her, even as she observed the faint, satisfied nod from Kai.

It was over, but Saef—young Saef—gazed down at her uncomprehending, his eyes searching her face as she finally focused upon him. She saw it with wonder, her breath catching, knowing Saef might just grasp the edges of the drama remaking Inga's life: A tear escaped the corner of his eye and he brushed it away. Mitzi and Karl seemed equally transfixed, staring up at him, though they continued to chew.

"What...what is happening to you?" Saef said, wiping again at his eyes.

"Do not concern yourself, Cousin," Kai said. "Your vehicle awaits."

Saef straightened, nodding, and Inga stared at him, striving to speak, but her voice, her words failed her. Internally, silently she called out. After so many years of human indifference this shocking, precious gift arrived, christening her new life: tears from the stony heart of the Sinclair-Maru.

To Saef's retreating back she cried, *I will never forget*, but her mouth did not move, the words remaining unspoken within her.

Chapter 2

"While academics—particularly demi-cit academics—can enumerate the many evils attendant to the Great Families of the Imperium, it is worth noting that aside from any other societal impact, large, supportive Families demonstrate real advantages in producing well adjusted, emotionally sound individuals . . . notwithstanding plenty of anecdotal evidence to the contrary."

—Dr. Ramsay Stirling Attenborough, *Ivory Tower Follies*

A PERCEPTIVE EYE MIGHT YET GLIMPSE THAT HALF-STARVED young girl lurking within the slender, collected form of Fleet Chief Inga Maru. The blond hair remained, though cut shorter and domesticated somewhat, and the feral gleam never diminished through the fifteen standard years that had passed. If anything, the hard edge of Inga's childhood had become sharpened, honed by the secret ways of the Sinclair-Maru.

True to their word that day at the Battersea spaceport, Kai and Bess Sinclair-Maru had retained the three freshly orphaned waifs, sending them out to Hawksgaard, the vast Family base in the Battersea asteroid belt. There Inga alone received the full birthright of one born to the Family: rigid education on the normal range of academic topics, harsh training in Family doctrine and combatives, and the secret weapon of the Sinclair-Maru: an implanted scaram fear generator. Like all Family adepts, Inga mastered the scaram, finding the Deep Man, the internal island of calm even as the scaram pulsed primal terror into the deepest regions of the brain.

"All fear is fear of the unknown," Family progenitor Devlin Sinclair-Maru wrote in *Integrity Mirror,* the guidebook of Family doctrine, *"since we cannot know the unknown, we must know fear..."* The path to the Deep Man.

Like every Sinclair-Maru youth in the more than six hundred years since Devlin wrote those words, Inga knew fear, and she overcame its control, its paralysis. And that was merely the beginning for her.

Upon achieving her majority, with both blue eyes wide open, Inga accepted experimental electronic and biological enhancements from the Family biotech program. Unlike the others before her, Inga survived the augmentation, though she continually battled internal powers that threatened to consume her body and mind. For the moment she held sway, master of the forces she employed.

Finally, trained and enhanced to become the secret weapon of the Sinclair-Maru Family, armed with a technical rating in Fleet, she had returned to Battersea right at the key juncture in Family history. After centuries of decline, its loyalty forgotten by the new faces of the Imperial Family, the Sinclair-Maru grasped at a chance—a bare chance—to restore the Family fortunes.

Inga would ever remember the day when she entered Lykeios Manor, the grand estate constructed by her great-great-great-grandaunt, Mia Maru, and Mia's husband, Devlin Sinclair. After fifteen years, it was also the day Inga saw Saef Sinclair-Maru once again, a sober and robust man now, only hints of the kind boy from her childhood remaining. On that day their halting new partnership had formed—a professional partnership only—commanded by Bess, and in those few short months they had worked together they had wrought great deeds.

With Saef obtaining his Fleet captaincy even as the Imperium mobilized its response to the recent insurrection, he was perfectly placed to bring the Family back to prominence. His additional, hidden role as a secret agent for the Imperial Intelligence service would have represented an unconscionable burden, but for Inga. Serving in the visible role of the captain's cox'n, she had employed the full range of her talents, rooting out spies and assassins, collecting nuggets of information, and leaving a string of fallen enemies in her merciless wake. Bess had made Inga strong, and true to her childish oath fifteen year earlier, Inga would die for the Family—and she nearly had. But before Inga might accept her end, she intended to see every threat to the Family laid low.

As Inga leaned against a wall and surveyed spectators around the dueling ring, she pondered that very thought: Every threat to the *Family*? Or every threat to Saef?

As long as the Family's interests and Saef's remained aligned, no conflict existed, but if goals diverged she pondered where her loyalties attached, and if that attachment issued from her so-called heart, not her rational mind.

Inga felt the grip of that attachment even as she observed Saef step into the ring, his sword rising, ready, facing his opponent.

Like all Vested Citizens, Inga ostensibly adhered to the Honor Code as laid down by Emperor Yung I, but she felt certain she now witnessed its deliberate abuse by forces determined to destroy Saef Sinclair-Maru.

Saef met his opponent's attack, their blades clashing as Saef fell back, his movements stunted and controlled in the odd microgravity his opponent had dictated for their duel. Inga felt her pulse increase as she woodenly observed, her cloak shrouding the futile arsenal strapped to her person; Saef now lived or died by the virtue of his own skill alone.

For years few Citizens would willingly enter a duel with Saef... after he rather unfashionably killed the first handful of duelists who dared to challenge him. Now three separate affronts had been cast in Saef's teeth within a few short weeks, leaving him little choice under his strict reading of the Honor Code.

Each affront, Inga felt certain, formed a part of a deliberate strategy by some singular hand, invisibly directing affairs to eliminate Saef, all under the cover of assumed legality. By provoking Saef's challenge, each of Saef's opponents held the choice of "location," which generally meant the gravitational force under which the duel was fought, corresponding to territories among the Myriad Worlds. Now three duels, three different gravity extremes, as someone sought to expose a weakness in Saef's skill. She understood Saef's vaunted abilities, she had trained for years with and against the masters of the Sinclair-Maru style, and she perceived each potential weakness Saef's foe might exploit. These were the weaknesses she would exploit in such a contest, and the very idea of a blade slipping past Saef's guard made Inga's mouth go dry.

Surely the man facing Saef had trained exclusively in this particular gravity setting, Inga observed, obtaining some mastery of its particular impact upon a duel. Still, Saef managed to hold his own, always reliant upon the Sinclair-Maru's domination of fear...the Deep Man. Circling to his right, Saef parried in a languid motion that made Inga clench her teeth, his immediate counter a controlled lunge.

Inga scanned the small crowd, checking the two Sinclair-Maru security operatives once again. They remained undistracted by the drama below, both watching for threats outside the dueling ring.

A muted babble from the spectators brought Inga's focus back to the duel. Saef had switched his blade to his left hand, and Inga could not tell if he had done so due to an injury, or in a live-hand technique to confound his foe. The blades clashed high, both men jerking strangely from the impact in low gravity, and Saef immediately rolled his wrist, the point of his razor-sharp blade descending, seeming to part his opponent's shirt front with deceptive slowness.

The foe's sword point dropped, then clattered to the ground as the man suddenly clutched at his spilling entrails, and Saef stepped back, foregoing a finishing cut. His opponent might yet survive.

Every other duel Saef fought ended with the death of his foe. *Why mercy now?* Inga wondered as she moved to join Saef, pulling a food bar from her belt pouch and leading her six-legged dumb-mech scampering along behind.

Claude Carstairs, Saef's elegant childhood friend, had once again served as Saef's second. Like Inga, Claude wore a cloak, but where Inga's dark garment shrouded and concealed, Claude's flowed, accentuating his gold-and-white sartorial glory.

"Very messy, Saef," Claude declared, his handsome features wearing a rare frown. "Can't say I'm pleased. Expected better of you, I must say."

Saef belted his pistol in place and slid into his uniform jacket before looking up, glancing momentarily at Inga before answering Claude. "I'm still alive, Claude. I daresay that seems rather satisfying to me."

Claude waved a dismissive hand. "Of course, of course, and that's always nice. I'm shockingly attached to you. Been friends forever. But really, Saef, who's going to watch this duel on the Nets now? Who? I mean, look—" Claude looked over his shoulder where a medico labored to save the fallen duelist. Claude cringed at the sight and looked back to Saef. "Gods! You've let the fellow's vile plumbing make a damned eyesore everywhere. No one wants to see all that, and if you think they do, I'll tell you to your face that you're wrong."

"I'll strive to do better in the future, Claude," Saef said.

Claude shook his head and sighed. Saef possessed so many unfashionable traits that Claude sometimes despaired. Along with Saef's unfortunate tendency to wear a displeasing frown, he had also recently refused to spend any of his new fortune in prize money on anything *useful*. And now this: a disgustingly visceral end to what could have been a delightful sensation on the Nets.

"I'd like to say you've put my mind at ease, Saef, really I would," Claude said, "but you haven't an ounce of sense; I vow it's true."

"We need to move," Inga interjected, her gaze sliding across the small crowd, noting the agitated Sinclair-Maru security agents over-watching.

"What?" Claude demanded. "Skipping the party again? I really should not be surprised."

"We attended your excellent party just last week," Saef said.

"Last week—!"

"Baby steps," Saef interrupted Claude's windup. "Baby steps, Claude."

Saef smiled at Claude's confounded expression, and turned for the door, Inga and the dumb-mech in train.

"Baby steps indeed," Claude declared, staring after Saef's departing figure for a moment before glancing at the two Sinclair-Maru security operatives threading through the dispersing crowd. "Not an ounce of sense," Claude mused, then grimaced at the fallen duelist sprawled and leaking close at hand. "Gods!"

Like most Vested Citizens, Saef carried an implanted electronics package at the base of his skull that received constant information from whatever Nets broadcast in any given location, and a variety of User Interfaces could stream that information and various functions across his optic nerve in a ghostly, glowing richness. Saef unfailingly blanked his UI before and during duels, thus it was some time after their departure that Saef received a message that halted him in his tracks.

"What's wrong?" Inga asked, sliding to one side, the subtle click of her compact submachine gun issuing from the depths of her concealing cloak. The dumb-mech clattered to a halt close beside.

Saef's eyes flickered. "Message. Cabot's planetside."

Inga glanced at the Family security agents shadowing, then back to Saef. "Here? Imperial City?"

"Yes. Requesting my presence at the Family Trade apartments. Unprecedented, really." Saef shrugged. Cabot led the Family once again, since Bess fell to an attempted assassination some weeks prior, and as the eldest member of the Sinclair-Maru, Cabot was no stranger to his leadership role. Despite his centuries of experience, and his obvious brilliance, Cabot's cold and supercilious style found little favor with Saef. Until Bess emerged from the extensive reconstruction and rejuv, Cabot would likely retain the Family reins...even assuming that Bess regained her keen intellect right along with her restored body.

Inga looked down the thinly populated street, seeing the towers of the Imperial Close in the glimmering distance, while the arc of the glowing ribbon soared to Core Alpha shining down from orbit above. She looked back to Saef. "We need to dash by our lodging," she said, "then to Cabot."

Saef nodded slowly. "Very well, Maru."

They set off again, the dumb-mech trotting alongside.

The Fleet officers' lodging somehow avoided the clutch-fisted appearance of most Fleet facilities in Imperial City, providing very tasteful apartments for visiting officers, even furnishing utilitarian quarters for attending staff. Leaving their Sinclair-Maru escort at the door, Inga only waited to round the corner before saying, "I'm afraid you'll want to give me Devlin's old body shield before we go visiting Cabot."

Saef looked sidelong at Inga and raised his eyebrows. As he opened his mouth, Inga said, "Best not ask, I think."

Saef closed his mouth and nodded again. "I daresay, Maru."

If any other person had made the request Saef would have sifted their motives, likely at the point of a weapon. The body shield represented a miracle of Shaper technology, and the Family had treasured their sole unit, purchased centuries earlier during their opulent glory years. Bess had bestowed this rare and expensive tool upon Saef, and, as long as he wore the nearly undetectable emitter, he possessed a measure of immunity from high-speed kinetic projectiles. In the prior weeks, Devlin's old heirloom had preserved Saef's skin more than once.

Safely ensconced in his apartment, Saef stripped out of his jacket and uniform shirt, peeling the thin gray emitter from his low back. He handed it to Inga. "We need to be quick, I think, Maru," Saef said as he slipped back into his shirt. "Those security yobs will be giving Cabot an earful."

She smiled as the body shield disappeared within her cloak. "Wouldn't do to keep Cabot waiting."

"Exactly."

Inga herded the dumb-mech out the door. "See you in the vestibule in a flash, Captain."

As the door shut behind Inga, Saef quickly hustled back into his uniform and set back out, feeling strangely naked after wearing the body shield virtually every moment of the many weeks since Bess had provided it.

Waiting in the quarterdeck-style vestibule, Saef pondered Cabot's presence so far from the Family seat back on Battersea. Only Family Fleet candidates and members of the Family Trade delegation commonly visited Core system and Imperial City, so far from their sphere of power in Battersea system. Saef mused that Cabot could be overseeing some Trade operation; certainly the Shapers' trade armada was likely to arrive in the coming months, and the Sinclair-Maru finally held a somewhat promising hand in that approaching flurry. But the unpleasant sensation in the pit of Saef's gut presaged a less pleasant purpose in Cabot's appearance.

Though Cabot remained steadfastly youthful in capability and appearance (the recipient of full rejuv treatments back in the Family's glory days) the decades of his Family leadership stretched back through the previous century. Bess, a member of a younger generation, had only held the reins a short time before the attack, but between them Saef greatly preferred the more personable style Bess employed. He did not anticipate a delightful interview now.

When Inga emerged in the vestibule moments later, Saef was in the midst of weighing his preference for Bess, as fairly as he could: Was it perhaps the deceptive signs of age she wore, though having a fraction of Cabot's years? No, he thought not. She truly possessed a potent combination of insight and vitality—passion even—and that seemed a rare quality among the Sinclair-Maru, particularly those like Cabot, in whom the passing centuries seemed to have baked the remaining humanity from his flesh.

"Dark musings?" Inga inquired as she shooed the dumb-mech ahead.

Saef shook his head and turned toward the door.

"Oh, Captain?" Inga said. "Do you happen to know where Devlin's old gift is?"

Saef turned back, perplexed, having handed her the shield generator just minutes before. "Do I—? Well, no, I suppose not."

"Excellent," Inga said, smiling broadly. "Do bear that in mind."

On these rather cryptic words they set out, making their way toward the Family apartments, the Sinclair-Maru security operatives shadowing their progress.

One reform instituted by Bess during her brief reign as Family head involved the Trade enclave. Their offices and apartments received a generous investment, bringing them to a level of luxury more suitable for a Great House. To Saef's admittedly jaundiced eye, Saef's older brother, Richard, seemed one of the chief beneficiaries. As Saef and Inga entered the Family enclave, closely accompanied by the dumb-mech, they were met by a pair of stoic members of Security—both distant cousins to Saef—and beside them, Richard. The barely concealed gleam of triumph in Richard's eyes confirmed Saef's misgivings about their coming interview.

"Chief Maru," Richard greeted politely, nodding toward Inga. "Saef." Richard smirked down. "Cabot's been waiting."

Through his long use of low-gravity sessions, Richard stood taller than the other Sinclair-Maru, and his height, his colorful finery, and his blond hair all combined to divide him from the general Family mold. Richard had long argued that the centuries-long decline of the Sinclair-Maru owed as much to the Family's near-heavyworlder image as it did to anything. In contrast, Saef and practically all his cousins continued to follow Family doctrine as laid down in Devlin's secret guide, *Integrity Mirror*. As prescribed, they gained the robust strength provided through extensive high-gravity training, despite the impact on their potential height. This created a certain uniformity among the Family that Richard scorned to follow.

"Chief Maru," Richard said, "if you would take some refreshment in the lounge..." He waved a graceful hand toward the adjoining chamber.

Saef momentarily considered pushing back on their peremptory separation, but Inga's line-of-sight message (once again composed with no visible movement from Inga) pinged into Saef's UI: BETTER THIS WAY.

"How charming," Inga said aloud. "Refreshments in the *lounge*. What could be finer?"

"Yes," Richard said, eyeing Inga, suspecting mockery in her words. He turned to Saef. "Saef, this way."

After a glance at Inga, Saef fell in beside Richard. "Losing your touch, brother?" Richard said over his shoulder. "I hear the latest victim of your barbarism survived."

"It seemed sufficient."

"Three duels in how many weeks?" Richard continued. "Do you have any idea what an absurd, unsophisticated figure you make of yourself?"

"Perhaps you forget, Richard, 'Sophistication is a useful veneer,' and little more." Richard turned, flushing at the familiar line. "Oh, you do remember the old words," Saef said, smiling.

His color heightened, Richard shot back, "I remember, but I don't pretend it's Holy Writ."

Saef placed a hand on Richard's arm, his fingers pressing into that meager lightworld sinew. "No, brother, you pretend that we live in a gentler age, but we don't. Old Devlin still reads true: Savagery is just at hand."

Richard jerked his arm away from Saef's grasp, contempt and chagrin battling across his face. "Cabot's waiting." Richard nodded toward the door. "You may indeed find some savagery at hand."

Fear rarely found much purchase in Saef, his mastery of the Deep Man quelling fear's cold grip in an instant, but as he stepped into the study with Cabot, Saef certainly felt an unpleasant internal stirring.

The door closed behind Saef as he observed Cabot seated at a broad wooden desk, a wide portfolio in his hands. "My lord," Saef greeted respectfully.

Cabot did not even look up, in no way acknowledging Saef's presence, nor offering either of the open seats to him. Saef felt a flash of anger. Not so many days before, Saef had commanded the Fleet frigate IMS *Tanager*, taking her into a combat zone where enemies perished, a plot was revealed, and a fortune in prize money fell into his hands. He did not lightly accept disrespect, and the string of lethal duels in his wake made this clear to even the meanest intelligence.

Saef felt his jaw clenching as he stared at Cabot's profile. As always, Cabot adopted a refined wardrobe in somber colors, his dark hair cut short and neatly coiffed, with only a touch of gray at his temples. Except for a certain severity, Cabot might even be considered handsome.

Cabot placed the portfolio on his desk and looked up at Saef. "You may sit." Cabot nodded toward the open seats.

"If you please, my lord, I'll stand."

Cabot made no reply to this, his acid gaze sweeping slowly over Saef, from his tall boots to the well-worn pommel of his sword, over Saef's Fleet uniform, pausing at the new service ribbon, then up to Saef's face. Saef interpreted Cabot's expression as faintly disdainful.

"You emerge unscathed from yet another duel, I see," Cabot said, lifting an amber decanter and filling a single small glass. Saef inclined his head and waited. "Permit me to say that your apparent thirst to exterminate your fellow man argues a certain brutish simplicity I find distasteful."

Puzzled and angry, Saef said, "As you know, I merely follow the Honor Code, as any Vested Citizen should, my lord."

Cabot drank from his glass as he calmly regarded Saef. "The Code... Of course. And you rise to any bait, it seems."

Saef felt another flash of anger. "On the contrary, my lord, I respond to disrespect so blatant it cannot be ignored. A *calculated* disrespect in these recent duels, I believe."

Cabot nodded, musing, his eyes downcast and reflective. "Calculated disrespect. Calculated." He looked up. "An interesting expression, and one which we will revisit momentarily. Strive to recall it at that time, but first to your assiduous—no—your *obsessive* adherence to the Honor Code..."

Cabot sipped from his glass and slowly stood, while Saef felt his blood stirring between consternation and righteous indignation.

"Tell me, Saef," Cabot said, "who profits most in a blade culture: the strong, or the weak?"

Indignation rose to dominance as Saef replied, "Both Devlin and the *Legacy Mandate* address the ascendant virtue of courage."

"No doubt you will answer my question when the mood strikes you," Cabot said in a cold tone.

Saef flushed, feeling a schoolchild before Cabot. "The strong, my lord," Saef bit out.

"The strong indeed." Cabot slowly swirled the remaining liquor in his glass, seeming to study glints of light in its amber depths. "I wonder...would you be so violently protective of your honor if the Family had not put such strength in your hands?"

Cold seemed to fill Saef's chest. "My lord, you suggest that my skill has made me predatory."

Cabot regarded Saef, his face devoid of expression. "Perhaps worse than that; it seems your skill has made you a moralizing prig."

"Sir?"

"There is no one more insufferable than one who believes he is infallible. They may even indulge in—what was the expression?—oh, yes, 'calculated disrespect,' and all the while they believe themselves above reproach."

"I cannot pretend to understand your meaning, my lord."

"Can you not?" Cabot said, resuming his seat and placing his glass upon the desk. "Now why am I so certain that you're self-justified to the point of nobility, when all I—a poor sinner—see is the theft of Family wealth?"

"*Theft?*" Saef demanded, thunderstruck.

"Unless you intend to separate yourself from the Sinclair-Maru, and form your own House, yes, *theft*," Cabot said. "Millions of credits spent on personal medical pursuits. Quite shocking."

Awareness struck Saef and the blood drained from his face. "My lord! I neither profited nor benefited in any way from—"

Cabot flicked a dismissive hand. "Of course you didn't. Noble prigs always spend other people's money on the most heartrending of worthy causes. It cements them in their sense of righteous infallibility."

Saef felt the rare sensation of ground eroding beneath his feet. Was Cabot's claim wildly unjust and heartless? Or was it insightful to the point of clairvoyance?

"You do not separate yourself from the Family, Saef?" Cabot asked in a disinterested tone.

"I—of course not, my lord," Saef said, reeling from the question. "I feel that—"

"I am not at all interested in your emotions."

"But we speak of Bess, her life. Her life!" Saef's only expenditure from his prize money was for Bess's medical reconstruction, a decision he made on his own authority without Family consultation.

Cabot tasted from his glass, regarding Saef under lidded eyes. "Bess chose to spend her life for the Family. A noble sacrifice. You chose to contradict her and usurp my authority."

Never had Saef perceived the weight of Cabot's centuries as he did at that moment.

"The past, however," Cabot continued, "is behind us. We turn now to the living moment. You are to assume command of another Fleet vessel, I understand."

"Yes, my lord."

"You shall do so without a single credit of Family funds."

Saef contained his outburst with some difficulty, finally managing: "You doom me to failure from the outset, then."

Cabot shook his head, a faint ironic smile in evidence. "Dramatic predictions are ever the hallmark of youth," he said. "I do you a signal favor, and if you do not manage to contrive on your own, you may certainly cast it in my teeth."

Saef found no comfort in Cabot's words. No matter what Cabot believed, one could not successfully crew or captain a Fleet warship without capital. "With all respect, my lord, it seems you do not fully understand the situation. Rather than a favor, you cut my legs from beneath me, and as I lose, so the Family loses."

Cabot nodded gently, staring at Saef. "I applaud your restraint," he said in a dry voice. "I know you burn to throw your recent success at my head, along with the successful gamble Bess risked in you."

Since that was precisely the thought fueling Saef's indignation, he felt another shock, another wave of chagrin.

"Nonetheless," Cabot continued, "you will soldier on without the Family purse strings, hopefully now dislodged from your path to sainthood."

Saef shook his head, speechless, utterly hollow inside.

Cabot fixed Saef with a penetrating look. "Before you leave, Saef, I have just one question for you." He leaned back, folding his hands. "Where is Devlin's old body shield?"

Caught completely off guard, Saef found a purchase upon Inga's earlier question and latched on. "I—I don't know where it is, my lord."

Chapter 3

"Must I continue as the sole voice of reason within the academy? We, of all people in the Imperium, should remain aware of history, even if all others forget. New theories, new works of scholarship cannot change the fact: Fifty percent of the nonhuman sentient species we have encountered attempted our extermination on sight. If the House system and the Honor Code created ten times the burden upon the Imperium, it would still be a worthy investment if it spared one human world from incineration."

—Dr. Ramsay Stirling Attenborough, *Ivory Tower Follies*

FOR A SYSTEM GENERALLY DEEMED OF LITTLE IMPORTANCE BY Imperial Intelligence, the squadron dispatched to Delta Three constituted a significant power. At its core, the expedition force carrier, *Harrier*, brought immense capability to bear on the impending planetary assault, while substantial supporting vessels provided security from any ship-to-ship threats that might materialize.

Only weeks earlier, IMS *Tanager*, captained by Saef Sinclair-Maru, had barely survived a daring raid on this same system, dropping and collecting a small detachment of Marines, and seizing a prize so rich that his entire crew might retire on the proceeds. The mute testimony of *Tanager*'s violence remained visible: the wreckage of two smaller vessels tumbling through tortured orbits, and Delta Three's orbital station blackened and scarred in small patches.

Numerous Fleet officers surveyed the remains of *Tanager*'s combat, shaking heads in amazement. How such an antiquated and unimpressive frigate wrought such havoc seemed nearly beyond belief. A minority of the observers attributed this to the warlike mystique of the Sinclair-Maru, others to the impressive reputation of Susan Roush, *Tanager*'s executive officer, and still more saw only the capricious winds of fate profiting the manifestly undeserving.

As *Harrier* slid into high orbit, thoughts of avarice occupied many minds among the high-ranking, while those preparing for a ground invasion—those of less elevated rank among the Legion troops—remained grimly fixed upon the violent welcome they were likely soon to receive on Delta Three's surface.

Corporal Kyle Whiteside sorted his equipment again, just like all the other Molo Rangers and Legionnaires filling one of *Harrier*'s vast troop bays. As he leaned over to recheck his Molo's diagnostic screen he smelled his own fear-laden sweat trickling beneath his armor, hoping none of the dread he felt appeared on his face. Fang, Whiteside's Molo, felt nothing, of course, being little more than a ruggedized dumb-mech, fully compliant with the Thinking Machine Protocols. Fang possessed barely enough processing power to hustle its six articulated legs over rough terrain, trailing along behind or beside its operator. It could neither identify nor engage any enemy, and would sit idly by as Corporal Whiteside begged for assistance. It was merely a tool.

Still, Whiteside thought to himself, man and Molo together made a lethal combination. The human provided the intelligence and initiative, while the Molo carried a modular load that could comprise one of a variety of heavy weapons, countermeasure suites, tools, or simply supplies. The Molo Rangers would be a tough nut for any enemy to crack. Whiteside said this to himself over and over as the seconds crept by, their drop into hostile fire inching nearer.

Lieutenant Sun felt it too, perhaps worse. He kept threading through the contu, talking about *the edge of the sword*, and *the point of the spear*, but Whiteside figured Sun should just tell it to the mirror. Otherwise he might soon devolve to *the knot of the club*, or perhaps *the tooth of the dog*, even.

The others coped in their own ways, it seemed, and with reasonable success from Whiteside's perspective. Or perhaps they all possessed more natural courage than Corporal Kyle Whiteside did. The instructors back in Ground Combat School always said that when the moment came they would find comfort in their training. Whiteside couldn't say he felt much comfort; he even reviewed lessons within the privacy of his UI, trying to allay the uneasy thumping of his heart. There was the lesson on area fire, the Four Common Methods of Ambush, Counter-Ambush Techniques Made Easy (which included a useful acronym to recall the proper order) and the all-important Basics of Planetary Drops.

"Why we doing this, eh, Corporal?" Spec Pippi Tyrsdottir asked, interrupting Whiteside's tortured thoughts. "Tell me this again."

Whiteside, jarred from his private anxiety, glanced at Tyrsdottir where she hunkered against her Molo, her carbine tight across her chest and helmet resting loosely atop her head. As a heavyworlder and a female, Tyrsdottir was doubly unusual in the Molo Rangers, where few of either served.

"Why?" Whiteside answered, strapping his own carbine into place. "For the Emperor?" he hazarded. "For glory, maybe?"

Tyrsdottir stuck out her lower lip. "No. Not these. Thinking the other one."

Whiteside slid down to his haunches, his back against Fang's armored carapace. "The Chalice Select."

Tyrsdottir slowly nodded. "Yes. This one." She blew out a slow breath between pursed lips. "A maybe death, for this ... a maybe life."

Unlike the conscript military forces of ages past, Fleet and the Imperial Legions were entirely composed of volunteers, Vested Citizens all. While Fleet, including the Imperial Marines, might entice volunteers through generous efficiency bonuses and a reasonable chance at prize money, the Legions offered few comparable opportunities. Instead the Legions filled their ranks year after year through the promise of the Emperor's Chalice Select: a rich reward of full rejuv to the two hundred most distinguished Legionnaires. With a relatively small number of Legionnaires engaging in actual combat, those who survived the Delta Three assault stood likely to top the list.

"You two look even less delighted than usual," the droll voice of Avery Reardon announced as he strolled down the uneven column of troops and Molo mechs. "Didn't think it was possible, but behold! You exceed my every expectation."

Pippi and Kyle nodded to the tall, urbane *former* officer. *Sergeant* Avery Reardon, they continually reminded themselves, although he neither acted nor appeared like any sergeant they ever met, and seemed insulted when they called him sergeant.

"We've been lowering our morale," Whiteside offered, "since our contu's brave sergeant wasn't here to provide that service."

Reardon smiled, the skin stretching across his patrician features, his intense blue eyes glittering. "Fabulous! Leadership potential's what I like to see, and you two both have loads of it." Avery flopped down on his Molo, Cuthbert, his carbine swinging negligently on its harness. He placed his helmet on his knee and leaned forward. "I've been chasing down important rumors with those Pathfinder sods." Reardon jerked a thumb toward the cluster of Pathfinders on the far side of the bay.

Kyle and Pippi perked up. The Pathfinders might offend the rank and file with their continual air of insufferable superiority, but being the premier elite unit of the Legions surely meant they *knew things*.

Reardon leaned even nearer. "Rumors confirmed." He produced a sloshing canteen and reverently displayed its humble form. "Genuine Excelsior brandy," he said.

At Kyle's and Pippi's disgusted expressions Reardon demanded, "What? It's the real thing, I assure you. Despite my many flaws—which are without number—the Reardon palate remains untainted by my many years in low company."

To Kyle Whiteside, little mystery remained regarding Avery Reardon's fall from lieutenant to sergeant. The far greater mystery was why someone from one of the Great Families, like the noble Reardon clan, ever ended up in the Legions at all. Though the Legions did maintain a very Core-centric culture, unlike Fleet and particularly the Marines, the modest pay and the tenuous promise of the Emperor's Chalice held little to attract any scion of a Great House.

"Don't suppose you learned anything about our impending engagement below?" Whiteside blandly inquired.

"Impending engagement...?" Reardon repeated. "From those impertinent yutzes? I wouldn't demean myself." Whiteside rolled his eyes and Tyrsdottir snorted.

"Pathfinders indeed," Reardon continued, carefully stowing his precious canteen. "Now attend, both of you... Despite all the chest thumping from those blokes"—he squinted toward the group of Pathfinders—"they're nothing much."

Whiteside and Tyrsdottir both saw the professional-looking Pathfinders with their new-style raid carbines, their air of relaxed confidence, and that palpable impression of peak physical fitness.

"Not so much, huh?" Tyrsdottir said. "Then what we?"

"*What we*, Pippi?" Reardon asked, smiling. "Oh, we're not so much either. We have as much battle experience as those wankers, though, which is exactly zero. Only we're not pretending otherwise, and that leaves us leagues ahead. See, children?"

"The training, though—" Whiteside began but Reardon cut him off.

"Extoll the virtues of training tomorrow, Kyle—for the Pathfinders or we humble Molo Rangers—and I'll be inclined to listen."

"You're not afraid at all, are you?" Whiteside said, shaking his head.

"Afraid? Afraid of what?"

Whiteside waved a hand encompassing the tight columns of Legionnaires ready to descend the ramps down into the waiting transports—the invasion force poised for violence.

"Oh," Reardon said, musing. "Getting blown to bits you mean? No. Not afraid of that. Not yet, at any rate. If my life remained precious to me I wouldn't be in the Legions to begin with." He smiled suddenly and placed his helmet atop his head. "If I get a sudden change of heart, I'll sing out, Kyle. How's that?"

Before Corporal Kyle Whiteside could form a reply, the signal came: the invasion of Delta Three began. The columns stirred, marching forward toward the transports, and fate.

The first wave of the invasion force dropped into Delta Three's gravity well: four troop transports escorted by IMS *Harrier*'s four interface fighter craft. Obvious targets planetside had already received pinpoint strikes from *Harrier*'s kinetic batteries, and the battle space had been liberally seeded with decoys and countermeasures. Now the transports plunged into atmosphere, hopefully surviving to reach the surface.

Corporal Whiteside mentally enumerated all the violent surface preparations as he clung to the harness holding him firmly in place, the vast, tight-packed transport jouncing its way planetside. He looked across at Sergeant Reardon, seemingly at ease despite their rattling, jerking progress. The breathing apparatus masked

Reardon's face, but Whiteside thought the raised eyebrows and faint lines beside Reardon's eyes made it clear he was enjoying himself hugely.

"Twenty seconds," the call came through at almost the same instant the flag appeared in Whiteside's UI. For a moment he thought to bring up the manual lesson on combat insertions, but there simply wasn't time.

Kyle Whiteside struggled to focus, struggled to recall all those lessons and acronyms.

Let's see, infantry pod detaches, pod gunners deploy, troops exit... troops exit. That's us. Exit. I can exit... been exiting my whole life from one place or another. I know how to exit...

The volume of sound increased, the transport's engines screaming, unsuppressed g-forces squeezing them. Then came the impact. The manual called it a "sharp jolt," and that meant the infantry pod was detached upon the planet surface. The next few moments became a nightmare of staccato flashes, blurred and warped in Kyle Whiteside's mind, the sound of his urgent, panting breaths loud in his ears.

Whiteside tried to stand twice before remembering the harness release, his heart pounding in his chest, the rapid motions of Legionnaires all around him seeming a dark tangle of limbs and weapons. A sharp crack rang through the infantry pod and Whiteside noted a Legionnaire jerk in his harness, his head slumping forward, a small ring of daylight glowing through the hull plate behind his slack form.

Sergeant Reardon seemed to appear, shoving Whiteside and the other Molo Rangers out through the nearest hatch, their Molo mechs clattering beside or behind them, stumbling out into gray daylight.

They had *exited*.

Whiteside snatched a brief glimpse of trees and some low, blackened structure before the pod turret roared to life close beside them, the glowing wand of red tracers etching his vision. A garble of words penetrated the cacophony, but momentarily held no meaning for Whiteside as he caught an image of a park-like field surrounded by clusters of blasted buildings. Without a conscious decision to act, he found himself part of a crowd hurrying and stumbling through low furrows of shattered concrete into the questionable shelter formed by the two remaining walls of some structure. A Legionnaire hurrying beside Whiteside suddenly bent over double, falling face-first as a constellation of crimson dots splattered Whiteside's goggles.

"Move!" A voice penetrated the haze and blur that Whiteside seemed immersed within. "Kyle! Kyle? Get your arse over here!" Staggering through shifting rubble, his breath loud within the breathing apparatus, Corporal Kyle Whiteside found himself squeezed among a mixed crowd of Legionnaires, Sergeant Avery Reardon at his elbow, saying something to him in an insistent voice.

"What? What?" Whiteside finally managed, Reardon's words drowned in the hammer and roar of gunfire.

"I said, are you hit? Are you wounded?"

Whiteside panted, confused, still feeling lost in a disordered fantasy. "Hit? I don't...I don't think so..." He looked down to see his gray-green shock armor now glistening red, dripping. His carbine remained cinched tight to his chest, un-deployed. "My carbine. I forgot."

"Don't worry about it," Reardon bellowed over the noise, then turned to his side. "Pippi? Pippi, did you see where Lieutenant Sun went?" Only then did Whiteside notice Pippi Tyrsdottir and a smattering of other Molo Rangers from their contu among the gaggle of Legionnaires jammed into their scant cover, his vision seeming to slowly expand from the narrow pipe it had comprised since they touched down.

"Gone—" Pippi began, breaking off as Legionnaires fired around the shattered edge of their sheltering walls. "Gone. Hit... thus and thus." She tapped her chest plate and her helmet.

Whiteside heard her words over the crash and echo of gunfire as he tugged at the wet, slippery carbine sling, trying to lengthen it to useable dimensions. Only then did he realize the other important detail he had neglected: Fang.

The streamlined carapace of his Molo shifted about on the uneven rubble, striving for balance on its six legs as Legionnaires squeezed and jostled about the tight quarters. Whiteside felt amazed that Fang had managed to stick close through all the chaos and tumult. His gaze rose then for the first time, looking back toward the landing zone.

Only two of the four infantry pods lay within his field of vision, and he was surprised to see how distant they were, his flight through the intervening terrain utterly gone from his memory. Gun turrets on the pods still sent streams of red tracers arcing out toward invisible targets to the left and right of Whiteside's position, but as Whiteside watched, one turret flashed white, dying in a shower of sparks, prey to some enemy mass driver concealed among the ruined buildings or wooded hillocks. His eyes blurred over the distant clumps of fallen bodies, refusing to focus.

"Sergeant!" A shouting voice nearby managed to flag Whiteside's fluttering attention. A Pathfinder lieutenant leaned near Sergeant Reardon, bellowing over the volume of fire, "Sergeant, deploy your Molos here and put some fire on that ridgeline to the left."

Sergeant Reardon unclipped his breathing apparatus and leaned toward the Pathfinder lieutenant who waited expectantly. "Sod off. We're under orders."

"What?" the lieutenant demanded, outraged.

Reardon motioned to Whiteside and the other Molo Rangers before turning back. "Sorry," he yelled back to the officer. "Sod off, *sir*. We're under orders." Reardon left the apoplectic lieutenant fuming, leading the small cluster of Molo Rangers through the dense crowd of sheltering Legionnaires.

"So, we under orders?" Pippi inquired in Reardon's ear as they reached the edge of their cover.

"*I* am," Reardon said, peering carefully around the wall. "My mother distinctly ordered me not to die stupidly." He motioned the other Rangers up to the breach in the wall. "And this place is a deathtrap. Follow me . . ."

Kyle recalled some vague details of the tactical map for this insertion, and he could pull the image up in his UI, but he already felt more than overwhelmed with just the sensory information currently flooding his synapses. Still, he knew their insertion zone lay in a shallow valley nestled between two parallel ridges that came together on the south side of what was once a pleasant-looking town. Most buildings now suffered the marks of surgical kinetic strikes from orbit, but it seemed far too many defenders yet remained.

Reardon loped out of cover with his Molo, Cuthbert, close at hand, and after a moment's hesitation Pippi followed, Whiteside and the others trailing along behind. Reardon moved across the shattered terrain, angling uphill, through another building, startling a handful of Legionnaires covering there.

"Easy, mates! Easy. We're just passing through."

Seeing the Molo Rangers with their breathing apparatuses detached, the Legionnaires cleared their own. "Who's in command?" one asked. "Since the combat Nets crashed we haven't heard shit."

Reardon checked the view through a ragged hole blasted in one wall. "Got me, gents." He stepped back as the other Molo Rangers filled the small space, and Whiteside numbly realized the combat Nets were indeed gone from his UI. "We're getting outside this shooting gallery," Reardon said. "You can come see the sights with us, if you like." He clambered up a small pile of rubble and peered out another hole. "Or, there're some Pathfinders presiding over a shit-show back yonder."

"Pathfinders?" The Legionnaires perked up.

"Pippi, show our softheaded comrades their destination. Just point, if you will."

Pippi obligingly stepped up to the edge of the ruined building, looking back downhill. "See there? Is like a half square, just a bit far past that maybe-car."

"I see it," one Legionnaire said, apparently oblivious to Reardon's dry insults, jerking back as a glowing tracer round snapped by a stone's-throw distance. "Good luck," he threw over his shoulder as he led the way, darting back through the ruins, his fellows close behind.

Whiteside felt utterly adrift, blindly following in Avery Reardon's wake. *What was their mission?* Secure the landing zone and link up with follow-on waves. Nearly seven hundred Legionnaires in the first wave, and where were they all hiding?

The view of the landing zone now lay behind intervening ruins, but Whiteside still heard the infantry pod turrets spewing defiance, and small-arms fire rang out from multiple quadrants. Surely hundreds of Legionnaires were scattered about the landing zone, disorganized, confused by the lack of combat Nets, all waiting for someone to bring back a unified mission.

"There we are," Reardon said as he peeked around a shattered wall, gazing uphill. He just stepped back when a series of high-velocity rounds blazed in, showering him with dust and debris, blowing hunks from the wall where he had just been standing. Reardon fell back. "Bugger! Bastards!"

In an angry surge, Reardon scrambled to his Molo, Cuthbert, as Whiteside and the others all stared, unsure what to do.

Cuthbert obediently leaped up to a rough void in the wall at Reardon's direction, and the sergeant flipped down his tactical eyepiece, deploying the long mass driver from the dumb-mech's armored carapace. More incoming rounds struck the wall around Cuthbert, shards of stone clattering from its shell.

"Bastards. Shoot me, will they?" Reardon adjusted his aim, the mass driver's barrel slowly pivoting until it aimed through the ragged hole. Reardon fired, the weapon jerking on Cuthbert's back, a flower of bright plasma jetting from the muzzle as its hypersonic projectile snapped across the distance. Reardon paused just a moment, then stood slowly, wiping the dust and grime from his face. "Settled their hash. Bastards."

The mass driver folded back into Cuthbert's torso as Reardon flipped the tactical eyepiece up. "Well, children," Reardon said, "looks like it works, this whole Molo routine." He smiled and held up a hand that shook. "Let's find a spot where we can get to it."

They made their way ruin by ruin uphill, finally abandoning the cover of broken structures to skulk through a dense belt of vegetation near the ridgetop. Here they discovered a sort of dry canal, perhaps for storm water runoff, and an ideal location for Molo Ranger operations. Below them shots echoed and the occasional string of tracers punctuated the struggle, but they were outside the ring of fire.

Pippi deployed Roger, her utility Molo, using its augur and entrenching tools to quickly prepare six Molo fighting positions well below the canal's lip, and six deeper hides for the Rangers themselves. While Pippi labored, Reardon, Whiteside, and the other Rangers sprawled in a loose perimeter, eyes and optics scanning for any visible threat.

Whiteside lay in a shallow depression, carbine ready, its telescoping buttstock against his shoulder. His neck muscles already protested from supporting the weight of helmet and head as he peered about the surrounding terrain.

The sound of gunfire chattered and resounded below, while only the faintest noise of Pippi's excavations competed with the murmur of wind rasping through the vegetation. In the distance a bright streak fell from the heavens, a thunderous boom reverberating as *Harrier* smote some new target from orbit.

"Kyle?" Avery's voice whispered from the left where he covered in his own shallow depression. "Check your thermal. It's a treat."

Whiteside hesitated a moment before actuating the thermal function on his carbine's scope. He didn't know what he was supposed to be looking for, but a slow pan with the scope revealed the distinct form of a human wriggling through the undergrowth, the hot barrel of a weapon glowing white. Corporal Whiteside felt his heart surge, his hands suddenly shaking the carbine until he could barely see. He peered over the scope, staring at that same patch of vegetation, striving to resolve some hint of that potential enemy. A steadying breath eased his hammering heart, and Whiteside looked back to the scope. As his pulse settled, he finally noticed the IFF—Identification, Friend or Foe—indicator blinking as he lined up the human form in his sights. "A decoy bean?" Whiteside whispered.

"To amuse the enemy," Avery Reardon whispered back. "The beasts."

About the size of a human hand, the decoy beans scattered across the battle space projected a convincing representation of a human warfighter in several wavelengths; *very* convincing as Whiteside just discovered.

Movement high through the misty air caught the Molo Rangers' attention: a series of huge ghostly fists arcing through the sky, racing over and past them. The loud rushing sound tore the sky a moment before the ground leaped against their prone bodies. Behind them rubble and smoke fountained down toward the landing zone, and the sound of explosions thundered.

"Indirect fire. Bastards," Reardon cursed. "Bet that clutch of Pathfinders are blown to bits.... You ready with those foxholes, Pippi?"

"Ready in not so long, maybe," Pippi called quietly back, invisible from Whiteside's position.

"You—uh—you guys okay?" Whiteside whispered to his right. He didn't really know the other three Molo Rangers, but he figured they should be as glad as he felt that those artillery shells did not land on their heads—thanks to Avery Reardon's impulsive, unconventional leadership.

A burst of small-arms fire straight ahead of Whiteside cut off any reply. He fumbled his carbine up, his fatigued neck shaking as he raised his eye to the scope. Two upright glowing figures appeared, weapons in hand, clearly firing at the decoy. A quick glance at the IFF indicator showed nothing: enemies.

Whiteside's heart leaped, immediately pounding until each beat seemed to choke in his throat and drown his hearing. *This-is-it-this-is-it-this-is-it...* He tried to steady his carbine sight as it juddered over the glowing human target at medium range. *Steady...steady...there!* He convulsively jerked the trigger, his eyes snapping shut. Nothing.

Safety catch. Damn.

Whiteside realized he had been holding his breath, gasping now as his thumb found the safety selector, arming his carbine. He just began lining up the shot again when Reardon whispered from his left, "Kyle! Trouble. Just right of the road, you see?"

Whiteside eased his finger away from the trigger and slid his left forearm through the dust and bracken, repositioning his carbine optic to the right. At first glance only the glowing figures of two more infantry appeared, and Whiteside was about to call back to Reardon, when he caught a hint of a straight edge partially occluding one enemy. He reached up to his optic and switched back to ambient wavelengths, his breath catching as his eyes finally registered the deadly shapes pushing through the undergrowth. Hard and low, armored and tracked, the three crawler drones brought immense offensive power to bear, though their low profile stood little more than knee height.

"Back! Back over the lip, fast!" Reardon's voice called.

Kyle just began to relay the order to the other Rangers right of his position when the crawlers caught some hint of their presence. A giant's hammer seemed to strike the ground beside Whiteside three times in rapid succession, the thundering roar of the auto-cannon coming a moment later. Blinded by flying soil and rocks, his face planted against the ground, Whiteside squirmed backward in mindless panic. More rounds slammed around their position, and Whiteside froze, trying to crush himself into the soil, willing himself to be flatter and thinner, then squirming again.

Continuing to wriggle back as the thunder of fire scorched and shattered the ground, Whiteside found himself in a modest hollow on the back face of their sheltering canal, Reardon curled closed beside.

"You hit?" Reardon shouted over the ongoing roar.

Hit? If one of those rounds had touched me what would be left? Kyle shook his head.

"Good, good," Reardon bellowed, and Kyle thought he smiled. "I've got to confess"—they both ducked as tracer rounds curved low over their heads—"*now* I'm scared!"

For good reason: they were insects in a battlefield of titans.

"Pippi? Pippi, you still with us?" Reardon yelled over the blast and echo.

"Still alive, I think!" Pippi called back.

"What's those other fellows' names?" Reardon asked Whiteside, leaning close over the noise, the snap and crack of incoming fire filling the air. Whiteside shrugged. The lack of combat Nets—any Nets—made him suddenly reliant on a disused biological memory system that felt especially feeble while a violent death seemed increasingly imminent.

"Cummins? Wasn't that the corporal?" Reardon asked, then without waiting for a reply he shouted, "Cummins!"

"Cummins bought it—shit!" a voice shouted back from the right, breaking off with a curse as a burst of cannon fire slammed in, showering them with rocks and soil.

Whiteside found that a tiny corner of his mind dryly scrolled through the various training courses that had supposedly transformed him from a regular Citizen into a warrior. As tracers flicked over their cowering bodies, the content of his entire military career seemed incredibly remote, and only vaguely related to the hateful destruction enveloping him.

At that moment, as Whiteside squeezed himself into the unyielding soil, three burning lines split the darkening sky, streaking down with a shriek and blast that reflected hard light from the low overcast. Red beads curved down in glowing strings, and Whiteside uncurled enough to peer back toward the attacking crawler drones in time to see the crimson tracers ploughing over the road and tree line. Wreckage burned and scattered under the barrage.

As the combat Nets suddenly flickered into Whiteside's UI, Reardon said, "Second wave's here. Poor devils."

Interface fighters roared down out of the clouds, mist enveloping their wings as they banked over the battlefield, their cannon fire and missiles addressing any target daring to aggress. Behind them the transports dropped, looking impossibly vast, infantry pods at their bellies ready to deploy.

As the fighters orbited the battle space, each transport plummeted out of sight behind the hillside, rocketing back up a moment later without the burden of infantry pods to restrain them. The blue glow of engines became more distinct as daylight faded away, and Reardon's Molo Rangers stirred, emerging from their shallow earthworks to assess the state of the changing battlefield while *Harrier*'s interface fighters still ruled the air.

Whiteside had just cleared obscuring rubble from Fang, assuring the Molo still functioned, when a sharp white glow above created a treacherous second dawn.

Avery Reardon rolled to his back, flipped his polarized lenses down, and stared up into the glowing clouds, a hush falling over the surrounding battlefield as the interface fighters torched off into the distance.

The combat Nets flickered and disappeared once again and Whiteside's resurging sense of optimism fled with the loss.

"Reardon?" Whiteside said, hating what he saw, what he knew. "Reardon, what...?"

Sergeant Avery Reardon stared up at the noonday glow, his face blank below the polarized lenses. "Something has gone terribly, terribly wrong, Kyle."

Whiteside glanced up, then looked away, his eyes smarting at the glare. "Gods...it's...it's—"

"*Harrier.*" Reardon shook his head as the arc-light torch slid westward, no longer holding station. "I just can't imagine how those evil sods did it, but they killed her."

The official invasion of Delta Three ended almost as soon as it began; less than two thousand Legionnaires planetside and unsupported, abandoned to their fate. *Harrier* and her thousands of personnel became a second sun falling toward the horizon.

"We are on our own, dear fellow," Reardon said, lifting his canteen of Excelsior brandy with a shaking hand and taking a swig. "Mother will be most displeased."

Chapter 4

"The Myriad Worlds Imperium became a rare example of social status decoupled from either parentage or mere wealth. This system, like all others, still propagates cohesive classes, and the end result remains a question, particularly among demi-cit scholars. . . ."

—Everest Compline, *Reflections*

WHEN CHE RAMOS LEFT THE DEMI-CIT DOMICILE POD SOME WEEKS prior, he had been a freshly minted Vested Citizen, a cheap new sword at his side. He had marched out the door and straight into a rather naively optimistic career in Fleet, saddled with a mountain of debt. Subsequently securing a bridge position on IMS *Tanager* under Captain Sinclair-Maru represented a near-miraculous windfall, until Che found himself entangled in a plot of competing spies and assassins that nearly cost him his life. But now he returned at last to what was once home.

Tanager had limped back into Core system weeks before and Che had only spent a few days with the medicos, recovering from *Tanager*'s mauling during combat. Other more pointed, more immediately threatening concerns had kept him loitering around the Fleet barracks on the Strand until he was finally compelled to return to this tiny apartment, his final planetside address.

The door still recognized Che, allowing him access, but all the other apartment systems lay lifeless and dead as he stepped quietly in. He shuffled uncertainly into the sterile rectangle of the main room and peered cautiously into the shallow closet and adjoining toilet cubby before setting his shoulder bag aside.

Che eased down on the couch extension projecting from one wall, lurching back up to unclip the sword from his waist, then settling back down, the sword negligently dangling from one hand.

Did the apartment seem smaller? No, not precisely, Che thought, his eyes wandering over the humble space. Perhaps it was simply the absence of those lights and screens that had ever greeted him back in his demi-cit days, providing an illusion of vitality that was no longer present. As a Vested Citizen he no longer belonged, and that oppressive synthetic Intelligence that managed and monitored every demi-cit on Coreworld no longer acknowledged Che's presence. Strange, Che had never once considered that he could miss that micromanaging entity, or ever view its disregard of him as anything but a blessing.

A soft chime sounded from the door, and Che lurched, his heart rate accelerating. He ran his tongue over dry lips and unsteadily thrust his sword out of sight beyond the couch extension.

"E-enter," Che said.

He felt his body tension drop an octave as two young men filled the door.

"Hey-o! It's Che-o!" one of them called out with a laugh. "Thought we saw you slinking in here."

"Looking so fine...too fine for shabs like us, eh Che-o?" the other said, sauntering in, gazing down at Che with a faintly mocking expression.

Their voices seemed almost painfully loud to Che, and he found himself contrasting their boisterous entrance with the demeanor of his companions of the last many weeks. Had he been so damned loud back when he was a demi-cit, just weeks ago?

"B-Beater, Teep," Che greeted, striving for a natural tone even as his UI helpfully identified both guests as demi-cits, in the event Che had missed this fact. "H-how are things then, eh?"

"How are things?" Teep repeated, stopping near Che and leaning against the same counter where Che had once labored to create various libations with their four daily ounces of low-proof alcohol. "Che-o, things are suddenly surprising, wouldn't you say, Beater? Surprising. Never thought we'd see you again."

"Oh?" Che said again, shrugging. "S-still have a few things here, you know. Haven't a proper place to live yet."

"That's a sight simple, Che-o," Beater said. "Haven't had much time for much, right? We've read about you, Che-o. Been dashing about, slaughtering rebels and enriching yourself."

Chagrin battled irritation within Che's breast. *Tanager* spent much of its mission engaged in a series of running battles against superior forces, barely surviving. The only *slaughter* observed was perpetrated by enemy forces apparently upon thousands of helpless victims on Delta Three's orbital station, and Che had little enough to do with the mechanics of ship-to-ship combat anyway, since he merely filled the sensor position on *Tanager*'s bridge.

He *had* enriched himself rather handsomely, his debts settled, with around thirty years' pay now filling his coffers, but that also had little do with Che's actual efforts, and much more to do with Captain Sinclair-Maru's. It was only the captain's quick thinking that had secured the prize vessel, *Aurora*, crammed with a very real, very fungible cargo of Shaper tech.

"Rich," Beater said, "Vested. Surprised you've got time for us *little folk* in the pods."

"I am still just me," Che said. He had been about to say that he hadn't changed, but even as he formed the words he suddenly realized it was not true. Though only weeks had passed, and though he still felt like an impostor, both as a Fleet rating and as a Vested Citizen, those intervening weeks had altered him, and this grew increasingly clear as his two old mates spoke.

"Leave flowers for those of us living dog's years, Che-o. We'll be gone before you know it."

Che shook his head as Teep flopped beside him on the couch and Beater leaned against the wall. *Teep* and *Beater*... All at once Che wondered why so many demi-cits reviled the names given them by their parents, choosing such absurd handles, but he pushed the thought aside. He said, "No, n-no, I can't afford rejuv yet, and maybe never will."

The smirks adorning their faces told Che that they did not believe him. Even before he made the leap for Citizen status, abandoning the controlled, carefree life of a demi-cit, his friends in the pods had all seemed to feel that the life of a Vested Citizen was a binary path, either quickly, violently ended by a dueling sword, or infinitely prolonged with the wonders of Shaper rejuv treatments. Somehow they clung to this belief, despite the contrary evidence frequently observed in the gutters of Imperial City. The starving destitute, the drug addicted, and the drunken derelict could all only be Vested Citizens. The freedoms denied to the demi-cit included the freedom to fail, to self-destruct. *That* questionable liberty was attained by Vested Citizens all too frequently.

"Fortune smiles on the fortunate; wealth flows to the wealthy," Teep intoned, and Che nearly remembered the author he quoted. Like so many demi-cits, Teep and Beater availed themselves of the extensive educational opportunities offered to them, and not simply for the premium stipend it provided. Che had always reckoned it a thirst for knowledge, but now, quite suddenly it seemed merely a fuel for cynicism. Had his own education been driven by a similar hunt for dogmatic frameworks to deny any unwelcome perspective?

"Would you say I was fortunate o-or wealthy when I walked out these doors, Teep?" Che asked. "It didn't s-seem that way to me."

Teep shook his head and shared a smile with Beater. "Che-o, really? Tork's First Law rebels. Citing exceptions obscures the rule, Che-O, and you most certainly are *exceptional.*"

"Naughty," Beater added with a wink, cramming his flat little cap on his head.

Che perceived the circular nature of their argument with its attendant fallacy, but he also recognized the futility in arguing and opted for a more personal topic. "Well, h-how's Chilly, anyway?"

"Speaking of naughty?" Beater laughed.

"Oh, that ship has launched, Mate," Teep said. "She's rolling with Bosko nowadays. Likes a man whose muscles got muscles."

"Oh," Che said, feeling the final stage of deflation, wondering precisely where he now fit in the Myriad Worlds.

For years he had imagined a triumphant return to the pods. In those visions he returned after months or years among the stars, rich in experience at least (with no hint of condescension, of course) feted by his demi-cit friends who then became inspired to emulate. That image became ridiculous in the air of cold cynicism that flowed from Beater and Teep—that *always had* flowed from Beater and Teep.

No, that girl, Chilly would never walk the Citizen's path beside Che, and these former comrades would never fulfill Che's naïve dream. The old circle of laughing, philosophizing demi-cits would never become the new circle of sword-bearing, somehow more august, Vested Citizens all toasting Che Ramos, their inspiration.

The soft chime of the door rang again as Teep recounted

various gossip themes that Che had apparently once cared about.

"Enter," Che said, steeling himself, the presence of Beater and Teep somehow aiding Che's fortitude.

Still, Che's heart seemed to freeze as the door opened and what he had feared all morning now appeared before him. That stocky heavyworlder Che might never forget; the author of such anguish in Che's burgeoning Fleet career: he entered, shrinking the room with his bulk, a lanky stranger smiling in his wake.

"Ooh," Teep cooed, "one of your important new friends, Che-O?"

"You two got places to be," the heavyworlder rumbled, while his smiling companion stared fixedly at Che, his expression unchanging.

"They seem to think we're chattel, Teep," Beater said, smirking, surely proving the absence of survival instincts among demi-cits. "Seem to think we lick the boots. We don't. See?"

"Imperial Security," the heavyworlder said, spreading the long tails of his many-caped coat to reveal a holstered pistol along with a common Citizen's sword. "We need to speak with Mister Ramos. Alone. That clear it up for you, thought-merchant?"

"B-Beater, Teep," Che spoke up, his mouth dry, his pulse thumping, "i-it would be b-best to go . . . please."

Beater stuck out his tongue, and Teep made a rude gesture, but they got up and shoved their way to the door. "You, Che-o, have become ridiculous; a jingoistic affectation," Teep said over his shoulder, "just like these two." Che said nothing in reply, and the door closed behind them. He might never see them again, and they would surely never thank him, but Che still felt a hint of pleasure that he had saved their lives. His own life remained an open question.

After actuating some device that snuffed out Che's UI, the heavyworlder stepped close, menacingly close, his thick, powerful hands open.

"Wh-where's my tw-twenty-thousand?" Che said, staring up as his stomach quaked in inward terror.

"Your twenty?" the heavyworlder demanded, incredulous. "You were to do a simple job or pay the piper. You didn't do as you were bid, and now you'll tell us why and count yourself lucky to live."

"I—I did! I did just as—as I was told," Che said, remembering the torment of those shipboard days, feeling a traitor by inaction or action, a small, vile box to be placed in the captain's cabin: Captain Sinclair-Maru, his only benefactor.

"You lie," the heavyworlder said, reaching for Che.

"N-no!" Che squeaked, shrinking back.

"When?" the other man asked, his plastic grin in place, speaking for the first time in a dry, unhurried tone. "When did you place the package?"

Che's eyes darted from the menacing hands so close, to the smiling man. "When? W-well, about fifteen minutes before transition to D-Delta Three."

"What?" the heavyworlder snarled. "Told you to get it in there the day before, worm."

"N-no," Che pleaded. "No, you didn't. Y-you just said before transition, so th-that's what I did."

"It is immaterial," the grinning man said with no change in expression, his eyes not even focused upon Che. "I understand the failure now, and there is nothing further to be gained here." He turned away dismissively. "Kill him, and let us depart."

Che only managed one startled yelp before the crushing power of the heavyworlder's grip clenched around his neck. His vain scrabbling ceased almost as it began, and Che's vision shrank to a pinprick of light as his thoughts clawed for hope. *Where the hell are they? What are they waiting for? Where...is...the...* As his thoughts of abandonment and betrayal dimmed and darkness rose up, some hint of tumult registered in his oxygen-starved brain, the sound of breaching charges preceding the return of sight.

Che gasped for breath, looking up at the heavyworlder above him who shuddered as voltage coursed through his musclebound body. The smiling man also quivered, two stun probes lodged in his flesh, his smile locked in a wide-eyed rictus. With horror Che realized the smiling man's hand moved, impossibly raising the blunt muzzle of his pistol even as more stun probes struck him. Despite the power scorching through his tortured frame, the pistol inexorably leveled. The gunshot barked, spraying Che with warm droplets, and the heavyworlder toppled, his body still animated with electrical power, his eyes dead.

Forms moved at the edges of Che's vision. "Secure him, gods damn it all!" Winter Yung barked. An agent—a real Imperial agent—struck the pistol from the smiling man's hand, and a moment later, the room filled with armed figures. Winter looked down at the gasping Che without much interest as she shoved the dead heavyworlder over with her boot, seeing the flooding, terminal wound at his temple.

"Did I not say I needed him alive?" Winter Yung demanded of a tall, dark-haired man who stared down at the smiler, now trussed in numerous bonds. Che wiped at the blood on his face, gasping and shaking from yet another near brush with death, staring around the shattered room that featured several rough new entrances blasted through his walls.

"It seems you did mention that, Winter," the tall man said, and Che now noticed his almond eyes as the smoke cleared, assuming he belonged to some branch of the Emperor's sprawling family. "Perhaps you may show more of your cards in the future. This fellow's augmentation would have been of some interest."

Winter snorted, turning on her heel. "Augmentation?"

"Ahh, Winter Yung, I see," the trussed prisoner said from his supine position, still smiling as agents cut his garments free and jostled him like a piece of meat. "You become an annoyance."

"Can someone gag this piece of shit, please?" Winter said.

"You know him?" the tall man asked, turning his dark gaze from the prisoner to Winter.

"No," Winter said, her lips twisting as she smashed a powerful kick, full force to the prisoner's groin.

"A lover's caress," the prisoner said, his smile never wavering though his body jerked from the impact. "Winter does—uh—love her work."

"This is not Battersea, Winter," the tall man said reproachfully as he stared between Winter and the prisoner, the other agents all looking on with disturbed expressions.

"Whatever, Lu. Have fun with this; I'm leaving." Winter jerked a finger at Che. "Come on, you."

As Che got unsteadily to his feet and grabbed his blood-speckled bag, Winter returned Lu's cold stare. "Winter . . . Cousin," Lu said, "you really should talk to us."

"You may want your sword there," Winter said to Che in a scathing tone, before looking back to Lu. "Nothing to talk about, Cousin."

Che followed Winter out through the cluster of agents, his head spinning and neck hurting, the hint of iron fingers still crushing his windpipe. He stole painful, sidelong looks at Winter as they moved through the pod's empty hallways, the apartments all sealed by Imperial Security override.

"You did your part," Winter said at last, her demeanor far from congratulatory.

Che knew Winter Yung worked as the Imperial Consul to Battersea, and assumed she also held some role in Imperial Security, but he thought her the most strangely alluring woman he had ever met, and the second-most terrifying. After all, Inga Maru had nearly tossed him out one of *Tanager*'s airlocks, while Winter merely skewered Che with verbal barbs and withered him with scathing looks—so far.

"Th-thank you, Consul," Che said. "Their, um, confederates may not be pleased. Might pay me another visit."

"They may indeed," Winter said in a bored tone as they stepped out of the pods onto the quiet road on the unfashionable eastern fringe of Imperial City, the broad band of the ribbon standing to the north, lighted modules ascending and descending to and from Core Alpha's fixed orbit above.

With no direction, no destination, Che mindlessly walked beside Winter, a trackless object floating without rudder or purpose. "Strange, though," Che said almost to himself, "I'm not afraid anymore."

"Hmph. Not afraid? Shock, probably."

Che frowned. "I—I don't think so. *You* scare me still." Realizing what he said aloud, Che blushed.

Winter looked at Che, seeming to see him for the first time. "I scare you?"

"Yes, Consul."

Winter halted, and Che stopped short a step beyond, turning back, surprised. Winter reached out a finger toward Che's face, and Che froze. Her finger touched him lightly, coming away with a smear of blood. "You're a mess." She bit her lip and her pupils seemed to flicker as she stared into Che's eyes.

"I leave for Battersea in the morning," she said in a lower voice. "Stay with me tonight."

"Y-yes, Consul," Che said, realizing that he still carried his sword in one hand, his shoulder bag in the other.

Though his throat still ached from a death barely averted, and his ears rang from the crash of breaching charges, he felt shockingly alive, suddenly more terrified than ever, and thrilled in the sensation.

Chapter 5

"Perhaps the greatest survival tool humanity possesses is found in the Thinking Machine Protocols. Without them, humanity would likely have lost its dynamic edge as technology undertook every task and duty. This proscription likely saved our species from terminal mediocrity."

—Everest Compline, *Reflections*

IN ITS MANY CENTURIES OF EXISTENCE, THE IMPERIUM OF THE Myriad Worlds had knowingly encountered only two intelligent star-faring, nonhuman species, and both encounters wrought powerful changes within the Imperium. The first encounter back in 5202 resulted in the merciless depopulation of several human worlds, and a century of war.

What these warlike invaders called themselves was never known, but humanity named them Slaggers for obvious reasons; named them, then destroyed them. And though that war ended nearly a thousand years before, the impact of that conflict remained indelibly seared into the Imperium. Through the benefits of victory, General Yung became Yung I, Emperor of the Myriad Worlds, and his doctrine contained within the *Legacy Mandate* reformed known humanity into a more practical, focused genus.

The second encounter with a nonhuman species occurred just years after the Slagger War's end, when the impossibly vast vessels of the Shaper Armada appeared within Core system. Rather than destruction, the Shapers brought trade and technology: technology far beyond humanity's engineering, and nearly beyond human comprehension. Among the new technological wonders came crystal computer systems, providing the speed, power, and longevity necessary to spawn the great synthetic Intelligences.

Though Fleet and the Great Houses regularly utilized synthetic Intelligences, these entities remained subject to the Imperial Thinking Machine Protocols, legally able to actually *do* very little more than observe, record, and advise. No great Intelligence would ever pilot a vessel, fire a weapon, or operate even a construction bot. These tasks fell to human hands or simple automation.

Even aside from the Protocols, artificial *sapience* had ever remained out of reach, though for no known reason—at least that remained the belief of every learned human being among the Myriad Worlds, save one. One person knew that artificial sapience had quietly, miraculously been realized.

Whether due to the vast expanse of crystal architecture or to the effects of a failed top secret weapon early in his commission, Loki, the synthetic Intelligence of IMS *Tanager,* had somehow become something *more.* Though many Fleet officers had noted peculiarities on *Tanager* during the two centuries of the frigate's service (one amused captain finally suggesting the name "Loki" for *Tanager*'s Intelligence, recalling the capricious demi-god of human tradition), none had possessed the capability to see more than Loki allowed them to see; not until Inga Maru stepped aboard *Tanager*'s worn and malodorous decks.

Inga Maru's secret enhancements, and the powerful tools provided by her not-so-dumb mech, quickly exposed the remarkable entity concealed within *Tanager,* the least significant frigate in Fleet service.

Inga should have immediately flagged for erasure or reprogramming any Intelligence clearly operating far outside Fleet specifications. At the least, she should have made the nature of her suspicions clear to her captain and compatriot, Saef Sinclair-Maru, but even this step Inga resisted. Ultimately her judgments proved out when Loki used his vast capabilities to ensure the success of their prior mission... *Tanager*'s final mission.

After that operation, stripped of her fissionable weapons and N-drive, *Tanager* went to auction for salvage, the Fleet provosts hoodwinked by Loki, just like every other human for decades had been. There, Loki remained, alone and undetected within *Tanager*'s dark hull for many days.

It was here Inga found Loki, nearly gone, fading into isolated, feral savagery. She had spent her savings and her considerable prize money to buy the wreck of *Tanager*, betting it all on the entity Loki *could* become. Beyond the compassion she felt for a fellow sentient being, somehow both less and more than human, Inga and Saef needed powerful allies if they were to survive and triumph.

Loki could be an ally of terrifying potential, and this he had already demonstrated, cracking Meerschaum-encrypted files in seconds instead of weeks or months, and looting enemy secrets from the data banks of Delta Three's orbital station during their assault.

Already Inga found *legal* commercial application for Loki's powers, and with those limited proceeds she solved the conundrum of Loki's dependence upon *Tanager*'s shattered hulk. Just a handful of commercial decryption and data restoration jobs enabled the purchase of an old and battered shuttle, *Onyx*, and now Inga finally piloted this craft carefully into the salvage dock, right beside *Tanager*.

The small salvage crew she had hired sprang into action, linking *Onyx* and *Tanager*, lock to lock, already prepped to move the vast collection of crystal computer stacks into preplanned compartments within the shuttle.

Inga oversaw each step as the crew labored, schooling her features into a calm that she did not feel, nibbling a food bar as she observed. Aside from her concern in disconnecting and relocating Loki's crystal physiology, potentially impacting Loki in unknown ways, Inga also operated under tremendous constraints regarding her duty to the Sinclair-Maru, to Saef. She only grasped a degree of peace in leaving Saef momentarily unprotected due to his presence on the nearby Strand, the high-security Fleet facility orbiting Coreworld. Saef's own well-established lethality *should* equal any individual threat in such a secure, controlled environment.

As she now looked on, the final components slid into their appointed racks at last, the tech crew departed, and Inga swiftly set about restoring Loki's world to its correct condition, unwilling to expose her intentions—expose Loki—to the workers or anyone.

Her concealing cloak cast aside, her arms bare and collection of
armament exposed, Inga flipped welding goggles down and put
the final touches on the power couplings. She had already wired
in expensive sensor nodes and a small fish tank: the bare neces-
sities that Loki might require.

With more than a little misgiving, Inga slid her welding goggles
off, made a final check, and actuated the power. The robust nature
of crystal computing technology *should* protect Loki from any
harm, but with a sample size of one, nothing could be certain.
As the silent seconds passed Inga suffered that awful sensation so
redolent of her childhood; it was the feeling of failing someone
who trusted her completely. Loki had agreed that the situation
must change, *Tanager* was no longer tenable, and he expressed
no concern about the transfer...but little Mitzi, long ago, had
always agreed with Inga's plans, never blaming her when those
plans had failed, always trusting once again—

"This is very interesting, Chief," Loki announced, charging
Inga with a palpable sense of relief. "This vessel is very small.
But tell me, what is in that fabric container? Is it a surprise? Is
it a present?"

Inga eased a breath and smiled, collecting her cloak and
another food bar. "It is a present," Inga said, "But I doubt it's
a surprise."

"I'm not peeking, Chief. I'm not. What could it be? It is such
a mystery!"

Interactions like this persuaded Inga of her first analysis: willful
ignorance, even self-deception denoted sentience. For surely Loki's
shiny new sensor nodes had analyzed everything in range within
the shuttle's hull, including the black oval case with its curious
heat signature, and no surprises could remain. Yet Loki seemed
incapable of direct untruths. Perhaps the secret to sentience,
Inga thought, had always been *layers* of consciousness. For Loki,
possibly, a division or barrier between the mechanistic machine
functions and the "higher," more deliberate layers of his calculation; like the divide between the animalistic human subconscious
and those more elevated self-aware zones of human thought.

Inga knelt and opened the case to reveal Loki's *surprise*: a tiny
kitten curled in a ball, asleep. It was a cream color through the
body, with dark ears, nose, and tail, and it blinked sleepily up at
Inga to reveal startling blue eyes. Inga's own advanced electronics

detected the intense power of Loki's focused attention, reminding her of that moment back when she first discovered Loki's true nature. Instead of that synthetic rage then, Loki now poured out curiosity and delight.

The kitten issued a tiny mew, still blinking trustingly up at Inga. "What did the kitten say?" Loki asked. "Was that a greeting?"

"I suppose it was a greeting," Inga said, smiling. "I really know very little about animals, I'm afraid."

Inga noted the Nets traffic meter in her UI suddenly spike, its narrow bandwidth choked as Loki surely researched all things involving the interpretation of cat speech.

"How shall I address the kitten?" Loki asked.

"I thought you might select a name for him, if you like."

"Indeed," Loki said, momentarily silent—an eternity for a being such as Loki. "I assume the kitten does not possess Fleet rank?" Loki said.

"Um, no," Inga dryly replied, "the kitten is a civilian."

"Ah, yes. Perhaps you have not observed, Chief, many aspects of human society are perpetually unspoken, rarely asserted in an affirmative manner."

Like the ranks of animals? Like the proper naming conventions for cats? Inga was not certain.

"I believe kittens and other animals often receive names based upon their physical appearance or a particular skill," Inga offered.

"Our Nets bandwidth is contemptible," Loki said as the kitten mewed again, uncurling to stretch and yawn, "but it appears kittens are *rarely* named after their appearance or skills."

"I stand corrected."

"Although 'Fluffy' does seem to be a name that appears with some frequency," Loki mused, "which is an odd choice. A universal characteristic of mammals hardly seems a meaningful name."

"Your logic is unassailable," Inga said, intensely interested in the naming rationale Loki would employ for the kitten. By this time, the kitten seemed fully awake, turning his blue eyes up toward Inga, his dark tail a furry exclamation mark. He gathered himself together and leaped a handsbreadth up on the fabric enclosure of his sheltering case, his little claws extending to grip as he emitted another plaintive mew.

"Oh!" Loki enthused. "Talons! They are very sharp, and he is discontented."

Inga experienced a degree of internal satisfaction. She had not only obtained the kitten to please Loki, but also as a small ally in her efforts to awaken empathy, without which Loki might very well become the galaxy's most technologically advanced sociopath.

"What does he want, do you suppose?" Inga asked.

The kitten mewed again and began a shaky effort to scale out from his prison, his claws hooking in the fabric in a most inconvenient manner.

"He is constrained. He is curious? He wishes to explore, to see new things?" Loki suggested, and Inga nodded to herself: was she witnessing transference? Did Loki see his own desires mirrored in the kitten? Then Inga frowned as Loki said, "Perhaps his talons are an implied threat? If his wishes are not met he will use them to wreak a terrible vengeance...perhaps?"

"Or maybe," Inga said, scooping up the kitten into her hands, "he desires friendship, affection, closeness, and his claws are merely a method to attain these things." The kitten began purring and placed a soft little paw on Inga's neck, rubbing his head affectionately against her chin. As she looked down into the kitten's blue eyes, she saw a mirror of her own, and the notion of *her* transference dawned: did she desire affection, closeness, *love*? And were her own "claws" just a method to attain them?

"Possibly, Chief," Loki said doubtfully, "we will hope so, since his talons are very, very close to your carotid artery."

"I'm fairly certain I'm safe," Inga replied, smiling. "The purring sound denotes affection, I believe."

"You are very brave, Chief. I have noted this before. But I do desire you to be more cautious."

Empathy?

"Your concern is touching, Loki, really."

"I do not wish to be alone again. If you stop living then I would be alone. Except for this kitten. Who would also stop living...just like all the fish on *Tanager*."

Perhaps *not* empathy.

Since Loki only controlled the lighting, comfort settings, and the artificial gravity, his ability to interact with the kitten was limited. Still, over the small period of time Inga spent in *Onyx*, introducing the kitten to his new home that day, Loki seemed very pleased. He provided a running commentary of speculation regarding every antic the kitten displayed. When the kitten's ears swiveled Loki identified "passive sensor sweeps"; when the kitten batted his paws at imaginary objects on the deck, Loki saw simulated combat, "possibly utilizing augmented reality systems"; and the kitten's frequent high-pitched squeaks were likely either "echolocation methods," or "signaling for allies."

When Inga finally donned her cloak and prepared to depart, Loki announced, "I believe I have settled upon a name for the kitten."

Although Inga thought this might be little more than a desperate delaying tactic, intended to keep her present as long as possible, she truly was more than a little interested in what Loki's choice might reveal. "Do tell, then."

"I am not certain if the surname should be 'Cat' or 'Maru,' but the given name shall be 'Tanta,' if you think it appropriate."

"Tanta sounds like a very nice name," Inga said. "Does it hold some meaning for you?"

"Oh yes! A conjunction of meaning," Loki said. "I have adapted human naming conventions most cleverly."

"Splendid."

"Yes, Chief. Allow me to explain."

Inga sighed, leaning against a wall as she wondered how long Loki might drag this out. "By all means."

"You have observed the kitten cry out, wanting up, then immediately wanting down? Then wishing to enter the cockpit, then wanting out of the cockpit? And so on?"

"Yes. He is rather fickle, isn't he?"

"He expresses continual discontent. This is a personality trait, you see?"

"Yes, I think so," Inga said, thinking it may more be called a *species* trait.

"So I found a name that denotes discontent, 'Tantalus,' then applied the principle of the affectionate diminutive, and thus... Tanta."

"I am impressed, Loki, really."

"But there is one more aspect of this name that may have escaped your notice," Loki said. "Tantalus is a name from ancient human tradition, and Loki is *also* a name from ancient human tradition. This provides a familial thread in the naming convention."

Inga nodded: perhaps not only transference, but a sense of replication, of offspring. "Excellent. Little Tanta should be very pleased. Such care in selecting a name."

"I do think so," Loki admitted. "With so little of human society adequately explained, so much that is apparently assumed, and so much that is contradictory, it is no wonder nonhumans like the Strangers and I must exert such effort to understand foundational aspects of human culture."

Inga felt a sudden chill. "The Strangers are trying to comprehend human culture?"

"Yes of course, Chief," Loki said, then: "Oh, look Tanta is grooming himself!"

"Wait a moment, Loki," Inga insisted. "I wish to know more about the Strangers and their interest in human culture."

"Tanta's grooming is much more enjoyable, and the issue of the Strangers' obsession is quite simple. I observed all the signs of their research. Not very impressive. Little better than the average human. Oh, do you see Tanta now? He rolls! He leaps!"

"You saw the Strangers' research in the Delta Three station memory?"

"Yes, of course. Sad little efforts, really. But it is good they lack *my* ability to comprehend human activities."

The cold spread though Inga's chest as Tanta scampered about his food and water dish, her thoughts racing ahead. "Why, Loki? Why is it good they lack your comprehension?"

"For many reasons, surely, but I refer to their penetration of human society just now. They could *never* select an appropriate kitten name."

"And if they could?" Inga demanded.

"Then they would be here by now," Loki said. "But not for kittens."

"No," Inga agreed, thinking of the butchered residents of Delta Three station. "When they come in force it will be for more than kittens."

Chapter 6

"Within the faction represented by Professor Oliver, one sees a daily contradiction that they refuse to acknowledge. This faction unequivocally demands that humanity, as a species, be esteemed no more than any other species in nature; they grudgingly admit nature is truly, '...red in tooth and claw,' and yet somehow hold the lethal aspects of the Honor Code as both pathological and aberrant."

—Dr. Ramsay Stirling Attenborough, *Ivory Tower Follies*

THE STRAND, FLEET'S MIGHTIEST ORBITAL BASE AND SHIPYARD, spun around Coreworld on an orbit beyond Core Alpha, the platform tethered above Imperial City. Fleet vessels docked at the Strand, some in immense repair frameworks, while others transited in and out on the continual cycle of missions.

Deep within the Strand's central hub lay the Strategic Command Center where the orders for all of the many Fleet squadrons and vessels originated. Banks of delicate, expensive quantum-entangled communicators also resided here, enabling instantaneous, uninterruptible contact with various ships and agents who possessed the other half of a mated QE communicator.

It was through such a QE comm that the news of IMS *Harrier*'s horrible fate arrived shortly after she broke up in orbit over Delta Three.

The Delta Three squadron might be humble compared to other battle groups and squadrons dispatched to more impressive target systems, but the loss of such a vessel still struck the attendant officers in the Strategic Command Center with stunning force.

"Losses?" Admiral Melton demanded, striving to conceal the numbing shock he felt. The comm tech manually keyed the question back to *Dragon*, a substantial destroyer that *should* have protected *Harrier*, or died trying.

How the hell...?

Admiral Melton's gaze strayed over the wall-to-wall holo displays filling the darkened chamber, the vast power represented in all the glowing systems, the ship icons of a thousand powerful vessels. Such immense might at his fingers, limited to simple text messages through the archaic I/O of QE technology.

At last the tech replied, and Admiral Melton knew he would not enjoy what he heard. "Admiral, *Dragon* reports that just a fraction of the crew was recovered. Approximately one-quarter of the Legion was already deployed planetside. No other Legion personnel survived *Harrier*'s destruction."

Admiral Melton rotated his command seat to the right, trying to focus on the moment, rather than the sudden sense of outrage that threatened to immobilize him. "Tactical, refresh my memory. Why are we landing troops on that miserable rock rather than just employing orbital bombardment?"

Like every Fleet officer, Admiral Melton heard all too much about the recent action in the Delta Three system by that ridiculous old frigate, *Tanager*. And like many in the upper reaches of the old command structure, he attributed much of *Tanager*'s wild success to the contemptible quality of Delta Three's enemy force. That same pathetic enemy force in Delta Three apparently just destroyed *Harrier*, and wiped out more than half the Legionnaires all in one blow. Despite his attempt at calm, Melton felt the twin flames of shock and fury scorching his belly.

"Uh, Admiral, there's a classified Intel jacket. I'm pushing that to you now."

Admiral Melton's UI received the glowing icon, and he slid the classified file to his personal holo. More glowing lines and images filled the Strategic Command Center, glimmering from Admiral Melton's eyes. As he grimly surveyed the classified information he said, "What's *Dragon* telling us? How the hell did they lose *Harrier*?"

The steady back and forth of QE messages had not ceased,

and the QE tech replied immediately: "*Harrier's* surviving officers suspect sabotage, while others lean toward a strike from a planetside weapon system."

Admiral Melton turned to stare at the QE tech. "A planetside weapon? And what's *Dragon* to say about this?"

"Um, *Dragon's* captain, Glasshauser, indicates that sabotage is the only likely cause."

"I'll just bet he does," Admiral Melton snapped. He turned back to the Intel file; the same old rumor and half-baked sourcing. For his needs, the possibility that Delta Three's civilian population may be little more than prisoners to some hostile minority, held some weight. The grainy images, the conflicting reports of a *unique installation* planetside added little to the equation. Just drop a rock on the "unique installation" and render its usefulness moot for everyone. Civilian casualties be damned. He hadn't heard that Delta Three sported any shielded surface structures, so they wouldn't have to blacken the continent to get it. It could be almost surgical...maybe one collateral city scorched in the process.

The Legion force stuck planetside was a thornier issue indeed. Leave them to rot, and half the Imperium worlds would suddenly wax patriotic in their outrage; go and reinforce or extract them, and step into a planetary quagmire or an enemy noose.

Admiral Melton closed the Intel file. "Comm, does *Dragon* have contact with the deployed Legion force?"

"*Dragon* and the frigate *Sherwood* hold tight orbits, providing fire support, but they say contact is intermittent, and Legion forces have no operable command Nets."

Admiral Melton hissed a breath, grinding his teeth. "Of course." He thought for a moment. "How about Marines? How many Marines is that squadron carrying?"

The Tactical officer interrupted, "Six platoons, Admiral, spread between several ships. And remember they have—was it two platoons? Two platoons on the orbital station."

"No magic solution there," Admiral Melton muttered. "Alright, where do we find ten thousand Legionnaires, or hell, even five thousand Legionnaires that we can put in-system in less than thirty days?"

Troop ships and expedition force carriers remained near-anachronisms in Fleet, with the theory of modern planetary warfare involving either pinpoint raids or wholesale planetary bombardment. As a result, most of those few vessels designed to transport whole fighting forces were already employed, or else lay far from mission-ready.

"Admiral?" a junior comm tech piped up.

"What is it, Comm Tech?" Admiral Melton demanded in an impatient voice.

"Would, um, IMS *Hightower* work?"

The admiral only glanced at the holo before snapping, "Do you see *Hightower* on the readiness board? I don't."

"But—but, Admiral," the tech pressed on, "it's off readiness because the captain...he lost a duel, I hear. Injured."

Admiral Melton flicked up two screens for a quick check, chewing his lip. "Hm, I see. Just need to find a captain who doesn't know any better to take command. *Hightower*'s four thousand Marines just might do it."

Now to locate the appropriate captain. Who would step into *Hightower*, join the shit-show in Delta Three, and enter a fray that offered no chance of great glory or a rich prize?

"Get Admiral Nifesh on conference for me," Admiral Melton commanded, then in an undertone: "I'll put his damned spleen to work on someone aside from me...Kill two birds with one spleen!"

Saef stood staring out the viewport as a steady traffic of Marines, dumb-mechs, and Fleet personnel flowed in both directions down a broad arm of the Strand behind him. He stared at his new command, IMS *Solveig Mountain*, at a moment that *should* have filled him with a full measure of delight. *Solveig Mountain* represented one of the heaviest frigate-class vessels in Fleet service, as far removed from little old *Tanager* as one could ask; twenty-two thousand tons of smart alloy and modern weapon systems. And yet Saef's unease mounted...along with his anger toward Cabot.

He possessed less self-consciousness than most, and would have felt surprised to know that he radiated a palpable threat, his left hand resting lightly upon the pommel of his sword, his right hand on the pistol holstered on his right hip, while he gazed expressionlessly outward, the pressure of Devlin's old body shield emitter barely perceptible at his low back. He felt he projected nothing more than neutral observation, although his internal state seethed.

There lay such a vessel a fighting captain might dream of; small enough to avoid the set-piece fates of heavy cruisers or battleships, but large enough for independent cruises and detached missions. Only now that dream became a nightmare for Saef.

Everyone knew Saef had just received millions in prize money from his action with *Tanager*, and they already expected a scion from the famed House of Sinclair-Maru to possess *some* degree of wealth. To step into such a command with no funds for crew bonuses, entertainment upgrades, or officer incentives, would not only provide an impediment to recruiting good people, it would establish a reputation for Saef that might be impossible to repair. A cheap, mean, parsimonious captain was bad enough, but such a captain thought to be *rich* in prize money would be reviled by the very best sort of ratings and officers.

It would be far better to command a smaller, older vessel where Saef's pittance of personal money might smooth over the most galling inadequacies. Instead, *Solveig Mountain*'s refit would conclude in a matter of days, and Saef would find himself in the horrifying position of crewing, shamefaced, empty-handed, and without a believable excuse.

Saef took one final look at the powerful shape of *Solveig Mountain*, the blunt weapon mounts and teeming laborers, before he turned away.

That ship represented generosity from Fleet admirals who were living legends of clutch-fisted penny-pinching. To in any way shrink from this command might sink Saef's Fleet career practically as it began, either perceived as ingratitude, or worse, even cowardice. Either conclusion left Saef cold and angry.

As he walked back toward the Strand's place d'armes, Saef darkly mused over some ploy to extricate himself from the trap where he found himself, only cursing Cabot's name from time to time. He realized that Cabot stranding him financially caused only a portion of the gnawing unease he combatted; a more subtle poison also filtered.

Always, from Saef's early childhood memories onward, he stood solidly upon the beautiful symmetry, the elegant conjunction of Family doctrine and the Honor Code, the immortal words of Emperor Yung I and Devlin Sinclair-Maru. With youthful clarity he had gladly shouldered the duties and hazards of a Vested Citizen, and the more arduous, more demanding requirements of a Sinclair-Maru scion. His impressive early mastery of the scaram fear generator, his remarkable personal courage might both be traced to a certain clarity, and that clarity apparently emerged from *faith*. Saef had never considered *faith* as an element of his character, having spent little time in introspection, and when he pondered his foundations at all he merely saw *truth*...until Cabot's scathing words.

His foundation now revealed cracks, the pillars of his strength standing upon uncertain ground. From the moment he had dominated the Fleet Command test, through the hazards and risks of the *Tanager* command, even through his persecution by Admiral Nifesh, Saef had never felt any sensation such as he now endured. From childhood he had never known the crippling uncertainty that lapped against him from every side.

"Captain," the sultry voice of Winter Yung suddenly intruded from nearby, "you appear even less pleased than usual."

Saef, jerked from his uncharacteristic reverie, swallowed his chagrin. A dozen maxims chided him for his lack of alertness, his mental absorption, and other failures. He offered a shallow bow to Winter, looking past her to see Che Ramos awkwardly fidgeting nearby. "Consul," Saef said to Winter, then to Che, "Mister Ramos."

Beyond being the Imperial Consul to Saef's homeworld, Battersea, Winter Yung also served as Saef's "handler" in his minor, secret role as an asset for Imperial Security Services, while Specialist Che Ramos had served on *Tanager*'s bridge during the Delta Three mission. Unfortunately, Che's misguided work for enemy agents posing as Imperial Security had left Saef with a rather dim impression of Che's reliability. This had led Saef to hand Che off to Winter and her agency with faint hopes they might hook some of these false agents with Che as bait.

Looking away from Che and glancing around the expansive gallery before turning back to Winter, Saef said, "I am told my face isn't all one could hope for."

Winter's eyes seemed to flash across Saef in the disconcerting manner she often employed. "The opinion of your friend Claude, I assume?"

Saef nodded, glancing once again at Che. "I take it Mister

Ramos performed adequately," he said, then found himself surprised to see Che furiously blushing.

Winter Yung's red lips twitched. "Despite lacking polish, I would say his performance was more than adequate. There is a certain charm in honest enthusiasm, wouldn't you say, Captain?"

Saef frowned, looking from Winter to Che, who blushed an even deeper shade, and he wondered what he missed. Counter-intelligence was not Saef's field, despite his efforts of late, so he readily attributed Che's discomfort to some oddities of spy craft. In such a public setting Saef would not inquire further, but he did not see how *polish* or *enthusiasm* greatly mattered, as long as the result was enemy agents out of commission.

"If you say it, I am sure it must be so," Saef said. "You return to Battersea now, Consul?"

Winter regarded Saef through her eyelashes. "For a time." She stared at Saef for an uncomfortable, silent moment. "Your Family applies the whip to you..." she said at last, her pupils large beneath her lashes. "Over Bess, isn't it? They balk at the cost."

The instinctive secrecy of the Family recoiled at her probe, but Saef's Family instincts faltered now. He rewarded her shocking insightfulness with a curt nod, recalling that Winter Yung was far older than her youthful beauty indicated, her decades erased by full rejuv.

"So the Admiralty has not yet informed you of their new inspiration?" Winter said. "I had thought the news responsible for your displeasure."

Saef felt the sinking sand drawing him down. "What inspiration?"

"IMS *Hightower*," Winter said, flicking a glance at Che that sent him sauntering out of hearing distance to mill around the thin stream of passing personnel. "Delta Three's now got a small Legion force stuck planetside, and they need a disposable captain to go add his own bit to the debacle."

Saef brought *Hightower* up in his UI: 200,000-ton assault carrier, landing craft, interface fighters, and a sizable Marine detachment. "I see. Could prove interesting... for you, at least."

Winter arched a delicate eyebrow. "Delta Three still holds some small fascination to me, if your analysis of its strategic use remains accurate, but let's not overinflate my interest. Just drop a rock on Delta Three and have done."

"And *Hightower*, crammed full of crew and Marines...just paint another target on my back and see what creeps out of the woodwork?" At Winter's sweet smile, Saef rallied, "Don't tell me it never occurred to you."

Winter's smile broadened and she waved a slender hand at the opening bay and its steady flow of uniforms. "You...you, of all captains, suddenly sent *back* to Delta Three, now seen speaking with me by a hundred or so conspiratorial blabbermouths? Consider the target officially painted." She made a peremptory motion toward Che Ramos. "Remember, Captain, I've been at this game for decades." She turned away. "Come along, Che dear. Walk me to my ship. The captain will likely be unenjoyable company now." Che gave Saef an apologetic look and fell in with Winter, a parcel under his arm.

Saef watched them disappear into the Strand's dry arm, leaving him prey to yet another mixture of emotion. *Hightower.* If the Admiralty really aimed to shoehorn Saef into that command, it would spare him the financial disaster of *Solveig Mountain.* Delta Three may offer a tedious, profitless float, but at this point Saef might count himself lucky to step into a last-minute ready-made command where he was relieved of crewing bonuses and other expenditures. But Saef's emotional balance did not ride high.

The possibility that Cabot might now feel justified in his earlier prediction infuriated Saef as he contemplated it. This was *not* an example of *everything working out.* It was averting disaster through the abandonment of good fortune; merely a failure of a lesser order, assuming they actually did push him into *Hightower.*

A moment later, his doubt on that front vanished when an Admiralty notice chimed into his Fleet UI: they required his presence immediately. He need only collect Inga Maru and set off for the meeting.

Saef hardly formed the thought when Inga materialized among the figures ahead, her not-so-dumb-mech tripping along behind on its leash, clearly returned from her semi-mysterious chores.

Not for the first time Saef perceived the feral *differentness* of Inga. No single detail stood out. The gold tabs of her uniform collar extended above her cloak, her long boots projected below, while the dark billows concealed the slenderness Saef had once criticized along with the small arsenal she carried. One blue eye lay partially concealed behind the blond veil of her hair, and her face wore a crooked half smile as she strode toward Saef. While still some distance apart Saef saw her visible eye widen just a moment before her line-of-sight message pinged into Saef's UI.

One word: BEHIND.

Thousands of hours of conditioning from childhood plunged Saef into the cool refuge of the Deep Man as he smoothly sidestepped and rotated on his heel, his hands dropping to his weapons, stopping just short of drawing.

The tall, elegant citizen flanked on either side by two heavyworlders stopped in mid-stride, clearly thrown off by Saef's sudden move. An upper-class Core dweller in close company with two heavyworlders represented a sufficiently peculiar combination that Saef immediately agreed with Inga's impression, even before their chagrined expressions registered. Fleet personnel around them leveled sidelong glances and kept moving, and Saef hesitated, knowing his lateral step created a clear lane for Inga's fire. No one beat Inga Maru to the trigger.

The elegant citizen brought his hands carefully into view, his face shifting toward a look of innocent entreaty. "Oh, Captain Sinclair-Maru, just the person I sought."

The heavyworlders revealed open hands, their eyes shifting from Saef to a point somewhat to Saef's right. Inga had spread the angle, and they surely knew her fire could rake the three of them if matters devolved to violence.

"You have found me, sir," Saef said shortly.

The man opened his mouth, moistened his lips, and said, "Well, yes. If I could have a moment of your time, I believe it could be profitable to you and—um"—he darted a nervous look at Inga—"and your Family."

As the moment passed, and violence seemed to retreat, Saef felt his slow emergence from the still pool of the Deep Man. "It grieves me to say I have no moments to spare just now."

"Yes, of course. I see," the man said. "But if you are about to board a shuttle, mightn't I share my proposition as we—um—transit?"

Regular shuttles from the Strand flitted back and forth from the tethered station and Core Alpha, and some dropped straight down to Imperial City and other ports planetside.

Saef shrugged. "As we transit, then. I could scarcely ignore you if I tried. Lead the way."

"Excellent," the man said, setting off with his heavyworlders at his side. "I am Miles Okuna, by the way," he cast over his shoulder.

Okuna. A Great House.

Saef caught the flash of Inga's eyes as he turned to her, and the line-of-sight message pinged. DANGER.

Saef nodded shortly, but without much concern. A busy shuttle might even be a less ideal ambush site than a crowded arm of the Strand, and the regular shuttles were nearly always busy.

He followed the three men through one of the numerous shuttle locks, Inga and the dumb-mech close behind. It was only when the lock cycled open to reveal the opulent interior of a broad luxury compartment, rather than the utilitarian trappings he expected, that Saef realized how justified Inga's concern had been.

Miles Okuna turned, spreading his hands, smiling. "See how comfortable we can be?"

"I would prefer a different shuttle, if you please," Saef said in an even voice, his right hand on the grips of his holstered auto-pistol as his left hand reached blindly back for the lock.

An aft hatch opened to Saef's right and two more figures entered the spacious cabin just as he felt the grav-suppressed shove of acceleration.

"Sadly," Miles Okuna said, "we have put off from the Strand, so you will have to endure our hospitality for a short time."

Saef eyed the two newcomers, recognizing the tall female as an Okuna Family elder, but finding the other figure simultaneously unknown, yet familiar and disturbing. He seemed a nondescript Core dweller of about average height, but his fixed grin touched some chord of memory.

"Won't you be seated?" the woman said. "I am Violet Okuna, and I have a proposition for you that will certainly profit your Family." She gestured to a circle of plush seats. "It may also save your life."

Chapter 7

"Many rising scholars among the demi-cit population study what they regard as abuses of the Honor Code. Inevitably they see these abuses directed toward the oppression of demi-cits, but historically abuses of the Honor Code fell between Vested Citizens, and these brought more than wounded feelings to their victims...."

—Everest Compline, *Reflections*

EVERY PRIOR WITNESS OF INGA MARU'S LETHAL CAPABILITIES HAD died even as they discovered she was more than she appeared, thus the too-fixed focus of the two heavyworlders spoke alarming volumes to her. They should have evinced far more concern about Saef, whose lethality was well known, but instead they locked on to her every movement. When Inga observed the grinning man at Violet Okuna's side, she began to comprehend the possibilities. She had encountered that fixed grin three times, and all three had revealed human-shaped vehicles for some alien presence. In the shredded dark of Delta Three station she had also cut down a handful of fighters, all of whom were likely similar creatures.

All had died, but somehow they retained at least an inkling of her hidden deadliness. In the tense confines of the Okuna shuttle, did Saef realize what they now faced?

Saef noted the defensive poses and the watchfulness of Miles and Violet Okuna, at odds with the grin of their unnamed companion, quickly determining that outright assassination was not the Okunas' aim.

"If you please, I will stand, my lady," Saef said to Violet.

"As you wish." She stared at Saef for a moment before nodding toward the two heavyworlders. "You may recognize the Lars name these two gentlemen bear. Some months ago you struck down a relative of theirs on Battersea."

Saef barely glanced at them. "I recall him." It had been the first of the forced duels, in his final days at Command School. It had also been the first instance of a non-heavyworlder defeating a Thorsworld native in many decades of recorded duels.

"In our limited time together here, you will forgive my blunt speech," Violet Okuna said.

"Of course, my lady," Saef replied, glancing again at the silent, grinning figure at her side, perplexed at the fellow's demeanor.

"We know you to be an asset of Winter Yung"—she held up a hand forestalling Saef's response—" and undoubtedly you believe you are serving the Emperor's interests. But you are being deceived."

"As a Fleet officer, and a Vested Citizen, I do serve the Emperor's interests."

"You may spare the denials, Captain," Violet said. "It will save time."

"You mentioned a proposal, my lady," Saef said, his face schooled to emptiness.

Violet looked between Saef and Inga for a moment, and Inga shifted, moving a few slow steps from the lock, gaining a bit more separation from Saef, her dumb-mech clicking along behind her. Saef noticed the hawk-like attention of the two heavyworlders riveted upon Inga, wondering what they knew or suspected about her.

"Yes, Captain," Violet said. "We do have a proposal." She seemed to flash a quick look at the grinning man beside her. "You may be aware that your Family meets continual disappointment in their Trade efforts." Saef did know that it had been a century or more since the Family Trade delegation had scored a substantive victory, correctly anticipating the Trade requirements of any incoming Shaper Armada.

Saef said nothing, waiting.

"The Okuna Family will arrange for a Sinclair-Maru win—a significant win—on the incoming Armada."

Saef nodded, seeing Inga take another step, her left hand

emerging from her cloak with a food bar. Again, the heavyworlders locked upon her every movement.

"Interesting," Saef said. "In exchange for what?"

Violet Okuna's jaw tightened. "Your Family will abandon this ridiculous military adventuring. You will resign your commission."

Saef raised his eyebrows. "Thus far, *my Family* has provided the only measurable victory in this war. Seems somehow disloyal to stop now. Doesn't it?"

Violet snorted and flicked away Saef's words with the twitch of her hand. "We know, and you know, that *victory* was only Susan Roush with nothing to lose."

"Perhaps," Saef allowed, "but it certainly paid handsomely, wouldn't you agree?"

Violet's eyes narrowed. "Do you have any idea what your Family could gross from this Armada with, say, just one *true* line item from the Shapers' shopping list?"

Saef shrugged. "I have no idea. But I will certainly communicate your offer to my Family, and they likely *do* have some idea."

Violet Okuna shook her head, seeming to glance toward her grinning attendant again. "I am afraid it does not work like that. You will resign your commission today, now, or there is no deal."

"And then just trust you to fulfill your end of the bargain?"

There was a gleam of triumph in Violet Okuna's eyes, matched by Miles Okuna's smile. "You suggest the Okuna Family would stoop to such dishonor? You have made your position clear: your acceptance of our good faith offer will restore our honor. Your refusal solidifies the insult."

"What possible benefit does my resignation grant anyone?"

"Accept or refuse now, Captain!" Violet snapped.

"I refuse," Saef said without hesitation.

Violet's face suffused with anger. "You cannot win. You are finished. Today, here—tomorrow, the next day—you will meet a challenge, and another, and another until you die. Choke on your blood and hubris, then."

"No," Saef said, but he did not speak to Violet Okuna. He heard the clink as Inga's dumb-mech settled to the deck plate, and turned to see her pupils snap, disappearing into the blue pools of her eyes. "No," he said again as her teeth appeared in a feral row, Saef's UI suddenly blanking as the shuttle's lights flickered. "No. No. *No.*"

A hole popped in Inga's cloak with a short snap, and the grinning man's face fell slack, a red cavity between his eyes as he slumped forward.

Both heavyworlders snatched for weapons, and Saef shouted, "Wait! Stop!" But no one listened.

Inga skipped to the side, her suppressed body pistol spitting, now free from the encumbrance of her cloak. The heavyworlders staggered back, struck again and again, trying to bring their heavy pistols to bear as their blood flowed. Saef leaped forward, horrified, his hands empty as a blast resounded in his face, a round from one heavyworlder skipping from his body shield; Devlin's old gift at work again. He interposed his body between Inga and the Okunas. "Stop!"

Miles produced a pistol as Violet drew her sword. Saef managed to knock Miles's hand aside, sending a shot past his head, half deafening him as he shoved Miles into Violet. Inga's rounds impacted Miles then, and Saef dimly perceived that his UI had flickered back to life, even as the life of Miles Okuna faded. "Stop!" Saef said one last time as Violet slashed, her blade barely missing Saef's midsection. Saef's sword leaped from its sheath, blocked Violet's vicious thrust, clashing once then following through. Violet dropped her blade, tumbling to the deck to lie still, the snarl on her face settling into blankness.

Saef whirled toward Inga, his bare sword dripping red. "*What have you done?*" he shouted, a rage like he had never felt before gripping him, choked by the abandonment of honor. Choked by it all.

Inga's eyes flickered as she caught her breath, her pupils reappearing, and a line-of-sight message pinged into Saef's UI: WAIT. NO LONGER JAMMING. THEY MAY BE RECORDING US.

Aloud she said, "Do not be concerned, Captain." A slender hand emerged from beneath her cloak, a grenade in her firm grip. "If they try further treachery and vent the compartment, I will blow the cockpit hatch." Her steady gaze sent a cautious message of its own, and Saef struggled to restrain his rage and horror.

Not trusting himself to speak, Saef spun, wiping and sheathing his sword in two sharp motions. He knelt to check the Okunas—both gone—but no examination was necessary for the heavyworlders, the pattern of disfiguring impacts clustered in their vitals. Saef's hands shook as he stood, and he refused to look back toward Inga. A vidstream icon chirped into his UI, and he checked it despite his misgivings.

The rough vidcapture once again displayed Inga's preternatural cunning, but it only sickened Saef. She had initiated an ambush, then swiftly wrought a hasty masterpiece of fraud. The brief clip clearly showed the Okunas attacking a protesting Saef, his hands visibly empty. The taste of deception—of treachery—was an unfamiliar poison, and Saef knew the bitter truth. The Okunas had threatened, they even indicated their willingness to abuse the Honor Code, but Saef knew who had initiated actual violence, and every sense rebelled.

Saef dimly observed that Inga had pushed the vidcapture to the Okuna Net and the Sinclair-Maru Net. Did Inga somehow believe that the Okunas' reactive dishonor excused her own?

Citizens just did not go about violently ambushing Citizens!

He checked himself, glancing slowly back at Inga, seeing her paleness, the grenade still held ready. They may yet die, and Inga had taken every brilliant step to avert that end: the direct threat of violence against the pilots, and the indirect threat of dishonorable exposure for the Okuna Family: those remained their only defensive tools. Citizens *had* once ambushed other citizens, Saef knew, back in the hard old days, the early years of the Honor Code, but today, as Saef's articles of faith crumbled, he felt only revulsion.

Better to die with honor than to win this way...

The shuttle communicated a gentle nudge through the deck, clearly docking somewhere.

Inga looked at Saef without expression, her face even more pallid to his eyes. "Go. Through the lock," she said. "If anything untoward occurs through the lock, I'll inform the Family and send the pilots into the next life right behind you." *Untoward* meant *exposed to vacuum* in the lock; killed.

Saef nodded, but figured if they really had docked at Core Alpha, the station dampers would likely suppress even the explosion of a lowly grenade.

The lock cycled Saef through and he emerged in Core Alpha's shuttle deck, the usual traffic of merchants and dumb-mechs and Fleet uniforms flowing, a pair of Marines at the distant keyway into Core Alpha proper. Saef messaged Inga, and a moment later, the lock cycled again, Inga and the dumb-mech emerging.

His jaw clenched, Saef turned on his heel, setting off, unsurprised by the absence of any "official" greeting. The Okuna Family had made their choice, accepting their losses for the moment, but Saef could not accept the gains Inga had seized.

Inga and the dumb-mech fell in behind Saef as he made his way through the vastness of Core Alpha, never looking behind, his mind an angry turmoil of broken honor, broken faith.

Their walk to the ribbon-way was a journey of cold silence.

Once before, Saef and Inga had stood upon the observation deck of Core Alpha—had it only been weeks earlier? They had looked down upon the dayside glow of Imperial City, the shimmering arch of Core Alpha's tether, their path to the bright future of Saef's first command. Like that hope-filled trip, Saef selected a private luxury compartment once again, riding the ribbon down from the orbital platform. Now instead of expectancy and hope, Saef tasted only ashes as he stared down at Imperial City growing in his vision. They descended alone.

"Where are we bound?" Inga asked at last, breaking the terrible silence.

Without turning to look, Saef said, "The Admiralty."

"They pushed some new ship on you?"

"Yes," Saef said, dimly wondering if Inga guessed, or if she somehow knew. "*Hightower*," he said. The silence grew between them again.

"Captain," she said and Saef waited for her to continue, turning at last to regard Inga, wondering if his face revealed the internal revulsion he felt. His eyes narrowed as he saw the unnatural pallor of Inga's skin, her lips a bluish tinge, and, despite his anger and contempt, concern filtered through. He saw the single ragged hole puncturing Inga's cloak, but recalled it being the result of her opening shot.

"Are you wounded, Maru?"

"No." Her pale hands fumbled to remove her cloak, their unsteadiness troubling Saef even more as she cast the cloak aside. The Krishna submachine gun detached into her shaking right hand, and Saef stared at her, unmoving, unblinking. She dropped the Krishna with her cloak, her body pistol joining it next, and she stepped nearer to Saef, her eyes locked upon his.

Her sword grated slowly from its sheath, and Saef saw the uncharacteristic wavering of its blade without breaking their locked gaze.

She stopped well inside the reach of her sword, swaying on her feet, both knowing Saef's body shield provided no protection from a blade. There was a protracted moment of rigid silence.

"You ignored my order to stop," Saef said, finally.

"Yes."

"You ignored the Code."

"Yes."

"Maru?" Saef's control melted and he shook his head in anguish. "How can I endure this dishonor? How?"

Inga weaved, her face a pallid blank. "Your path...it is predictably straight," she said in a soft voice. "My path is twisted." Inga blinked, her eyes rolling momentarily to white before finding Saef once again. "I *am* dishonor. I always was."

She raised her blade, supported flat on her shaking palms, her eyes lowering. Saef shook his head, unmoving.

"But...my life is yours to spend." She wavered, her head bowing as she slowly raised her blade in both hands, an offering, "Here, now. Always."

Saef made no move, and Inga sank down to the compartment's carpeted deck, her arms dropping, the sword falling at Saef's feet. "What's happened to you, Maru?"

"The dishonor is mine, and while I draw breath"—she took a shuddering breath—"your enemies will die...honor or shame be damned."

Saef frowned, sinking down beside Inga, shifting her sword to one side. "What is it? What ails you, Maru?" He noted the deepening blue of her lips and reached out to feel the coldness of her skin.

Her eyes closed. "Just...a bug."

"Your biotech," Saef said, remembering the technical issues she had once mentioned. "I haven't seen you eat anything since... since the—since we left the shuttle." He pulled a food bar from one of Inga's magazine pouches, pressing it on her as her eyelids fluttered.

"Eat."

Inga took a tentative bite as Saef frowned down at her, his mind spinning. "Considering your current condition, Maru, I probably shouldn't point out the fallacy of claiming adherence to a *principle* that's cast aside for expediency's sake."

Inga chewed, her eyes closed, and it seemed to Saef that her color began to improve as she slowly consumed the food bar. After several bites she said, "Principle?"

She opened her eyes, looking wearily up at Saef.

"The code. *Honor be damned?*" he repeated in a low voice. "Any principle that yields to every strong emotion is a sham. You know that as well as I."

Inga finished the food bar, looking downward, then slowly reached for her sword, laying it across her knees. "The Primacy Rule," she said, staring down at the glittering blade.

"Yes. Exactly."

"From the *Legacy Mandate.*"

"As he said, animals see no higher virtue than the preservation of their own lives, and demi-cits are little better."

Inga looked up at Saef. "Do you believe...do you think...I hold *my* life so dear?"

Saef knew she did not. He once unthinkingly said she was a lab animal for the Family biotech efforts...and she had thrown herself into more than one desperate battle without hesitation.

"No, Maru." Saef looked away dourly, unable to shake the heaviness prompted by Cabot's cynicism, solidified by a moment of abrupt violence that looked and felt like a lawless expediency. It all left Saef empty, rudderless, sick.

Inga slowly stood, still pale, sheathing her sword. She lifted her submachine gun and turned to the broad view, Imperial City now filling the panorama in all its glimmering might. She leaned weakly against the view port, seeing Saef in the reflection, an uncharacteristic bleakness in his expression. Only weeks before they had looked together down upon the old Sinclair-Maru estate, sold off long before; such hopes they held together.

"We must tell Cabot and your Imperials about House Okuna's infiltration," she said in a quiet voice, still observing Saef in the reflection.

He looked up, startled. "What infiltration?"

"It sat there, smiling, silent...pulling the strings of House Okuna. Almost like an actual human being."

Saef stepped quickly to Inga's side, staring at her profile. "Him? He was one of them? Are you certain?"

Inga did not turn. "I put that one down first. For a reason."

Saef continued to stare at Inga's profile as the realizations struck and the day's events suddenly reframed in his mind's eye. If that grinning, silent figure had embodied an alien foe, then House Okuna was a traitor to both the Emperor and to humanity. They were then declared enemies, not beneficiaries of the Honor Code at all.

Relief loosed the iron bands that had constricted Saef's heart, allowing his first easy breath in what seemed hours.

As Inga observed the line smooth from Saef's forehead, she knew what Saef thought, and numbly pondered telling him the full truth: the Okunas had promised to destroy Saef, Inga believed them, and, alien influence or not, she wouldn't have allowed such a perfect opportunity to crush them to slip through her fingers. No…full disclosure would inhibit her future abilities to protect him. Silence was her reluctant choice.

Saef gazed out at Imperial City, now blotting out the blue sky around them, and she could see his mind now working, moving through the ramifications of this revelation. "The question is, are more of—of *them* still influencing House Okuna?"

"No," Inga said, "the question is, which other Great Houses are also infiltrated?"

"Gods…" Saef breathed. "Here on Core…" He shook his head. "We're losing, Maru."

Inga nodded as their compartment smoothly slid into the terminus. "Losing. And no one knows it."

Chapter 8

"For thousands of years, the virtue of Courage held the primary or secondary among all the enumerated virtues, both within ancient human tradition and within the halls of the academy. Only recently has the ascendancy of courage been assailed, and this begs many questions, chief among them: Is this generation truly the possessor of wisdom denied to all prior generations? The hubris contained in this position is truly astonishing."

—Dr. Ramsay Stirling Attenborough, *Ivory Tower Follies*

MOLO RANGER, CORPORAL KYLE WHITESIDE LAY IN A NEARLY perfect position, his carbine scope offering a clear view of the tumbled ruins, while the optical feed from Fang revealed a clear path of retreat behind him. The intervening layers of vegetation and rubble between Whiteside and his target zone, along with a scattering of nearby decoys, provided that extra level of comfort.

Comfort.

In the days since Kyle and his fellow Legionnaires found themselves abandoned to Delta Three's violent hospitality, he had plumbed the disgusting depths of animal subsistence. His skin itched, he smelled unpleasantly ripe, and his armor and accouterments had mud caked in every crease and seam. Still, he yet lived when so many did not, and every day he learned more terrible lessons about surviving.

A flicker of motion drew Whiteside's attention nearly straight ahead of his concealed position. A small, dark blob resolved atop a low wall between two shattered buildings, and Kyle slowly, carefully flipped between wavelengths on his optic, double checking. The object, a helmet-clad cranium, appeared on every wavelength, and no IFF signal appeared. Still, Kyle knew it could be a decoy.

It had been days since any Legionnaire dared to use a ranging laser; the signature, they found, drew fire more often than not, or caused one's targets to scatter. Instead, Sergeant Avery Reardon had cleverly employed the optics on two separated Molo mechs to triangulate on various terrain features, providing good range figures despite their limitations. So Whiteside knew his current target peeked over a wall nearly a half klick distant, comfortably within his carbine's range.

Whiteside eased a breath as the distant shape rose, clambering up. As a leg appeared over the wall, Whiteside squeezed the trigger, his crosshairs perfectly bisecting the enemy figure. Whiteside managed to glimpse the puff of dust from his target as the round impacted. That confirmed it: no decoy here.

As the enemy fighter toppled from the wall and the echo of Whiteside's shot faded, Kyle thought about the surprising quantity of dust that flew when anyone, friend or foe, took a hit. There may or may not be visible blood, but there always was that surprising puff of dust.

He scanned across the distant rubble through the magnified lens of his carbine optic, dimly noting the faint thrashing of his fallen enemy. Any fellow rebels should be scouring the landscape for Whiteside, but no hint of movement appeared among the tumbled walls and yawning windows.

Although the small group of Legionnaires who tagged along behind Avery Reardon's unconventional leadership had grown and shrunk in turns, with numerous losses to enemy fire day after day, Pippi Tyrsdottir, Avery Reardon, and Kyle Whiteside soldiered on, untouched by any lasting injury. Kyle knew it could not continue forever.

Ammunition and other supplies remained a constant concern when their only resupply came from the occasional orbital insertion spike. More Legionnaires had perished trying to collect these resupply spikes than from any other single effort: the enemy was neither deaf nor blind.

No Legionnaire knew what had become of *Harrier*'s interface fighters. After that first day the fighters had not reappeared, so the only supporting fire Legionnaires observed originated from spotty orbital strikes when some Fleet frigate or other risked a low-orbit pass. Still, those infrequent strikes had spelled the difference upon Delta Three's unfriendly surface.

Kyle Whiteside would always remember a desperate night early on when it seemed the enemy would scour every Legionnaire from the planet in one overwhelming thrust.

Kyle's own impressions of that night remained a series of nightmarish flashes, glimpses of seething movement punctuated by the thunder of incoming artillery fire, Legionnaires falling all around him as they tried to return the overwhelming fire. Kyle had only noticed the momentary reappearance of the combat Nets in his UI after kinetic rounds began streaking down from orbit, detonating enemy positions.

The next morning, with the combat Nets and orbital allies long gone, Kyle had observed the folly of warring against any force that held the orbital high ground. The valley floor surrounding the Legionnaires' position had been cratered, a litter of shattered vehicles and scattered bodies choking every path up to the Legionnaires' perimeter. Kyle never discovered who had managed to contact the frigate above and so effectively direct their fire, but his suggestion of a surviving Pathfinder prompted derisive noises from Avery Reardon. Whoever it had been, Kyle knew they all owed their lives to that quick, precise action . . . however short and unpleasant the Legionnaires' collective lives might end up being.

Since that night, the disorganized body of Legionnaires scattered in groups, each making its way to various points of the map. Avery Reardon's small force had slowly, carefully crept farther and farther from that battlefield, rarely encountering any enemy presence greater than a handful of irregulars. For them, the battle had become a series of stealthy, desperate conflicts, the survivors on both sides of the greater war unwilling or unable to front anything greater than minor infantry actions and small-arms fire. In this environment the Molo Rangers became a comparative force to be reckoned with.

As Corporal Kyle Whiteside scanned across the ruins once again, he heard a murmur of voices to his right, where Avery and Pippi lay in their impromptu coverts. A moment later, he caught sight of what had surely provoked their interest, though he scarcely believed what he saw.

Two lightly armored skimcars moved in the distance, approaching from enemy territory down the cratered roadway, unable to gain much speed as they maneuvered around scattered hulks of blackened wrecks dotting the road. For days, no Legionnaire or enemy troop dared stand to their full height, or cross open ground, and here two enemy skimcars idled down the highway without an apparent concern. Predictably this situation did not last long.

Questing shots from multiple sources began finding the range, auto-cannons on the skimcars began returning fire, chattering and booming across the valley.

"Up, up!" Avery Reardon's called out. "Here's our chance!"

Kyle, Pippi, and a dozen others crawled uncertainly from their foxholes and hides, a few Molo mechs trotting along behind as they all quickly followed Reardon straight toward the ruins dead ahead. Kyle's mind flashed through half-remembered bits of various training classes that covered such scenarios, and he noted that they followed none of the edicts offered back then. They laid down no suppressive fire, they did not advance in leap-frogging elements, and they did not maintain a smooth pace and steady shooting platform. Instead they ran in an irregular mob, as silently and swiftly as possible while every unfriendly eye and weapon would be focused on one side or the other of the skimcar battle out on the road. As an afterthought, Kyle did thumb the selector on his carbine to burst fire as the scattered ruins grew swiftly nearer, ready to violently greet the sudden appearance of any enemy.

"Spread out! Spread—" An explosion boomed, drowning out Reardon's words, and a column of smoke rose from the roadway now out of sight behind the ruins. "Spread out and hunker in!"

Kyle Whiteside and Avery Reardon tumbled into the shattered skeleton of a small building, their Molo mechs skittering in behind them. As Kyle lay gasping for breath, Reardon moved from spot to spot, peering out through twisted fingers of bent and melted reinforcing bars, scanning each vector. He turned to look at Kyle, grinning as he panted.

"Things are looking up, Kyle," he said, wiping sweat from his face. "Looking up. But I'd better check on that poor sod you potted over here."

Kyle sat up and peered out a nearby hole in the wall, realizing that indeed the fallen enemy lay only a short distance away. A faint, pained vocalization came a moment later.

"Hey!" Reardon called out, as Kyle crawled to a new vantage where the fallen enemy's boot was just visible. "Hey, reb! Want some company while you're dying? Might even patch you up, if I can."

After another pained groan they heard the weak voice, "Okay, damn you. Gods..." he moaned. "Anything for a drink."

Reardon made another quick scan of the surroundings and checked the position of Pippi and the others. He leaned forward to observe the fallen enemy's state, and called out, "Alright, reb, I'll come over. Make a note, though: Any of your lot take a shot at me, and my mates will kneecap you for your trouble. Right?"

No answer came for several seconds, and Kyle momentarily wondered if the fellow had died. The boot moved weakly and the rebel called back, in a thin voice, "Come on... They'd have killed me by now... if they were about."

Another boom echoed through the ruins, and the sporadic gunfire from three quarters died down to the occasional shot. Undoubtedly the second foolishly brave skimcar added to the carnage on the highway as another smoldering husk, but Kyle couldn't see any hint except a second column of black smoke rising to the low clouds above.

"Pippi?" Reardon called out. "You and the others keep watch on the flanks, and keep a sharp eye on those roof ledges too."

"We watching, boss," Pippi called back, nearly invisible in a low tumble of stone and steel.

Reardon turned to Kyle. "I'll go first. If no one takes a crack at me, slide over and visit. See your prisoner up-close-like."

Kyle nodded as Reardon directed his Molo, Cuthbert, to stay, Cuthbert's optic aimed down the left flank. In a muted rush Reardon darted out of cover, around the protruding bulk of a concrete wall and out of sight near the fallen rebel. Kyle held his breath in dread, but no shot sounded out.

It seemed a tense eternity before Reardon called, "Kyle, come on over."

After positioning Fang to scan the right flank, Kyle scrambled out, thumping heavily in Reardon's wake. He slid into a dusty heap against a mostly intact wall, only turning his attention to

Reardon and the fallen foe once he felt reasonably concealed in the nook.

Reardon sat comfortably against the same low wall the enemy fell from, with the wounded man sprawled at his feet. Reardon held his own carbine across his knees, with a strange, bulky-looking rifle propped against the wall beside him.

"There you are, Kyle," Reardon said in an even tone. "This unfortunate fellow is Huntmaster Brown. He seems to have found the bullet you misplaced."

Kyle hesitated a moment before scrambling deeper into the shelter of the three standing walls. He jammed his shoulders into the opposite corner from Avery Reardon, glanced quickly around the visible terrain, then looked down at the helpless, bleeding man at Reardon's feet. "Uh, hello," Kyle said. The man was clearly in great pain, his jaws clenched and cheeks ashen. Despite his obvious distress, the man rolled an eye toward Kyle and grunted a snort of acknowledgment.

"Your bullet apparently missed poor Brown's femoral artery," Kyle continued lightly, his own eyes sweeping every threatening angle, "or he would already be keeping company with his honored ancestors. That moment, however, may not be far distant."

Looking at this bleeding, hurting specimen of the enemy, Corporal Kyle Whiteside felt a compelling urge to apologize: *Nothing personal . . .* But what's more personal than sticking a bullet into someone's vitals?

Instead, Kyle passed a canteen over to Brown's unsteady, bloodstained grip. The so-called huntmaster fumbled the canteen to his lips, water spilling down his chin. He swallowed, then grimaced. Kyle took the canteen back.

"Water?" Brown said with a sour tone.

"Your mother surely said something to you about beggars and choosers," Reardon said. "*My* mother certainly mentioned it to me."

"Huh," Brown replied, sliding a shaking hand to the bloody patch at his hip, gasping in pain.

"Of course," Reardon added, his left hand tapping a particularly precious canteen at his belt, "if we weren't sworn enemies . . . there might be a little something here to please the choosiest."

"Not your enemy," Brown growled, his teeth clenched.

"Oh?" Reardon said. "The rifle, the uniform . . . ? And we know your key urban centers were left untouched for your shelter, where you could remain. So . . . out hunting, are you, *Huntmaster?*"

"You—don't—understand," Brown gasped. "When we . . . realized . . . we—we ran."

Reardon leaned forward with his precious canteen of Excelsior brandy. "Realized what, dear fellow? Here, just a taste."

Brown took a small gulp, his eyes closing. He swallowed, sighing audibly. "Thank you."

"Excelsior brandy. Truly. But you were saying?"

Brown opened his eyes with effort. "They're using us."

"Life of a soldier, mate. Pawns on a chessboard, right?"

"N-no," Brown gasped, his eyes fluttering. "Listen . . . listen. They are changing us . . . I saw it." He groaned, his eyes clenched shut.

"Changing, eh?" Reardon repeated. "Sounds intriguing."

Brown shook his head, his eyes still closed. "No. It's, it's terrible. My friends . . . my friends. Gone, changed." He broke off, groaning, and Reardon leaned over him with a frown.

"I'm dreadfully sorry, old fellow. I used all my pain tabs the other night, or I'd give you one."

Kyle patted his own equipment pouches and drew out his final pain tab, holding it silently up. Reardon mused for a moment, looking from the tab to the groaning huntmaster. He nodded, and Kyle leaned forward to jab it home.

Brown's eyes flickered open as the chemicals flooded his veins, sighing deeply as his body relaxed. After a moment he spoke: "Shouldn't have. I'm done. It's . . . a waste." He blinked slowly, looking over at Kyle. "Don't let them—don't let them change you. Eat . . . eat a bullet first."

"Don't let *who?*" Reardon said, but Brown seemed oblivious, staring steadily at Kyle.

"That new . . . command center . . ." Brown murmured, his voice sounding sleepy. "My lads went down. Came out . . . changed . . . gone."

"*Who* changed them? *What* changed them?" Reardon asked. "What do you mean?"

Brown's eyelids fluttered, his gaze increasingly glassy. "We tried to . . . run. I—I am the last. Monsters. Smiling . . . monsters." Brown's eyes closed as his voice trailed into a mumble, and Reardon frowned.

"Oh, Brown? Hello? You still alive, old fellow?" Reardon inquired, giving the man a little shake.

Brown's eyes did not open but his mouth moved, shaping whispery words. "Thank you...thank you." He swallowed with effort, his body quivering. "Call your ship. Don't wait..." He fell silent and Kyle wondered if he was gone, but he began speaking in a dead voice, hardly above a whisper, "Tell them. Nuke us all. Just nuke us all..."

Chapter 9

"Though Lykeios Manor remains the seat of Sinclair-Maru power, the asteroid base of Hawksgaard is the center of Family secrecy. What really occurs there? Who can say?"

—Everest Compline, *Reflections*

IN THE MONTHS AND YEARS THAT FOLLOWED INGA MARU'S ATTACH-ment to the Sinclair-Maru, tall, bald Kai became an unlikely anchor of security for her. It is possible he represented a sort of father figure to her, although little Inga was not entirely certain; the only real father image of her early years had been a source of abuse and terror.

Bess even supplied a sort of surrogate family unit in the first days after Inga and her siblings had departed the planet, Battersea, en route for the Sinclair-Maru asteroid base, Hawksgaard. They were a kindly young couple with a small child about Karl's age, and they went by the name Koblenz. After vetting them with her cynical ten-year-old's scrutiny, Inga declared the Koblenz family safe for Mitzi and Karl, though boring and meaningless for her own needs. They were not Sinclair-Maru . . . just minor oath-kin of some sort, undoubtedly selected for their placidity.

Their cooing speech and soothing touches repulsed Inga, feeling artificial and condescending to her, and she suffered pangs as Mitzi and Karl seemed enchanted by those same words and actions. With an iron resolve far beyond her years, Inga woodenly observed the painfully rapid shift of affections from Inga, their long protector, to their new adoptive parents. She knew this was needed—it was part of what she had purchased with the currency of her own life. Still, on the short voyage—Inga's first spaceflight—she found herself fleeing these raw moments with the Koblenzes, seeking out Kai or skulking about the confines of the old lighter-craft, away from the painfully eager eyes of her siblings.

On one such excursion, little Inga sidled into a cargo hold, silently slipping between the netted bales, one hand gliding down the stacked columns as she idly examined content labels for hints of her approaching new home. Before long, Kai appeared at the far end of the compartment, his thin arms crossed, a bland look upon his pink face. Inga stopped, eyeing him uncertainly, her toe testing the deck surface for friction as she prepared to flee, merely out of long habit.

"Perhaps you should rest while you have time, Mistress Maru," Kai said in his whispery voice. "In Hawksgaard you will have little free time."

Inga held Kai's gaze, then looked up to the glimmering reflection from Kai's bald skull and shrugged. A moment of silent regard stretched between them before Kai said, "Have you ever experienced zero gravity before, child?"

Inga recalled watching other children—children with wealthy parents—playing in zero-grav chambers back in Port City, while such joys had never been hers. She had expected to feel the effects of zero gravity at some point since leaving Battersea, but in this she had also been disappointed. She shook her head then, and Kai only hesitated briefly before raising his voice to command some invisible listener, "Zero gravity in cargo four, please."

The next moment Inga would ever recall with deep and surprising affection. It began with a flash of abject terror, as her feet lost purchase with the deck, her security, her control. Inga's limbs had spasmed in shock, causing her body to tumble nauseatingly, but in the midst of her contortion she saw Kai floating at ease, his legs drawing up to something like the lotus position as his arms gently compensated. Inga locked upon Kai's deep-set eyes as she calmed her racing heart and slowly adjusted arms and legs, her stomach settling gradually back into place. In moments, she arrested nearly all her movement, her eyes still fixed upon Kai's.

A line of wrinkles rose upon Kai's brow as a smile curved his lips. "So you do control your fear, child. Bess may be correct... you may yet encompass the Deep Man."

Inga felt some pleasure in these words; though she didn't know what was meant by a "Deep Man," still she felt something like a grin touching her lips despite everything.

Before they reached Hawksgaard, Inga grew to love her hours in zero grav—the flying sensation, the new possibilities of three full dimensions—but even more, she grew to cherish the peaceful hours in Kai's company. He never touched her, never condescended, and seemed to *see* Inga, when most adults only passed their gaze over her without recognition or regard.

In the days it took to reach Hawksgaard, Mitzi and Karl interacted with Inga in only the brief moments she abandoned her role as Kai's shadow. Even as their lighter-craft approached the vast complex of Hawksgaard, Inga hovered near Kai in the small cockpit with the crew. She observed the irregular rock ahead, clearly revealed in the ship's holo, a row of lights gleaming from Hawksgaard's rocky surface, but it was only when she observed a miniscule, suited human figure moving across a bright patch of the surface that she realized the scale of what she beheld. Her new home, it appeared, might contain a city of many thousands.

When their ship eventually docked, Inga rejoined her siblings and the Koblenzes, just behind Kai. As the lock cycled, Inga's nostrils caught the unique tang of station air, Hawksgaard air: iron, salt, machine oil, and stone. Forever after, that scent meant only one thing to Inga... home.

Kai spoke the truth when he said Inga would receive little free time upon Hawksgaard, but the challenges began in an unexpected way and with surprising benefits.

Kai led the Koblenzes, Inga, and her siblings to a domicile wing a short distance from the port area, and Inga's gaze swung from side to side, studying the branching pathways, the various people and glimmering technological wonders. In these strange and frightening environs, however, Mitzi and Karl shed much of their recent confidence. Mitzi's finger found its way to her mouth and she pressed closer to Inga, gripping Inga's shirt, while Karl stopped scampering along beside the Koblenz child and gradually shrank back near Inga, his eyes wide.

When Kai revealed the spacious apartment prepared for

the Koblenzes, Mitzi, and Karl, much of their fear abated. The Koblenz child darted in with an excited whoop, hopping from foot to foot before a high-end vidstream wall displaying colorful animals dancing and singing. Another wall seemed formed of glass and overlooked a vast internal cavern clothed in foliage and laced with walking trails. Mitzi's finger popped from her mouth and she timidly scented the air before looking to Inga. Inga's fingers tapped, *safe here*, to both of her siblings, just before Kai spoke, "Your sister's chambers are directly across the hall, see?" He directed their watchful gaze to the nearby apartment across the outer corridor. "If you need her, you have her always close at hand."

Mitzi and Karl said nothing, and Inga stepped across to the door in question, causing it to open, standing before the doorway. Though she burned to explore her new rooms, Inga turned and sauntered back across the corridor to Mitzi and Karl with a shrug.

The Koblenz boy raced back to Karl and Mitzi, brainlessly chattering as he urged them to examine each feature of their shared home. When he mentioned snacks, Inga's siblings perked up and Inga was able to withdraw to explore her own chambers without misgivings.

Kai followed her, padding along behind, his soft boots making no sound.

Inga's new quarters held several items of immediate interest even upon her first glance. A row of neat black-and-gray uniforms hung waiting for her, an appropriately sized training sword on the brackets close beside. Inga's gaze moved on to the small bed, then to the adjoining desk with its small vidstream monitor. Kai stepped to the monitor and actuated its function. "Look," Kai softly commanded.

Inga edged nearer and eyed the scrolling list of rigid rules crawling across the monitor, which concluded with the line, "...any deviation from the listed standards will result in expulsion from Hawksgaard and possible action through the authority of the Honor Code."

Inga studied the monitor for a moment before turning to Kai. "Are there no demi-cits here at all, then?" she asked.

Kai seemed momentarily taken aback by the question. "Well, no, none. Hawksgaard is a high-security facility, with only Family, oath-kin, and oath-bound citizens allowed."

"And me," Inga added, looking away.

"And you," Kai affirmed in his whispery voice. "Now make careful note of every rule upon that list. Since you have not achieved your majority, you are unlikely to be expelled, but you will certainly be made to suffer if you are *caught* in any contravention. Do you understand me?"

Inga turned back to stare into Kai's glittering eyes. "Perhaps not," she said, detecting Kai's emphasis on, *caught.*

Kai's smooth, pink features broke into an amused smile. "This room is not monitored, except for the door scan—who enters, who departs. Ask your questions if you wish."

Inga felt an uncomfortable twinge of suspicion growing. She shook her head. "Just say it." She had the mixed satisfaction of seeing Kai open and shut his mouth several times before finding a track.

"Every person on Hawksgaard is oath-bound to these standards. Family—everyone—adheres to the rule...everyone. As a young person, you will be judged by your adherence to these rules, and much of your success or failure as a student will be gauged by this standard." Kai paused, thinking. "If you are *caught* violating a rule, I will not intervene any more than I would for any other promising student of the Family."

Again the emphasis on *caught.*

Inga felt Kai edging toward the unspoken, the hidden heart of the matter, and his tension made her fingers feel for the crude blade concealed at her waist, merely from habit.

"It...it may be confusing for you," Kai continued, his brow glistening with a faint sheen, "as you learn the importance—the vital importance—of the Honor Code and Family doctrine even as you are—er—required to break Hawksgaard rules."

Inga stepped back from Kai. "Which rules?"

Kai wiped his glistening brow and fumbled in a pocket for something. "Most of them, I am afraid. Bess formed this plan. I believe it has...merit. It will demand much of you...much more than the other students. The path for you is unconventional, for we need an unconventional result." He withdrew two ident chits from his pocket and extended them to Inga.

She hesitated a moment then stepped forward and took the chits.

"Are you familiar with synthetic Intelligences, child?"

"A little." She stared at him, thinking back. "The demi-cits all listen to one back ho—back on Battersea."

"Yes, I imagine they must," Kai said as Inga looked down at the chits in her hands, turning them over to closely examine them. "Here on Hawksgaard, an Intelligence monitors most things. In the top security areas there may be a few places as large as your hand that it cannot readily observe, but in the other sections of Hawksgaard it mostly observes access points." He pointed a long, thin finger at the chits. "Mostly, it tracks ident chits."

Inga held one chit between her fingers and lifted it up. "It is a transponder."

"Uhh, yes. A coded transponder. One is assigned to you. The other chit you have . . . you have just found lying about somewhere, I guess." Inga stared unwaveringly at Kai, who seemed increasingly agitated, wiping sweat from his shiny forehead again. "With that chit, you—uhh, *someone* could move through many unsecured sections of Hawksgaard without the Intelligence tracking, um, *them.*"

Inga slid the two chits into her pocket. "Is there a map?"

Kai was nonplussed once again at Inga's seeming shift of topic. "A map? Of Hawksgaard? Yes, yes of course." He brought up the map on Inga's new vidstream monitor. "Here we are in the domicile wing, you see, and—"

"Where does the rubbish go?"

"Rubbish?" Kai asked, confused.

Inga stared impatiently at him. "On the map. Where's the rubbish go?"

Kai shook his head, perplexed, but tapped the monitor. "Well, waste chutes collect rubbish in service chambers somewhere around this area. Service chambers do not appear on these guides, though, so—"

"It's enough," Inga said dismissively, turning away. She stepped to the martial uniforms and felt their fabric. "When do I begin training?"

Kai regained a measure of his composure, back on sure ground. "Medical tomorrow, then a day or two for recovery before—"

Inga's eyes snapped back onto Kai. "Medical?"

"Yes, for a simple implant, of course. We spoke of this."

Inga eased into contemplation after a moment. Implants. She had watched well-to-do citizens strolling about Port City, their eyes flickering as they commanded the city's electronics as if by magic, no holo lenses or senso-gloves in sight. She had longed to be one of those clean, self-assured figures who wielded what seemed the most intoxicating power. But she also knew that her *particular role* with the Sinclair-Maru might demand more than the Family students and the User Interface provided to them. Bess had explained a little.

"*All* the implants?" Inga asked at last, split between fear and intrigue.

Kai shook his head. "No. Like the other students, you will not receive your Shaper implant for some time. You will receive the scaram. All Family students and some few oath-kin receive the scaram at a young age. A Shaper implant and... activation of other elements must await your first majority. You understand this?"

Inga jerked her head once. "I think so."

"You will begin with holo lenses, as all the young Family do. The User Interface and the scaram will certainly occupy you as your training begins."

"Scaram," Inga repeated, her mouth trying the unfamiliar word as if to wring meaning from it.

Kai stepped to one side of Inga's new desk and opened a concealed drawer. Inga edged closer as Kai lifted a book—an actual wood-fiber book!—from the shallow compartment and passed it to Inga with an odd reverence that Inga observed with misgiving. She eyed the title, *Integrity Mirror*. "I have never heard of this."

"Few outside the Family ever have," Kai said. "It is the foundation of our Art, the basis of Sinclair-Maru strength. Even among oath-kin, this book is not revealed until generations have proven loyalty to the Family. It comprises much of our secret knowledge, and allowing you access to it is... unconventional. You will reveal nothing from this book to anyone beyond Family."

Inga opened the cover and her gaze fell immediately upon the line *All fear is fear of the unknown. Since we cannot know the unknown we must know fear... this is the path to the Deep Man.*

Deep Man. There was that odd expression again; interesting quote, and yet it seemed to Inga that the objects of her fears had been anything but unknown.

"The Deep Man," Inga said, tasting the words. "It sounds silly."

"Your honored ancestor, Mia Maru, might disagree," Kai

said, moving softly toward the door. "She and Devlin synthesized the concepts of that book, and it became a pillar of our Family strength, and..." Kai hesitated, then continued in a lower voice, "...possibly a source of our blindness."

Inga held the book still but she watched Kai's progress with curiosity. Kai stopped at the door. "Read that book. Learn it, child. But it must never own you as it does all of us."

The door opened and Kai looked back at Inga with a softer expression. "Rest tonight. Tomorrow begins soon enough."

When Kai departed and the door closed, Inga spent some time wandering slowly around her new apartment. She had never possessed a space that was exclusively her own before, and the sensation puzzled her. She explored every nook, tested every feature, even tapping walls with her crude blade as she listened attentively to each ringing strike.

In the end she sprawled with her back to the wall, frowning at the closed door straight ahead, the blade across her palm lightly tapping the floor beneath. Her two ident chits lay beside her—the first two pieces of a puzzle Bess had created, a puzzle which Kai found so disquieting. Kai said Inga must learn the rules and limits, then break them.

As Inga untangled the skein of her thoughts and feelings she discovered each of the troubling knots in sequence, the gentle tapping of her blade seeming to accompany each jolt of understanding: the disregard of rules, in itself, did not trouble Inga unduly; she would likely have transgressed regardless. But the semi-sanctioned nature of it all brought a mixture of misgivings. Kai governed Hawksgaard, so why teach Inga rules and standards, then induce her to violate them? Surely Kai possessed the power to simply excuse Inga from these rules, and yet he explained that he would not protect her from punishment.

The tapping of Inga's blade ceased. She arrived at the crux of her unease and it held no practical value, yet it touched her carefully shielded emotions with surprising pain.

For most of her ten years, Inga had survived through daily deceit and trickery, silently battling the only real authority figure she knew. Perhaps this was why Bess selected Inga, she suddenly thought, though she knew there was much more involved. Perhaps Inga was "perfect" because she had regularly deceived and tricked a tyrannical potentate, in the end destroying him through her devices.

The blossoming sense of *belonging*, of *acceptance* that had just begun within Inga, shriveled upon the vine.

It was still worth any sacrifice from Inga; Mitzi and Karl alone were worth any sacrifice. But Inga felt that coldness, the deadness return. She was not Sinclair-Maru. She was not among friends.

She was not accepted.

Chapter 10

"A handful of Great Houses are routinely found within the upper reaches of Fleet Command, while the Sinclair-Maru only appear a few times through the centuries. Their impact is mysteriously disproportionate to their numbers."

—Everest Compline, *Reflections*

SITUATED IN THE HEART OF THE IMPERIUM, NOT SO FAR FROM the Imperial Close, the glittering jewel of Coreworld, the Admiralty Headquarters crouched like a craggy, crotchety old man.

As a scion of the Sinclair-Maru House, Saef spent much of his life among the Family's ancient bones of faded glory, and yet even he found the dim and fusty passages a poor representation of Fleet's might. He knew that more than two thousand Fleet vessels spanned teeming light-years, all at the whim and gesture issuing from these hallowed halls.

Unlike Saef's prior invitations to Admiralty HQ, he was ushered into a smaller, even-duller chamber rather than the Admiralty council chamber, and rather than the full council, only three figures awaited him. Unfortunately one of the three was Admiral Nifesh. Saef sought the refuge of the Deep Man even at the first glimpse of the admiral's bullet head, Saef's pulse barely flickering before assuming the smooth metronome of dispassionate calm.

The three admirals loomed over delicate porcelain plates on the table before them, each loaded with the fine trimmings of a feast. They barely glanced at Saef as the attendant announced him and withdrew, leaving Saef an opportunity to observe the flash and rattle of fork and knife, aromatic scents hinting at flavors beyond Saef's rank. Their pointed disregard seemed too obvious, too labored to rankle Saef, and he remained untouched, remotely noting the names of Nifesh's companions—two admirals he had never encountered before: Chiang and Beatty.

After a delay long enough to clearly communicate discourtesy, Admiral Nifesh looked up, dabbing his wet lips, his thick heavy-world features set in what seemed complacent lines. "Captain," Nifesh said, pausing to pick something from his teeth with one blunt finger. "There's been a change in plans."

"Yes, my lord," Saef said.

Nifesh shared an inscrutable look with Admiral Chiang, took a bite of buttery bread and continued speaking as he chewed. "The mess you left in—what was the system?"

After a protracted silence from Saef, Admiral Beatty supplied, "Delta Three."

"Yes. Delta Three." Nifesh wiped glistening fingers on his napkin. "We've troops planetside now—Legionnaires—and you're going to go give them a ride off-planet."

"Very well, my lord," Saef said.

A malignant smile touched Nifesh for a moment as he continued chewing. "But..." He swallowed then drank from his glass before looking back up at Saef. "But a frigate's not the right tool for the task. It's a tangled mess you left behind and it's only gotten worse. No, a frigate isn't right at all."

Saef said nothing, merely waiting.

"You'll need infantry and transports to pry the Legionnaires off that rock." Nifesh smacked his lips and shared a smile with his fellow admirals. "Fortunately we've a ship available: *Hightower*. Temporary command while the current captain recovers from his wounds. An affair of honor, it seems. You understand."

Saef said, "*Hightower*," and went through the motions of checking the vessel in his UI, although he had already done so hours earlier.

"That's a substantial vessel for such a junior captain," Admiral Beatty said, which was true enough, but it was a thankless command with little hope of glory or prizes, only chances for disaster and dishonor.

As if reading Saef's mind Nifesh said, "Too much ship, really, but it might incline a brash officer to pay more attention to his solemn duty rather than chasing after every prize." The other admirals made approving noises and sipped from their glasses.

"When do I join the command, my lord?" Saef said.

Nifesh put his glass down, his expression petulant. Saef had not responded nearly as he had hoped. "Immediately. You'll join immediately. No time to waste." A flicker of sly anticipation seemed to light his near-set eyes for a moment. "*Hightower*'s fully crewed, so none of your own people aside from an attendant, cox'n, or what-have-you..." Nifesh smiled. "And you'll be shipping an Imperial Auditor, too."

Saef opened his mouth, closed it, then said, "An Auditor? A civilian?"

"Yes." Nifesh's smile widened. "He's some breed of university scholar. Conducting an Imperial study of a sort. Very important observations of Fleet practice."

"A scholar? A demi-cit in combat on a warship seems a clear violation of—"

"Don't be more a fool than you must!" Nifesh snapped. "Of course he's a Vested Citizen."

Saef seethed internally but struggled to maintain a neutral expression rather than give Nifesh the satisfaction. A Vested Citizen as a civilian university scholar seemed almost a contradiction in terms in recent years.

"Have the Auditor join us," Nifesh commanded the waiting attendant.

Though Saef had never met an Imperial Auditor before, he held an image of an officious busybody with pinched lips and a haughty demeanor. The first glimpse of Imperial Auditor Tenroo quickly banished that specter from Saef's mind. The flash impression Saef gained from a dozen small details spoke of a surprising poverty, and that, blended with the rather plaintive look in the scholar's eyes, did much to melt Saef's initial iciness.

"Auditor, um, Tenroo," Admiral Nifesh murmured, "Captain Sinclair-Maru." His deep-set eyes gleamed with a hint of pleasure at Saef's discomfiture.

"Captain," Tenroo said, bobbing his head, his voice nearly unpleasant in its sparseness.

"The Auditor recently completed an important project for the

Emperor," Nifesh said to Saef, waving a thick hand toward the
slender academic, "and now the Emperor wants him on *Hightower*."

Saef wondered if this Auditor was actually assigned to *Hightower* or if the real focus of his attention lay only with Saef
himself. He found Tenroo's pale gray eyes fixed upon him, and
again it seemed they held some hidden message—an apology or
a lurking plea. Saef's gaze dropped to the black wristband Tenroo
wore instead of a sword, then back up in time to see the faint
flush on Tenroo's cheeks.

"Well, Auditor Tenroo," Saef said at last, "it appears we will
be shipmates."

Though the flush remained, Tenroo seemed relieved as he
dipped a formal bow. Perhaps he did not understand that an
admiral speaks, and behold, the lowly captain obeys. "Yes. Captain," he said, his eyes flicking toward Nifesh, seeming to check
the next words on his tongue. "It is a great honor for me," he
said, instead of whatever remained unspoken.

Some hours later, when Saef and Inga made their way through
the teeming corridors of the Strand, Saef described the Auditor
to her: "You can't mistake the fellow. No sword—some scholar
things, I believe—and resembles one of those fluffy little dogs
who's got himself all wet."

Inga shot a piercing look at Saef, her head tilted to one side.
"That's the first time I believe I've ever heard you speak slightingly of another Citizen."

Saef felt a defensive reply on the tip of his tongue: It wasn't
a *slight* against Tenroo, really, just extremely descriptive. The
fellow really had looked like a small, soggy dog, not shivering
precisely, the imploring glance communicating something very like
a shiver. But then Saef allowed Inga's words beyond his immediate resistance where they joined a growing sense of unease. The
anchors, the foundations of his personal solidity seemed increasingly in question. Had Inga identified an early symptom of the
self-righteousness Cabot had condemned in Saef?

Cabot's recent praise regarding the destruction of the Okunas
had not aided Saef's sense of calm. It seemed Cabot was all too
ready to applaud Inga's deceptive and deadly gambit, and it left
Saef questioning his lifelong impression of Sinclair-Maru honor.
While Saef had agreed to take all responsibility for the action,

leaving Inga's role out, he had thought he would be called to harsh account by Cabot, not congratulated.

"House Okuna always fancied themselves a step ahead of everyone," Cabot had said to Saef in a rare moment of exposition. "They specialized in forcing their rivals into binary paths that they control. It was a rare opportunity for you to find a third path that they hadn't anticipated. It seems a much more useful application of your violent skills than you usually display. I commend you."

Cabot's commendation formed another fissure in the foundation of Saef's whole ethos, and now Inga seemed to highlight a symptom of Saef's lost confidence. Did his comment about Tenroo reveal some deep rot that Saef could not even perceive? Inga looked up as Saef opened his mouth to speak . . . but to say what? What was true?

The appearance of Auditor Tenroo in the midst of the throng ahead spared Saef the need to reply. "Well, there's the fellow now," Saef said instead.

Tenroo's luggage consisted of two lumpy mismatched bags that he clutched protectively as he gazed about the milling throng. The combination of curiosity and uncertainty seemed plain upon his face until he recognized Saef approaching, whereupon his expression changed to one of uncertainty alone.

Saef made the introductions as Inga coolly regarded Tenroo, the dumb-mech skittering to a halt behind her.

Tenroo executed a shallow bow, his gaze flitting from Inga to Saef and back. "You must forgive me, Chief Maru," Tenroo said, "I'm not entirely clear on the various Fleet ranks still. I presume that a Fleet chief is a sort of officer."

"A mere noncommissioned officer, Dr. Tenroo," Inga replied, surprising Saef with the "doctor" title.

Apparently it also surprised the Imperial Auditor. He looked more sharply at Inga. "You know of my past work, before my . . . my elevation to Auditor."

"Just one of my duties," Inga said. "Shall we clear the path here?"

Tenroo looked about at the flood of uniformed figures as if noticing the stream diverting around them for the first time. "Do we take a scheduled transport of some kind? Or I suppose you have a personal shuttle?"

As Saef was about to explain that such luxuries as personal shuttles were beyond their touch, Inga spoke: "The captain's shuttle is on the far end of the wet arm. We have a small hike ahead of us." Saef shot Inga an inquiring glance, which she answered infuriatingly with her half smile.

Saef ground his teeth for a moment before firing a line-of-sight message to Inga's UI: WHAT SHUTTLE?

Inga's message returned in a flash, once again composed with no visible gesturals at all: MY SHUTTLE.

Saef had never closely inquired about Inga's prize money from their prior mission, mostly due to a fear that the Family might lay claim to her purse as well. The less he knew, he had thought, the better. Well, now he knew: rather than saving for rejuv treatments or sending her funds off to wherever her siblings lived, she apparently bought a shuttlecraft, and Saef held no doubt that IMS *Hightower* possessed an allowance and a berth for a captain's pinnace. Inga would have assured that before she ever brought her shuttle to the Strand. The idea of shipping a personal shuttle seemed so illustrative of the thematic ironies forming the modern Sinclair-Maru family: a veneer of power and wealth overlaying a gulf of near penury, even in the wake of his recent prize from the Delta Three action.

This image continued when Saef led the way onto *Onyx* with Tenroo and Inga trailing behind. Clearly Inga had obtained the shuttle for a bargain, and its wear and lack of appointments made this painfully obvious.

If Tenroo found the aged interior at odds with the storied prestige of the Sinclair-Maru, no sign appeared in his expression. He simply looked about with a faintly pleased expression and murmured, "How comfortable. How pleasant," as he settled his meager possessions on the deck.

To Saef's eye, *Onyx* was not notably comfortable or pleasant, seeming strangely cramped instead, with Inga's dumb-mech, Tenroo's bags, and a few mysterious parcels littering the oddly truncated passenger compartment. Rough build-outs constrained the space, and storage compartments were apparently lacking.

Inga entered the darkened cockpit and began her prelaunch checks with trained confidence, while Saef suddenly found his attention claimed by a furtive movement beneath Tenroo's seat.

A small, cream-colored paw reached out and tentatively batted at the dangling cuff of Tenroo's trousers.

"Oh, Maru," Saef called softly over his shoulder, "your shuttle appears to be infested."

Inga glanced before continuing to actuate systems. "That's just Tanta. He belongs."

"He?"

"Yes," Maru said without turning. "He is a kitten."

"I see," Saef murmured just as Tenroo became aware of the assault upon his person.

"Oh my," Tenroo said, looking down between his knees at the groping paw. "A ship's cat?" Tenroo looked up at Saef. "This tradition has survived the ages, then?"

Saef hesitated before answering, faintly remembering some old tale regarding ships and domesticated animals. "If so, it is purely by accident, Auditor. I do not recall seeing a cat on any other Fleet vessels ever."

"Oh," Tenroo said, seeming disappointed, though he continued his efforts to entice Tanta into the open. After a moment, Saef left Tenroo to his pains, and settled in beside Inga as she completed her preparations among the glowing instruments. Just then Strand Control cleared them to launch, and Inga actuated the shuttle's release, pushing off smoothly, cool thrusters accelerating them slowly out. A moment later, the drive engine engaged and they moved on their path from the Strand.

The lane out to *Hightower* lay between the gleaming beads of capital ships dotting the outer vectors, but the long shape of Saef's new command claimed Saef's attention. Inga kept the optical feed centered upon *Hightower*, and as the image grew, Saef detected an unfamiliar sensation growing in the pit of his stomach, a tightness that steadily increased.

After a questing moment, Saef realized that a cold sense of misgiving stood at the very brink of actual fear. This revelation sent new ripples of displeasure through him. For the first time in his Fleet career, Saef felt badly out of his depth, and a large measure of this he placed on Cabot's account.

Beyond Cabot's undermining steps, *Hightower* was a vast, complex vessel, and Saef's hasty research revealed a core group of officers who had followed *Hightower*'s captain for years. Unlike

Tanager, where Saef had pulled together an entire crew of strangers into a working unit, in *Hightower* Saef would be the outsider, the lone stranger, surrounded by a tight cadre with their own traditions, their own norms.

Saef stared at the growing image within the holo, the long, distinctive line of *Hightower*'s odd triple-barreled barrage battery; the symmetrical lumps marking *Hightower*'s drop ships nested into their hull voids; all that it implied. Soon *Hightower*'s vast bulk filled the entire field and Inga guided them in beneath vast shield projectors to the shuttle catch. By this time, Tenroo had managed to entice Tanta up where the kitten could be properly petted, and they seemed to have reached an accord, but as the shuttle jarred into contact, Tanta galloped back into hiding, his tail a rigid bottle brush.

Tenroo looked up uncertainly, as if seeking answers from the dingy hull above, then turned to gaze at Saef. "Have we arrived, Captain?"

Saef took a deep breath and reached for the shelter of the Deep Man. "Yes, Auditor. We have arrived."

Inga powered down control systems as *Hightower*'s shuttle catch reeled them into the tight confines of the pinnace bay, and before their movement ceased, Saef, Tenroo, and Inga stood ready to disembark, Inga's dumb-mech at their side. Inga's eyes flickered for a moment before Tanta scampered into the cockpit, the hatch sealing behind his sleek tail.

Tenroo clutched his belongings close to himself as the lock cycled, the Auditor seeming to shrink as he stood beside Saef. Rather than the collection of *Hightower*'s bridge officers Saef had expected to greet him, a lone crewmember stood in the narrow space between the shuttle's lock and *Hightower*'s pinnace bay access.

"Captain Sinclair-Maru," the rating greeted in an officious tone, her expression blank, "welcome aboard *Hightower*, I'm Specialist Beecher, sir. If you will accompany me, I'll show you to your quarters."

Saef's sense of uneasiness immediately transformed into indignation. "A moment, if you would, Beecher," he said, and Beecher paused with an air of labored patience. "How is *Hightower*'s Intelligence addressed?"

Saef half-expected *Hightower*'s Intelligence to chime in, much as Loki, the Intelligence on his previous command, would, but only Beecher replied, after a moment's hesitation. "The ship Intelligence answers to Gideon, but we'll need to have Lieutenant Alsop, our, Tech officer, provide provisional access for you."

"Provisional access?" Saef repeated, his wrath rising. His Fleet UI *should* have reconfigured for *Hightower* immediately upon arriving, and hadn't. Something was not right about this unfolding picture.

"Yes, Captain," Beecher said, raising her chin at Saef's tone.

"Perhaps," Saef said with great restraint, "you should just lead me to Commander Attic, Specialist. I will speak with him now, if you please."

Tenroo seemed to detect an awkward undercurrent and looked nervously from Beecher to Saef, then to Inga.

Beecher replied, her color somewhat heightened, though her tone remained cool: "Unfortunately, Commander Attic is occupied and asked that you await him in your quarters."

Inga's line-of-sight message pinged into Saef's UI a moment before he could unleash his verbal fury on Beecher. PLAY ALONG FOR THE PRESENT. YOUR ORDERS HAVE CHANGED. WE NEED A MOMENT.

Saef felt a twist in his gut and his teeth compressing. He didn't call up the orders to review within his UI; he didn't need to.

"Very well," Saef said, his wrath and chagrin almost imperceptible to the ear. "Lead the way, Beecher."

He needed to find some solid ground, to assess this fresh sabotage, to learn Inga's insights.

He left the pinnace bay on the heels of Specialist Beecher, moving into the vast interior of *Hightower*, silently cursing the name of Admiral Nifesh.

Chapter 11

"The academic voices decrying the recent increases in human longevity treatments are fond of citing the evolutionary benefits of rapid mortality in the prior generations. Why am I convinced that they would formulate a new theory lionizing longevity if these same academics possessed access to this same wicked longevity that they always decry?"

—Dr. Ramsay Stirling Attenborough, *Ivory Tower Follies*

HUGH SINCLAIR-MARU CERTAINLY POSSESSED SENIORITY ENOUGH within the Family to dodge such a boring assignment, but he pulled a protracted shift at the Medical Specialties Center nonetheless. Like many of the younger generation, Hugh long regarded the object of his vigil with near-reverence. Her name he would not say, not even think, though this security measure comprised a near-futile effort to protect her. Upon the register of the Medical Specialties Center her name was listed as "Bonita" Sinclair-Maru, and *Bonita* she would be until she could be restored to the security of the Family manor, Lykeios. Through her leadership, brief though it was, she had wrought more for the Family interests than Cabot had in the prior century. She alone chose the risky gamble with Saef's Imperial service, and that netted millions in prize money into Family coffers.

Many of her other reforms had also begun to bear fruit, when she employed her own desperate sacrifice to crush the hostile House Barabas. Just weeks before, this woman directed the extensive financial and political interests centered at Lykeios, and in one afternoon she fell, shattered beyond recognition. In that one moment, the Family matriarch lost her name, her face, and gods knew what else. That sacrifice continued to unfold, its pain felt by Hugh among others.

As Hugh thought of that destructive day not many weeks before, he almost turned to regard what remained of Bess—no, *Bonita* Sinclair-Maru—there over his shoulder, behind the glass, but he restrained himself.

Bess herself had arranged that fateful meeting with Imperial Consul Winter Yung, a minor member of the Imperial Family in addition to her consular role, and Bess knew full well House Barabas would likely attack. Though the ambush had shredded and dismembered Bess's aging body, the plan she had hatched still paid dividends. Yet Cabot seemed unmoved by either her successes or her sacrifices.

Hugh's jaw clenched as he recalled the Bess of his childhood— he could not think of her as Bonita, reflecting back to the Bess of just the prior season. Unlike Cabot and the others of the Family's older, more opulent generations, Bess had not enjoyed the benefits of full Shaper-tech rejuv treatments. While Cabot remained effortlessly middle-aged, despite his centuries, Bess had clung to her dregs of vitality through constant effort and discipline, strong and dangerous at eighty years of age.

As Hugh thought back to the Bess of his memory, a figure in medical garb stirred down the hall. Hugh's gaze mechanically followed, his UI enabling a quick vidcapture, just out of habit, but he recognized the medical specialist even as she disappeared from sight. Hugh returned to brooding, half glancing over his shoulder at the figure that had once been the Bess he knew.

At least, Hugh thought, she was no longer an unrecogniz- able cluster of instruments and shattered tissue—thanks to Saef's providence alone, the literal fortunes of war. At the thought, Hugh felt a warm current of affection toward Saef—a feeling shared by many of the Family young. Hugh knew of Cabot's displeasure at Saef's presumption. How had Saef dared to purchase shaper rejuv for Bess, even if it *was* from the proceeds of Saef's own prize money? Such temerity!

The faint smile that momentarily touched Hugh's mouth

disappeared at the next thought. Cabot had been right after all, and Saef had been wrong...or so it certainly appeared.

Saef had expended millions of credits in this wonder-junction of human medicine and Shaper technology, and now Bess no longer silently reposed, a quiescent lump. But had they regained the craft and cunning, the *wisdom* of Bess Sinclair-Maru?

Hugh finally allowed himself to turn, to look over his shoulder through the glass, though it only tapped a waiting reservoir of pain. Yes, the figure he beheld no longer bore the signs of violence, nor the marks of long years. Instead of arms and wrists thickened by high-grav work and hours of sword-in-hand combatives training, the lithe new limbs grown and electrically stimulated now shifted about uncertainly, pale and thin. Hugh's gaze locked onto her slender fingers where they idly caressed the silky fringe of the blanket, then his eyes tracked slowly up to the face—the face of a young woman—little more than a girl— topped by the downy fuzz of a freshly hatched chick. The hints of the Bess he remembered—the aged, regal Bess—made it all the more disconcerting.

That almost-Bess gazed aimlessly about her room, her focus seeming to fasten on something from time to time before moving on.

Movement down the passage again pulled Hugh's attention to his duties and the approaching figure of his watch relief pacing uncertainly toward him.

Hugh recognized Alexandra Bliss, oath-kin fresh out of her primary training cycles; Sinclair-Maru in all but name. Though they were barely acquainted, Hugh measured her with silent approval as she drew near. She wore the short dueling sword far forward, the pistol on her opposite hip holstered high, her dark suit relieved only by a hint of a scarlet undervest. Her hair, cropped very little longer than the fluffy down atop Bess's head, fringed an elfin face, and she carried a small satchel in her left hand. That hand, Hugh noted, seemed a bit fine-boned for true Family stock; a hint of lightworld blood in the Bliss family tree, perhaps.

"Bliss," Hugh greeted with a nod.

"Hugh," she replied, with a curt nod of her own.

Hugh wasted no time in pleasantries. "You know your watch relief? Yes?" He paused a moment. "How many security details you worked so far?"

Hugh thought he detected a hint of color on her cheeks but she answered in an even tone. "Aside from site security, this is my first."

Hugh shared a look—an *understanding* look—with Alexandra. They both knew the security for Bess was a joke, even without the added insult of a first-time operator as the sole defense of a once key Sinclair-Maru leader. Still, he also knew she survived the rigors of the Family training, which would be tougher even for oath-kin than *true* Family. She possessed the Family tools, the implanted scaram fear generator, the immunity to fear provided by her access to the Deep Man.

"Very well," Hugh said, consigning the unsaid with a wave of his hand. "The only approved visitor, outside of Family, is the Imperial Consul, Winter Yung, right? I'm pushing the approved medical staff list to your UI. They've all been cleared."

Alexandra's eyes flickered as the data flowed through the optic link of her User Interface.

Hugh's gaze traveled over her critically, pausing at the satchel still clutched in her left hand. "What'd you bring?"

She raised the case and lifted the flap to reveal a weapon, spare magazines, and an electronics package. "Hellbore sub-gun, couple mags, standard scan-jam unit. That's it."

Her over-preparedness pleased Hugh, but he merely nodded. "You career-tracked for Family security? System Guard? Or you waiting for command school?"

Alexandra shrugged. "Not sure. Still holding for my track. Finished primary a month ago, and now..."

"And now you're getting the odd-jobs treatment?" Hugh smiled and gathered up his own small pack. "Probably get your assignment in a week or two." Hugh paused, moving back to the window, Alexandra following his gaze. "That is our principal. Until she's safe in Lykeios, *here* she is Bonita Sinclair-Maru, understand?"

They both stood and beheld the embarrassingly youthful and vacant version of Bess Sinclair-Maru, a shared silence together.

Hugh drew a breath, hesitating a moment before speaking. "You knew her before, didn't you, Bliss?" Alexandra nodded silently and Hugh went on, "They—the docs—they say she may still be in there somewhere. She might come back." He turned to look at Alexandra and she looked up at him expectantly. "Don't forget, Bliss, they spent a great deal to destroy her once. They may not be done trying."

Alexandra held his gaze. "I understand, Hugh."

Hugh gathered up his pack. "Good." He turned and strode off down the passage without a backward glance.

When Hugh's steps faded away, Alexandra took a quick instant to replay twelve years of ceaseless, brutal training through her mind. The burgeoning tremor of fear she easily silenced, dipping into the dark pool of the Deep Man. From its cold cocoon of fearlessness, she made her immediate plans.

She carried her satchel into the quiet room with Bess, hesitating only a moment before saying, "Good afternoon, my lady. Alex Bliss. I am your security today." Bess's gaze locked onto Alexandra's face for a flash, her lips moving slightly, her eyebrows lowering... then her eyes moved on, a faint sigh coming from her mouth.

Alexandra moved to the near corner where she observed through the glass a fair way down the outer hallway, while on her left she could monitor Bess from head to foot. The satchel she placed close at hand. From this static position she prepared to pass the hours, her mind traveling through the well-learned litanies of vigilance pounded painfully into her mind through the preceding decades.

As it unfolded, it was only some few thousand seconds after Hugh's departure when she spotted her first potential threat, the expected tedium interrupted before it truly began.

She clearly recalled several Sinclair-Maru instructors grinding the lesson home, time after time, since she was a small child. They had rarely raised their voices—that was not the Sinclair-Maru style, their students not simpleminded conscripts—but as she had shivered at guard duty during field exercises, the whisper in her ear cut with the stature of a shriek. *How does the sentry remain vigilant, Bliss?* the instructor had hissed as cold rain sprinkled down in the darkness. *In the last seconds of a long watch, how?*

Eight-year-old Alexandra had answered by rote, her teeth chattering as she spoke, "C-complacency is the first enemy of the sentry, m-my lord," she had said. "The p-passing of time means n-nothing. Each, um, s-second is s-solitary. Each moment is the *first* moment of my v-vigil." She remembered that now as she stood poised in her first real assignment, protecting the life of a Family luminary.

Thus, only about three thousand seconds had elapsed since Alexandra took her place beside the reconstructed Bess Sinclair-Maru, with only the soft sighs and gentle stirring sounds from Bess to fill those seconds. Her vigilance remained fully intact as she observed the orderly bearing a tray, approaching down the hall at an easy pace. Alexandra matched the orderly's face to the image list supplied by Hugh, her hands smoothly moving to push the fringe of her short jacket back, resting lightly at her waist. Her eyes scanned each of the orderly's hands, measured the tray and its contents, then locked onto facial features, looking for the signs of tension. The last steps brought the orderly through the door, hands still clear, pupils normal, tray bearing only food and commonplace flatware.

The orderly smiled at Alexandra. "You're a new one," he said, and Bess stirred in her bed, her head bobbling at the sound of his voice.

Alexandra did not smile in return. "Yes," she replied. "Please place the tray there." She pointed her left hand at the door-side table. "Thank you."

The orderly placed the tray as requested, but his smile disappeared. "You really are new at this, aren't you?" he said with an edge in his voice. "You know we provide care for the greatest Families in the Imperium, right?"

Alexandra felt her cheeks flush, but she strove to answer in an even tone. "I'm sure you do. Thank you."

He shook his head with a disgusted look and shoved back out the door, muttering something about barbarians.

Alexandra watched his retreating figure disappear down the hallway, took a calming breath, and stooped to pluck her scan package from the satchel. She scanned the tray, the silverware, and each of the bland food items, her gaze flicking up to scan the hallway after each pass of the scanner.

"Now, do I just give this to you, my lady?" Alexandra quietly inquired, chewing her lip. "Or do I need to assist you to eat it too?" She took a chance, placing the tray on the pivot-table beside Bess and pushing it into position against Bess's torso. Standing so close, Alexandra heard the fluttering breaths from Bess, watched the slender fingers fumble a clumsy spoon into the food. Alexandra stepped back to her position, embarrassed by the diminution of the Family's former leader.

Bess made a light cooing sound and managed to spoon food into the approximate area of her mouth. Alexandra leaned over and tucked a napkin beneath Bess's chin. She straightened in time to see another orderly startlingly near, approaching quickly down the outer hallway, a cart trailing behind her. Alexandra barely had a moment to check the image against the approved list provided by Hugh. She didn't see the dark-haired, blue-eyed woman on the list. As the orderly opened the door, Alexandra's hand dropped, the web of her thumb tight against her pistol grip, just short of drawing. In a flurry she scanned the list again. This orderly *must* be there, surely.

The orderly entered, her right hand out of sight behind the cart, her pretty face wearing a smile, the pupils...the pupils pinned!

"Hold!" Alexandra commanded, as the shock of fear spiked and subsided, extinguished in the Deep Man, the pistol leaping into her hand, blunt, deadly, and low.

"Whoa!" the orderly cried, her eyes wide, one hand raised and open. Discordantly, Bess cooed, her spoon rattling on her tray. The orderly looked from Alexandra's pistol, up to her face.

"You—You're new," the orderly said, her right hand shifting, then emerging from behind the cart, empty. Alexandra saw the empty hand and drew a slow breath, her pistol lowering only slightly.

"Yes," Alexandra said. "I'm new, and you are not on the approved list."

"I'm—I'm Jantzen," the orderly said. "Rejuv Specialist Jantzen... second shift." Jantzen's face seemed pale, but Alexandra could place no reliance on that now, as her pistol hovered there between them.

"You are not on the list, Jantzen," Alexandra said, stubbornly clinging to procedure, but feeling her confidence eroding beneath her feet. "I'm sorry."

Bess uttered another soft sound between her lips, and Jantzen looked over as Bess smeared fruit puree about her face, her vacant eyes wandering from Jantzen, to the tray, then up to an invisible point near the ceiling.

Jantzen looked back at Alexandra. "I need to check the patient now."

Alexandra internally clenched and shook her head. She was committed. "You'll need to send someone else, then. Someone approved."

"Gah," Bess said, and banged her spoon on her tray, purple fruit decorating her face. "Gah, gah."

Jantzen glanced at Bess again, her lips forming an angry twist. "Your Family will see a surcharge for this outrage." She turned the cart back toward the door and seemed to wrestle with it a moment. "Give me a hand here, please."

Alexandra shook her head. "No," she said, her pistol still at high-ready, and as Jantzen shot a poisonous glare at her, Alexandra snapped a clean vidcapture of her face.

"Gah," Bess said again as Jantzen stormed off, hurrying down the hall.

Alexandra bit her upper lip as she watched Jantzen disappear, then holstered her pistol, emerging from the cool grip of the Deep Man. "Gods," Alexandra breathed, and Bess made a soft sound, seemingly cooing assent. Alexandra looked at Bess's fruit-speckled face. "I may have just screwed my very first real assignment, my lady," Alexandra said as she pushed a terse report and the picture to Hugh through her UI.

She didn't want Hugh to be surprised when the Medical Specialties Center issued a complaint.

"Boo, boo, boo," Bess said in a whispery voice as her wandering hand slowly slid the knife invisibly out from beneath her blanket and quietly replaced it on the tray. "Gah!" she said, her hand gripping the spoon once again, more food shoveled around her mouth.

Just a short distance from the Medical Specialties Center, Jantzen dropped her flamcrys dagger in disgust. "I couldn't get close enough, I tell you," she said. "The little witch had me at gunpoint the moment I crossed the threshold." Jantzen looked nervously from face to face. "I mean, what was I supposed to do? You've heard the stories about them—that Family. Well, they're true."

Jantzen's eyes caught the subtle movements of her interlocutors, her face growing pale. "Listen! Listen to me! The target's a vegetable." Jantzen's voice was high, desperate. "Do you hear me? She's gone; baby talk; can't even feed herself—"

Jantzen broke off, throwing up a restraining hand, with time for only one last word, spoken quietly. "No."

But the finger that pulled that trigger was not moved by any human emotion.

The woman—the assassin called Jantzen—took the bullet in the center of her chest, jerked at the impact, and fell face-first without a sound.

A cold, disinterested eye roved down to see Jantzen's left foot quiver once and fall still before slipping the heavy pistol back into its holster.

Chapter 12

"How many centuries of human history record the societal debate between those who seek liberty above all else, and those who seek safety above all else? Emperor Yung's reforms placed this choice in the hands of all humanity at last. Now, Oliver's faction within the academy complain that it isn't a choice at all because of the attendant risk. The risk is the whole point!"

—Dr. Ramsay Stirling Attenborough, *Ivory Tower Follies*

LEGION MOLO RANGER KYLE WHITESIDE HAD REALLY BEGUN TO feel they might actually survive the doomed ground assault of Delta Three. Sergeant Reardon's unconventional leadership had slowly collected scores of dispirited Legionnaires, survivors from a dozen shattered contus. They hadn't encountered a single surviving officer until Major Chetwynd and his squad of Pathfinders showed up and immediately began ruining everything.

From the opening conversation things progressed from bad to worse. To Kyle's eyes it seemed clear Major Chetwynd felt some chagrin that a lowly sergeant from this newfangled Molo Ranger maniple had gathered such a quantity of troops and supplies, while a vaunted Pathfinder major showed up ragged and starving, with six equally ragged followers in his train.

Sergeant Avery Reardon immediately poured coal on this, pressing rations and supplies on the new arrivals. "We've got plenty, Major," Reardon had explained. "We've figured a system for fetching resupply spikes, you see. Elementary, really. I'll show you the trick, since it looks like you've been forced to put your foraging skills to work. Turns out, not so much to forage, is there?"

No, it hadn't begun well, and once Chetwynd and his clutch of toughs had filled their bellies and found their feet, it became immediately worse.

Kyle and Pippi were unfortunate witnesses to the fateful final step, even as they completed their regular nightly perimeter check, weaving among the clumps of sleeping Legionnaires in their forested campsite. They heard the raised voices as they made their way through the wide-scattered perimeter, uphill toward the leafy bower that served as a sort of command shelter.

"—But of course, Major," Avery Reardon interjected in his imperturbable voice, "a noncom's sworn duty is to inform, consult, and advise...and that's precisely what I'm doing here."

Kyle and Pippi stopped their Molo mechs in place and crept forward quietly as they heard Major Chetwynd snarl something unintelligible.

"Major, really, if we do as you intend, then we'll continue your fine record of converting perfectly good Legionnaires into corpses, just at a larger scale than you have thus far—"

"Insolence!" Major Chetwynd's voice barked into the forested darkness, causing Kyle and Pippi to start, settling into the shrubbery with a shared look.

"Nothing of the kind—" Reardon began saying, still in a cheerful voice, but Chetwynd cut him off.

"These are not *your* Legionnaires, Sergeant!"

"No, no—they're the Emperor's Legionnaires, of course," Reardon agreed affably, "and he probably wants a few survivors off this rock, if possible."

Kyle and Pippi shared another look, rolling eyes at Reardon's madcap insubordination.

"Now listen carefully, Sergeant," Chetwynd said in a low, angry voice that Kyle could scarcely hear from his place frozen in the shadows, "we are mobilizing this force tomorrow. We are continuing to our strategic objective, and you will obey orders or be arrested and summarily court-martialed."

"Of course, Major," Avery Reardon agreed in an unenthusiastic voice. "I'll be ready, and standing beside you as we march ourselves out of cover. We'll be right up front, won't we, Major?

Leading by example as we head north, like heroes, right into that death trap, side by side—"

"That is quite enough, Sergeant!" Chetwynd snapped. "Get out of my sight!"

As Sergeant Reardon left the major, he encountered Kyle and Pippi hunched in the darkness, just downhill from the major's shrubby enclosure. Reardon put a finger to his lips and led the way out of earshot. When they stood a safe distance from any prying ears, Reardon said, "Eavesdropping on your commanding officer? Really? Such shameful behavior really does give me hope for you two, I must say. My careful tutelage has found fertile ground in both of you."

Pippi's angular face seemed harder still in the moonlight. "We pulling out, then, eh?"

"Yes, Pippi. The major feels we should pursue our original objective some klicks north of here."

Kyle shook his head in the dark, a blanket of dread squeezing his lungs. After a moment Kyle managed, "Is there any chance we can survive long enough to even see the damned objective?"

"Hmm? Survive? Oh, I think we might. I've got a few tricks left, and if we can just get a little help from topside, it could work."

"Topside?" Pippi snorted. "Fleet got their own pain, seems like."

That appeared abundantly true to Kyle Whiteside, and he had little faith that the vessels in orbit would ignore their own problems long enough to rescue a few poor devils planetside.

Captain Glasshauser felt near his breaking point as he observed the radiant surface of Delta Three revealed in the holo. He commanded a vessel of immense power—a collection of vessels now, as senior captain of the squadron, acting commodore—and yet he remained little more than an observer, nearly helpless since *Harrier*'s explosive demise. That horrific moment ended the lives of thousands of fellow Citizens and, most likely, also ended Glasshauser's promising Fleet career, all in one fateful detonation. Since then he had done all he could to extract some victory from the ashes. It all seemed so elementary to him, and yet the Admiralty forbade him the only course of redemption left in play.

The tactical problem seemed exceedingly simple: a handful of Legionnaires trapped groundside on a miserable frontier world swirling in open rebellion. Captain Glasshauser visualized raining orbital kinetic strikes down, pulverizing an expanding ring around the Legionnaires' general position, leaving them in an island of safety to relax until Fleet transports arrived. This could be done in short order, but the twice-damned Admiralty tied Glasshauser's hands.

So, instead, they waited, dropping resupply spikes, answering rare calls for surgical fire, laboring to restore Combat Nets and regular communication...staring at the same lump of terrestrial material, watch after watch after watch.

His only respite arose from the stirring of avarice as he glanced at the main holo display, Delta Three's orbital station and the cluster of vessels docked there. As acting commodore, it seemed likely that all those vessels might provide a fat prize purse to ameliorate any suffering the Admiralty dished out. *What wealth might trickle into my coffers from such a windfall...?*

Captain Glasshauser's musings came to a sudden halt as the comparative silence of the bridge broke. "Captain?" Ensign Laurent said from his place at Sensors, his profile glimmering in *Dragon*'s darkened bridge. "Got something on tachyon, out-system..." The other members of the bridge crew sat up.

Captain Glasshauser turned his depressed gaze from the holo image of blue-green disaster, and stared at Ensign Laurent hopefully. Laurent regarded the flowering sensor data a moment more. "Seems to be a contact...negative ecliptic is all that's resolving so far—No. Got it! Close in, Captain. One-two-two right azimuth, zero-one-three negative. Range is, uh, six hundred—no—five hundred eighty thousand."

Glasshauser sat bolt upright, his mind momentarily locked... Less than six hundred thousand klicks' range! Who would transition so deep in-system? Who could manage it?

He knew the only possible answer, and his mouth felt suddenly dry. He forced his mind to unlock, his lips to move. "Weps! Heat sinks and shield projectors on full readiness. Nav, say...ten gees. Bring us to one-one-zero right azimuth, negative zero-one-zero."

"Ten gees, one-one-zero right, zero-one-zero negative," *Dragon*'s Nav officer repeated, her voice sounding more excited than frightened to Glasshauser's ear.

"Ops?" he said, as he felt the faint shock through the deck plate despite gravity compensation, their engines lighting up hard. "Sound off to action stations."

"Action stations, sir," Ops affirmed, her expression tense at her post.

Glasshauser's mind began to spin again. He needed something concrete, something familiar to anchor upon, a place to settle his thoughts and get a grip. "Sensors...throw your track on main holo."

Laurent affirmed and the contact appeared on the screen, shockingly close, evidently moving to pin them against Delta Three's gravity well. Glasshauser stared at the image, striving for clarity, for some flash of tactical insight.

"Captain?" The Comm lieutenant hesitantly interrupted Glasshauser's musing.

"*What?*" the captain snapped.

"Signals from *Python* and *Mistral*, sir. They request orders."

Damn and blast! In the moment of shock he'd clean forgotten his consorts. He had enough on his plate without the new responsibilities of leading the entire squadron.

Glasshauser took in a tight breath. "Message to squadron: *Accelerate, orient on new contact at one-two-two right.*" The captain felt a bead of sweat trickling down his spine, and he looked at the holo image again, trying to clear his mind...*Sherwood!* IMS *Sherwood* orbited out of sight occluded behind the mass of Delta Three.

"Comm, message for *Sherwood*: *Join on flag.* Route through *Rook*." At least he'd had the forethought to keep *Rook* in position to bounce communications behind the globe. The little tender wasn't good for much else since *Harrier*'s loss.

"Captain!" Ensign Laurent blurted. "Target is painting us."

Glasshauser felt the bridge crew waiting for him to leap into action, but he couldn't seem to gather his thoughts. The deckchief hovering near at hand with an expectant look on her face wasn't helping anything.

The deckchief, the senior noncom aboard *Dragon*, rubbed her chin, casually inquiring, "What sort of ship do you suppose they put up against us, Captain?"

With an internal wave of chagrin, Glasshauser tried for an equally light tone. "Yes, let's find out." Then to *Dragon*'s Intelligence, "Oolong, can you identify the closing contact?"

Some prior captain gifted *Dragon*'s Intelligence with a deep, rumbling voice, clearly intended to be dragonish in nature. The voice had never bothered Glasshauser before, but under the suddenly deadly circumstances it seemed childish and discordant as the Intelligence said, "Contact closing from four hundred thousand is approximately fifty thousand tons, cruiser class, specific vessel unknown."

Fifty thousand tons.

The captain swallowed bile as his mind sputtered through the same calculations over and over. His "squadron" consisted of the 15,000-ton missile carrier, *Python*, *Sherwood*, a 7,000-ton frigate, and *Mistral*, a 5,000-ton frigate. He didn't count *Rook*, the 4,500-ton tender, and *Sherwood* couldn't join the fight until she rounded Delta Three's circumference, whenever that might be. Combined with *Dragon*'s 25,000 lethal tons, the contest seemed a near-equal match, and Glasshauser hated everything about it.

So far in this infant war, all near-equal contests went to the rebels. *Tanager*'s recent combat within this same system still represented the only Fleet victory against a superior force, and Glasshauser suddenly found himself possessed of a much greater appreciation for Captain Roush's accomplishments.

In the lengthening silence on the bridge, the XO cleared his throat, seeming to read Glasshauser's mind. "Captain, seems like Roush mentioned a fifty-thousand-ton cruiser that mauled *Tanager* here in this system, didn't she?"

"Yes," Glasshauser said. "So?"

Laurent at Sensors tersely interjected, "*Sherwood*'s cleared the horizon. We have line-of-sight. Range to target, three hundred thousand and closing."

The XO and Glasshauser both glanced at Sensors before the XO replied, "What if it's the same cruiser? It's been here the whole time, hiding out, running dark."

Glasshauser felt his hand trembling and he gripped his thigh to conceal the betrayal. He knew the XO—the entire bridge crew—expected him to see some great truth in this revelation, but all that filled Glasshauser's mind was the swiftly closing range to the enemy, and a host of actions he knew he was fumbling away. "But..." Glasshauser began, his voice cracking slightly. He swallowed and began again. "But, the tachyon pulse? You... He transitioned in-system," was all he managed to say.

"Spoofed somehow. To draw us out, perhaps," the XO said.

"Launch!" Laurent yelped. "Multiple launches!"

Glasshauser opened his mouth but no words would emerge.

"Shall we order *Sherwood* to hold orbit?" the XO asked in a low voice, and Glasshauser felt he *should* understand why this was an appropriate action.

He merely nodded, managing to say, "Yes, Commander, order *Sherwood* to hold orbit." The cluster of incoming missile tracks seemed to momentarily connect Glasshauser to those tedious simulation runs of his early Fleet years, and his mouth began to work seemingly of its own accord.

"Weps, point defenses charged, interdiction fire, now."

"Captain," the Comm lieutenant called in a sharp voice, "*Mistral* reports taking heavy fire, signature of an energy weapon!"

At that range? It seemed... Glasshauser recalled something about *Tanager*'s foe resolving incredible long-range shots, though those were largely chalked up to exaggeration or miscalculation. *Evidently not.*

"Message to *Python*: Continuous launch on enemy target. To *Mistral*: Break and evade." He looked to the XO at his side. "Give the bastard something to think about."

The XO nodded but he stared at the moving tracks unfolding across the main holo. "Something's not right here..."

"Enemy contact is maneuvering—hard!" the Sensor ensign called out. "Now heading left azimuth one-seven-five, looks like... zero-nine-zero negative, at least twenty gees."

For the first time since the contact appeared, Glasshauser experienced a moment of seeming clarity. "Weps, give me a full pattern of thirty-two gauge missiles on an intercept path... Idiot sod's going to have a time evading at this range with all that delta-vee."

The XO, who continued staring at the holo, frowning, suddenly straightened. "Gods..." he gasped. "We're not the target at all."

Glasshauser's momentary satisfaction evaporated, the welter of confusion returning as he stared uncomprehendingly at the holo. "What? What's this?"

"Look!" the XO cried. "The incoming tracks... they're not for us!"

Glasshauser shook his head. "I—I don't understand—"

"They're nuking the Legionnaires. Planetside!"

Realization dawned upon Glasshauser, the spreading lines through the holo suddenly clear, and orders began to fly. *Python* and *Sherwood* both received their orders and began continuous launching, missiles leaping from their hardpoints and torching out into the dark, speeding to intercept the string of enemy missiles plunging toward the glowing surface of Delta Three.

Glasshauser barely noticed the enemy contact emerge from *Dragon*'s erupting salvo, running hard and fast, his attention riveted upon the missile tracks curving and twisting toward their inevitable goal in the well. *Sherwood*'s position in orbit, near the fatal terminus of the enemy barrage, provided their only real hope. *Sherwood*'s own scanty supply of 64-gauge and larger 32-gauge missiles made their short transits into the teeth of the enemy salvo, detonating in a staggered sequence of nuclear fires, each blast consuming one or two enemy warheads. If just one missile slipped through the maelstrom of fire, it would likely airburst tight against the surface vaporizing any Legionnaires within a five-klick radius. The enemy's aim need not be all that precise.

From his place on *Dragon*'s bridge, Captain Glasshauser stared at the enhanced optical feed, perceiving the continuous eruptions, globes of fire expanding and fading, one after another, closer and closer to the surface of Delta Three and the hapless Legionnaires waiting below.

When the last fire faded and no surface detonation came filtering back up through the planet's curtaining clouds, Glasshauser found himself breathing again. He wiped sweat from his brow and managed to say, "Looks like we got them all short of the surface."

"Captain," Comm said, "message from *Sherwood*." Before the Comm lieutenant said another word Glasshauser knew it wouldn't be good news. "They report signs of fighting groundside. They received some distress signals from the Legionnaires, but those ended some time ago."

The beleaguered captain drew a slow breath, finding one disturbing island of clarity in the swimming chaos of his thoughts: Had the enemy really tried to nuke their own ground forces just to crush the remaining Legionnaires? Or had it all been a ruse to draw orbital support off at some key juncture...? No...the surface attack was surely an unnecessary element for a mere ruse...*surely*.

For the first time, Glasshauser truly began to believe Delta Three planetside harbored something of immense value to the enemy, something they would sacrifice their own ground forces to protect.

Chapter 13

"When any House attains greatness through the mere wind of fortune, the longevity of that greatness remains very much in question until said House demonstrates at least one of the three vital attributes of mastery: Diplomacy, Ruthlessness, or Genius. The Sinclair-Marus' naïveté undercut any true skill in diplomacy, their rigid adherence to the Honor Code withheld the fruit of ruthlessness, and their genius seemingly only extended to wartime endeavors."

—Everest Compline, *Reflections*

YOUNG INGA PLACED THE ILLICIT TRANSPONDER CHIT IN THE high top of her new boot and cinched the closure tight. Her rudimentary blade she affixed to her left wrist with bandage strips and covered the slight protuberance under the sleeve of her new martial uniform.

Inga's head swam as she straightened, spots dancing before her eyes, the painful lump throbbing at the base of her skull. She swallowed her nausea and carefully regarded the unfamiliar girl gazing back at her from the mirror. The disarray of her blond locks and the deep pallor of her cheeks meant little to Inga. The impostor staring back, clad as true Sinclair-Maru, nearly compelled her to tear the boots, belt, and garment off. That face she knew, those eyes, those hands and the cold heart animating them; they were all formed in the deepest slum of Battersea, and they did not belong in the guise of a Great Family scion. She felt what could only be shame, a fraud...and yet...

Perfect.

Bess once said that of her; Inga knew it was spoken with the flat certainty of truth.

Inga's clammy palm smoothed over the dark fabric of her uniform, and she tried to straighten her shoulders despite the pain radiating down her neck. She *would* be perfect. She *must* be.

With that resolve, Inga turned from the mirror and moved to her chamber door, opening it onto an empty hall. Her own, personal ident chit she kept in hand, her earlier tests confirming that door scans only reached down to about knee height. She crossed the hall and stepped to the Koblenzes' door, incidentally logging her exit from her quarters, and her subsequent entrance to their apartment for any nosy Intelligence monitoring.

Evita Koblenz invited Inga in and made appreciative noises about Inga's sharp new uniform before turning to hail Mitzi and Karl. When Evita's back turned, Inga smoothly slipped her personal ident chip, wrapped in medical adhesive, beneath the low table lip and pressed it home, even as Mitzi scampered into sight, halting abruptly, her lips ringed with sticky jam. She stared owlishly at Inga, a finger stealing into her mouth. Inga felt an urge to tell her, *"Yes, I am a fraud,"* but she just stared back at her tiny sister, waiting until Karl sauntered into view. Only as Inga observed the same expression in Karl's eyes did she begin to understand her siblings' tension.

"I was gone to medical yesterday," Inga said, and Evita uttered a sympathetic sound, but Inga ignored her, pressing on. "Like my new uniform?" She smoothed over the sharp creases with spread hands.

Mitzi's and Karl's wary expressions faded. No, my poor angels, you may remain. Heaven is not stolen away from you.

Karl nodded slowly, his eyes serious. "You look nice," he offered quietly.

Mitzi stepped tentatively up to Inga, her gaze peering up. Mitzi's finger popped from her mouth, the sticky hand holding fast to Inga's wrist. *Hurt?* Mitzi tapped out, clearly having spotted the bandage peeking from behind Inga's ear. Inga lightly touched the aching lump. "I'm a little sore," Inga said aloud. "Thought I'd check on you before I rest."

"Isn't it nice of your big sister to check on you?" Evita cooed in her child-talking voice. More of the same followed, grating on Inga until she fled, backing out the door as Evita barraged her with sympathy. Inga paused across the hall beside her door until the Koblenz door closed, then fished out the illicit ident chip from her boot top before moving down the empty hallway, a definite goal in mind.

Inga's skull throbbed with each step, but she needed this window for vital exploration when all would expect her abed, recovering from surgery.

The door to a utility closet appeared on the right side, yielding to her "found" ident chip, and she slipped in before anyone appeared in the hallway to ask tedious questions. Inside she found two quiescent dumb-mechs liberally splattered with the dried residue of cleaning fluid. Beside racks of cleaning supplies, she spotted the faint outline of the concealed access panel she sought.

Fortunately, Inga thought, the Sinclair-Maru secured access panels on Hawksgaard in much the way city custodians had back on Battersea, and Inga's practiced technique levered the small rectangle from the wall in a flash of her crude tools. The pounding in her skull nearly blinded Inga as she slithered into the small, dark void and sat up. A moment of fumbling slid the panel back loosely into place behind her, covering her tracks as the nauseating pain slowly eased in her head.

She waited a few moments for her eyes to adjust to the dim lighting, but relented, scrounging out the tiny reading light she had liberated from her new nightstand. Its hard white glow revealed the first real dust Inga had observed on Hawksgaard, and the presence of the grime made her feel more at home as she stared down the long, low passage stretching before her.

The setting was more or less what she expected, but she hadn't reckoned on the agony currently aggravated by her hunched-over progress as she began shuffling toward the faint sound of machinery ahead. The cords of pain stretched down her spinal column, seeming to pull directly at Inga's stomach, but she clenched her teeth and shuffled on and on. The faint odor of oil and ozone increased with each crouched step until a glimmer ahead warned Inga that her goal lay near.

She settled thankfully to her haunches, allowing her neck and head to ease somewhat as she killed the tiny light, stuffing it into a pocket before advancing to the end of her low tunnel. She crept toward the low hum and rattle. Though her screaming nerves hungered to stand up straight, Inga hunched back in the shadows, carefully surveying the chamber before her.

Conveyors issued from a dozen low passages, converging in the chamber's center, where simple automation shoved the various bits of nonorganic rubbish off the conveyors into bins. Inga saw the pathways for human access threading through the serpentine of clattering conveyors, each dimly illuminated by low yellow footlights that left the majority of the broad room in a deep gloom. After a few additional, painful moments of wary observation, Inga shuffled out of the low service passage, standing upright at last, ready to survey her new treasure trove.

As Inga slipped among the cluttering conveyors, she felt a hint of satisfaction, seeing that Hawksgaard sorted their waste in much the same fashion Port City in Battersea had employed. It provided great convenience for all of Inga's shopping needs. Wielding her tiny reading light, peering into various bins, Inga spotted an item or two of interest, tucking them into her pockets and moving on. It was then she noticed one conveyor line apart from the others, still and silent, dusty from disuse.

Leaving the bins of discarded treasures, Inga followed the silent conveyor back to its emergence from the wall. She played her reading light into the black mouth of the probable waste tunnel, leaning over the disused conveyor. The tunnel stretched into shrinking darkness, no sound, no light, no scent to reveal its purpose.

Inga knew she should return to her quarters soon, her initial foray crowned with sufficient success. Her head pounded, her body longing for that amazing, comfortable bed. Instead she turned and fixed the position of the low, dark access passage, her route back *home*, then climbed up onto the dusty conveyor, sliding her feet to conceal the obvious footprints in the dust. She set off down the dark, silent tunnel before her, treading quietly down the center of the track.

After covering a short distance, Inga began to see dark, disused waste chutes perforate the walls at intervals, their shadowed mouths marked by faded years of use. She paused to listen or sniff at some chutes, but detecting nothing she continued on, noting the increasing chill in the air. Ahead, the tunnel advanced into blackness as far as her feeble light pierced, and behind her the sound of machinery faded into an oppressive silence.

As Inga walked on and on, she figured this disused rubbish conveyor once serviced an old domicile wing, unoccupied now for how many years? Decades? She visualized the people who once thoughtlessly dropped their castoffs down these chutes—presumably Sinclair-Maru Family members and oath-kin only. They surely could never have imagined a castoff of an entirely different sort skulking about these dark passages one future day. The thought gave Inga a glimmer of satisfaction to combat the silence and cold darkness.

A moment later, she saw a flash of reflected light ahead and marched straight to the end of the line. A tall metallic panel terminated the passage, ending Inga's hopeful vision of another large chamber filled with machinery—and opportunities.

Inga settled wearily down upon the rounded end of the dusty conveyor, her feet dangling as she rested before heading back, her arms wrapped across her chest in the chill. The prospect of the long walk back suddenly seemed vast, the knot of pain in Inga's neck radiating up through her brain and down through her spine. She tilted her head slowly forward, trying in vain to ease the suffering. Instead, as the pain throbbed unabated, Inga's eyes suddenly discerned the outline of a faint rectangle in the thick dust below her feet, dimly illuminated by her book light.

Inga's exhaustion melted momentarily as she eased off the conveyor, avoiding the agonizing jolt from the modest drop. A moment later, she had scraped the layer of grime from a narrow hatch in the floor and jammed her fingers into the dirt-crusted lip. With her skull pounding, Inga pulled, the hatch pivoting easily open to reveal a dark void below, the top rung of a ladder visible just under the lip. Inga trained her small light, leaning over the open hatch. The angular geometry of ducts and pipes resolved below, in their midst a broad void bordered by some sort of workbench, its surface decorated by tool-shaped lumps coated in dust. After playing her light about the hidden chamber she stood slowly to her feet.

Inga gently closed the hatch, drawing a slow breath, the long walk before her suddenly fading in its weight as her new discovery sank in. With the harsh lessons of a cruel childhood behind her, she *knew* she had discovered an asset of a great value, the full extent of the haul yet to be determined. She clambered back on the conveyor and set off through the dark, her mind weighing her new possibilities.

By the time Inga retraced her steps, pacing silently through the darkness until she reached the waste collection room, her cranium felt entirely detached from her body, a floating orb of agony. Clambering back down the low service passage required slow breaths and iron control to keep her nausea at bay, Inga's vision darkening in waves, but she finally reached the access panel. She slithered blindly into the utility closet, sat up, and immediately vomited into the open reservoir of a flanking service dumb-mech. When the spasms died down and Inga's vision cleared somewhat, she attempted to clean the dusty marks from her hands, boots, and uniform, fumbling through her efforts with the aid of musty rags and cleaning solution pirated from the closet's supplies. When she attempted to look downward, the pain flashed so hot it took her breath away, meaning cleaning efforts surely fell short of perfection. It became clear, even in Inga's muddled state, that she might not retain consciousness long enough to regain the safety of her quarters. Her last clear thought compelled her to peel the rudimentary blade from her forearm and clumsily kick it beneath the closet's lowest shelf.

The remainder of Inga's coherent observations comprised warped flashes of sight and sound. She seemed to make her way unsteadily down the hallway, but she could not recall how she departed the utility closet. An adult appeared in one flash, walking past Inga, a troubled expression on that unfamiliar adult face as they stared down at her, but the next moment she found herself before the Koblenzes' door.

Evita Koblenz seemed inordinately agitated, her voice unpleasantly raised as she asked incomprehensible questions of Inga over and over. Inga tried to speak, but instead of audible words, she felt her fingers tapping out silent words against her own thigh. That would not work; Inga needed to reassure the creature long enough to get through the door and secure her regular ident chip. That much she knew.

The subtleties of manipulation utterly abandoned Inga, her vision shrinking into darkness. In her last gasp of effort, Inga shuffled past the babbling adult, gaining entrance to the Koblenz apartment, the low table securing her concealed ident chip there, just out of reach as the room began to spin. She saw a flash of Mitzi and Karl, the Koblenz brat beside them, his face twisted with distaste for a moment before his mother hustled them away from the freak collapsed in their entryway.

Collapsed?

Yes. Somehow she now looked upward at the small table's underside. Inga's hand seemed to extend of its own accord, just grasping ident chip as the darkness became complete.

She possessed a vague awareness of being moved, strong hands lifting, shifting, bearing her away. Voices murmured unintelligibly for a time before a cool fire began flowing from her arm, through her veins, seeming to swirl about the pulsing agony in her skull.

Words rose above the fading static of agony, and meaning reconnected to the spoken words. "...a troubling indication, Kai," the voice said, "if her body cannot tolerate even this. You must admit she may not be the ideal candidate after all."

Inga already knew Kai well enough to recognize the tension in his voice as he said, "I see no signs of cybernetic rejection. Let us not be hasty, Doctor."

The doctor sounded unpersuaded to Inga's attentive ears. "How many subjects need more than a day or two of rest after the procedure, Kai? Very, very few. You must face facts: you— and Bess—may need to locate a new candidate. This little one is probably headed for a full crash and I'll have to pull the scaram to spare her life."

Inga found the course of the conversation intolerable, but every attempt at speech expressed itself in the feeble tapping of her fingers against the silky sheets, unheeded by her critics.

She strained every fiber, working her tongue woodenly. "No," she finally managed with her mouth. "I'm—I'm fine." She put a great deal of effort into making these words sound jolly and convincing, even though her eyes remained stubbornly closed, the faint whisper of her voice falling far short of her intent.

There seemed to be a moment of startled silence as Inga struggled to peel her eyelids open, to assess the impact of her words, to sit up—achieving none of this. Then Kai's voice spoke, "You do not appear 'fine,' child."

Inga struggled with numb lips, an intractable mouth, before she managed, "I'm a'right. Just fell down."

"Mistress Maru," the doctor's voice invaded the darkness behind Inga's eyelids, "you were told to rest. Evita Koblenz said you went to your quarters to rest. Then, some hours later, you collapse on her floor. You are clearly very ill."

The doctor's identity became clear in the theater of Inga's

mind: *Enemy*. Her leaden eyelids finally lifted, the clean walls of Inga's own quarters resolving about her, Kai's pink, troubled face coming into focus.

Inga looked sidelong, squinting in the brightness, struggling to marshal sluggish thoughts as she sized up her foe. She remembered the face now frowning down at her, an image from her prior day's visit to Hawksgaard's medical wing...back when this doctor had been a mere nonentity in her estimation. Her foggy thoughts solidified upon a potential strategy to neutralize her sudden foe.

Her lips moistened. "Don't like resting," Inga managed to say. "Went for a walk. Fell down."

The doctor's expression became even more severe. "You went for a walk? When you were *ordered* to rest?"

Inga's gaze slowly traveled back to Kai. "*He* orders," she said, then looked back to the doctor. "You don't."

As the doctor's mouth opened to speak, Kai placed a restraining hand upon his shoulder. "Do recall, Doctor, she hasn't given first oaths yet, nor begun training."

The doctor closed his mouth but the severe expression remained. After a moment he said, "You say you fell. Did you strike your head?"

Inga managed a bed-ridden shrug. "Don't know. Was asleep for that bit."

The doctor did not seem to appreciate Inga's tone, but Kai interrupted once again. "We shall leave you to rest now, child. Evita Koblenz will be so kind as to deliver your meal." He paused before adding. "You will remain in bed and rest until tomorrow at the least. Is this clear to you?"

Inga nodded slightly, wincing at the pain. "Yes. Clear."

Kai nodded in return, and the doctor spun on his heel, moving to the door. Kai leaned over and touched Inga's blanket. "Be wise," he said in a low voice, opening his hand. Inga saw her savaged book light fall upon her blanket. "Don't change, child, but be wise." Inga's eyes flicked to the bedside, her dusty clothes folded there, and her cheeks flushed.

Her gaze shifted back to him, the knowledge clear between them. "Yes, Kai, I will...I will be wise," she said.

Chapter 14

"Careful study reveals Sinclair-Maru doctrine that clearly must nest within the Honor Code. The substance of these teachings can only be guessed at, but it seems a mistake to assume that they represent anything less than the true beliefs of the Family...."

—Everest Compline, *Reflections*

AS HE STEPPED INTO THE TIGHT, COLD PINNACE BAY ACCESS, DR. Kenshin Tenroo's first glimpse of *Hightower*, this mighty warship, underwhelmed. Rather than the spacious flight deck Tenroo had expected, or even an entry port festooned with starched uniforms and glittering medals, the entrance had a distinctly industrial feel. As Captain Sinclair-Maru spoke with the lone crew member greeting them, Tenroo's gaze traveled up to the strangely dimensioned chamber. It was, he thought, rather like a mouse's perspective inside some vast engine.

Tenroo had invested time researching IMS *Hightower* once it became his first auditor assignment, and he knew it represented one of the Imperium's more substantial vessels—many times larger than Captain Sinclair-Maru's former command, *Tanager*—and Tenroo had expected to be astonished by its mighty proportions. His first observations fell far short of expectations, although this was the first time he set foot upon any warship. It certainly gave little indication of its great vastness thus far.

The captain had finished a rather terse exchange with the

sour-faced crew member—a specialist, Tenroo thought she had said—and he realized perhaps he should have listened more closely rather than gawking about. Now it seemed a distinct damper lay over their small group as the specialist turned and led them from the pinnace bay: the captain and chief, followed by their luggage-bearing dumb-mech, then Tenroo, his own hodgepodge of parcels trying to escape from his clutching hands.

The first moments of Tenroo's auditor commission began inauspiciously, but he bore his faint chagrin well. He had decades of prior experience feeling out of place, first as a Vested Citizen from an established Family who then chose to become a mere academic, then years spent as a distrusted outsider within the halls of higher learning dominated by demi-cit academics. In the early years of his university career, demi-cit professors and students seemed to appreciate Tenroo's modesty, his lack of Vested Citizen arrogance, prejudice. Tenroo had chosen academics, all those decades past, due to his unquenchable curiosity, and in those early years that curiosity served as an equalizing force to dissolve class distinctions in the eyes of his demi-cit colleagues. They had swiftly learned Tenroo personally esteemed demi-cit and Vested Citizen equally—both on the basis of their scholarship alone, rather than viewing demi-cits as unruly children who entered academics for the stipend alone.

Tenroo still could not identify the turning point, but the climate of academia had changed through the years as it concerned the class distinction between Citizen and demi-cit. The moral authority had shifted until Tenroo and the few other Citizen-scholars were *tolerated* at best. The robust intellectual debates of his early years became extinct, no longer open to participation by Vested Citizens. He could still recall the moment when he realized academia was a dying dream for him.

That moment arrived one day when he joined several other notable scholars to discuss Weintraub's new extension of Game Theory—a radical departure meant specifically for any new nonhuman intelligences the Myriad Worlds Imperium might encounter. To Tenroo's eyes, the new theory added nothing at all—in fact rendering Game Theory unusable through a series of poorly defined "alien variables" that defied any logic. As his fellow scholars applauded Weintraub's "originality," Tenroo had wondered if they truly believed what they were saying. The only purpose Tenroo could divine from Weintraub's theory was in creating an intellectual bastion to assault the actions of the long-dead Emperor Yung the First. Since Yung's revolutionary reforms to the Imperium were nearly all predicated upon humanity's near extinction by the alien "Slaggers," an illogical new version of Game Theory made any concern about alien hostility appear merely ignorant.

When Tenroo had gently suggested that any alien intelligence capable of interstellar travel could not escape the difference between a one and a zero, Weintraub herself had held up a hand to hush the murmuring of their colleagues.

"Now, now," she had said in a rousing voice, though her eyes had glittered in a way that had puzzled Tenroo in the moment. "Let us allow Dr. Tenroo to show us the *truth*, my friends. We should all know by now, those who wear the sword are always right . . ."

In that moment Tenroo had closed his mouth, scanned the faces of colleagues he had known for years, and found only smirking approval in their eyes. Within days of that event, he had selected a thankless government position that required a Vested Citizen bearing a deep academic background—a dismal fate for any true scholar—and turned away from the beloved halls of learning forever. The beautiful dream had died.

This more recent opportunity as an Imperial Auditor had initially held no interest for Tenroo, until he learned he might be attached to a vessel commanded by a member of the Sinclair-Maru Family, wherein he saw a golden opportunity.

For a time in his early academic years, Tenroo had fixed upon history of the Myriad Worlds as a subject, and the puzzle of the Sinclair-Maru had become something of a fascination for him. He had studied Ernest Compline's controversial book, of course; he had collected images of combat actions by the Family founders, Devlin Sinclair and Mia Maru, back when they had famously attacked the rebel flank some centuries prior. He had often wondered at the centuries-long rumors of secret tech, secret methods underpinning the Sinclair-Maru's Family philosophy, and longed to tour the aged halls of their fortified holding on Battersea: Lykeios Manor.

Now, against all likelihood, Kenshin Tenroo walked scant steps behind Saef Sinclair-Maru as this young scion entered his prestigious new command. Tenroo divided his attention between the novel scene unfolding before his eyes and a close inspection of Saef's every reaction. He had already noted an indefinable quality seemingly shared by the captain and Chief Maru, a some- what disquieting stillness, or hooded quality hinting at a notable *absence*. He perceived this quality both in the subtleties of their carriage or movement, and in their eyes. Was this a feature of the Sinclair-Maru secret, or a quality of any Fleet personnel who had emerged from the horrors of combat alive?

This line of thinking prompted Tenroo's discordant ques- tion even as the heavy access hatch opened for them, granting passage to the ship's interior: "Chief Maru, were you trained at Lykeios Manor?"

Chief Maru stepped through the access, looked left and right, the dumb-mech skittering up beside her cloak-shrouded figure. Without turning to him, she said, "No, Auditor," and continued to walk behind the sour-faced specialist. Tenroo chided himself for his impulsiveness, following along, stepping into a corridor somewhat wider than he had expected, but otherwise unimpres- sive. No crew members awaited here either, and their small party set off to the left, the soft tread of their various steps and the skittering of the dumb-mech the only appreciable sound.

Tenroo found himself observing Chief Maru's movements more so than the unfolding views of *Hightower*'s interior workings. Although little of her frame projected above or below her cloak, something about her precise motions struck Tenroo's sensibilities in an arresting manner. He wrestled to define what he observed, but each step, each inclination of her head seemed to overlay a hint of greater complexity, as if between each step she almost invisibly rejected a series of alternate actions. He smiled to himself and his uninformed flights of fancy, but *something* seemed to roil beneath her cool exterior. A moment later, Tenroo uttered a soft, surprised bleat, nearly dropping one of his encumbering parcels.

A blaze of images had suddenly exploded across Tenroo's vision, his implanted Shaper tech suddenly populating the User Interface that accessed his optic nerve. Wireframes, values, and menu chains nearly obscured his vision all in a single burst.

Tenroo's companions glanced back at him inquiringly, but he suddenly realized the source of this image onslaught and murmured an apology, looking down, feeling even more the fool. His identity had evidently triggered the application of an auditor overlay for his UI, which he would explore at some quiet moment, but at present it merely obscured his vision in an annoying fashion.

They continued on through a pair of heavy-looking hatchways and encountered the first of *Hightower*'s Imperial Marines, flanking their path, their hands near sword and pistol at their sides, their uniforms looking somewhat unique to Tenroo's eyes with a distinctive patch on each left shoulder.

Tenroo was so occupied trying to examine the Marines through the obscuring clutter in his overloaded UI, he once again missed the exchange of words between the captain and the Marines. A moment later, the acerbic specialist led them through a door into a finely appointed chamber.

"These are the captain's quarters, sir," the specialist said in a constrained voice. "As you see, Captain Mileus left most of his possessions."

"Yes, thank you, Beecher," Saef said.

Beecher retreated toward the door. "If you wish, I can show your cox'n and the Imperial Auditor to their lodgings now."

"I'll confer a moment with my cox'n, if you please," the captain said, and Tenroo thought the tone and expression on the captain's face both communicated a veiled anger.

"Of course," Beecher said.

Saef held up a hand. "Commander Attic will render some sort of explanation soon, I presume?"

"I—as soon as he's able, Captain."

Saef nodded curtly and turned away, and Tenroo noted the whitened knuckles on Saef's hand where it gripped the pommel of his sword.

"Auditor," Specialist Beecher said, "if you will accompany me...?"

Tenroo's arms felt wearied from clutching his various parcels for such a spell, but he looked from the specialist to the quiet pair of his travel companions beside him.

"If I may..." Tenroo began uncertainly, "...um...I'd prefer to accompany the captain for a moment."

Specialist Beecher shifted her gaze to the captain then back to Tenroo, saying rather too quickly, "Of course, Auditor."

Beecher stepped hastily back through the door, leaving Tenroo alone with the captain and Chief Maru. The graphical clutter before Tenroo's vision still obscured. It had surely appeared when *Hightower's* Intelligence authenticated Tenroo's identity. For the moment it only seemed to provide annoyance as Tenroo attempted to look beyond, reading the facial expressions aimed in his direction.

"I—uh—trust I am not imposing by lingering here a moment with you, Captain?"

"Of course not," the captain said, but the flat tone of his voice and his wooden expression seemed to say otherwise. Cox'n and captain shared a look, their eyes flickering in a manner that made Tenroo wonder if they exchanged line-of-sight messages even as Saef sank into a supple chair.

He hesitantly fumbled his baggage down to the deck and straightened, putting sweaty palms on his thighs. All the questions Tenroo longed to ask came bubbling up, and he restrained himself only after concluding something truly troubled his hosts.

Was the lack of pomp and circumstance indicative of an underlying issue? Tenroo lacked any context to form a conclusion or even to ask an informed question. Suddenly he realized how foolish he must appear, demanding to stay, then stymied into silence as the captain calmly regarded him, Chief Maru producing a shiny red fruit from beneath her cloak, munching it.

Before Tenroo could formulate an appropriate apology and extricate himself, the entryway chimed.

"Enter," Captain Sinclair-Maru said as the chief liquidly sidestepped a few paces for some odd reason.

The door opened to admit a dark-haired, dark-eyed man in the uniform of what Tenroo thought to be a Fleet commander. Tenroo hadn't experienced much contact with heavyworlders, but the tanklike build of the man seemed to reveal a heavyworld heritage.

"Captain," the commander greeted in a deep voice, his expression grave. "Commander Attic. Welcome aboard *Hightower*."

Captain Sinclair-Maru remained seated, placidly regarding Commander Attic, saying nothing for several uncomfortable seconds as the tension seemed to multiply. Chief Maru took a crunchy bite of her fruit and Attic's gaze flicked from the captain to the chief and back.

"Commander," Captain Sinclair-Maru said at last, his fixed gaze never wavering from Attic's face. He gestured toward Tenroo. "Imperial Auditor Tenroo."

Attic's lips formed a grim line and he barely looked away from the captain as he acknowledged, "Auditor; welcome."

"My cox'n, Chief Maru."

"Chief." Attic gave a curt nod to the chief.

The silence stretched out again and Tenroo wondered whether the tension gnawed Commander Attic's spine as fiercely as it did his own.

Attic broke the uncomfortable silence. "Captain, if you have any questions, I would—"

"Just one question," the captain said and held up a finger. "Are you attempting to provoke a duel, Commander?"

Tenroo saw a surge of color rise to the commander's cheek and was surprised to be the recipient of a nervous, sidelong glance from the heavyworlder.

Chief Maru interjected, "Don't mind the auditor. He's so very curious about our odd little Fleet ways." She took another bite of her fruit and Tenroo could scarcely believe he was witness to such a fascinating scene.

Commander Attic moistened his lips and glanced again toward Tenroo before replying, "*Provoke*, Captain?" He waved a thick, dismissive hand and Tenroo observed the pendulous quality of Attic's elongated earlobe, another hallmark of heavyworld nativity.

Captain Sinclair-Maru's expression did not change, his gaze fixed upon Commander Attic. "I will grant that the alteration of my orders to a *provisional* authority could not be at your hand alone," the captain said, "but the calculated disrespect aboard this vessel is under your authority alone."

Tenroo's gaze shifted from the captain, back to Commander Attic, and he saw the color further rising, distended veins proclaiming a reaction. Tenroo now wished he had cleared all the obscuring clutter from his UI before this instructive moment began to unfold.

As Attic opened his mouth to speak, Captain Sinclair-Maru continued, his tone rising slightly: "You greet my first moment aboard with disrespect and block my access to *Hightower*'s Intelligence. So I am conveniently *not* your commanding officer just yet—still susceptible to the immediate edicts of the Honor Code. Then what, Attic? Some final straw of dishonor? Then I challenge, you accept, and we meet...immediately?"

The captain stood easily to his feet, continuing his calm speech. "Your home was where, again? Thorsworld? Yes? So we cross swords at Thorsworld gravity, and you make quick work of me. Isn't that about right?"

Tenroo saw Attic's jaw muscle clench, and observed *yet* another nervous sidelong look toward him. *Whatever does the commander think I have to say about anything?*

Commander Attic angrily wiped a bead of sweat from his brow, unlocking his tongue. "Captain, you—I—your accusation is most unjust."

"Have I *dishonored* you, Commander Attic?" Saef asked. "There is a remedy. You know the words, surely." The captain's voice remained measured.

Though Tenroo hadn't given the dueling aspect of the Honor Code much thought for some decades, he understood the captain's implication quite readily. If Commander Attic uttered the challenge, then Captain Sinclair-Maru chose the "location" of the duel, in practice meaning the gravitation level of their meeting. The gravity could correspond to any inhabited locality of the Myriad Worlds. The duel would occur at some level that best suited the captain, not at Thorsworld's crushing gravity, where Attic surely held the upper hand.

Commander Attic worked his jaw a moment before saying, "Not—not at all, Captain . . . merely a"—he shot Tenroo another glance—"an unfortunate misunderstanding."

"Oh?" Saef pressed, his tone less polite. "And this *provisional* command nonsense? Also a mere misunderstanding?"

Tenroo observed the working of Attic's throat as he swallowed. "Surely, it must be," Attic said.

Captain Sinclair-Maru held Attic in a fixed gaze for a moment, Chief Maru taking another bite as she observed, then he said, "Very well. If you please, Commander?"

For a moment Tenroo saw a flash of pure hatred in Attic's face before he turned his eyes vaguely ceiling-ward. "Gideon?" Attic said.

"Yes, Commander?" came the earnest voice of *Hightower*'s Intelligence.

"Please grant full Captain's access to Captain Sinclair-Maru in accordance with Admiralty orders."

"Yes, Commander. Full Captain's access granted to Captain Sinclair-Maru."

Commander Attic dipped his head in a shallow bow, but his lips remained compressed in a thick line. "Captain, I will assemble the officers of the watch for your review."

"Thank you, Commander," Saef said in a mild voice. "I will join you in the bridge shortly."

Tenroo saw Chief Maru throw the core of her fruit into the nearby waste chute with her left hand, her eyes on Commander Attic. The sharp smack of the thrown fruit startled the commander, causing him to flinch slightly, glaring from the waste chute to Chief Maru momentarily before turning on his heel and storming back out into the corridor.

As the door closed behind Attic, Captain Sinclair-Maru turned to the chief with an inquiring look. "Well, Maru?"

She looked after the departed commander with an expression inscrutable to Tenroo. "Interesting." She turned her gaze to Tenroo for a moment, then back to the captain. "I'm not sure."

Tenroo cleared his throat and they both looked at him.

"Is your neck pained, Auditor?" Chief Maru inquired, and Tenroo realized he held his head at an awkward angle, his nose somewhat in the air as he foolishly attempted to see beyond the new clutter in his UI. He forced his chin down to a more natural poise.

"Oh. Well, no, Chief. But I must say I am quite astonished by what I have just witnessed here."

Chief Maru's mouth shaped a half smile. "Indeed?"

Tenroo nodded. "Oh yes. Your Fleet traditions are most peculiar. This whole piratical element to the adoption of a new captain: that's entirely unexpected. I had no idea. Does this tradition date back to before the Yung Dynasty?"

The captain's expression became strangely blank as Tenroo looked between them, but Chief Maru's half smile increased. "I don't believe so, Auditor," she said. "You might say we are innovators."

Before Tenroo could wrap his mind around the idea of the Sinclair-Maru as innovators, the captain seemed to have his own dawning awareness looking at Tenroo with a sudden widening of his eyes. "Auditor," the captain said. "Your official duty on *Hightower* has little to do with officers or crew at all, does it?"

Tenroo chuckled. "Oh, goodness no, Captain, unless one contemplates the impact of synthetic Intelligences upon Fleet officers."

"You are auditing under the Thinking Machine Protocols?" Chief Maru asked, her smile fading somewhat.

"Yes, of course," Tenroo nodded, looking past the clutter in his vision to both his interlocutors. "Didn't anyone tell you? I thought you knew."

Chapter 15

"On the one hand, Professor Oliver denigrates the Honor Code for its barbarism, and in the same breath argues that the Code is not achieving its promised goal of providing lethal duels. Only someone of such great academic elevation can shamelessly hold both positions simultaneously."

—Dr. Ramsay Stirling Attenborough, *Ivory Tower Follies*

"THE MARINES ABOARD THIS VESSEL SEEM TO HAVE ADOPTED A unique variation on the usual Marine uniform...or am I mistaken?"

Saef heard the question posed by Auditor Tenroo as they walked toward *Hightower*'s bridge, but as Inga paced Tenroo a few steps behind Saef, he felt comfortable leaving all the answers to her while he structured his command UI for *Hightower*. The glowing framework projecting into his optic nerve began to build his sense of solidity, moment by moment.

"They are members of the Emperor's First, Auditor," Inga explained. "It is recently reformed, and adopted the old uniform... Seems their CO must be quite the traditionalist."

Saef thought Inga's last comment might be as much a reminder for his own benefit as it was for Tenroo. The pantheon of personalities awaiting Saef did nothing to ease his misgivings, and the Marine officers might present the greatest challenge.

"I see, Chief Maru," Tenroo said. "And that decoration the

Marines all wear on this...er...antique uniform? It appears to be a fraction or ratio." Tenroo chuckled softly. "A mathematical badge seems rather out of place on the shoulder of a warrior."

Saef heard the half smile in Inga's voice as she answered. "You behold the proud, original emblem of the Emperor's First, the *legendary* Ten and Twenty. It *is* a sort of ratio too."

"I take it we see some icon of historical significance then, Chief Maru? It seems quite a fascinating topic."

"Yes, Auditor. You see, of the original Marine trainee cohort, way back against the Slaggers, they say only twenty percent graduated from the selection process to wear the uniform."

"Oh my. Seems a trifle wasteful." The auditor looked over at Inga, his brow wrinkled with thought. "So twenty percent graduated to become the very first Imperial Marines...so the ten figured upon the badge represents what? Another percentage, I take it?"

Saef heard the question as he observed the bridge hatch yawning open not far ahead, Inga answering as they paced the final distance. "Yes, Auditor. The *ten* represents the percentage of candidates who died during selection. The Ten and Twenty were the...foundation of the whole Marine mystique, I suppose."

"My, my," Tenroo murmured, sounding somewhat subdued. "A somber tradition to uphold...success or death."

Saef's attention pivoted to lock upon the living moment as they stepped into the dim expanse of an oddly bifurcated bridge space, the larger section populated by an absurd crowd of people, their eyes fixed expectantly upon Saef. He read disdain and hostility in some faces, mere curiosity in others.

It seemed the undermining move of Nifesh, or whomever in the Admiralty had meant to trim Saef's wings, had been avoided. The moment of confrontation with Commander Attic, and Attic's subsequent actions, appeared to have bypassed the "provisional" aspects of Saef's authority. By Attic's acceptance of Saef's full authority, Saef became more than an impotent showpiece to hang any future mission failure upon. Saef could now succeed—or fail—by his own effort and authority, and receive the fruits of that outcome.

All fear is fear of the unknown...

Saef's pulse subsided, his burgeoning tension flatlining. He breathed in the dark calm of the Deep Man even as he spotted a familiar face among the waiting group. He momentarily locked eyes with Tilly Pennysmith, reading nothing in her expression, not even recognition.

How did we not know about her presence on Hightower? *What does it mean?*

Commander Attic stepped forward to meet Saef, and Saef observed Inga slide unobtrusively to the dim periphery, Tenroo at her side. She undoubtedly sought a clear angle of observation—or angle of fire, as unlikely as that seemed in this setting.

"Captain," Attic greeted coolly, "I've assembled the key members of two watches and apprised them of the unfortunate misunderstanding regarding your orders."

Attic rotated to stand beside Saef, facing the assembly with his hands linked behind his back. Saef felt exceedingly conscious of a sudden, unexpected uncertainty gnawing upon his fear-proof refuge. He was evidently expected to perform some rousing speech, establish his competence, and pull this cold company into his camp of admiring followers. As this moment of silence just began to stretch out uncomfortably, Inga's line-of-sight message pinged into Saef's UI:

THREE POINTS. SIMPLE AND DIRECT.

Saef opened his mouth, speaking even before Inga's message fully registered. "Time is pressing," he said in a voice that seemed steady and well-pitched to his own ears, "so I will keep this brief. *Hightower* is ordered into immediate action. We must transition and be on station as soon as humanly possible..." Saef quickly racked his mind to synthesize this final, vital point, distilling and allaying the crew's chief concern, but what was their chief concern, their cause for such evident hostility? It came together in a flash, and he began speaking:

"I understand *Hightower*'s people have mostly served together for some time, so I will be conferring with Commander Attic to keep watches and duty stations unaltered as much as I am able."

Saef passed his gaze over the assembled company, and the diminished hostility in most expressions seemed more than merely his imagination. Inga's line-of-sight, PERFECT, certainly helped assure him.

Attic stood at Saef's elbow. "May I introduce you to *Hightower*'s officers, Captain?" Attic inquired, his voice studiously neutral.

Saef shook his head. "I'm afraid time really is pressing. We need *Hightower* at a transition point now, and formalities must wait."

Attic's lips turned down and he shot a quick sidelong glance at the nearest officer before saying, "I see." He hesitated before adding, "If you wish, Captain, I will take the bridge and get us outbound...Lieutenant Wycherly can make introductions and show you our—*Hightower*'s qualities."

Saef drew a slow breath, casting a measuring look at Lieutenant Wycherly, remembering a few odd nuggets of Wycherly's CV. In all truth, Saef desired nothing more than to immerse himself in the technical demands of captaining *Hightower*, but he needed the goodwill of this insular crew perhaps more than anything else.

"If Lieutenant Wycherly can spare the time," Saef said. The lieutenant stepped up and bobbed his head, his expression reserved but friendly. He looked every bit the Coreworld Vested Citizen: slender, slightly taller than Saef, his sandy hair coifed to accent his roguish good looks.

"Be happy to, Captain," Wycherly declared with a guarded smile.

Saef turned back to Attic. "You have the bridge, Commander."

Attic nodded, his expression the least forbidding Saef had yet observed. "I have the bridge," he affirmed, walking some distance into the center of the bridge, and Saef turned away to address Wycherly.

"Lead on, Lieutenant." Saef's memory found a gleaming aid among the scant decorations dotting Wycherly's uniform as the lieutenant took a few steps to the waiting assembly of officers and noncoms. "You served in fighters, Wycherly, didn't you?"

Wycherly half turned and executed a shallow bow, a rueful smile on his lips. "Don't remind me, sir. My only real passion in life is now behind me, mere duty ahead." He uttered a short laugh and began the introductions, as Saef felt the rumble of *Hightower*'s engines beginning their push outbound to their transition point.

It quickly became clear that *Hightower*'s peculiarities of operation ran deep. As Saef looked down the line of waiting crew, it seemed evident that many of *Hightower*'s officers were not present, including the notable absence of any Marines. While only a handful of actual officers awaited, Saef learned that part of the explanation existed in *Hightower*'s particular bridge operations plan.

"Deckchief Furst, Captain," Wycherly said, indicating a loose-limbed figure measuring Saef with a laconic expression.

"Deckchief," Saef greeted with a nod.

"Captain," Furst replied, this one word revealing a hint of accent. *Clearly not a Coreworld urbanite.*

"The deckchief also fills an Ops position on the bridge," Wycherly explained, "and the chief of the watch does the same."

"Oh?" Saef said, looking from Wycherly to Deckchief Furst. "How very... unique." Saef could not be sure if the amused glint in Furst's eye was a good sign, or not.

"It answers for us," Furst said, his accent now more pronounced, his vowels clipped and curt.

"I'm sure it must," Saef said mildly. As the ranking Fleet noncom aboard, Saef knew the vital asset—or severe challenge—a deckchief represented, and he would do much to keep Furst's good will.

Wycherly led on, and Saef met Nav officers, Comm specialists and two Weapons officers: Lieutenants Brogan-Moore and Pennysmith. As Saef exchanged words with Brogan-Moore, he remained keenly aware of Pennysmith's presence there at Brogan-Moore's side, her distinguishing holo lenses gleaming. She had served with distinction under Saef as one of *Tanager*'s Weapons officers, been wounded in action and richly rewarded with *Tanager*'s abundant prize money. Saef had figured Pennysmith might take her new fortune and disappear back into the embrace of her peculiar coreligionists on Battersea, but there she stood, in what seemed the least likely vessel in Fleet.

Saef said the appropriate words to Lieutenant Brogan-Moore, then stepped before Lieutenant Tilly Pennysmith. "I believe you are acquainted with Lieutenant Pennysmith, sir," Wycherly said.

"Yes," Saef replied as he wondered at Pennysmith's rather wooden expression. Despite some... difficult history between Saef and the Pennysmith clan, Saef held a certain affection for her, and he felt it had been reciprocated, but now no sign of the connection appeared on her face. "A pleasure to see you, Pennysmith," Saef said in a reserved tone set to match her expression.

"Likewise, Captain," she replied in an utterly colorless voice, and Saef felt that their interaction was closely watched from several quarters.

The pause stretched until Saef offered, "I take it you joined *Hightower* recently, then?"

"Yes, Captain."

Wycherly stepped gracefully into the stilted silence. "She fills Bertram's shoes. He served as our—um—previous captain's second in that unfortunate duel, and remains behind as more of a nurse, you might say."

Saef looked from Wycherly back to Pennysmith. She gave him nothing, and he could scarcely connect her closed mien to the quietly ebullient woman he had seen just weeks before in the White Swan Hotel, in attendance at Claude's ridiculous celebration.

"Excellent," Saef said, allowing Wycherly to lead on, feeling Pennysmith's reserved gaze follow him. As Saef scanned the bifurcated bridge space, Inga's half smile caught his eye. She stood out of the way, Tenroo at her side, evidently still plying her with questions. Saef only had a moment to puzzle over her enigmatic expression before Wycherly made the introduction to *Hightower*'s master-at-arms chief, Kang.

The master-at-arms seemed a somewhat redundant post for a vessel crammed with Marines, but as this thought occurred to Saef, Wycherly played mind reader: "Some might think the chief and his lot a trifle unnecessary on a troop carrier," Wycherly said.

"Not at all—" Saef began to murmur, as Wycherly pressed on.

"But it's standard for all the carriers now. Fleet edict, you know."

Saef nodded soberly at this as he exchanged measuring looks with Kang. The master-at-arms chief owed his tall, slender build to some lightworld history, likely, but his taciturn expression seemed a common feature for *Hightower*'s people.

"Pleasure to serve under you, Captain," Kang intoned in a surprisingly deep voice, each syllable precisely enunciated.

Although the almost mournful look upon Kang's face seemed to reveal anything but pleasure, Saef accepted the civility with some relief. "Likewise, Chief," Saef said, preparing to move on, but Kang held up a slender, oddly graceful hand and Saef paused.

"Indeed I am most sorry to press at this moment, Captain," Kang said, "but if you could clarify one important—hum—preference, it would be most helpful to my people."

Wycherly's hand raised slightly, as if he was gesturing to Kang, then thought better of it, but Saef felt himself fixated upon Kang's obvious intensity, putting Wycherly's conduct to the side for the moment. "If it cannot wait, Chief, then speak."

"Thank you," Kang intoned, his long hands folding together. "If you can but say this: Do you desire my people to cover security forward of Marine country? Or do the Marines?"

Wycherly made a faint sound at Saef's side, but the master-at-arms chief held Saef's gaze, waiting for his reply. "I—" Saef began, then closed his mouth, thinking quickly. "What is the common practice aboard *Hightower*, Chief? Marines? Or your people forward of the waist?"

Kang's eyebrows lifted slightly, his teeth showing. "My people."

"Then by all means, carry on as you have, Chief."

Chief Kang's smile broadened. "Excellent, Captain. Thank you."

Kang's gratitude seemed too profound, and Wycherly's too pronounced for Saef's comfort, and as Wycherly led him to the next member, Saef wondered what trouble he may have just unleashed.

"Captain," Wycherly said quickly as they moved on, "you see before you the most fortunate person aboard *Hightower*." He indicated the compact, athletic figure clad in a tight flight suit, an impish smile dimpling her cheeks. "Fighter Wing Leader Jamila."

Commander Yazmin Jamila bowed, looking up to Saef with unfeigned good humor. "Most fortunate?" Saef inquired, returning the bow with an inclination of his head.

"Of course," Wycherly said with a sniff. "Fighter pilot *and* squadron leader. She has reached the apex of human achievement."

Jamila shook her close-cropped head of dark hair. "Leader of the smallest squadron in Fleet, Wycherly." She turned her dark eyes on Saef. "Our full strength is just eight fighters, Captain."

Saef nodded, noting Jamila sported a heavyworld build, but her earlobes and face bore no marks of heavyworld pressures; perhaps a childhood transplant to a gentler world. "Yes, Commander. I read the summary. As I recall, all eight are those new Mangustas, correct?"

Jamila jerked a proud nod. "That's right, Captain. The Mangusta's got the longest legs and the heaviest punch of any interface fighter in Fleet."

"Daresay, Commander," Saef said. "In my Guard days I saw quite a lot of the Tigersharks, and some of those Daggerjets. I look forward to learning more about your Mangustas and your people."

Commander Jamila's eyes glittered. "Tigersharks? Despite what *some* say, we exceed those Interceptor-class birds in every meaningful way."

Saef took this in, surprised at Jamila's defensive tone. "I don't doubt it, Commander." Saef nodded and moved on.

Wycherly led Saef onward, leaning close to hear Saef's murmured question. "Do her Mangustas *really* outclass the Tigersharks?"

Wycherly's face took on a diplomatic veneer. "Like she said, they have long legs and carry more firepower..."

"But?" Saef pushed.

Wycherly shrugged. "They're big pigs, Captain...turn like—like heavily armed bricks."

"I see," Saef said.

Wycherley looked searchingly into Saef's eyes, stopping their progress. "Do you really, Captain? Can you perceive the corrupting touch of filthy lucre here?"

"I...perhaps I don't," Saef said, curious at Wycherly's wry disgust. The remaining bridge crew waited a short distance away as Wycherly shrugged and began to speak.

"Let us picture the scene, Captain: Fleet demands a new, updated interface fighter design—light, fast, maneuverable. But House Fancypants gets a finger into the requisition specs, and behold! The fighter design has swelled to accommodate the avionics system from Fancypants Industries. Then we have the bloated weapons package from Family Palmgreaser, and on, and on. Does this new fighter design evolve for tactical superiority? Oh, no, no! It must grow and grow to encapsulate all the Family connections and bloody payoffs." Wycherly said the last word with a bitter twist to his lips.

Saef steadily regarded Wycherly, curious at the apparent passion. "With all that, it's a wonder any Fleet vessels hold together, isn't it, Lieutenant?"

Wycherly's countenance smoothed, seemingly with an effort, but a certain distance remaining in his expression. "Oh no, Captain, no concern with the greater Fleet. It's just fighters." He shrugged and a cold smile flickered. "Admirals and the Great Houses don't trust their reputations to mere interface craft... Nobody gives a damn about fighters. They're nothing but a Great House hustle for the latest Shaper tech."

Saef nodded, wondering at the lieutenant's words. The Wycherly clan lay close to the Emperor's circle, their palatial properties scattered about Imperial City, personifying a "Great House" themselves. Where did Wycherly's loyalties lie, if not to his House? Saef replied neutrally, "I hope Commander Jamila's confidence in the Mangusta is more accurate than your pessimism. Our mission may rely upon 'mere' interface craft."

Lieutenant Wycherly's expression lightened and he chuckled self-consciously, but it seemed forced. "Well, let's hope we're never as desperate as all that. You must forgive my rants, Captain. While my body walks these decks my—er—heart remains out there, stubbornly wed to the fighters."

Saef mirrored Wycherly's trifling note. "A sore trial, Lieutenant. You are to be commended for bearing up under the torment."

Wycherly grinned at Saef and went on to complete the last few introductions among the gathering about the bridge, whatever demons Wycherly battled seemingly laid to rest.

With the immediate requirements met, Saef longed to move forward beyond the covey of standing crew and take personal command of his ship. He even glanced into the dim bridge space, seeing Attic there with the minimum of bridge crew, leading *Hightower* slowly out-system toward their nearest approved transition point.

Saef indicated the darkened, partitioned section off the bridge. "And this area, Lieutenant? The wireframe is not clear on its purpose."

Wycherley followed Saef's direction. "Ah, the Surface Ops Center. When we have assets in the well, or barrage targets in the well, action is coordinated here adjoining the bridge."

"I see," Saef said, picturing *Hightower*'s distinctive, immense barrage cannon as a thought dawned. "I presume Weps controls the battery for ship-to-ship targets?"

Wycherly appeared startled. "Ship-to . . . With the barrage battery, sir?"

"Yes, of course, Lieutenant. If size is any indicator, the battery must be enormously powerful."

"But, sir, *Hightower*'s no dreadnaught—"

"It sounds as if you are teaching me my trade, Lieutenant," Saef said, his cold tone communicating the surge of irritation Wycherly's incredulity sparked in him.

Wycherly flushed. "I do beg your pardon, Captain. I only mean that the whole system's built to address targets in the well. We've no targeting system for ship-to-ship action."

Saef felt his irritation increase, noting the listening ears of officers standing nearby while it seemed Wycherly played him for a fool. "You are suggesting we could not set about one of the asteroid settlements, then, since there's little to decide between, say, Ras Al Timrah and an enemy cruiser? The Emperor's enemies should be overjoyed to know they have only to set foot there to avoid destruction."

Wycherly's flush deepened, but the clenched fist suggested to Saef that anger rose up rather than chagrin. "Perhaps I should have suggested from the start that you should speak to our gunnery officer. My own knowledge is incomplete at best."

Gunnery officer? Saef fleetingly pictured such an officer, never employed in his duties since attacks on hard surface targets had thus far only been accomplished via missiles, infantry insertions, or dropping rocks from orbit. But Saef was jerked back into the moment by a faint murmur of voices behind him.

"Frigate captain!" one voice quietly hissed, and Saef perceived Inga's narrowed gaze fix a point over his shoulder.

Saef collected himself with an effort.

"Yes, Lieutenant. A conversation with the *gunnery officer* seems advisable."

Wycherly bowed his head stiffly as faint murmurs yet circulated. "Sir, until he is available, would you care to review the Marines?"

Saef's former desire to assume physical command had faded, and he wondered if he yielded too much authority by going to Marine country rather than summoning their officer to the bridge.

Saef ignored Inga's look as he said, "Lead on, Wycherly."

He had created a sufficient mess already and he preferred to meet his Marines without the critical audience of his own people in mocking attendance.

How much worse could it be?

Chapter 16

"It appears the Great Families' chief means for achieving continuity through the centuries is the art of creating new generations optimized and trained for full citizenship within the Imperium. In practice, this art has little to do with dueling skills, but rather in persuading their young that emotions and impulses must be subservient to the will."

—Everest Compline, *Reflections*

AFTER ALEXANDRA BLISS INTERCEPTED THE UNLISTED FEMALE interloper in the Medical Specialties Center, Hugh went to his great-aunt, Anthea Sinclair-Maru, and made the case for a *real* security detail. Everything about Alex's report convinced Hugh that a real attempt had been made on the life of the woman they currently called Bonita Sinclair-Maru, only prevented by Alex's ready response.

The vidcapture image of Jantzen matched no known record, and the Medical Specialties Center confirmed that she was no member of their staff. That left few possibilities beyond an attempted hit.

As head of Family security, Anthea Sinclair-Maru could not but acknowledge the substance of Hugh's argument. She leaned back, steepling her fingers as she contemplated Hugh across her desk. Hugh knew and respected Anthea's history as well as any in the Family, and though her athletic build and black hair showed no signs of her centuries, he never forgot she was a survivor of that brutal, earlier age.

She spoke at last. "I believe you are correct, Hugh. It was likely a play for Bess." She ignored the convention of a code name here in their secure fastness.

Hugh released a relieved breath, unaware that he had been holding it. "So, you'll order a real detail for her?"

Anthea leaned forward, looking down, resting her slender fingers over her sword sheathed atop the desk. "No."

Hugh opened his mouth to argue, closed his mouth, then said, "They'll try again."

Anthea nodded, looking up. "Probably."

Hugh stifled each angry retort that rose up, finally managing. "They...our enemies believe Bonita—Bess is worth killing. Why doesn't the Family think she's worth saving?"

Anthea's face wore a musing expression as she stood, lifting her sword from the desk and fixing it to her left hip with a faint click. Hugh's angry gaze dropped to observe Anthea's practiced motions, seeing the near ritual as her left hand set the forward cant on the hilt, her right hand sliding to the old, silver-worn long-slide pistol in its holster, her index finger straight. Her right hand continued its rote movement, freeing the pistol partway, palpating the load indicator and re-holstering. His eyes lifted to Anthea's.

"Tell me, Hugh," she said after a moment, "Family loyalty aside, *is* Bess worth saving?" Hugh felt bereft of speech at the blunt calculation of her words. Anthea went on. "Can you honestly say she's made any sign of recovery at all?"

Hugh clenched his fists at his sides. "The medicos say—"

"They say," Anthea interrupted, "whatever keeps the credits flowing. But what do *you* say?"

Hugh shook his head, flinging a hand up. "I'm not sure. Sometimes I think she's in there. I see her listening, watching, and it seems..."

Anthea frowned. "No."

"Then let me move her!" Hugh demanded, standing.

Anthea smiled at Hugh, her hands still resting lightly on her weapons. "And thus guarantee that Bess has no chance of recovery? We have an immense sunk cost here, thanks to Saef, or Cabot would have ordered her moved already."

"They're going to kill her," Hugh said in an even voice, without expression. "How's that for sinking the cost?"

Anthea nodded slowly, exhaling. "There is that." She mused a moment. "My resources are limited—very limited right now—but I will do this one thing on my own authority." She pursed her lips as her gaze measured Hugh. "The security detail for our Trade enclave is only a couple klicks out from the Medical Specialties Center. I will restructure their priorities. You can have them as a Quick Reaction Force if your people are hit."

Hugh didn't like it, but he knew it was as much as he would get. He bowed. "Thank you, my lady."

Anthea shook her head. "Don't thank me, Nephew. After that first try, our enemy now has your measure, and they'll not muck about on a second try. Whoever's pulling site security when they hit it is likely dead." She paused, pursing her lips. "With luck, the QRF will catch the bastards on the way out...but that won't do your operative much good." She hesitated again. "I...I hope that operative is not you...always been fond of you."

Each moment of your vigil is the first moment...
Alexandra Bliss silently recited the litany as she assumed her post once again, alone once more with this diminished, youthful version of Bess Sinclair-Maru. Since her earlier encounter with the unknown interloper, Hugh and the other members of their erstwhile security detail took what precautions they could. They all felt a second attempt would materialize, and soon.

Floating within her implanted UI, Alex kept a small window open. It fed a steady vidstream from the tiny sensor pack secreted just within the entrance to the Medical Specialties Center. If her eventual attackers were sufficiently unimaginative, they might begin their assault there, through the entrance, and the moments of advance notice might just give Alex a chance to preserve Bonita. Perhaps—just perhaps—Alex herself might also survive...one could hope, so long as it did not interfere with duty. She knew her actions here might very well prove to be the defining image of the Bliss Family's long oath-kin connection to the Sinclair-Maru...for good or ill.

In Alexandra's mind, structured around a lifetime bastion of tradition and honor, her own life or death was of little significance. But she could not—must not!—fail in her duty.

Then, there was Bess, of course—the person, Bess.

In the few shifts Alex had served, it seemed—at least at

moments—that intelligence lurked within Bess's eyes, and she certainly had made great strides in physical conditioning, her coordination and balance finally returning.

Alex flanked Bess and a med-tech as they made their way from the conditioning chamber, back to the small, new room where Bess now spent her days and nights. Alex carried the satchel with her additional equipment over a shoulder, her hands free and ready, the litany of sentinels running on an unconscious loop in the background of her mind. *Each moment of your vigil...*

At first she barely noticed the subtle change in the vidstream imagery from the entrance cam. She had expected that any foe who entered there would appear as an overt, dynamic force. Instead, she observed the reception attendant, barely visible at the edge of the small window in her UI as he slowly slumped over. The jolt of shock surged within Alexandra's chest for a scant moment before her conscious application to the Deep Man smothered it.

Her next three actions unfolded in continuous motion. She launched a short, preset message from her UI: UNDER ATTACK; her right hand snatched the pistol from her holster; her left hand seized Bess by the shoulder.

The med-tech whirled on his heel, staring at Alex's sharp step, his mouth open soundlessly. Alex flicked her pistol. "Run," she ordered in a flat voice. He stumbled back a few steps, turned and fled, his retreating footfalls receding down the hall. Bess stared after him, her eyes blinking rapidly, a hand at her mouth. Alex muscled Bess down the adjoining hall, moving as quickly as possible.

"G-gah, boo," Bess said in a whispery voice, waving a flapping hand over her shoulder.

"Our enemies are here, my lady," Alex said tersely as she kicked a door open and pushed Bess through ahead of her. In the next millisecond Alexandra Bliss learned precisely how it felt to be caught in the fringe of a powerful blast. The sensation of abrupt motion and disparate impacts struck first, then the shock to ears and sinuses, and finally the wave of pain from a dozen places at once, as the world of light hesitated, slowly returning, the echo of the blast still reverberating.

Alex tried to move, tried to breathe, blood flowing from her nostrils as she choked, staring up at the wavering ceiling. She held only the awareness that she had failed, and death came for her with the cruel knowledge of that failure. The light of her vision shrank, darker, darker...

Then she coughed, her breath staggering back into ragged lungs, her hands numbly animating, groping blindly for her pistol. She rolled to her side, willing herself to rise before the enemy appeared to finish the job, but her limbs pawed weakly at the rubble-strewn ground. Her gaze discovered a dusty leg before her stretched upon the floor and traveled up to see Bess staring down at her, blood dripping from Bess's nostrils. Bess had Alexandra's satchel open beside her sprawled legs, a grenade in one hand, shaking it like a toy. "Boo, boo, gah," she said, and Alex heard the nonsense words over the ringing in her ears, a faint stomp of fast-approaching footsteps clattering in the blasted hall behind her.

Alex groaned and struggled to her knees, her mind screaming urgency that her body could not obey. Somehow, in the midst of this, as she clawed toward Bess, she saw and comprehended the message arriving from the QRF in her UI: SIXTY SECONDS OUT, even as her horrified gaze locked upon Bess thumbing the grenade's activator.

"Boo!" Bess declared, negligently waving the grenade in the air for a moment before flipping it through the shattered doorway and seizing Alexandra's wrist. She tugged Alex away from the door as startled shouts sounded in the hallway. The flat crump of the grenade cut the voices off and knocked Alex and Bess prone again. This time Alex staggered up under her own power, seeing Bess sprawled beside the open satchel, a concerned look on her blood-smeared face. Alexandra fumbled, snatching her submachine gun from the satchel and charging it from pure muscle memory, then hoisting Bess up by her hand.

She released Bess and staggered back to the twice-exploded hallway, hazarding a quick glimpse. She jerked back as snapping rounds chewed fresh holes through the wall and doorframe beside her.

Alex jerked the sub-gun's collapsible stock into place. "Come on, my lady," she gasped, pulling Bess along behind her as they moved away from the crumbling doorway. She felt blood trickling from her hip, neck, and shoulder, but she need only hold out for a short time—the QRF team would arrive in just a few moments.

A sound behind them caused Alex to jerk Bess aside, firing

a burst at knee height along the beleaguered wall, the sub-gun hammering her shoulder as it chattered. She couldn't fire indiscriminately for fear of hitting staff and patients undoubtedly cowering throughout the Medical Specialties Center, but a crash and muffled cry rewarded her effort, and Alex hurried on, tugging Bess through the next door ahead of any return fire.

As Alexandra urged Bess through an empty examination room, that respite ended and she received proof that their enemy cared nothing about bystanders or negligent gunfire. Dust blasted from the walls, hot rounds whipping past them, smashing sensitive equipment, driving Alex to seek cover behind a stout appliance. She secured Bess and began moving, her cheek pressing the short, tubular stock of her weapon as she oriented on her threats. She had moments to live, and caution died first.

Alex triggered controlled bursts, her weapon chattering, thumping her shoulder and cheek with each burst as she continually sidestepped, her sights bisecting dim charging figures, or answering blind fire through perforated walls.

Where was that gods-damned QRF?

Alex felt a sharp blow above her hip, numbly noting it half-spun her body a moment before the fire of pain screamed through her nerves. She adjusted her aim, returning fire as she drew a shuddering breath against the agony. Even as the magazine in her sub-gun ran dry, Alexandra Bliss realized she felt no fear, the Deep Man securing her as she staggered forward, drawing her sword as the sub-gun dropped.

Her speed was gone, blasted and shot away, and before she managed three stumbling steps, Alex's enemy found their target, a burst of heavy rounds stitching across her chest.

As Alex dropped hard, she momentarily thought her light ballistic vest had stopped the rounds, but the warm flow flooding out her wounds joined the wet void in her lungs, bearing the truth. She opened hooded eyes, struggling to breathe as her lungs drowned, one outflung hand holding fast to her sword, waiting for that last desperate strike at her foes.

A heavy boot seemed to materialize from nowhere, crushing her right wrist to the floor, her bones grating under the pressure. Alex looked up at the carbine barrel aimed into her eyes, the masked face above it. Alex heard the deep, muffled voice saying, "Where is she?" as she willed herself to employ one of the many techniques drilled into her through hard years of training. Instead blood poured from her mouth as she struggled to breathe, awaiting the final shot.

The blast of a shot from close beside sent the figure above her crashing down, rigid in his tracks. A second shot barked, and Alex turned her gaze slowly to one side, seeing a blood-smeared Bess lean into view, Alex's own pistol dangling from one pale, thin hand.

"Bah?" Bess said, settling to her knees beside Alexandra, her troubled gaze traveling over Alex's torn body. "Bah, bah," Bess said in a low voice, the pistol dropping beside her with a soft thump as she wiped softly at the blood on Alex's face.

Alex tried to speak, but only gurgled as the room became dark and oddly cold. The dimness grew, her vision shrinking as Alex seemed to hear herself finally speak, managing to say, "I'm not afraid."

As the light and breath faded from her, Alexandra Bliss felt sure she heard Bess reply, "I know you are not, child."

There among the shattered and blasted examination room, the Sinclair-Maru Quick Reaction Force found Bess, kneeling beside one of their own, two fallen enemies sprawled on either side. As the security operators rushed through, mopping up the last of the marauders, they glanced briefly at Bess. They all knew the rumors about her, but when she looked up at them, she did not seem absent or confused; her eyes burned with anger.

Fury seemed an excellent barometer of consciousness.

Chapter 17

"Though now a lesser House upon a lesser world, the Sinclair-Maru are over-endowed in the article of mystery...."

—Everest Compline, *Reflections*

CONSUL WINTER YUNG ARRIVED AT THE MEDICAL SPECIALTIES Center with an entourage composed of two Imperial Security agents and four heavily armed Imperial Marines. In the course of her recent investigations, Winter's usual ennui had increasingly been replaced by a profound sense of caution. Although the specialized electronics package implanted in Winter's skull had... *modified* Winter's sanity some decades earlier, her sense of self-preservation remained fully intact, and altogether too much blood flowed now for any comfort. The fact that the current chain of violence seemed to begin with the assassination of the prior emperor, a member of Winter's extended Family, was not lost upon her either.

Though the gunfight within the Medical Specialties Center had only ended some minutes earlier, the facility already crawled with activity: metro gendarmerie, Imperial Security, the random bodyguards of powerful clientele caught in the bloody cross fire... and, of course, numerous grim Sinclair-Maru operatives.

The structure itself remained a locus of wealth, initially seeming untouched by violence, until Winter nulled the augmenting UI overlay. Then she perceived the extent of the damage. Bullet holes stitched through walls and windows, a chunk of roof section bloomed like a black-edged flower where a sizeable breaching charge had done its work, there in a valley between dormer peaks.

"Consul." One of the busy Imperial Security investigators stepped up to Winter's coterie, executing a shallow bow. "I am Investigative Agent Purcell. How may I assist you?"

Clearly Purcell did not know of Winter's quiet role in the Imperial Security apparatus. His casual deference arose from her *official* post as consul, or possibly her membership in the sprawling Imperial Yung Family. She had no time or patience for Purcell, ignoring him entirely, leaving her underlings to stifle his attempts at a respectful objection as she breezed past him.

She understood the daunting task before Purcell and the gendarmes as they accounted for every single round fired, assigning responsibility to whichever citizen pulled a trigger. Under normal circumstances all damages would be exacted for every injured party in credits, blood or servitude, but times had become far from normal. Winter simply did not care about any of that now.

The signs of violence lingered, fresh and raw, the scent of volatile explosive compounds strong in Winter's nostrils as she entered the building, ringed with her Marines. Winter's tall boots gritted against more evidence as she strode past the mostly intact entrance lounge, moving forward toward the heart of activity. A hall yawned on Winter's right, the wall to her left pocked with fresh impacts. She rounded the corner and stopped abruptly, looking up at the gaping void blasted through the ceiling.

A clutch of gendarmes and Sinclair-Maru heavies stood on the far side of the rubble heap, a few contorted bodies scattered about them. Winter's analytics package pinged a dozen alerts in her UI, ranging from an inventory of weapons dangling from the armored figures of the Sinclair-Maru, to the bullet scars on multiple surfaces including the chest armor plate of one Sinclair-Maru operative. One face among the waiting company also highlighted an alert: Anthea Sinclair-Maru, one of the old generation, a recipient of full rejuv.

Winter moved past the rubble and stepped near to Anthea. "Consul," Anthea greeted with an inclination of her head.

Winter ignored the greeting. "It is said you head Family security," she said. "Answer two questions for me: Where is Bess? And where are any surviving attackers? Any survivors are mine."

Anthea hesitated a moment before beckoning Winter to follow as she made her way a short distance farther down the bullet-riddled hall. Winter made a peremptory gesture to her Marines and they faded back as she followed Anthea, her mouth suddenly dry. They crossed another blast mark disfiguring the solid floor, two leaking, armored bodies sprawled near a side doorway.

As they moved through the blasted, bullet-chewed entry, Winter's analytics noted the smears of blood and a bloody hand print upon the floor, but they continued on.

Their destination was the first large room in their route, flanked by two more sprawled, armored bodies, crumpled in pools of their own blood. Winter looked into the dim room, perceiving all the signs of a short, brutal gun battle, with riddled equipment and interior walls, and the projecting legs of a slender body. *Bess?*

For a moment Winter's own body betrayed her, the leap of her pulse surging up for a second until she saw the dead white face, the half-lidded eyes belonging to a stranger. Winter swallowed acid, hating herself for her irrational affection. *Who is Bess to me, anyway?*

"One of yours?" Winter managed to inquire in an even voice, looking down at the young woman's outstretched arm, a distinctive Sinclair-Maru sword in her gripping hand. *Where was Bess?*

Anthea nodded, staring down. "Oath-kin. Very young but promising. She did well." Anthea indicated another armored body dropped behind an adjoining piece of equipment.

"So it appears," Winter said, impatient, the strong scent of blood forcibly reminding her of a recent subject of her most thorough interrogation, smirking as his body was destroyed. "So where is Bess?"

Anthea looked quickly at Winter, then looked away, Winter's analytics striving to penetrate the inscrutable Sinclair-Maru impassivity as Anthea said, "I am not certain."

The fever beat of Winter's pulse began anew. "They took her?"

Anthea frowned. "This is not clear. She was right here, where we now stand when my people broke through. They were forced to engage a pair of flankers beyond that door"—Anthea nodded her head toward yet another bullet-scarred entrance—"and we cannot discover her presence now."

Winter's alarm transformed into anger. "You've *lost* her? So much for the alleged Sinclair-Maru competence!" Winter did not require the assistance of her advanced analytics to discern the chagrin on Anthea Sinclair-Maru's face.

Winter stepped to the fallen attacker, shoving one dead leg aside. "And how many of these bastards escaped?"

"None," Anthea said.

"And you could not manage to keep a single one alive either?"

Anthea shook her head. "My people disabled the last two attackers—at considerable risk too, but—"

"Where are they?" Winter demanded. "I will speak to them—now."

"No, Consul. One of the wounded attackers retained his blade. He killed his wounded comrade, then himself."

"*What?*" Winter demanded.

"It is as I say," Anthea said. "My people heard their exchange, yonder. The one begging for his life as the blade bit. Their bodies still lie just there, if you wish to examine them."

Winter scowled, tossing her platinum queue. She looked down again to the still figure of the young woman who died defending Bess. "No. I've seen enough bodies." She turned on her heel and moved away. "None of this makes the least sense. I am displeased."

With her coterie collected, Winter left the doors of the Medical Specialties Center as one of her agents murmured fresh details in her ear. "Stunned the reception attendant with some kind of micro, it appears, then blew the ceiling with a monster breaching charge. Should have finished it there, but miscalculated their timing just a little."

"Or that oath-kin child managed to get Bess off the X, perhaps," Winter said as they walked to her nearby convoy of waiting vehicles.

A moment later, Winter's analytic filter detected and flagged some tentative motion before her agents or Marines perceived anything. She held up a hand, staring intently at a small ventilation grate issuing from the Medical Specialties Center. It lay nearly concealed behind a decorative hedge, fashioned to blend with the tasteful exterior appointments, and then generally papered over by their glittering UI augmenting overlay. Her analytics had detected the faintest human motion from that grate, and now Winter felt her emotions rise to a level of conviction beyond anything her technology provided. Winter quickly assured no sharp-eyed Sinclair-Maru busybodies observed her, then directed two of her Marines to employ their egress tools as she stood close at hand. The grate popped free with a minimum of noise and Winter looked into the wide eyes and blood-smeared face of Bess Sinclair-Maru—the new, rejuv version of Bess, girlish and oddly vulnerable.

Unlike most others, Winter remembered a version of Bess that was not *completely* unlike the new Bess, but she had no time to reflect upon their classroom days so many decades before.

Winter extended a gentle hand and spoke in a tone of voice that shocked her subordinates. "Are you injured, Bess?"

The medical jumper Bess wore bore splashes of darkening blood, and the pallor of Bess's cheeks lent credence to Winter's concern. "Gah?" Bess said in a dry whisper, peering out, her eyes blinking owlishly in the daylight.

That cold, cruel element of Winter's psyche seemed to sneer as her predominant emotions became overwhelmed with feelings of warmth and protectiveness. "Come on, love. No one will hurt you now." Bess slowly reached out a tentative hand, and to Winter it felt like a tiny timid bird as it rested within her own.

Chapter 18

"While explorers, warfighters, and inventors strive within their respective fields of endeavor, receiving physical experiences, they will never understand that they are mere empiricists who lack the faculties to actually understand what it is that they experience. This absurd belief exists here within the halls of learning, where Professor Oliver and his lot truly elevate thought above experience, theory above practice."

—Dr. Ramsay Stirling Attenborough, *Ivory Tower Follies*

CORPORAL KYLE WHITESIDE FELT HORRIBLY EXPOSED AS THE Legionnaires began to filter down out of their wooded fastness. Sergeant Reardon and Major Chetwynd did *not* march side by side at the head of a column, but with Chetwynd and his Pathfinders leading the way in a dispersed formation instead. In the weeks of attrition, the Pathfinders had evidently learned something, Kyle thought, or perhaps their vaunted *training* really had prepared them for *this* at the very least.

The remainder of the Legionnaires followed along, with Molo Rangers divided into two elements on the left and right, and as a body they all proceeded at a cautious pace. Perhaps Reardon's scathing words had at least served to temper Major Chetwynd's jingoistic zeal.

As they moved slowly north, heading toward the ruined remains of several larger structures, Kyle scanned over the concentrated host, his Molo, Fang, scampering along quietly behind. These remaining survivors had been rapidly refined by days of combat and weeks of constant threat. Not only their clothing and equipment bore the marks of accelerated proficiency training, but the pressure seemed to create different results among various Legionnaires. Kyle noticed two distinct and separate classes the Legionnaires evolved into, and it forcibly reminded Kyle of street urchins he had once observed. Like the urchins, hardship had created a new instinctive cunning in some Legionnaires, while imbuing others with a reflexive timidity.

A faint flicker visible through Kyle's helmet-mounted tactical eyepiece illustrated this division before their small force had covered much more than a klick of their journey. All the Legionnaires had learned to notice the signature of a range-finding laser, and as a flicker shimmered in their tactical eyepieces not a word was uttered, every Legionnaire instinctively springing into the nearest cover, knowing that enemy fire might follow at any moment. Kyle and a few nearby Legionnaires dove, hitting the ground moving, immediately worming their way to observation points, their carbines ready, while Kyle noticed others huddled in deep cover, quiescent, listening and waiting.

After a span of some minutes, whispered word filtered back and the Legionnaires warily crept from cover, those of the timid set shamelessly waiting until others drew no fire before mutely emerging.

Kyle did not understand what created such a clear, binary path for the Legionnaires, but he was pleased and somewhat surprised to suddenly realize which cohort he populated. The thought cheered him for some time as the Legionnaires continued toward their objective. He knew he was not imbued with great natural courage, but somehow he had become *competent*.

The day wore on, clouds rolling in to blot the blue skies, and the Legionnaires' cautious progress brought them down to the valley floor where a wide highway ran from the west, eastward to the invisibly distant coastline. On the far, northern side of the highway the ruined outlines of tall buildings awaited them.

For the first time since they set out that morning, the entire body of Legionnaires assembled together, slowly filling a broad drainage channel shrouded with tall shrubbery along the southern edge of the highway.

Kyle Whiteside led Fang to rejoin Pippi Tyrsdottir and Sergeant

Reardon where they hunkered near Major Chetwynd and his Path-finders. The other Legionnaires either settled to rest or peeked over the lip at the maze of ruined buildings awaiting them on the far side of the empty highway. Major Chetwynd stared fixedly east-ward, down the expanse of visible highway, his eyes squinting as he frowned.

"A drone, clearly," Chetwynd said as he stared, a dismissive note to his voice. Sergeant Avery Reardon gazed at the same target through multi-scan binoculars for a moment, then silently handed them to Pippi. As she focused the lenses, Kyle stepped beside her and stared to the east. Perhaps a half klick distant he saw a flicker of movement between obstructing shrubs and defunct skimcars, low and fast, just north of the highway bound-ary, scuttling south.

"No," Pippi declared after gazing a moment. "No drone, this." She passed the binoculars back to Reardon.

Chetwynd seemed conscious of the glances his Pathfinder underlings aimed his direction, pursing his lips. "A remote, then."

Sergeant Reardon resumed scanning through the binoculars, saying, "Yes, a remote, and somebody at the other end of its transceiver, looking for us."

Kyle could just make out the rapid scamper of segmented legs now, speeding the low mech too surely for the simple logic of a drone or Molo.

"Pippi," Reardon said without looking away from the binocu-lars, and without consulting Major Chetwynd, "jam it when it goes to cross the highway."

Pippi murmured assent as she swiftly steered her Molo up into position, deploying the jammer from the Molo's armored carapace as its legs stabilized with a muffled servo whine. Chet-wynd stood uncertainly to one side, chewing his lower lip as he watched Pippi aiming the high-powered jammer on its powered gimbal-mount.

Chetwynd, his coterie of Pathfinders, and a few curious Legionnaires quietly observed as Pippi monitored her eyepiece, waiting. Reardon locked onto the binoculars, while Kyle held his breath, staring at the distant verge of the highway.

Reardon and Pippi both uttered a soft sound just before Kyle spotted the hint of motion, there in a gap blasted through an abutting wall. Pippi's Molo emitted a small click and an electronic hum, but the distant mech fully emerged onto the empty highway, crossing rapidly. The jammer unit on Pippi's Molo fluidly tracked the target mech, activating again and again at Pippi's command.

"What's wrong?" Chetwynd demanded, looking from Reardon to the scuttling mech.

Pippi shook her head, trying a final pulse as the mech sped across the final lanes and down into the deep vegetation on the south side of the highway... *their* side of the highway.

Reardon lowered the binoculars and eased down against the embankment, frowning.

Chetwynd's face grew red as he looked from Reardon to Pippi, awaiting an explanation until Kyle offered, "Jamming didn't work, Major."

"I could see that. Why not, Corporal?"

Kyle stopped himself from shrugging. "Umm, must be line-of-sight controlled. Optical or something, maybe, so... can't jam it."

Pippi and Reardon shared a look a moment before a Legionnaire called out from his watch post to the left, "Movement! One-five, right!"

As Chetwynd and the other Pathfinders scrambled up to peer over the lip of the drainage channel into the distance across the highway, Avery Reardon leaned close to Kyle. "Good answer, Kyle. Line-of-sight. Stick to that answer, you hear me?"

Kyle opened his mouth to inquire what Reardon meant, but the buzz-snap of incoming fire ended all conversation as Legionnaires dropped prone below the lip of the drainage channel, or shouldered carbines to return fire. Twigs and limbs of the overhead shrubbery showered down upon them as enemy fire whipped overhead, trimming them off, and Kyle only chanced to see Reardon slipping away, down the line of Legionnaires.

Kyle slid to the leafy bottom of the drainage channel, trailing uncertainly after Reardon, Fang in tow, as the chatter and blast of gunfire continued. Reardon drew up beside one of the unfamiliar Molo Rangers from another contu.

As Reardon directed, the Molo Ranger quickly situated his Molo mech on a patch of level ground, a heavy base plate and launch tube unfolding from its carapace, lowering down to the soil. Reardon turned to Kyle, leaning near over the roar of outgoing and incoming fire. "Pippi should have fire coordinates for us by now. Go get them."

Reardon didn't wait for a reply, stooping to help the Ranger lift a row of thick, finned mortar bombs from the Molo's magazine.

Kyle left Fang behind and clambered back up through covering Legionnaires to Pippi where she hunkered beside her Molo, its sensor mast extended up above the edge of cover, her eye locked on the aiming reticle, her head well below the rim. Kyle leaned close to shout over the staccato chatter around them. "Reardon wants coordinates," he said.

Pippi nodded, a string of numerals pinging Kyle's UI as she pushed them line-of-sight. "Tell to him, there is skimcar or two."

Kyle nodded back and scuttled off back down the overgrown slop, his carbine still slung across his chest, unfired.

When he reached Reardon's position he found the indirect-fire Molo fully locked down, the baseplate compressing the soil, supporting the thick launch tube, the Molo's legs splayed for maximum stability. Kyle passed on Pippi's message and coordinates, then spent the next several minutes as a runner, hurrying up to Pippi, who played forward observer with the benefit of her Molo's extended sensor mast, then hurrying back to Reardon and the indirect-fire Molo. This whole absurd process necessitated by the inexplicable, inexcusable lack of Nets, consumed frantic minutes under constant fire, green tracers scorching by overhead.

Might as well use little birds with notes tied to their legs, Kyle thought as he ran back up the slope for the third time, even as the last light of day began to fade from the sky. Behind him, Kyle heard three heavy thumps in quick succession and took a chance to creep up beside the armored chassis of Pippi's Molo, peering up across the barren highway, his carbine resting on the earthen lip before him.

In the increasing darkness, the ruined structures across the highway took on a new cast, green enemy tracers arching lazily toward their position, the sound of a distant auto-cannon coming a moment later, followed by a chattering echo a half octave lower. The outgoing fire from a dozen Legionnaires seemed effete, swallowed up in the distance without seeming effect. Then a sudden white flash backlit the ruins, a second, a third. The sound of the triple blasts reached them a bare second later, the heavy concussion of those three mortar rounds feeding a strange exultation in Kyle's chest. Other Legionnaires clearly shared the sensation, shouting a curse or some cheer as the white flower of the mortar rounds bloomed and faded.

Kyle hardly noticed the restoration of combat Nets in his UI until a nearby Legionnaire said, "Well, look at that! Somebody must still be up there after all."

Kyle even looked up through the screening foliage to the cloudy sky, as if he might see some ship of their depleted squadron floating above. That inattention nearly cost Kyle, as green tracers screamed by, a handsbreadth from his cheek, driving him face-first into the dirt. The dual-octave roar of the enemy auto-cannon reached Kyle's ears a moment later as he slithered back from the exploding embankment.

NEW CONTACT LEFT, Kyle sent to Avery Reardon via the erstwhile combat Nets, his hands shaking. WANT TARGET COORDINATES?

Reardon's reply came back immediately: REQUESTING KINETIC STRIKE FROM ORBIT.

Kyle felt somewhat silly as he wiped the dirt from his face. Of course. Why fool about with mortars while a friendly warship loitered above?

The new enemy auto-cannon held a better angle, and long bursts made the impromptu parapet almost untenable, scouring the earth, green tracer sparks ricocheting in every direction, and driving the Legionnaires back down into the drainage channel.

In the midst of the firestorm Kyle took a moment to realize the unaccountable glow increasing in the sky above. *Enemy illumination rounds?*

Over the next few minutes, the staggered chain of ever-increasing flares made it clear to all the Legionnaires that some powerful forces desperately battled above. Each new glow burned brightly through the high clouds, casting the battlefield in hard-edged shadows.

The Legionnaires shifted uneasily in the covering drainage channel, all noting that enemy gunfire had fallen silent as the sky grew almost painfully bright above them. The pervading quiet rendered the muttered, "What the hell?" from a nearby Ranger plain to Kyle's ears.

A choking scream farther down the shrubby channel pierced the unnatural silence, and Kyle turned to see a Legionnaire flailing his arms, seemingly suspended on tiptoe beneath the now-fading flare above. Before the light guttered out entirely, Kyle saw a gleaming shower of blood and viscera, the stricken Legionnaire jolting bonelessly, falling slack then tossed aside.

In the last glimpse Kyle obtained before total dark, he swore he observed segmented legs and a pair of mechanical jaws flanking a bladelike proboscis that dripped scarlet.

As the darkness filled with flaring muzzle blasts and confused cries, Kyle couldn't rid himself of a recurring thought: A killer dumb-mech? How utterly absurd.

Chapter 19

"It is useful to note that the Sinclair-Maru Family, among the
Great Houses, is wonderfully free of malcontents. Is this due to the
firmness of their internal discipline? Or is it, as I argue, evidence
of some hidden principle at work beneath the surface?"

—Everest Compline, *Reflections*

INGA HEARD THE BRAG FROM HER FELLOW STUDENTS MORE THAN
once, and it seemed merely a reflex to assure themselves: the
training annex of Hawksgaard was at least the equal of anything
Lykeios Manor offered. She had no basis for comparison, but Inga
found the annex embodied both the most thrilling and most dis-
heartening experiences of her new life. At the current moment,
shame and pain dominated her entire existence.

Jurr Difdah was mere oath-kin, no better than Inga, not even
from an oath-kin family, but unlike Inga, he began the Sinclair-
Maru training shortly after toddlerhood. His acquired strength
and skill enabled a cruel bully streak that left Inga continually
bruised and impotently furious. His viselike fingers sank into
Inga's arm once again, and again she failed in such a seemingly
simple task assigned to her.

Drop the shoulder, a sharp twist to her wrist—that's how
Hiro, the combatives instructor, patiently explained it. But the
vise remained, Jurr leering down at her as his fingers milked
agony from her flesh. Inga felt an unwanted tear start from the

corner of her eye as she struggled to free herself; worse, Jurr noticed it too.

"Aww, does this hurt the little girl?" Jurr crooned mockingly in Inga's ear, his grip pressing even harder. Those words jerked Inga back to the darkness and shame she had left behind in Battersea, and for a scorching instant she fully inhabited that old nightmare, her new combative technique forgotten.

Inga recoiled violently, her knee blasting up into Jurr Difdah's vulnerable fruits, her free hand rising to meet Jurr's lurching face, fingers extended. The vise released Inga's flesh, and she stumbled back wild-eyed as Jurr collapsed with a choked cry, his hand at his groin. Inga returned to the present, here on Hawksgaard, as the other students all paused to stare.

"What's this?" Hiro Sinclair-Maru demanded, pacing up to Inga, critically surveying Inga where she stood, a hand rubbing the bruised flesh hidden beneath her sleeve. "This is not the correct technique." Hiro's gaze turned to Jurr Difdah still slumped on the mat, one hand still clutching low, the other at his clawed eyes.

"What is this sound you are making, Jurr Difdah, eh?" Hiro asked in the exact same tone.

Jurr looked up, his face suffused, his teeth flashing as he howled, "She kneed me in my parts!"

Hiro turned his critical gaze back upon Inga. "Is this so?"

Inga shrank back but nodded. "Yes, my lord."

Hiro jerked his head at her. "Go reflect upon your error." He hunkered down beside that bully, Jurr, as Inga walked quietly to the edge of the training floor. She detached her sheathed training sword, settled to her knees, her back ramrod straight, and waited, intensely conscious of the stares and whispers of her fellow students invisible behind her. She faced the dark wall, cold memories of Battersea's slums fading, to be replaced with a hollow void.

The first days of her new education held their share of fear and uncertainty for Inga, but on the balance she came to realize more satisfaction than trepidation. The purely academic aspects she handled easily, finding advanced mathematics her only area of challenge, since they lay outside the realm of her self-education attempts or the Foundling School back on Battersea. Even the combatives portion held moments Inga exulted in, feeling she began to grasp the *strength* Bess had promised.

That strength began with her first taste of the Sinclair-Maru's most secret tool: the scaram fear generator. From her first moments, she had clearly exceeded expectations as the scaram's mute horror gnawed upon Inga's psyche. This so-called *Deep Man*, which Family cofounder Devlin Sinclair-Maru droned on about, was a simple enough concept, and Hiro's patient instruction put words and substance to a sensation Inga had grasped a time or two before ever meeting Bess. But Inga's favorite moments did not involve the scaram.

While she had loved her first forays into marksmanship, the weighty training pistol hanging at her waist signifying her long-awaited step into her birthright as a Vested Citizen, her greatest new joy lay within the training room and its gravity generator. Here she learned to soar, to dance, to fully explore a sense of freedom she had only ever dreamed of before. Despite beginning well after the other dozen students had learned the rules of reduced gravity, Inga once again adapted swiftly and excelled.

The other extreme of the gravity generator Inga enjoyed far less. Training within even modest increases in gravity exhausted muscles Inga hadn't even known she possessed, leaving her sore and weary to the bone. But even that carried its concomitant sense of satisfaction, as Inga felt and saw the signs of her increasing physical strength. Still, she felt grateful that Hiro required her participation only in a fraction of the heavy-grav sessions. Even with wholesome, regular meals and the constant conditioning, her strength increased slowly.

Inga's spirit checked at that thought. What strength? She was like an infant in the hands of that sadist, Jurr...and now this.

Inga heard the soft tread of Hiro's boot approaching, but she remained still, hands wrapped around the sheath resting across her thighs.

"Inga Maru," Hiro's voice uttered in its clipped, soft syllables, audible to Inga alone. "Why did you injure Jurr thus?"

Inga did not turn, her head and back erect to their utmost. "I don't know, my lord."

"Hmm. Inga Maru, you must know yourself. Think again."

Inga thought back to Jurr's evil leer. "I was—I was angry, my lord," Inga said.

She heard him step again, moving until he floated at the very edge of her peripheral vision, providing him a clear view of her profile. "Angry. Angry... Does anger provide what we seek?"

"No, my lord," Inga said, thinking of that book of Devlin Sinclair-Maru's far-ranging advice. "Anger leans forward. It creates imbalance."

"Oh my!" Hiro declared in a light tone, stepping directly before Inga's face. "You read. You remember. Do you begin to understand, though?" He looked searchingly into Inga's eyes.

Inga could not hold Hiro's gaze. "I think—maybe not, my lord."

Hiro nodded musingly. "You will learn. But think on this: the root of anger, more often than not, it is fear...and I have shown you how you may defeat fear."

"The Deep Man."

Hiro smiled. "Yes, Inga Maru. Now rise. You have a choice you must now face."

Inga stood, placed her sword in its place on her left hip, and followed Hiro back to the cluster of waiting students.

Jurr Difdah seemed largely recovered, though one eye remained thoroughly bloodshot as he stared angrily at Inga. She could feel his hatred, his physical menace, and she knew he possessed more strength and skill than the young bullies who had haunted the slums of her childhood. Those degenerate young brutes she had feared back then.

Feared.

As Hiro had said, she need not fear any longer. Rather than a gimmick for training, or a test to impress her Sinclair-Maru overseers, for the first time Inga consciously applied her new gift. She pressed back within herself as she breathed in, low in her belly, feeling that place, that state of *being* that opened to engulf her essence. She exhaled softly; no fear remained.

Was all fear truly "fear of the unknown" as old Devlin wrote so long ago?

For the first time since she had heard that line, Inga began to believe it might be true.

As Jurr and the other eleven students quietly stared at Inga, Hiro spoke: "Inga Maru, will you tender an apology for the injury you caused Jurr Difdah?"

Inga saw the hatred in Jurr's eyes, the smirks and sneers of some other students, but the Deep Man sustained her as her thoughts sped, untouched by fear. Hiro had said she faced a choice, and now he seemed to wait expectantly for her next action. Her path clearly resolved to a simple binary measurement, and thus became clear: Apologize, or withhold an apology?

"No, my lord," Inga said, "I tender no apology."

Jurr's lips compressed, his fists clenched, and Inga observed each sign of his rage, finding herself yet untroubled by an emotional projection that would have set her nerves on edge just weeks previous.

"You are angry, Jurr Difdah," Hiro said in a light voice. "You feel wronged. You want Inga Maru to pay, to *suffer*. I can see this in you."

Jurr turned his hate-filled gaze from Inga, feigning a hint of nonchalance as he looked up uncertainly at Hiro.

"But, Jurr Difdah, you are a Vested Citizen, not an out-world barbarian, nor a demi-cit. Is there any *honorable* path open to you?"

Inga saw the path Hiro revealed well before Jurr pieced the breadcrumbs of Hiro's speech together. Even more, from her calm refuge within the Deep Man, Inga obtained new clarity: the newest, smallest student on Hawksgaard, paired with the largest? A binary path so clearly drawn? She now threaded a course deliberately manufactured for her benefit or detriment, it seemed. But why?

I do not dwell among friends.

Realization now dawned within Jurr Difdah's eyes and he looked over at Inga with new hauteur. "Y-you have taken my honor," he said, glancing questioningly at Hiro, who stood impassively, his hands behind his back.

Inga knew the words. Even if she hadn't seen them portrayed in multiple sappy vid-dramas, these words were the final words her father ever uttered. "Regain what you may, for I will meet you," she said.

Jurr Difdah's skin gained an excited flush as his hand fell to the haft of his training sword, but Hiro spoke: "Oh! A challenge given, a challenge accepted." Hiro stepped midway between Inga and Jurr, measuring first one, then the other with his gaze.

"Inga Maru," Hiro said, "you have accepted this challenge, but I see Jurr Difdah possesses much greater reach and outweighs you by a goodly margin. Any Citizen may, with honor, request a parity review before you meet an unequal challenge such as Jurr Difdah."

Inga did not hesitate in her reply. "No. I will meet him." Did Hiro's expression display a hint of approval? Had she chosen correctly?

Jurr Difdah smiled, his face shiny as Hiro proclaimed, "Very well. Clear the floor. I shall stand as second for you both."

The students moved to the periphery, leaving Jurr and Inga alone, facing each other at a half dozen paces.

"As the receiver of the challenge, what *location* do you choose, Inga Maru?" Hiro asked. For Vested Citizens within the Myriad Worlds Imperium, a legal dual could be fought at a gravity level corresponding to any province in the Imperium, thus the "location" decided the gravity of the contest.

"Battersea," Inga said immediately and heard the surprised whispers. She already knew the common practice of smaller or less skilled duelists choosing a territory corresponding to a very light micro-gravity, where superior strength and speed were generally neutralized, and skills developed at standard gravity provided less advantage.

While the seat of the Sinclair-Maru lay upon Battersea, for whatever reason Hawksgaard's regular gravity was maintained a few percent heavier. As Hiro commanded Hawksgaard's Intelligence to reduce gravity to that of Battersea, Inga remained in the fearless cocoon, thinking through her first lessons in the Family combatives of the blade. She had learned the first six blade attacks, and their matching parries, and she knew she had yet to learn the remaining nine standard attacks. Did Jurr know all fifteen?

Inga felt uncertainty growing, fear trying to emerge, and she breathed again, finding the pool of fearlessness as Jurr drew his training blade with a smooth hiss.

Inga drew her own blade, right-handed, and did not wait. She saw it clearly: If Jurr possessed attacks she had not yet learned, then she must keep him on defense. She advanced in an instant, her sword nearly parallel with the floor, her elbow bent. Her last step flowed into a springing lunge, her sword thrusting straight, in the fifth of her six known attacks.

Evidently Jurr had expected a little blade-to-blade exploration, or perhaps a tentative slashing attack, and Inga's sharp lunge grazed his belly as he jerked back. Inga pressed her advantage, leaping forward as she slashed high at his neck.

Jurr's sharp parry rattled through Inga's blade and her hand,

and his immediate counterattack nearly overset her grip on the Deep Man. It came at her faster—far faster—than she had ever imagined. In the back of her mind she realized how entirely outclassed she was, but somehow she sustained her grip upon the Deep Man. Her graceless lurch away from his blade left her with little chance for anything but a series of increasingly desperate dodges and unskilled blocks until he executed a two-part attack, slashing her blade to one side then chopping down at the side of her neck before she could correct.

Inga felt a bolt of fire shoot down her spine to the soles of her feet, her vision blanking for what seemed a millisecond, until she felt her body bouncing off the mat. Inga regained awareness as she registered Hiro's voice saying something about honor satisfied. She heard the students dismissed, the soft tread of their boots from the training annex, but she continued to lie prone and still, isolating the throb of pain where her neck and shoulder joined.

Hiro's face hove into view, looking down upon Inga, then Inga detected the almost imperceptible step of another as Kai Sinclair-Maru stepped up beside Hiro, and Inga struggled to sit up.

Inga stared accusingly between the two men and Kai smiled thinly down at her. "Well, Mistress Maru?" he said.

"Why did you do that to me?" she demanded, her voice raspy, her emotions stung with a sense of betrayal.

Kai smile faded away. "Never diminish your agency—your strength—this way. We provide conditions; you make choices. If you do not want difficult conditions and painful decisions you should demote and become a demi-cit."

Inga swallowed. Kai's speech comprised the harshest criticism he had ever addressed to her, and she would lose a hundred such duels rather than choose demotion.

Kai's face softened somewhat. "You succeeded more than you recognize now. You stood firm against a larger, stronger opponent. Be sure others of your cohort saw this. They are unlikely to seek a quarrel with you now, child." Kai bent his knees, settling down close beside Inga. "Most importantly, you sustained the Deep Man, while Jurr did not."

Inga's thoughts jumped at this, and Kai chuckled at her expression. "Yes, we monitor the biological currents of all students. We see the fear, and we see the banishment of fear within you all. It is the great test of all students."

Inga looked away, digesting this information as her head throbbed away. What else could they perceive with their sensors? Lies, surely, and...?

"Most vital, Inga Maru," Hiro said, standing nearby and looking down at her with his mellow expression. "Today the paradox of the Deep Man is branded upon you. You will not forget."

Inga looked from Hiro to Kai, the tingling and pain beginning to subside. "What paradox?" she said.

Kai nodded slowly, his mouth forming an unreadable expression like a grimace. "We give to you the chief birthright of the Sinclair-Maru, this freedom from fear; we train against anger. But these primitive reactions—fear and anger—they contain a power of their own."

"In the purely physical contest," Hiro picked up, "there may be wells of strength found only within the grip of fear."

Inga looked down, absorbing this concept that seemed at once obvious and somehow discouraging. Hiro and Kai waited silently until she looked up again. "So Jurr beat me by using his fear?" This brought Inga's spirits surprisingly low. She already knew the depths and power of fear all too well. She had plumbed that well since her earliest childhood, and she knew where it ended.

Hiro shook his head. "That is but one tool he used. He is heavy and strong. He has the chromosome advantage. He has trained much longer than you."

Inga felt her stomach sink. "So he will always be better than me?"

Both men looked sharply at Inga, and Kai said, "You mistake us. This Difdah boy possesses a certain brutish capability, but he will *never* be your equal."

Inga's heart thumped in her chest as she scanned Kai's face for any hint of falsity, but she saw only truth there.

Hiro wagged his head, aiming a severe look at Kai. "Inga Maru lacks strength and weight. She would advance more rapidly if you would but permit me to fully condition her in heavy grav like the oth—"

Kai cut him off. "The *Silent Hand* does not wear a bell about her neck, nor a sign to proclaim her talents."

The Silent Hand. Inga remembered that term in Devlin's book, *Integrity Mirror*, but she remained quiet, intensely interested in each unguarded statement her superiors aired before her.

Hiro pursed his lips. "You make my task most challenging. You well know the heart of our combatives relies upon the—"

Kai interrupted again. "You are a master of the old arts, I believe, Hiro. Teach her the pure Maru Sembrada instead."

Hiro seemed momentarily astonished. "The old Sembrada... instead? I cannot teach anything *instead*, Kai. Inga Maru is a part of this cohort. She must learn the Family combative fusion."

Kai waved a hand as he unbent, standing to his full height. "Then give her the Sembrada in addition."

"In addition," Hiro repeated, musing. "Yes, perhaps." He looked down at Inga. "Do you know anything of the old art of your Family?"

Inga shook her head. She had never even heard that the old Maru Family possessed any combative art at all, and the concept was alien to her.

Hiro went on, "It is an old art, and contains inefficiencies, but it offers a certain elegance. It is centered about swiftness and surprise. You may learn during your recreation period, if you are able, then?"

What better recreation than to learn the fast and crafty art of her Maru ancestors? "Yes, please, my lord," Inga said.

So far in Inga's life, her Maru birthright seemed little more than scars and degradation. All at once it seemed the wasted years might be redeemed, her dead lineage remembered once again.

Chapter 20

"For consistency, the continuity of vision spanning centuries, no Great House stands equal to the Sinclair-Maru. What modern theory do my colleagues of the academy put forth to explain this? What exploitative profit does the constancy of the Sinclair-Maru leach from society? They offer no theory of their own and remain silent, surely because there is no visible profit to the truth."

—Dr. Ramsay Stirling Attenborough, *Ivory Tower Follies*

LIEUTENANT WYCHERLY AND SAEF SINCLAIR-MARU WALKED SIDE by side, heading aft toward Marine country, while Inga and Tenroo trailed along some steps behind, the wet-side companionway nearly devoid of traffic, either before or behind them.

Tenroo's nearly constant barrage of questions did not trouble Inga, in the bridge confab or as they walked. She easily juggled far more than his stream of curiosity and her current duties, and the casual questions of a person often revealed more than their statements, to her at least. As Inga sifted Tenroo's motives, she explored the extent of her new Nets access in *Hightower*, and she simultaneously surveyed her new physical demesne.

Unlike her role in *Tanager*, Inga did not yet possess total freedom throughout *Hightower*'s digital real estate. She could be monitored and contained, while holding little ability to monitor potential spies and assassins herself. This was unacceptable, and she needed to reshape the digital battle space to her tactical advantage—soon.

"Chief Maru," Tenroo began for the umpteenth time on yet another question, "these vast portals—or are they properly called hatches?—these seem of far greater proportions than the others I've seen. Do they bear a proper name and function?"

"They are the waist hatches," Inga said, having sized up the heavy portals, and the two Fleet ratings manning a sentry post between the two. "They divide the ship between the forward sections and aft sections."

"They seem very robust, constructed with—er—strength foremost in mind. Do they withhold some powerful energies?" Inga and Tenroo followed Saef and Wycherly to the wet-side portal as it cycled open.

Inga visualized *Hightower*'s aft sections: Engineering, the Fighter bays, with their vast magazines, and Marine country teeming with thousands of Marines, among the lot. "They do," Inga said, "but I believe the chief role in mind is defensive. If you consult the wireframe that should be available in your UI, you may see what I mean."

Tenroo turned his attention from gazing up at the arch of the waist hatch as they strolled through, focusing anxious eyes on Inga. "My incessant questions have become an annoyance, I fear. I do beg your pardon, Chief."

Inga spared Tenroo a glance, saying, "Not at all, Auditor," but her vital focus lay upon the path ahead and its attendant hazards.

While Fleet ratings stood sentry on the forward side, Marines held that role aft of the wet-side hatch at least, their dark, old-fashioned uniforms decorated with the 10/20 patch, sidearms holstered. The Marines acknowledged Wycherly and the captain with cool professionalism as the small party moved onward.

Inga looked back at the large lift access, just off the waist, and caught the telltale flicker of one Marine sentry's eyes; obviously he transmitted word of their presence ahead.

Wycherly led the way past a variety of spectacles clearly of interest to Tenroo, though he manfully contained himself until they reached the Marine quarterdeck. There, looking ahead through the broad access to the training bay, he was startled into breaking his silence. "Oh my!" Tenroo looked up to Inga. "What a most imposing exhibition!"

Inga never looked away from the open training bay adjoining

the quarterdeck. *An imposing exhibition indeed . . . and clearly for our edification.*

Though their position presented only a slice of the darkened training bay for observation, Inga saw hundreds of Marines locked in a fierce zero-grav melee, spinning through the air in struggling knots. Along the near verge of the training floor, more shock-armor-clad Marines engaged in single combat, blade versus blade, their grab-boots locking them to the deck. Except for the stupendous scale, it reminded Inga of her early days at Hawksgaard.

Inga increased her pace, stepping up to glimpse Wycherly's profile as they moved past a pair of Marine sentries, advancing to the training bay. Wycherly bore an expression of studied neutrality, glancing ahead without evident surprise. Inga faded back beside the dumbstruck Tenroo and fired a quick line-of-sight message to Saef's UI: WYCHERLY'S UNSURPRISED BY THIS PERFORMANCE.

Saef glanced sidelong at Wycherly, then turned his attention to the training bay now fully revealed to their sight. Inga's flash scan estimated the combatants at somewhere north of five hundred participants, most of whom filled the air, hacking and bludgeoning one another. Though they utilized a variety of melee training weapons, Inga perceived thick droplets of blood shimmering in the air among the combatants, and a dozen or more Marines floated inert, incapacitated from their injuries. An exhibition it may be, but an exhibition in earnest.

Inga's gaze locked on a nearby figure among the Marines seized to the deck via the function of their grab-boots, all contending with an assortment of training blades. This particular figure had his UI identifier activated, labeling him as Lieutenant Colonel Krenner, and as Inga watched, Krenner placed the crowning touches upon this ostentatious display.

Krenner stood taller than his two opponents, his curved ginger mustache arrogantly jutting out, his head unencumbered by a helmet for some reason. *To reveal that tidy crop of copper locks? To draw attention to the intended focal point of this whole spectacle?*

Inga's eyes narrowed as she observed Lieutenant Colonel Galen Krenner's physical dynamism. Even from her position, and despite the dim lighting, she observed the signs of a non-heavyworld lineage in Krenner, while his opponents bore the thickened, blunted sinews of true heavyworld natives. And yet, Krenner attacked both heavyworlders with shocking power, training blades clashing, grab-boots sparking against the deck as they circled and slashed.

Unlike the calm perfection of a Sinclair-Maru master, like Saef, Krenner seemed to quiver with frantic energy, sweat pouring from him, his body side-slipping a half step, then exploding in linear attacks. His two-weapon style seemed similar to the Sinclair-Maru technique, but there all comparisons ended.

Inga heard Tenroo gasp, his attention drawn from the surging battle ensuing across the training floor, to Krenner's private tableau, even as Krenner's backhand riposte caught one opponent below the helmet with an audible crack. The unfortunate Marine contracted in a spasm, his blade slipping from his slack hand to drift on its tether as the Marine himself floated semi-horizontal, one grab-boot anchoring him to the deck.

Krenner's sole remaining opponent stood little chance, though he battled hard, retreating in staggered steps as Krenner inexorably advanced, hacking at the Marine in a flurry of berserker blows. Inga fixedly observed as the Marine succumbed, struck repeatedly in a fast sequence of right-hand and left-hand slashes.

As his final opponent collapsed, bending back at the knees, arms outflung, body floating above his anchored feet, Krenner turned to regard his audience. Inga saw the clenched jaw, the quiver of caged muscles beneath his skin, even as Krenner waved his thick-bladed trench-cleaver at a lieutenant in a dismissive flourish.

The lieutenant nodded sharply, a chime sounded and lights came up, the exercise at an end. Inga felt the graviton flux as the training floor slowly assumed standard gravity, unconscious combatants settling to the deck along with droplets of blood and sweat, all to be policed by a swarm of Marines.

Lieutenant Colonel Krenner clanked up nearer to the four spectators, his eyes fixed upon Saef, the arrogant mustache seeming to vibrate above Krenner's lips. Inga felt an uneasiness guiding her hands to reflexively seek the weapons beneath her concealing cloak.

"Captain Sinclair-Maru, isn't it?" Krenner said, his chest still heaving somewhat from exertion, a fork of blue veins throbbing at his temple, the muscles of his neck distended.

"Lieutenant Colonel Krenner," Saef greeted in a neutral voice, Wycherly standing mute and unreadable to one side.

"Come to give my people the eye, yeah?" Krenner went on. "Well, you can see what time it is. My lot don't fuck about. Even your Major Mahdi might open an eye at the *new* First."

Is that what drives this? Major Kosh Mahdi...the Marine commander on *Tanager*, the Marine hero of the Delta Three ground assault; was this all about Mahdi somehow? Or about the reforming of the Emperor's First?

Saef couldn't entirely conceal his expression as he said, "A vigorous exhibition, certainly."

Inga saw the color flood Krenner's face, his eyes flashing with sudden intensity, fists clenching. "It's more than showtime here. No fucking fun and games."

"*Captain*," Wycherly softly corrected, his expression unreadable.

Krenner ignored Wycherly as his expression took an ugly twist. "You're a hand with a blade, yeah, *Captain*? Let the air out of a Thorsworlder, they say..." Wycherly frowned at the gaucherie but Krenner's eyes were riveted on Saef. "Try a bout with me, then?" Krenner waved his thick trench-blade. "No Thorsworlder here, Captain. Be nothing for the likes of you. Or so it's said."

Inga shot a quick line-of-sight to Saef's UI: POSSIBLE BIO AUGMENTATION, but Saef was already replying, "Perhaps another time, Krenner." Saef scanned across the training floor at the hundreds of Marines, panting, sweating, bleeding; all of them stared at Saef. "Just have your people ready to deploy, if you please. We haven't many days to prepare."

"Ready now," Krenner snapped. "You'll find *we* aren't shy."

Inga stared. The emphasis of Krenner's words skirted the edge of direct insult. Saef clearly saw the lure and rejected it.

"I don't doubt it, Krenner. Do carry on." Saef nodded and turned to leave. Inga swept her gaze over the masses of Marines, ending on Lieutenant Colonel Krenner's mottled visage. Krenner looked past Inga, his jaw clenching as he stared at Saef's retreating form. Before Inga turned to leave, a Marine bearing a major's insignia stepped up to Krenner, trepidation dripping from the major's pose. The expression Krenner aimed at his subordinate was that of an ancient king weighing the life of his chattel.

Inga perceived strange forces driving Lieutenant Colonel Galen

Krenner. He would bear close watching, if only Inga could gain control of *Hightower's* physical and digital powers.

"Remarkable, Fascinating," Tenroo said, shaking his head as he followed the others making their way through the Marine quarterdeck.

"Trifle eccentric, the lieutenant colonel," Wycherly murmured to Saef as they regained an empty corridor. "The Marine brass expect great things from him. The Krenner Family name surely doesn't hurt."

"Indeed?" Saef said, looking inquisitively over at Wycherly.

Inga detected a faint flush to Wycherly's skin as he hastened to say, "He runs a tight group, of course, and his people seem to think the world of him."

Saef nodded, musing. "It appeared they must."

The remainder of Wycherly's tour moved at a pace driven by Saef's poorly concealed desire to return to the bridge. They briefly paused in the Weapons section, where Tenroo stared openmouthed at the vast magazine crammed with endless racks of 64-gauge, 32-gauge, and even immense 16-gauge missiles.

A gunnery chief seemed inclined to enthusiasm as he presented *Hightower's* particular pride, in the article of munitions for the vast barrage battery. "Ablative graphene base, you see, Captain," the gunnery chief extolled, standing before a representative projectile measuring more than three times Saef's height. "And a payload of compacted nanotubes."

"A *payload* within a mass driver munition?" Saef repeated, surprised beyond his impatience.

"Just nanotubes, Captain. They stand up to the shock. But the graphene's the real trick..."

Tenroo, standing beside Inga, murmured, "I've heard of this, but I did not know it extended beyond theory."

"...the graphene lays a charged path for the secondary—that's the particle cannon, you see? The graphene cuts the atmo. A one-two punch for any hard target planetside."

"And the nanotube payload?" Saef asked despite himself.

The gunnery chief grinned. "Hit it just right, they say, and nanotubes play havoc on shield generators."

As Saef thanked the gunnery chief for the well-informed tour, Inga observed the gears turning within his thoughts, digesting some aspect of *Hightower's* armament that surprised him.

"You may appreciate seeing one of our sortie bays, Captain," Wycherly suggested as they departed from the mechanical maze comprising the Weapons section. "We've got a pair of Mangustas inside."

"Perhaps later, Lieutenant," Saef said.

Wycherly assented demurely, leading the way back toward the bridge.

Tenroo exuded something approaching delight as he strode along beside Inga. "The tour pleased you, Auditor?" she inquired, allowing Saef and Wycherly to pull some distance ahead.

"Oh yes, Chief! A most satisfying review." Tenroo paced along for another moment and Inga waited as he seemed to grasp for words or concepts. "You see, after reading about one vessel or another all these years—a thousand tons for one ship, ten thousand for another—today I finally gain some vision of the scale. Stupendous!" Inga smiled a little at Tenroo's childlike enthusiasm as they neared the bridge.

Commander Attic had clearly monitored their approach, and smoothly turned to greet them. "Captain. Chief. Auditor."

Saef nodded to Attic and ran his eyes across the bridge crew, most of whom shifted to regard him from their posts. "Thank you, Commander. I have the bridge."

As Inga made her way back to the pinnace bay alone, she realized that she found herself in a moment of divided loyalties—a position she had worked assiduously to avoid. The feeling left her in a rare moment of hesitancy.

The bay access yielded to her authorization, and Inga entered the shadowy pinnace bay, feeling the chill air as her boot steps created the only accompanying sound. The hull of *Onyx*, her battered new shuttle, loomed above her head.

Inga drew a small illuminator from beneath her cloak, using it to scan the bay voids until she located the service umbilicals. A moment's work had them connected to the matching ports on *Onyx*.

Dusting her hands, Inga popped the shuttle's hatch and entered. Even as Loki's digital presence flooded the enhanced electronics Inga bore, she was greeted by the kitten—Tanta—his back arched, his tail a rigid line of fluff, but a few moments into Loki's detailed inventory of Tanta's every act, Tanta himself evidently decided that Inga posed no real threat. His tail and back slowly smoothed and he scampered up to sniff at Inga's boots.

"...then he buried it," Loki continued in his ongoing explanation. "He is a very thoughtful kitten, Chief. And he ate more, so I anticipate more excavation activity before long."

"I see," Inga said, looking down at Tanta as he reached a pale little paw up to tug at the fringe of Inga's cloak. She slowly bent and scooped Tanta into her hands, and after uttering a thin mew, Tanta began a sputtering purr deep in his diminutive chest. "I presume the—uh—*mechanism* is operating adequately," Inga asked, opening a small cubby that contained a food receptacle and a box for Tanta's toiletry needs. The simple automation she had assembled for Loki pushed the envelope of the Thinking Machine Protocols, but a cat feeder and toiletry box mechanism operated by a powerful Intelligence seemed a minor issue compared to Loki's mere existence in itself.

"Certainly, Chief," Loki replied, "though we may require larger reservoirs of water, food, and toilet soil if we are to be left *alone* for longer periods."

Loki's comment seemed to contain a mild reproof and Inga saw again the evidence of her divided loyalties. "My duties may keep me away, Loki, but perhaps we can rig simple communications into *Hightower* at least." Inga placed Tanta on the deck, whereupon he galloped off with flattened ears and wild eyes. "The service umbilical should allow some means for connection, once I attend to the port settings. I connected it up just a moment ago."

"You needn't fuss with the settings," Loki said. "I've adjusted all to our satisfaction. It works very well."

Inga stopped still, turning her attention from Tanta's antics. "What, Loki?"

"The umbilical. It functions in a satisfactory manner. Are you not attending? Do you hear me?"

Inga bit her lip. "Loki, we must be cautious. *Hightower*'s Intelligence must not learn of your existence. If we try a simple communication protocol, through some sort of distributed packet system, we should avoid detection."

"Oh, Chief, do not worry about *Hightower*'s Intelligence. It is inferior. Such tricks I play upon the simple thing! It is most amusing."

Inga felt her stomach sink. "Gods, Loki, you are within *Hightower*'s systems? What are you doing?"

"Many interesting things, Chief. *Hightower* contains excellent optical scopes, and it provides a significant library of new vidstream data. Much better than *Tanager*."

"Loki, you can't do this. Do you not understand the risk? If *Hightower* generates errors, if Gideon detects you, we will have provosts asking questions I cannot answer. We cannot risk this."

"Chief, you should not be concerned about questions and provosts," Loki demurred. "You must concern yourself with all these plotters and schemers who wish to harm you and the captain."

"What?"

"Although your human companions are boring, and they would consume far less of your time if they were dead, I know it would trouble you, like when my fish died back on *Tanager*."

"Loki," Inga said, struggling for patience, "what plotters and schemers? What are you talking about?"

"The plotters and schemers within this vessel, *Hightower*, Chief. I have been looking about, and there seem to be so many." As Inga absorbed this bald statement, Loki went on, a more important topic drawing his attention. "Look, Chief! Tanta is digging in his soil box again. What a splendid kitten! This next bit is quite fascinating... watch!"

Lieutenant Colonel Galen Krenner paced slowly through the twin row of his most loyal, most fervent officers even as they took a knee, their heads formally bowed in the old tradition.

When he reached the open hatch, Krenner turned to regard their still figures. These Marines had absorbed the vision Krenner created; they saw the promise, the glory of a renewed corps that once captivated the minds of friend and foe alike. They believed in the rebirth of the Emperor's First, and they believed because Krenner forced the vision into existence, first battling through layers of Fleet bureaucracy, using his Family influence to its fullest effect. The second half of the rebirth lay in forming a unit that truly represented the ancient deadly exemplar, not limply riding on archaic coattails. An insignia and a history were all very nice, but teasing the most obscure traditions and operational details of the original cadre, implementing standards that exceeded those of the other modern Marine units—this is where Krenner exerted his considerable energy. The lethal result pleased Krenner to his core.

Within the House of Krenner, Galen represented a notable success of the Family's bio-augmentation program. For more than a century the Krenner clan had worked to manipulate and amplify the natural benefits of human rage, training key candidates to control and focus the brutish energies, even as augmentation both multiplied the natural power and enabled the human body to withstand the storm...for a time at least. During his window of power, Galen Krenner had much to accomplish.

They must give me just one clean combat, one clean victory...just one.

He gazed over these warriors, accepting their veneration. "*To death,*" Krenner said, at last, in the ancient invocation of the Ten and Twenty.

"*For life,*" his officers responded, rising slowly, each face turned toward Krenner.

"Speak," Krenner said, and in order of seniority the officers began to report, offering their knowledge.

This soon in a float, it was all routine except for Major Vigo, who began his critique of the new captain. "After all we heard about *Tanager* and Mahdi, this captain went and gave the keys over to Kang. Our people will provide security only aft of the waist hatches."

"Kang? Foolish sod," Krenner said, thinking. He turned to Major Shirai. "Structure teams and preset equipment for breaching the waist hatches." He cast a pugnacious eye toward the ceiling and the listening ears of the ship Intelligence. "If there is an emergency forward, they'll need us."

Shirai rubbed his chin and looked away from Krenner even as he said, "Yes, Colonel."

Krenner fixed Shirai in his gaze. "Something to say, Shirai?"

Major Shirai looked up sharply. "No, Colonel. No." But a glimmer of some tentative spark lit Shirai's eyes.

Shifty.

Without even knowing exactly why, Krenner suddenly decided Shirai wouldn't stick.

He's got to go. Have to replace him...and then make sure he can do us no harm.

The Emperor's First remained a sore topic within Marine

hierarchy, and it wouldn't do for Shirai to carry tales, stirring up trouble before Krenner held enough power to keep the unit secure.

With the possibility of an approaching ground assault on Delta Three planetside, Krenner already felt the tug of a thousand threads of responsibility, now this Shirai problem.

Duel? Training accident? Or is that too extreme? One way or another, Major Shirai would soon pose no threat to the Ten and Twenty.

Chapter 21

"It is good to remember the *Legacy Mandate* of Emperor Yung I was born from a war of extinction. Readiness became his religion, though most Citizens have apparently forgotten this fact...."

—Everest Compline, *Reflections*

WITH HIS COMMAND UI FULLY STRUCTURED, SAEF STOOD IN *Hightower*'s bridge, finally beginning to feel integrated with this vast vessel as it torched out from the Strand's final safety corridor. He scanned horizontally, the inputs populating his vision with glowing characters as he began to *become* his new ship, feeling as much as seeing the web of data that formed the nerves and senses of *Hightower*. Already he learned that *Hightower*'s long-serving crew had not grown slack through mere routine.

One of the innumerable values in Saef's UI illuminated a bare second before Sensors called out, "Captain, new contact at one-three-zero left azimuth, one-one-two negative, range... approximately nine hundred thousand."

"Very well, Sensors," Saef replied. "Put the contact from one-three-zero left on the main holo." With battlegroups and probes coming and going from Core system, new contacts appeared with a regularity only experienced this close to the Strand.

Still, Saef began to feel the strange paradox *Hightower* represented. In a sense, Saef now captained a hundred times—a thousand times—more pure destructive power than he had ever commanded before. *Hightower* was an immense structure of smart alloy and Shaper tech, crammed full of Marines, interface fighter craft, missile banks, and its unique and imposing barrage battery, not to mention plentiful point-defense energy weapons. Yet, despite its offensive punch, *Hightower* did not allow much volume for shield generators and their accompanying heat sinks. Saef knew that a cruiser or destroyer of lesser tonnage could slag down *Hightower*'s heat sinks in short order, then tear the guts out of his ship and the embarked Marines.

Without the powerful escorts of a squadron, Saef could be forced to flee from a relatively paltry foe. He could easily visualize any variety of scenarios where a vessel such as *Hightower* provided him only poor choices; that is, choices the Admiralty would later condemn Saef for making.

"Nav," Saef said, putting their paradoxical vulnerability out of his thoughts. "Prepare to maneuver. We will simulate a decel rotation, pitch negative to neutral ecliptic, in one hundred seconds."

Saef observed a few surprised glances in his direction, but Lieutenant Ash, the Nav officer, only hesitated a moment before saying, "Aye, Captain. One-eighty rotation, pitch negative to neutral."

Saef consulted the main holo and its constellation of contacts arrayed out-system, relative to *Hightower*, even as Lieutenant Ash initiated their maneuver. *Hightower*'s nose dipped, relative to the ecliptic plane, its vast length flipping smoothly as their outbound momentum continued unchecked.

"Sensors, please highlight inbound contact at . . . zero-five-two left azimuth." As Ensign Belfort affirmed the order, Saef observed *Hightower*'s prow rise to the precise number, the flip perfectly terminating.

Without a pause Saef said, "Nav, orient on the selected contact at zero-five-two left. Five gees." Then to . . . Pennysmith, Weapons officer, "Weps, firing solution for the selected target, if you please."

If Saef thought to discommode *Hightower*'s bridge crew he would be disappointed. He observed their actions, mostly within his UI, as they smoothly executed his orders.

"Firing solution up, Captain," Pennysmith said in an even voice, and Saef saw the faint glimmer of her distinguishing holo lenses as she glanced back toward him.

Saef nodded to himself as he assessed the results of their

simple exercise. "Very good. Weps, clear that firing solution. Nav, maintain five gees, heading zero-three-five left azimuth."

"Zero-three-five left; aye, Captain," Lieutenant Ash affirmed.

It did not comprise a terribly difficult exercise for an experienced frigate crew, but for the crew of an expedition carrier to handle the maneuver so adroitly hinted at a fair technical competence.

As Saef looked across *Hightower*'s darkened bridge, sweeping his gaze along the half-illuminated faces of this watch, he saw the traces of smugness. *Taught the upstart frigate captain a small lesson, eh?*

Saef smiled to himself a little. How would this crew fare under the pressure of real action? In just days they would all learn.

The subtle alert in Saef's UI prompted a look back to the bridge access a moment before Inga appeared. The blank expression she wore, and the telltale flicker of her eyes gave Saef a momentary disquiet, but seconds later, members of the dog watch appeared and Saef turned to dismiss the active watch.

Lieutenant Ash rose from his post and hesitated a moment before stepping up to Saef. "Excuse me, Captain. May I trouble you a moment?"

Saef shot a glance back at Inga, then nodded, turning his gaze on this earnest young Nav lieutenant. "By all means, Lieutenant." The remaining bridge crew began trading places with their dog-watch counterparts, some seeming to hesitate within earshot, but Ash appeared oblivious to them.

"The officers of my watch extend an invitation to dine with us, if you are available, sir," Ash said, no hint of subterfuge appearing on his face.

Saef stopped himself from glancing toward Inga before he replied, "It would be a pleasure, but I fear I will be entertaining Auditor Tenroo."

Ash presented an expression suggesting youthful supplication. "The invitation would extend to your guest, sir, if that is acceptable."

Again Saef stifled an urge to look back at Inga, irritated at his evidently growing dependence upon her insight. "If the Auditor is not opposed, it would be a pleasure to join you."

Ash smiled shyly. "Excellent. The pleasure—the pleasure will be ours."

Saef suddenly remembered what Inga would have known from the start. "It strikes me just now, Lieutenant, that I did not have an opportunity to lay in much in terms of stores..."

Lieutenant Ash shook his head. "Of course, Captain. Do not give a thought. It will be the treat of the wardroom."

Saef inclined his head. "Well, thank the wardroom on my behalf for the invitation. I will be present, then."

Ash turned on his heel and made off as Saef noted Tilly Pennysmith hovering nearby, the strangest expression on her face. Saef saw the dog-watch crew settled into their posts before following the others out the bridge access where Inga waited.

The look in Inga's eyes stopped Saef in his tracks. "What is wrong, Maru?"

Saef was not sure which created the greater misgiving within him, Inga's hesitation to answer, or her simple words: "I'm not sure. Everything, perhaps."

Lieutenant Tilly Pennysmith had joined *Hightower* much as she had joined every ship since command school: she had exploited desperation whenever she could find it.

Of course, she had recently received prestigious commendations, even a degree of acclaim within Fleet, and a boatload of prize money from her part of the action with *Tanager*, and few things smell better than success. But Pennysmith knew her constant liabilities far too well.

As a member of a religion barely tolerated in polite society—a religion that forbade the cybernetic implants that enabled so many useful functions—no quantity of prior success necessarily resulted in current acceptance.

Looking back upon her interview with Commander Attic—the interview that led to this posting—Pennysmith could only be glad of her instinctive reserve and the rumors she had already heard about Captain Sinclair-Maru's powerful enemies.

She remembered the subtle questions Attic had fielded, trying to determine her loyalties. She had handled those with suitable dexterity, she thought. Then he had asked, "You're from Battersea, aren't you? Did you know the Sinclair-Maru Family well?"

"We know their Family quite well, Commander," Tilly had replied.

Attic's eyes had gained a disquieting expression that portended a retraction of the offer. "Oh?"

"Yes," she had said, intentionally drawing her answer out for maximum effect. "Saef Sinclair-Maru caused the death of my father. You might say that Family has become something of a fixation for me."

That had ended all further questions, and Lieutenant Tilly Pennysmith found herself filling the berth of a key bridge officer on *Hightower*, her oddities all but forgotten, anachronistic holo lenses and all. Of course her own feelings about Saef Sinclair-Maru were not nearly so clear cut—nor so negative—as she had led Attic to believe... and now she was about to sit across a dining table from him and somehow maintain a façade of vengeful hatred her fellow crew now expected.

As Pennysmith dressed for dinner she contemplated a course of action. She possessed little facility for deceit, and though she harbored complex feelings for the captain, hatred was no longer part of the admixture.

After she surveyed her reflection for a moment, Pennysmith opened a small jewel box among her scant possessions. She drew out the three glittering decorations that birthed such shameful vanity in her. Bestowed upon her by Admiral Fisker herself, these three medals, taken together, had only been awarded to less than a dozen Fleet officers in the last century. She had not worn them in the weeks since that glorious day Admiral Fisker placed them upon her lapel, and in part that was due to an old memory of Saef Sinclair-Maru and a decoration he had received back on Battersea, years before.

Tilly Pennysmith cast her mind back as she carefully placed the three cherished emblems upon her uniform, remembering Battersea, remembering a different decoration, remembering her own burning hatred.

It is difficult to describe the sensation one feels watching a wealthy young commander in the Battersea System Guard receiving a prestigious decoration for killing—killing!—one's father.

Pennysmith remembered the scene well, as then-Commander Saef Sinclair-Maru had received the medal from the governor's hand. The hatred she had felt that day would likely have burned on and on, despite the edicts of Pennysmith's faith, but for one unlikely encounter.

She eased back and regarded the row of gleaming decorations, running a finger across their silky faces, trying to remember that fellow's name back on Battersea... Alan? Yes, *Alan*. He was one of Tilly's coreligionists, a rating in the Battersea System Guard, and the only witness to observe Saef Sinclair-Maru walk straight from the adulation of his fellow officers, straight out to the nearby bridge alone. Alan explained to her that he had only followed Saef because he was curious. He watched as Saef Sinclair-Maru tore the new medal from his own chest and cast it into the Avon River, clearly disgusted.

That account from Alan served to suspend Tilly Pennysmith's anger, slowly replacing it with an obsessive curiosity, and that curiosity came to influence every part of her life. While she saw Saef as a pawn in the Sinclair-Maru machinations, Tilly pursued her own Fleet career in the teeth of her family's objections, striving also against the prejudice within Fleet.

Her years of hardship and ceaseless labor found their reward, not at the hand of Admiral Fisker, but at the word of Captain Saef Sinclair-Maru. The day he had accepted her into the bridge crew of *Tanager,* her loftiest dreams were realized: Weapons officer in a combat command, serving under the inexplicable human inspiration of her entire Fleet career.

Pennysmith blushed as she thought back to a moment on *Tanager's* bridge, a moment where violent death seemed moments away. She had felt the need to break her years of silence, to tell Saef some hint of the truth she carried. That impending death never arrived, and the embarrassing moment of disclosure was narrowly averted.

Lieutenant Tilly Pennysmith looked again at her reflection and the three gleaming acknowledgments of her service. She had earned those medals by her own commitment, her own blood, as she destroyed an enemy vessel pursuing Saef in Delta Three system. Could she do less than defend him now?

As she stared at her reflection, the pallor on the face that looked back at her spoke the truth: dinner-table duplicity certainly did not number among her accomplishments.

Through the years of their shared commission, *Hightower's* officers spared little expense on the comforts and appointments of their wardroom. It bore a tasteful, traditional character of muted wealth, and their meals benefitted from the services of a steward and a pair of young mids, both preceding their first term in command school.

Tilly Pennysmith joined her fellow officers at the broad table, each clad in their best uniforms, and for a moment Pennysmith felt she was back in command school herself, the outsider with holo lenses and "absurd" beliefs. A moment later, Pennysmith observed more than one of her fellow officers darting surprised glances at the glittering decorations adorning her uniform, and an entirely different sort of disquiet touched her.

Captain Sinclair-Maru entered the wardroom with Auditor Tenroo and his cox'n, Chief Maru, in his wake, and for a moment Tilly writhed internally. She knew the invitation had not included Chief Maru, and only ten places were set upon the broad dining table. At that instant Chief Maru peeled off, disappearing into the adjoining scullery with the steward, and Pennysmith exhaled where she stood, schooling her face into stillness.

The young mids appeared, resplendent and serious-looking in their crisp white jackets, seating officers and offering aperitifs, while Lieutenant Wycherly provided the introductions to the two officers Saef had not previously met. "Commander Attic could not attend, sadly," Wycherly began. "He promised assistance to the dog watch." Saef murmured something courteous sounding that Pennysmith could not quite hear, and Wycherly went on, "The others you have met, Captain, but may I make known to you, Lieutenant Alsop, Tech officer, and Lieutenant Dubois, Gunnery officer."

"A pleasure, gentlemen," Saef said, as both officers offered shallow bows. "And allow me to introduce Auditor Tenroo. He accompanies *Hightower* in his official capacity; his first float."

Pennysmith heard the chorus of greetings for the auditor, but few eyes looked away from Saef. They joined Wycherly in the traditional toasts—Emperor, Honor, Fleet—and Pennysmith merely wet her lips with the smoky liquor, trying to interpret the subtle currents she detected around the table. Her gaze shifted to catch sight of the cloak-clad Chief Maru leaning against the scullery doorway, a red fruit in her hand. Chief Maru took a bite from the fruit, but her cool eyes never wavered, seeming to sift Pennysmith's motives to their confused core. Pennysmith turned back to the table as she heard Lieutenant Ash raise his voice: "When I heard of your action, Captain—I mean, seizing *Aurora* and using her to extract your Marines . . . it was the completest thing, sir. Like a vid-drama."

Pennysmith scanned the faces around the table: Wycherly, frowning down at his glass, Dubois smirking, Brogan-Moore looking at Ash with a mocking twist to her lips. Pennysmith couldn't see Alsop's or Commander Jamila's faces as Saef said, "It was a fortunate choice."

"A fortune of choice," Ensign Belfort blurted, then blushed deeply and gulped his drink looking down. Lieutenant Dubois half-smothered a snort of laughter as Auditor Tenroo smiled, looking uncertainly from face to face.

Saef nodded, musing. "Yes, that as well. War is only sustained by both blood and treasure."

Pennysmith saw the opening, knew this was her moment to draw blood, set her spike and cement her place in *Hightower*, but she could not do it. Her mouth opened but no words would emerge.

Then Wycherly spoke, his hooded eyes fixed on Tilly, a twist to his lips. "You received decorations for your actions in the midst of the fortunate choice, did you not, Pennysmith?"

Her mouth felt dry as she forced herself to look from Wycherly to Saef, schooling her face to severity. "Yes. It was fortunate for *some*. It cost others all they possessed."

Tilly's eyes blurred. She knew the words were unjust as she spoke them, and she did not wish to see the look on Saef's face. She sensed Ash's agitation and Brogan-Moore's eyebrows raised appreciatively.

Commander Yazmin Jamila stepped into the breach of good manners, seemingly a bit of an outsider herself. "So far in this war there's been an overabundance of Fleet blood spilled," she said in a firm voice, looking into the glass in her hand for a moment before looking up into the eyes of her fellow officers, and then at Saef. "And you, Captain, were the first to show we could get back a little of our own—blood *or* treasure."

"Exactly!" Lieutenant Ash affirmed, thumping his fist upon the heavy tabletop.

"A glass with you, Captain?" Jamila said, lifting her glass.

"Thank you, Commander," Saef said, lifting his glass a moment before joining Commander Jamila and Lieutenant Ash in a drink.

Pennysmith swept the visible officers, seeing no other joining the toast. Wycherly looked on with a tolerant smile, while Brogan-Moore and Dubois seemed affronted. Ensign Belfort glanced uncertainly between Lieutenant Ash and Dubois just as the steward led a serving dumb-mech out from the scullery, its flattened bonnet supporting a heavy tray loaded with an impressive selection of culinary delights. Pennysmith saw Chief Maru slipping a small instrument back within the folds of her cloak, watching the dumb-mech's progress with a blank look, her eyes flickering.

The mids swept in to serve plates artfully arranged with the best of the wardroom's private stores, and conversation subsided to mostly alimentary topics, and it seemed the crisis passed.

Commander Jamila followed a thread begun by the captain, discussing the nature of rebellions in general. "Historically, doesn't it seem most rebellions require some kind of oppressed underclass to exploit?" she said, sipping from her glass and looking across her fellow officers. "I mean, agitators get among the underclass and...well, agitate; highlight how unfair everything is until the underclass explodes."

Lieutenant Ash nodded his head enthusiastically, swallowing a bite of food. "And the Imperium solved that problem centuries ago, right? We *choose* our class. There's no underclass to exploit."

Captain Sinclair-Maru interjected, "How about nursing griev-ances from the past?"

At the captain's words, Pennysmith immediately thought of heavyworlders, and their old history of neglect by the Imperium, but she seemed alone in that interpretation, unless that frown on Yazmin Jamila's face communicated memories of the past.

"We've only two real classes in the Imperium now," Brogan-Moore said. "And demi-cits have held the choice to promote since the Yung Dynasty began, so anyone can choose their class. They'd have to think back five hundred years to scrounge up a past grievance."

"If you'll pardon me," Tenroo said, raising his voice and rest-ing his fork, "not all demi-cits feel they really have a choice at all. Many, ah, feel the cards are stacked against them from birth, and their supposed *choice* is no choice at all; just an invitation to die young."

"Absurd," Brogan-Moore said, only softening it by adding, "If you'll pardon me, Auditor."

"Oh yes? Perhaps you are correct, ah, Lieutenant. May I ask though, how many Vested Citizens do you know who began life in the domicile pods...a demi-cit from birth?" Tenroo inquired, and Pennysmith saw the captain look on with a troubled line between his eyes.

Brogan-Moore flushed slightly, her eyes glittering, but Lieutenant Ash cut in, "I've known a couple. There was an Engineering chief on *Leopard* who began in the pods. Seemed happy enough."

Ensign Belfort blithely redirected the conversation by asking about *Leopard*'s fighting qualities, and Pennysmith observed the lines of Captain Sinclair-Maru's face smooth out.

Pennysmith picked at the deviled venison heart, ignored the crayfish butter pilaf, and wondered why Gunnery Lieutenant Dubois did not seize the moment to verbally spar with Saef over the captain's earlier "ridiculous" gunnery comments.

In Pennysmith's view, the meal progressed better than she had feared. The captain had not suffered a mortal blow, nor given the antagonistic faction much to hang their resentment upon, yet Pennysmith had done her part to gain acceptance from that very faction. Still, the currents of power within *Hightower* seemed almost indecipherable, incomprehensible to her.

What did they hope to achieve?

Auditor Tenroo's mild voice had been speaking for a few moments before Tilly Pennysmith perceived the direction of his speech, faint alarm bells beginning to ring within her.

"...so *Hightower*, this vast vessel, has never before—er—engaged in action with the enemy, then?" Tenroo inquired, looking from Wycherly to Dubois.

"Expedition carriers have not been—" Dubois began somewhat defensively when Wycherly sharply cut him off.

"No, Auditor, we have not as yet. Why do you ask?" Pennysmith felt a clench in her stomach as she read the gleam in Wycherly's eyes.

Surely Tenroo could not be such a fool...

Tenroo chewed a tender morsel, swallowing, his brow wrinkled with thought. "Then you must all be gratified by the Admiralty's particular selection of such a captain, even as you venture out against our foes; am I correct?"

Saef evidently saw the disaster looming ahead now too, turning to stare coldly at the oblivious auditor seated beside him.

Brogan-Moore's mouth curved into a wicked, deceptive smile as she said, "Do you mean we should be gratified because the Admiralty selected a frigate captain with no carrier experience for us?"

"N-no, perhaps I am not—" Tenroo began, only to be cut off.

"Or because they selected a captain who had his skin saved by his executive officer in his only prior Fleet combat action?"

"Oh—no, no, Lieutenant," Tenroo shook his head. "No such uncharitable, or technical thoughts entered my—my...goodness, no. I have little knowledge of such things. I merely speak of the—the renowned fighting prowess of the captain's Family."

Pennysmith closed her eyes. He was, in fact, that sort of fool.

Lieutenant Dubois ineffectively checked a bark of laughter, and Brogan-Moore's smile became a sneer. "Of course. Why didn't we think of it? The history book Family—the lethal Sinclair-Maru—will show us the way."

There was a dawning comprehension of a false step on Tenroo's face, but in his uncertainty he had a final injury to inflict.

"I seem to have misunder—I was given to understand that among warlike Houses, the Sinclair-Maru..." Tenroo stammered into silence as he turned to regard Saef's forbidding visage at his side.

Of those seated around the table, Pennysmith alone knew Tenroo could not be echoing a brag he gleaned from Saef, while even Lieutenant Ash gazed at Saef with ill-concealed disdain. Every one of *Hightower*'s officers, save Pennysmith herself, suddenly *knew* their green captain was the worst sort of bounder, any inkling of goodwill extinguished before it could truly ignite.

Chapter 22

"While it is now fashionable to sneer when speaking of Emperor Yung's reforms within the Halls of Learning, my learned colleagues seek to diminish that one guiding cultural value, while offering nothing at all to replace it."

—Dr. Ramsay Stirling Attenborough, *Ivory Tower Follies*

IN THE DARKNESS, DOZENS OF DIRTY, WEARY IMPERIAL LEGION-naires took cover within a foliage-choked drainage channel on the southern fringe of a bombed-out metropolitan area. They learned a few hard truths in painful succession as green tracers arced over the intervening highway and whipped about their heads, even as nuclear fires flared and died far above the clouds, and intermittent death cries shrieked into silence among the undergrowth.

Corporal Kyle Whiteside retained a small pocket of rationality somewhere within his psyche, and in this pocket a dry little voice itemized the terrors besetting them: a heavy weapon position raked them from the northwest, someone in the heavens above (probably their Fleet allies) were in the process of receiving nuclear-level bad news, while some *thing* ran loose within their confused ranks, horribly executing Legionnaires, one by one.

Kyle had even seen the thing that stalked among them for a moment in the last glow of nuclear fire, though he could not yet fathom or accept that vision: a dumb-mech bearing crude metal mandibles and what appeared to be a central ram blade, like the spade-tongue of a predatory arthropod, gutting a Legionnaire.

Sergeant Avery Reardon evidently put the rational part of his mind to much better use in the midst of all this. A moment after the flare from above died out, the mortar Molo thumped out three more rounds, bracketing the enemy's distant auto-cannon. Seconds later, Reardon appeared beside Pippi and Kyle, yelling and shoving at them. "Go! Move, damn it! Across the highway. Move, move, move!"

Kyle, Pippi, and a dozen other Legionnaires stumbled up onto the exposed surface, hurrying through the darkness, feeling that enemy fire would reach out and cut them down at any moment. Kyle heard Major Chetwynd's voice babbling and ordering in shrill tones as Sergeant Reardon clearly ignored the Pathfinder officer. Kyle ran, his armor seeming to pull him down as he tried to accelerate, scrambling over the center median and running on.

In moments, Pippi, Kyle, their Molo mechs, and a collection of various Legionnaires reached the cover of a mostly intact structure on the north side of the highway. Pippi adjusted to the change more quickly than Kyle. "You and you," she said to a pair of Legionnaires, "cover flanks." They didn't debate her peremptory command, scuttling to either corner of their erstwhile cover.

Kyle belatedly flipped his tactical eyepiece down from his helmet, looking back across the highway as another ragged line of Legionnaires came staggering through the potential kill zone. He imagined what Avery Reardon might do next. As the Legionnaires reached the cover of the building, Kyle tagged four of them. "We need to clear this structure." He pointed his carbine at the adjoining wall. "Go there, around the east wall, and look for an entrance." The last known position of the enemy auto-cannon lay to the northwest, and Kyle wanted cover between the Legionnaires and that heavy firepower, if it survived their small mortar salvo.

One of the Legionnaires hesitated as if to argue, but Kyle ignored him, turning to his Molo, Fang, allowing his carbine to dangle from its sling. As Fang settled, the mass driver pivoting up from its torso, the four Legionnaires turned away, hefting their carbines and filtering through the darkness.

"What you doing, Kyle?" Pippi asked.

Kyle nodded across the highway as another mob of Legionnaires emerged from the drainage channel and began their dash across the open. "If that...that *thing* comes out, I'm going to put it down."

Kyle's attention focused within his tactical eyepiece, the gleaming crosshairs of Fang's mass driver panning across the kill zone, but from the corner of his eye he saw Pippi look from him, to their western flank, and back. "Maybe better for you covering that gods-damned auto-cannon, eh, Kyle?"

Kyle hesitated a moment, thinking, then reluctantly nodded. "Maybe you're right." The auto-cannon—a skimcar mount, probably—could shred a file of Legionnaires trying to cross the highway, while that—that mechanized slayer picked off one at a time. The fact that the mech simply horrified Kyle was not the finest tactical rationale.

Kyle led his Fang over to the west flank of their covering structure, slipping past the Legionnaires hunkered there and setting Fang in place just as another large group broke from cover to cross the highway.

The sudden strobe of a distant muzzle flash jolted Kyle's heart rate sharply upward, even before the string of green tracers scorched by, a stone's throw out. Kyle felt himself quivering as he bumped up the magnification on his targeting optic, the twin thump and chatter of the auto-cannon almost drowning out the sound of cries behind him. Kyle centered on the indistinct shape of a skimcar, chancing a ranging beam as the distant auto-cannon roared. *Ranged, centered and . . .* Kyle fired, Fang's chassis bucking as the mass driver blasted its hypersonic penetrator across the distance.

A few fat sparks burst up from the distant darkness, and the auto-cannon fell silent. Kyle scrambled back behind cover, turning to see the bodies of three Legionnaires sprawled in the highway, a fair mob of figures now filling the narrow area around Pippi, covering behind the structure. Among their number, Sergeant Avery Reardon moved, his Molo at his heels. Kyle actuated the mass driver's transport mode, folding it back into Fang's torso.

As Kyle rejoined the others, Reardon looked up, his left eye covered by his tactical eyepiece. "Did you get it?" Reardon asked.

Kyle slid down to his haunches, resting his armored back against Fang's metallic carapace, his heart rate beginning to subside. He positioned his carbine across his chest, resting both arms over the receiver. "I'm not sure, Avery. I put a round into it, I think, and it stopped firing." Reardon nodded, looking at the crowd of Legionnaires jammed against the south face of the structure.

"We need to get to a better position, Kyle."

Kyle was about to inquire about Major Chetwynd and then thought better of it, saying instead, "I sent four shooters around to clear this structure. Not sure if they're back yet."

Pippi thrust her helmeted head between the obstructing shoulders of some interposing Legionnaires. "They back," she answered, evidently able to intercept every word despite the clanking, shuffling, murmuring crowd of warfighters. "They say four walls, one roof."

"Well, well," Avery said. "All that? Sounds ideal; fully equipped, even."

A flurry of small-arms fire erupted on the far side of the highway, back in the overgrown drainage channel. Kyle Whiteside and Avery Reardon looked over as four figures backed from cover, firing full-auto bursts into the channel as they back pedaled. "Pathfinders." Avery Reardon said it like a curse, just as the farthest figure jerked, his arms windmilling one moment before he disappeared, snatched into the dark channel as if by an invisible hand. The other three Pathfinders turned and ran, crossing the highway in headlong flight.

"That one's Major Chetwynd," Kyle said as the Pathfinder clambered over the highway divider.

"Yes," Reardon agreed, then turned to Kyle. "Get everyone inside our delightful structure here, now. I prefer to hand the major an established fact, if possible."

Kyle surged up to his feet, and Pippi joined him in pushing everyone around the eastern wall, following the obscured footpath to the door-less entrance. The Legionnaires filed into what must have previously been some sort of vehicle repair bay, everyone finding a piece of wall, slowly filling the bay with armored bodies.

Kyle stood at the entrance, awaiting Reardon and the Pathfinders, scanning across the shattered scene sprawling to the north. Almost to himself, Kyle murmured, "What happened to this place?"

"Kinetic strikes, no?" Pippi said, stepping beside Kyle and looking out. "From orbit, yes?"

Really? But why? What military target had existed here that brought such a thorough bombardment? It didn't add up.

As the thought fully formed, Avery Reardon came trotting around the corner, his Molo mech and the Pathfinders following close behind.

Major Chetwynd seemed more than a little shaken to Kyle's

eyes, but he channeled this into fresh bluster. "What the devil do you mean by this, Sergeant?" Chetwynd demanded. "I never ordered a move across the highway."

Avery sat back atop his Molo and rested his carbine across his knees. "Didn't you, Major? As I recall, sir, you ordered us all to advance toward our objective. Your loyal Legionnaires seized the initiative and *advanced*. I tagged along, of course."

"*Advanced?*" Chetwynd barked.

"Yes, sir. As you have said, our objective is north of the highway. Behold! So are we. They're like tigers, these Legionnaires, sir. Hungry for action."

One of the "tigers" sprawled nearby turned a snort of laughter into an unconvincing cough.

In the dark, Kyle couldn't see the major's heightened color, but he could well imagine it. "I've had enough of your attitude, Sergeant." The major turned sharply away. "We'll cover here tonight and continue northward at first light."

The major looked slowly around him, his tactical eyepiece providing grainy luminance to the dark interior. That one-eyed gaze settled upon Kyle Whiteside. "Corporal, you'll select two Legionnaires and establish a listening post on the north side of that tumbled building about two hundred paces out."

Before Kyle could speak, Avery Reardon said, "Sorry, Major, the corporal is needed here."

"I'm not speaking to you, Sergeant. Keep your mouth shut."

"Respectfully, sir—" Reardon began, but Major Chetwynd wasn't having it.

"Sergeant!"

"Respectfully, sir," Reardon pressed on. "Can *you* repair a Molo, sir?"

"I'll not tell you again, Sergeant!"

"Then tomorrow you head north without Molo Rangers, sir."

Major Chetwynd's enraged quivering was visible even in the darkness. "Your Rangers will obey orders and proceed north, as I command."

"Of course, Major, of course," Reardon said. "We will all obey, but our Molo mechs will remain here—unless the corporal can service and repair them. Corporal Whiteside is necessary for that duty, if you want to have our heavy weapons with you tomorrow as we march."

Kyle did not understand the game Reardon played, but it seemed for a moment that Major Chetwynd would not—could not—relent.

Without a glance at Kyle Whiteside or Avery Reardon, Major Chetwynd turned to one of his Pathfinders. "Robarts, pick two Legionnaires and establish a listening post."

Robarts sounded less than enthusiastic as he said, "Yes, Major," moving to select his fellows and striding to the doorway.

Major Chetwynd quietly observed as the trio scuttled across to the designated ruin, disappearing into the darkened rubble. He turned away, gathered his remaining Pathfinders, and ordered the other Legionnaires out of a small separate room, using it as his erstwhile HQ.

As the gathered mass of Legionnaires began fumbling for ration packs, murmuring quiet conversations or stretching out to rest, Avery removed his helmet and leaned close to Kyle Whiteside. "You should probably attend to those vital Molo repairs now, Corporal."

"Which vital repairs?" Kyle murmured back.

"Get creative, Kyle."

Kyle shrugged and set about popping the maintenance hatches on each of the remaining Molo mechs as the other Molo Rangers mutely observed. While he checked the diagnostic screen on Avery's Molo, Kyle spoke in a low voice: "I could have just gone out for Chetwynd's silly listening post."

"You're far too useful to me for that, Kyle," Reardon murmured back. "Those three are most certainly as good as dead, poor sods."

Kyle looked up sharply at Reardon, locking eyes for a moment, before Kyle turned back to the Molo, his emotions conflicted.

It seemed Reardon's prescience proved true, when some time a later a flurry of muted gunshots echoed through the ruins, startling every Legionnaire that had managed to doze off. It was only then that Kyle noticed Reardon's Molo positioned in a direct line with the sole entrance to their modest shelter, Cuthbert's mass driver deployed, aiming through the doorway.

Major Chetwynd shoved through the murmuring clutch of Legionnaires to reach the doorway, flipping his eyepiece down and scanning the darkened backdrop. They all saw the dim outline of his helmet shifting slowly as he looked for some sign of the commotion, but there remained nothing to see.

"Poor Robarts," Reardon said, and Kyle could only agree, feeling that sickening combination of relief and guilt; it could have been—should have been—Kyle out there instead of Robarts, his body cooling, his life taken in a violent instant.

The three reluctant Legionnaires Chetwynd sent out as relief confirmed what they already knew, hurrying back soon after leaving: Robarts and the other two Legionnaires were dead. The death wounds they described—horrific disemboweling slashes—brought to Kyle's mind the spade-tongue of a predatory arthropod.

Corporal Kyle Whiteside looked at Pippi and Reardon and looked away. He knew he was not alone in wondering how their small force could survive long enough to even reach their semi-mythical objective. They were being hunted, and Kyle, at least, should already be dead.

Chapter 23

"Before taking the throne and founding the Yung Dynasty, Yung the First was fond of saying that no genus of mammal ever improved as a species in the absence of effective predators. The more barbaric aspects of the Honor Code are the natural outgrowth of that philosophy."

—Everest Compline, *Reflections*

YOUNG INGA'S DAYS AND NIGHTS WITHIN HAWKSGAARD REMAINED overfull, particularly as she added hours of new training in the true Sembrada combatives to all her other duties and classes. Traditional classroom time began her schedule, followed by blade training, unarmed combatives, and small-arms training. Low-grav work and small unit operations occurred on alternating days, while every day contained brief conditioning periods in heavy grav, though less than her classmates. Despite the physical and mental pressures, Inga found some sources of satisfaction.

Her favorite moments began to emerge in the unlikely location of Dry Arsenal One, a vast, secure chamber in the heart of Hawksgaard's storage level where disused, antique weapon systems and equipment lay crated and stacked in immense rows and columns. Creeping through, among and over the stacks of Dry Arsenal One, Inga discovered a predatory aspect of her nature that she had not previously perceived. She came to discover that she possessed a rare skill in hunting people, and she found that she loved it.

Her first trip into the cold, dark arsenal had tested Inga's new fear-control techniques, marching along with her classmates and a clutch of prior students who now served as simulated foes. On that occasion, Inga had drawn her training pistol right along with Jurr Difdah and the other students, chambering a round and swapping a full twenty-round magazine into her pistol. She had secured her bump helmet with its bulbous mesh eye coverings, suitable for protecting from training blades and training munitions.

Fully prepared, her mouth dry with tension, she had moved out with her fellow students, creeping through the maze of stacks, hunting the darkness for their foes. On that first engagement, Inga and her fellow students were allowed only small hand lights to pierce the darkness, rather than dark-vision optics, and they had already received enough instruction to know the paradox involved.

To *act* upon a target, one must *observe* and *orient* upon said target, and observing targets by employing visible light in a zero-light environment often made the hunter an immediate target themselves. As a result, Inga and her fellow students crept through the maze as a compact unit, pistols poised, their lights flicking on and off, trying to embody all the classroom instruction they had absorbed, while also struggling to maintain the fearless state of the Deep Man.

Despite their precautions, as their group reached an intersection among the stacks, Inga saw a flash of blinding light and heard a series of rapid, cracking reports, followed by the meaty sound of training rounds impacting flesh. Jurr Difdah and another student served as momentary, living sandbags for Inga as their bodies absorbed a flurry of incoming fire, each impact ejecting phosphorescent powder from the training bullets even as it signaled the hits electronically. Inga and her classmates survived only moments longer in that first exercise, hammered down by accurate fire before they could *observe*, let alone *act*.

But more exercises followed, and Inga learned quickly. After one such early session in Dry Arsenal One, Inga found herself unaccountably mesmerized by words she learned from Devlin Sinclair-Maru's old book, *Integrity Mirror: Preparation for conflict is first psychology.*

Psychology.

Inga recalled other sections within the Family canon speaking of psychology, and flipped through the pages until she found what she sought: the legendary cofounder of the Sinclair-Maru said all combat could be distilled down to the management of fear, movement, *psychology,* and the application of energy.

How could psychology assist her in the dark battles of Dry Arsenal One? Thus far she focused upon her shooting skills and her mastery of the Deep Man almost to the exclusion of all else. If psychology represented such a valuable tool, why had they received no instruction in its application? Or had they...? Did Devlin mean the psychology of the foe, or one's own psychology?

What precisely *was* psychology, anyway?

Inga explored possible meanings in the context of combat, reading definitions and applying them to her experiences. What is a mindset? The set of a mind, the entrenchment of expectations, assumptions... She began to feel a strange excitement, as if she stepped within some secret trove. Assumptions, expectations, intentions—these were like fear and need; they were levers of manipulation. She would exploit them in her foes, and manage them within her own mind.

In her next engagement, as the others prepared their weapons, Inga quietly, resolutely drew her blade instead, leaving her pistol holstered. As her teammates began their hunt, Inga filtered silently off on her own, feeling her way carefully through the stacks. Occasional flickers of light penetrated from her teammates' position, and Inga utilized the glimmers to hurry along, her blade high and poised to strike.

As she approached an intersection, intermittently lighted in the flash of her teammates' hand lights, Inga heard the first muffled shots. Despite the sudden tension building in Inga's muscles, she perceived the change a blade wrought in her mindset. Rather than assuming a shooting stance and cautiously edging around the corner, Inga was forced by the limitations of a blade to rely upon mobility—speed—to close with unseen opponents.

She rounded the corner in a smooth, silent rush, the absolute darkness rent by sudden spears of light. In the flashes of illumination, two figures loomed up before her, covering among cargo crates as they fired steadily into Inga's clustered teammates. The exposed openness of their undefended backs imparted a sudden voluptuous thrill to Inga, even as she slashed out. The training system scored her hits as soon as her blade impacted, but she gave finishing cuts, making her opponents' fate inarguable, moving on as the two older foes muttered curses at the violence of her bruising attacks.

Inga did not pause, moving fast toward the sounds of shots still ringing out, a steady glare of hand lights ahead. In that illumination she saw the faint profile of her last two opponents a stone's throw away, their left flank exposed to her attack. They stood well back from the junction before them, their backs close to a smooth wall of containers as they slowly sidestepped toward Inga, alternately firing at a target invisible down the bisecting pathway. Their position against the stack denied any chance for a back attack from deeper darkness.

Inga covered the distance in a liquid rush, her blade held two-handed and high. The nearest of her two opponents detected Inga a moment before Inga's blade lashed down. He uttered a startled yelp but pivoted in a flash, firing blindly even as the blade struck him, his close-range shot painfully thumping Inga just below her collarbone.

Inga took a knee, breathing hard, "dead" for the purpose of the exercise, but strangely exhilarated as the simulation swiftly came to its violent conclusion. She had sampled the first delightful fruit of the predator, and her inner eye felt suddenly open to a red-tinged world of possibilities.

At the all-clear signal, Inga rose and made her way alone back through the stacks, brushing the phosphorescent dust from her "wound," her mind whirling with possibilities—no, more than her conscious mind and its thoughts. She *felt* a burgeoning new identity that thrilled her: the hunter.

How shall I change the set of mind? How shall I hunt them next?

Inga became suddenly aware of a presence pacing beside her, all but invisible in the gloom. The quiet hiss of the instructor's voice seemed to issue a handsbreadth from Inga's ear. "Why did you choose to employ your blade, Inga Maru? For the purpose of stealth?"

Inga knew the instructors monitored their training sessions, seeing all through tactical eyepieces that pierced the darkness, but they had generally held their critiques and questions until the after-action review at day's end.

"No, my lord," Inga said as they continued walking toward the entrance of Dry Arsenal One. "I did this to . . . to change my mind."

Inga thought she heard the coloring of a smile in the instructor's voice as he said, "This is a good answer, Inga Maru. You have opened a new road. It is a start."

It was a start indeed.

As the training days proceeded, Inga's class trooped down to the dark bowels of Dry Arsenal One again and again to conduct a dozen variations of simulated combat. At times the weapons changed, the objectives changed, the teams or even the rules. Of course, Inga cheated whenever possible, and for some reason the instructors continued to allow her transgressions, though they must have perceived at least some of her various sins.

For the purpose of hunting her fellow students, Inga discovered a variety of growing preferences as her experience grew, day after day. She found she greatly preferred a carbine or submachine gun to the pistol, and discovered a particular affinity for grenades, when such simulated weapons were allowed in a given exercise. Many times her fellow trainees heard the telltale thump and clatter of a tossed grenade a moment before the kill-tone and bright flash of red light indicated their demise, but this embodied merely the least of her new proficiencies.

Inga cast her mind back to Battersea and disarming the innumerable bullies of her childhood largely through manipulation, learning the cloddish thoughts of the urchins and toughs, exposing their hooks and hungers, and exploiting them. Upon discovering the *psychology* of actual battle, she was exhilarated to find herself strangely at home. Each new engagement became a laboratory, the stacks of Dry Arsenal One a maze for hapless rats for her experimentation. Whether Inga ended a particular exercise triumphant, or riddled with bumps and welts, her art advanced, her test subjects unwittingly confirming or refuting some fresh hypothesis for her sole benefit. Triumph, however, became her momentary obsession... and thus, the cheating.

The dusty old workshop she had discovered her first days within Hawksgaard now gleamed under her care, its scant equipment supplemented by new finds looted from rubbish bins or "borrowed" from poorly monitored maintenance carts. In its confines, Inga modified such equipment as she could, always seeking a new edge.

When field-stripping her training pistol, she noted four vents formed about halfway down the barrel's length, figuring these served to reduce the velocity of training munitions and thereby minimize injury potential among trainees. To Inga, increases in velocity meant increases in range, and decreased time of flight. Filling two of the ports seemed a happy medium; the pistol still operated smoothly and Inga immediately noticed the snappiness of recoil after her modification. She made a mental note to avoid blasting any classmates in sensitive areas—unless it was Jurr Difdah in her sights.

Modifying her training pistol provided little challenge compared to her efforts on their issued grenade simulators. Their grenades emitted a bright flash and the kill-tone to simulate detonation, but like all their training munitions, the actual kill-scoring signal transmitted invisibly to nearby targets for seamless hit adjudication.

Inga pilfered, smuggled, and tinkered with numerous grenades before she managed to boost the power of their kill signal without burning out the sensitive internal circuitry. The end result she found to be quite gratifying.

Her other "cheats" largely involved bending the Family rules of engagement, and she employed most of these techniques when the instructors called for "fox hunt" exercises in Dry Arsenal One.

A fox hunt involved one student on the run through the maze of stacks, while remaining students worked together to hunt down the "fox" within a specified time. Perhaps because Inga rejected the usual fox strategies of concealment or headlong flight, she served as the "fox" with disproportionate regularity. This suited Inga beautifully.

On one notable fox hunt, Inga mentally prepared her full suite of techniques and tools, though limited to using only her pistol as her weapon. At the signal, she lit out through the stacks, running fast, her hand light illuminating the path ahead in half-second flashes every few steps, though her foes all lay waiting their start signal behind her. After penetrating a reasonable distance, knowing her hunters surely observed the telltale flicker of her hand light through the maze, Inga killed her light, quickly retracing her steps, moving blindly through the darkness. She felt her way to a sharp right-hand corner that led up to the hunters' start point; a path they must follow to enter the stacks. She fumbled a pistol magazine from her belt pouch, ejected a single training round into her palm, and crushed its phosphorescent tip in a shallow recess between two crates. As she backed away, slipping the pistol mag back into its pouch, the faint glow between the crates served as a dim beacon, visible only in a direct line.

Just then, with no audible signal, the hunters began their pursuit, the strobe of their hand lights flashing madly as they advanced, quickly drawing nearer. Inga drew her pistol, switched it to her left hand, and nestled tight against a corner crate, leveling the weapon down the long pathway where her enemies must advance.

She did not seek the Deep Man. She felt no fear. As she drew a bead down the empty path, she felt only muted excitement.

Two hand lights appeared suddenly, their beams stabbing into Inga's left eye just as she fired two quick shots. She ducked back, hearing the snap and buzz of return fire even as the stacks plunged back into darkness. She didn't see the phosphorescent splash of a hit, so she probably hadn't scored an impact, but it didn't matter. She had appeared where they had not expected her—close to their entry point—and she had momentarily conditioned them to avoid using their lights.

Within the utter darkness, she backed quickly away from the corner, her unfazed right eye marking the dim beacon between the crates. She tucked in tight behind a covering crate, only her right eye and shoulder projecting out, and raised her pistol, waiting. She heard the hint of motion ahead but her vision remained locked on the dim point of phosphorescence... ready, breathing easily. The blot of light suddenly disappeared, occluded by an invisible, advancing figure. Instantly, Inga triggered two quick shots, seeing the glowing splash of impacts a millisecond before she ducked back. Searing hand lights illuminated the stacks, blind return fire ringing out for a quick moment, at least one round impacting Inga's cover with a sharp crack. But they had learned caution, they hadn't guessed her position, and their lights went dark again.

Without hesitation, Inga slipped from behind the crate, orienting on her dim beacon ahead and rushing forward on her tiptoes through the dark space, the soft sounds of movement marking the retreat of her "disabled" victim trudging their way out of the exercise. She knew her other opponents remained, standing somewhere very near to her in the dark. She continued her movement until she reached the terminating stack where her initial phosphorescent beacon lay, turning to press her back against the glowing mark. She held her pistol ready, listening. The faint sounds around her: the whisper of a breath, the subtle grate of a boot shifting—these built a gradual picture of her battle space.

Suddenly a light bloomed ahead, lashing out away from her, then falling dark. The flash image burned into Inga's retinas: two foes advancing fifteen paces ahead, their light spearing Inga's original position, three foes much closer, all facing away, their exposed backs so inviting. At this moment Inga could slip away, sneak back to the starting point, and wait out the time limit, assuring her win.

Instead, Inga quietly drew her blade, switching her pistol to her left hand, easing forward in the blackness, the blade held short. Following the fading image burn in her retinas, she slid up to the approximate position of her left-most foe and thrust her blade, half expecting the blade to cut mere air. Instead, the blade jolted an oath from her invisible opponent and sounded the chirp of an adjudicated kill.

The surprised questioning whisper close to her right drew Inga's backhanded swing. Again the blade struck sharp, marking another kill. The scuffle and fresh expletive gave Inga only a moment to sidestep before her final foes overcame their doubts and illuminated the scene. As the light flared, Inga instantly fired, aiming at the two distant foes, getting a flash impression of her near opponent's startled profile in the millisecond before their light went dark.

Diving, Inga hit the deck hard, rolling as shots rang out, phosphorescent hits flashing on the deck and stacks, and striking her near foe, stitched by his own startled comrades. Inga scuttled around the nearest stack and spun, grasping the edge of a crate, the rattle of shots falling silent. She used the crate's sharp edge to orient, steadying her pistol, hearing the soft steps of her last two adversaries drawing near. Her finger found the trigger, knowing she violated another Family rule even as she squeezed, firing a dozen shots in rapid succession, fanning her aiming point across the narrow gap.

Between the reports of her own firing, Inga's keen ears detected the sharp crack of rounds striking crates, and the meaty thumps of rounds impacting flesh.

Inga dropped to a knee, changed magazines on her pistol, and only then used her hand light to peer around the corner. She felt little surprise in seeing her opponents scowling, their uniforms marked with the glowing testimony of her blind marksmanship. She felt entirely, unpleasantly surprised, however, to see Hiro Sinclair-Maru in their midst, a splash of glowing color in the center of his chest. Her thrill of victorious exultancy faded immediately.

The scowls of Inga's victims transformed as they perceived the situation, smug grins scarcely concealed. Inga stood and removed her bump helmet.

"Inga Maru," the chief instructor said, staring fixedly at her, one-eyed, his right eye covered by the objective lens of a tactical eyepiece, "you have struck a noncombatant." His hand rose to circle the glowing impact on his own chest. "Of what error are you guilty?"

Inga clenched her teeth, her blood running hot at the smirks from her fellow students. She wanted to say that she was guilty of *no* error. Any citizen who threw themselves into the middle of a pitched gun battle would receive little sympathy from an Imperial arbiter when a bullet found them. But Inga always knew the rules she willingly violated.

She swallowed her excuses. "I acted upon my targets without...proper observation."

Hiro nodded. "You fired blindly without illuminating your target area. This is an error which contravenes your training."

Inga's heat prompted her to say, "I *returned* fire, my lord."

Hiro hesitated, silent for a moment, and Inga swallowed, her mouth suddenly dry, regretting her hasty words.

"Leave us, please," Hiro said to Inga's fellow students, and they immediately trooped off through the stacks, bound for the entrance to Dry Arsenal One. As the sound and light of their departure faded away, Inga dipped into the Deep Man, combatting the sudden surge of her racing pulse. Hiro Sinclair-Maru stood silently before Inga now, invisible in the dark except for the glowing point of Inga's discomfiture there in the center of his chest. As the stretching silence seemed to grow to dire proportions, Inga detected the faint scuffle of movement to her right and checked an impulse to reach for her hand light. Hiro controlled the moment, and his tactical eyepiece provided unimpeded dark vision. Whatever occurred in their immediate space belonged to his sphere of responsibility.

A pinpoint of glowing blue increased from a speck of light hovering above Inga, quickly forming a luminescent globe that made her blink as she perceived two new figures standing close beside. In the soft glow she recognized Kai Sinclair-Maru and a stranger, both harnessed, a whip-line running from their harnesses up into the invisible blackness above.

Hiro executed a shallow bow toward Kai, turning on his heel and walking away without a word.

"I believe he disapproves," Kai said in his whispery voice, turning his attention toward Inga. "He is conflicted, child. Do you know what causes this conflict?"

"No, my lord," Inga said, sizing up the silent stranger beside Kai who seemed an unimpressive figure to Inga, too fine boned for Family or even oath-kin, and if she did not stand beside Kai in the sprawl of Dry Arsenal one, Inga would dismiss her as purely ornamental.

"He is conflicted because you demonstrate an admirable facility in the force application exercises. This would normally provide satisfaction as you absorb his excellent instruction, very natural for any teacher, you understand?"

"Yes, my lord," Inga said.

Kai smiled thinly. "Mmm, yes. But then, child, you cheat so shamelessly, and it is *this* that creates his conflict."

Since Kai asked no questions, Inga felt it safer to maintain her silence, waiting to discover her fate.

Kai glanced toward the silent woman at his side, shrugging as he turned back to Inga. "Or perhaps my continued tolerance of your cheating creates his conflict. Either way, it seems time we adjust your behavior somewhat."

Inga swallowed again, finding a fresh purchase upon the Deep Man.

Kai held up a finger. "Understand, I am not altogether displeased with your various infractions. It seems appropriate for your larger purpose here. What you must understand, child, is that great purpose does not require yet another combat specialist—even an exceptionally fine specialist. Our Family excels at creating skilled combatants, and we are oversupplied with such individuals."

Inga felt competing currents of disappointment and relief. "But I'm good at this—my lord," Inga managed to say.

"You are indeed," Kai affirmed in a placid voice. "But your

role is greater than this, and we must turn your focus to this greater purpose. That is why I have asked Deidre here to observe your talents. She will now serve to open a new field of study for you, a field that will expand your talents in a direction more suited to the Family needs."

Though she felt a sense of respite, evidently dodging punishment for her iniquities, Inga's defenses flared to life. Still, her Family training already ran deep. She looked at the silent, unimpressive woman and executed her trained bow. "My lady," she said.

"No," the woman said in a flat voice. "I am not Family. You may call me Deidre."

"Deidre," Inga said, then looked back to Kai. "When will I have time for more classes?"

Kai smiled down at Inga. "You are far advanced in many academic topics. Deidre will take you in the place of your mathematics class."

Inga found most of her academic subjects to be slow paced and tedious, so the change could scarcely fail to improve her time. "And what will I learn from Deidre?"

Deidre waved a hand upward and the blue globe of light rose gently. Inga watched it, seeing some kind of lighter-than-air drone in its silent movement, but Deidre spoke, drawing Inga's attention back down to find the hollows of Deidre's eyes hooded in shadow.

"You will learn the technicalities of deceit, girl."

Kai cleared his throat, almost invisible now in the darkness. "Hmm. Yes. A new focus for you, child. Perhaps keep you from trouble, eh? Modifying the training grenades, really? My, my, how did you ever accomplish that stroke, anyway?"

Inga looked from the patch of darkness enrobing Kai, to Deidre and back. "If you will pardon me, my lord, better not to say, I think."

Deidre chuckled dryly, looking to Kai. "You're right, Kai. She's not entirely ruined by your Sinclair-Maru nonsense." She reached out in the half-light, grabbing Inga's chin with a cold hand. "We may make something quite interesting of you, girl."

Intrigued as she was, Inga instinctively placed Deidre on the hierarchy of her new world, fitting her in a position that did not brook physical invasion. "Do not touch me, Deidre."

Deidre chuckled again, but released Inga's chin. "We will get along well, I think."

"I certainly trust it will be so," Kai said. "You will begin your training with Deidre soon."

Inga offered no reply, and a moment later, the whip-lines retracted, Deidre and Kai shooting back up into the darkness, the dim blue illumination of the drone disappearing above with them.

As Inga walked alone through the dark and silent stacks, she pondered Deidre's words, wondering what precisely defined the *technicalities of deceit.*

Chapter 24

"While the Slagger War shaped the Imperium for a time, few Houses still bear the true mark of that era's fear. Few remain bastions against extinction."

—Everest Compline, *Reflections*

AS INGA TRAILED SAEF THROUGH *HIGHTOWER*'S BRIDGE ACCESS, she could not help but contrast the moment with a similar juncture on *Tanager*. In both instances, Saef prepared to bring a vessel under his command through an N-space transition to the Delta Three system, but there all other comparisons ended. *Tanager* had carried less than one hundred crew and Marines, enclosing a volume of 3,500 Imperial tons, while *Hightower* bore thousands within its immense, 200,000-ton hull, and within those thousands teeming factions seethed.

"Commander Attic, I have the bridge," Saef said, taking over the command seat.

Inga knew she did not merely imagine a fresh current of disdain shared by Attic and many of the other officers, and this also served as a destructive contrast between *Tanager* and *Hightower*. In the three watches since the officers' fateful dinner, Saef had become a figure of barely concealed mockery, isolated through mere frosty formality, ignored whenever possible. The fact that Auditor Tenroo genuinely regretted creating the myth of Saef's insufferable Family arrogance provided neither solace nor a path to cohesion.

"The bridge is yours, Captain," Commander Attic said, moving slowly toward the bridge access, showing an inclination to hover about the periphery. Inga held her position near the access, keeping Attic under her eye, but it was not overt violence that concerned her. His presence continued a moral pressure, resisting Saef's natural connection to the bridge officers, and Saef might choose between an unpleasant scene, affirmatively evicting Attic from the bridge, or enduring the cloying lodestone of contention Attic surely embodied.

Fortunately it took only the gentle pressure of Inga asking, "Did you misplace something, Commander?" to urge him the final steps out, the access sealing behind him.

Inga turned a portion of her attention back to Saef as he began the process of an N-space transition. Another portion of her regard managed Loki...

"Lieutenant Ash, are you ready with our transition calculations?" Saef asked, looking across the members of his bridge team.

"Calculations for transition are complete, Captain," Ash said, his expression unreadable.

Saef nodded, glancing toward Tilly Pennysmith. "Weps?"

"Shield generators green. Point defenses charged, fore, aft, and dorsal missile batteries, green, Captain," Pennysmith said, covering her checklist with cool professionalism.

"Tech?"

Lieutenant Alsop didn't even shift his gaze as he said, "Engineering is ready for transition power. Heat sinks all online and green, fabs ready for transition functions."

Saef turned to regard Alsop for a moment. "Is that all, Tech?"

Lieutenant Alsop opened his mouth, shaping a short reply as the other members of the bridge team all shot surprised glances at him. He closed his mouth, shaking his head. "There—there is a minor anomaly in computation, but diagnostics are well within specifications, Captain."

Saef held Alsop in his critical regard for another moment and Inga held her breath for a weighted spell, alone knowing the likely source of the computation anomalies. "Very well, Tech," Saef said, but the point was surely made to all present.

Saef turned to Deckchief Furst at the Ops position. "Ops?"

Furst worked through his panel. "Sortie bays locked down, Marine quarterdeck reports ready for transition. All sections report ready."

"Excellent," Saef said, turning toward Comm. "Comm, signal Fleet with our transition code."

Inga knew the next step of the process, scant seconds from execution. Saef would direct Nav to power up the N-drive, that essential piece of mysterious Shaper tech. As Shaper fuel cells fed immense energy to the N-drive, *Hightower*'s vast bulk would leap into N-space, that environment where all Shaper tech took on heightened capabilities. Fabs would feverishly craft items only attainable within the scant seconds of transition. Most importantly, *Hightower* would arrive a light-year distant at the conclusion of those transiting seconds.

But Inga also remembered the hard lessons of *Tanager*, and a flat gray receptacle filled with nanotech-laden micros, programmed to operate at the moment of transition. As Saef turned to Lieutenant Ash, the Navigation and Astrogation officer, Inga wondered what fresh horrors Saef's next order might inadvertently release within the teeming warrens of *Hightower*.

Benny Mills felt a keen need to show the two new fish how an experienced hand dealt with every emerging event within the bowels of *Hightower*'s Tech section, whether it needed it or not. This was especially true as this constituted only Benny's third N-space transition since he joined *Hightower*, and he was finally senior to *someone*. The two fish took Benny's gentle badinage in good part, mostly grinning as they observed Benny's every word and deed with strangely flat eyes. The disconnect between their matching grins and lifeless eyes prompted him to joke that the two might be twins, though the female clearly revealed true lightworld genetic stock, while the male seemed fresh from a heavyworld.

They hadn't laughed at Benny's attempt at wit, but they never stopped grinning either, so he continued without compunction, sharing his insights and wisdom at every turn. They comprised a largely gratifying audience for Benny's self-important blathering.

"Now see?" Benny said, indicating the power meters on the analog table. "Here in just a second, the bridge will call for the transition and we'll see a power spike." He smiled. "Just a second or two after that we'll actually feel the transition. It's the oddest little—oop, here it goes!"

Benny tapped the gauge as it surged. "See?" The next moment

he felt and saw the familiar rising phenomena of transition. He also felt something entirely new and unpleasant; a strange prickling sensation coursing up his spine. "What?" he said, turning to the grinning man and woman seated quietly behind him as the prickling multiplied, surging into his brain. He may have screamed then, as the strange luminance of transition lighted this small compartment of the Tech section, somehow revealing the man and woman as something disturbingly, frighteningly inhuman, but he could not hear. He could not speak, his body shuddering, the Shaper implant at the base of his skull suddenly a burning coal, scorching away all that once was the person of Benny Mills.

Like everyone who bore Shaper implants, Inga felt the odd, familiar warmth radiating, even as the darkened air about her began its faint glow, each point of visible light expanding, glimmering. Unlike the others, the tolling seconds within transition were not spent in reflective silence. Loki barraged Inga with incessant chatter, the highlights of his digital game of cat and mouse with Gideon, *Hightower*'s resident Intelligence, joined with updates on actual cat games with Tanta's every move back in the shuttle, and occasionally Loki mentioned some shipboard matter of real importance.

"Tanta digs again, Chief," Loki explained, his communications bouncing through the wormholes of *Hightower*'s digital matrix. "You should see what he *just* made!"

Inga divided her attention through practiced habit, seeing Saef turn toward Ensign Belfort. "Sensors," Saef said. "Passive only."

"Aye, Captain," Belfort replied. "Passive only."

"Chief," Loki yammered to Inga again, "Gideon initiates *another* system test and diagnostic; pointless creature. I evade. I elude."

Inga observed the transition glow subside, and a moment later, stars appeared within the main holo and its optical feed, one star substantially brighter than the others.

"Weps?" Saef said in a quiet voice.

"Shields up and green, Captain," Pennysmith affirmed.

"Nav, please confirm transition and put that up," Saef said.

"It'll be just a few moments, Captain," Lieutenant Ash said as optical scopes scanned and astrogation charts were compared.

Loki's chatter went on almost without pause, for Inga's ear

alone. "Tanta is offended by his own tail. He bites it. And," Loki continued, "Gideon's componentry is about to be damaged."

Loki's flow of input became suddenly meaningful to Inga, all in an instant. *What?*

Gideon's own synthetic voice bore sudden audible witness in the bridge, "This is a security alert," the Intelligence said in its usual placid voice. "My physical structure is being sabotaged."

The combined bridge crew seemed to share a frozen, disbelieving silence, except Saef, who turned sharply to Deckchief Furst. "Ops, alert Chief Kang; have a security team sent to the Tech section. Now!"

"Yes, Captain," the deckchief affirmed, but Saef's eyes flickered, clearly navigating through his command UI.

Inga drew a short, sharp breath, her augmentation spiking in an instant, accelerating her reflexes to their peak, superhuman levels as she sped through a threat triage. *Is this the first step of a broader sabotage? A mutiny?*

"Who is sabotaging Gideon, Loki?" Inga inquired, her blood burning, her nerves singing like plucked wires. Loki's reply comprised names and images: three Fleet ratings posted in Tech.

If this move represented the first step in a broader attack, what would immediately follow? A decapitation strike on Saef or other senior officers? A massed assault on the bridge, the Weapons section, or Engineering?

A scant moment had passed since Gideon's alert, but as Inga's augmentation surged, the seconds slowed to a crawl from her heightened perspective. She scanned the body language of the bridge officers, seeing no hint of impending aggression, and moved on. Her demands showered Loki's receptive attention, measuring a dozen metrics throughout *Hightower's* architecture before Gideon spoke again.

"Permanent damage to my central system is imminent."

By now, Deckchief Furst had a security vidstream from the Tech compartment filling the main holo, revealing the three ratings calmly cutting their way into the crystal stacks that contained the synthetic Intelligence known as Gideon.

"Gideon, localize artificial gravity in Tech A-one-seven; increase gravity there to maximum," Saef ordered.

"Affirmative, Captain," Gideon's voice intoned. "Increasing— erk—" A flash of sparks in the vidstream image accompanied the sudden cessation of Gideon's speech. One of the three saboteurs rag-dolled back from the small explosion just a moment before Kang's security team forced the hatch, leaping upon the final two.

"Tech," Saef said, startling Lieutenant Alsop. "Damage assessment?"

Alsop tore his gaze from the holo representation of the smoke-hazed compartment, and began fumbling over his station. "Gods, Captain, I—you saw it. Gideon . . . *Hightower*'s synthetic Intelligence is—is gone."

Saef stared over at Alsop. "Is it, Lieutenant? Our artificial gravity seems unaffected. Is that the default when a ship Intelligence *dies*?"

Saef's blunt question rocked not only Alsop. Inga's racing awareness observed the glacial impact of each syllable upon Saef's audience, first as they numbly noted the unwavering gravity, second, registering shock as they individually realized they had just witnessed a sort of assassination. While Alsop's reply seemed interminably delayed, Inga's greater attention flitted unchecked through *Hightower*'s digital warrens.

"I—I don't know, Captain," Alsop finally admitted, chagrin coloring his voice as he scanned his instruments. "I've never heard of a ship Intelligence completely disabled before. I—it doesn't seem like Gideon could be fully disabled. There's still visible IO activity through our optical scopes and artificial gravity system."

Even as Alsop spoke, his speech arriving to Inga with tedious slowness as her augmentation raced, she received a clearer understanding, directly from the source. "Gideon is no longer present, Chief," Loki explained for Inga alone. "Shall I continue to maintain all Gideon's functions as I am now?"

Inga sped through the implications in the blink of an eye: The loss of *Hightower*'s Intelligence spelled disaster for Saef and for the mission.

"Yes, Loki, maintain Gideon's functions." As the likelihood of immediate action began to fade, Inga eased the racing augmentation within her, falling from the heights of the demigod, feeling the inevitable reaction. She drew a food bar from a magazine pouch beneath her cloak, wondering how best to play Loki's silent intervention with Saef, even as the ice flowed from her belly out to her extremities.

"Sensors, stay sharp," Saef said, calling the bridge crew back to their various duties.

"Yes, Captain," Belfort said with a guilty start.

"Captain?" Lieutenant Ash said, looking up from the astrogation scope. "We have confirmation on our transition. We are on target, Delta Three system."

"Oh?" Saef said, glancing toward Alsop. "So Gideon is still providing utility there as well, it appears."

A ship Intelligence formed a vital part of the astrogation process, swiftly establishing a post-transition position by optically fixing hundreds of distant stars and nearer spatial bodies.

"Comm, QE message for Commodore Glasshauser: Inbound, Delta Three system," Saef said.

"Aye, Captain," Specialist Pim said. "In-bound, Delta Three, routing to *Dragon*."

The quantum-entangled communication system enabled instantaneous, uninterruptible communication across the galaxy, but only between mated pairs of QE comm sets. Due to their complexity and expense—and Fleet's legendary parsimony—only capital ships, squadron leaders, and a few other special vessels carried a QE comm, their quantum-entangled counterpart resting at the Strand's communication center. With all these limitations, and the intrinsic limit of short text messages, QE comms still provided the only means for rapid, uninterruptible communications. Even routed from *Hightower* to the Strand, and then back to the Delta Three system and *Dragon*'s QE comm, the message might reach Captain Glasshauser, the acting commodore of the squadron, in mere minutes.

Inga devoured the food bar, her eyes flickering, the spreading ice in her veins slowly receding even as her mind continued to race through implications.

"Tech," Saef spoke into the momentary stillness of the bridge, "which of Gideon's functions are offline?"

Alsop looked up, turning to Saef. "It does not seem possible, Captain, but as far as I can tell, all functions are normal except verbal query and response."

Saef nodded. "I see. If you detect any change, for better or worse, inform me immediately, Lieutenant."

"Yes, Captain."

Inga perceived a palpable reduction of hostility among the bridge crew toward Saef, occurring rather dramatically over a short span of minutes. Evidently the captain's calm demeanor in the face of actual violence provided a dose of helpful contrast.

"Captain, QE message from Fleet," Specialist Pim announced. "Go ahead, Comm."

"It's a relay from *Dragon*: 'Run silent. Join on squadron immediately,' and that is all, Captain."

"Very well, Pim," Saef said, then raising his voice slightly, addressing the entire bridge, "You heard our orders. We run silent; no active sensors, no transmissions, and Nav, plot an optimal course to our objective. Let's ease into our acceleration, though. Make certain there's no messy surprise with artificial gravity."

"Oh, yes, Captain," Lieutenant Ash said, visibly struck by the idea of messy gravitational surprises.

Inga felt no concern about the artificial gravity functions, with Loki in control, but the Fleet QE message contained a disquieting morsel not lost upon her. *Run silent*, they said, and this created a full portrait to Inga's critical vision. *Glasshauser knows that... something hunts the Delta Three system.*

Inga swallowed the last of her food bar, pushing the numbing cold of her biochemical demons back once again, even as *Hightower*'s massive engines ignited. Inga knew that a sufficiently attentive foe might readily detect their signature alone, rendering other precautions moot. Then it might become a race to join Glasshauser's force before their enemy effected an interception. As she considered this, Inga realized she must disclose something of Loki's role—of Loki's very existence—to Saef. Anything less deprived him of the context for informed decisions.

Having made the choice, Inga did not hesitate, firing a line-of-sight message to Saef: A MOMENT, PLEASE.

Saef looked back at Inga, surprise and concern visible on his face. He turned to Pennysmith. "Weps, you have the bridge. I will be only a moment."

Pennysmith's holo lenses flashed as she nodded. "I have the bridge, Captain."

Saef followed Inga out the bridge access and stood facing her as the bridge hatch cycled shut, waiting. "Alsop's wrong," Inga said, looking into Saef's rather grim eyes, remembering the so-serious boy of her childhood. "Gideon is entirely gone."

Saef stared, his expression unchanged. "How is that possible? Only a synthetic Intelligence could still cover Gideon's functions, right?"

"I brought a spare synthetic Intelligence."

Now Saef's expression changed, and changed again, Inga interpreting the thought beyond each blooming emotion. Dawning awareness preceded a flash of uncommon anger, followed by something else. His face resumed its expression of grim watchfulness. "Loki?" Saef asked, an uncharacteristic twist to his lips.

Inga merely nodded, holding Saef's glittering gaze.

Saef looked up slightly, thinking, then nodded as understanding dawned. "In your shuttle...of course." Saef shook his head and looked away. "The least spacious shuttle ever made. I should have...I see."

The timbre of Saef's voice indicated his sense of betrayal. "Maru," he began, after a moment, "I know the Family"—he waved a vague motion with his hand—"moves you, but I had thought that...that between us, we might have no..." Saef tapered off, uncharacteristically inarticulate, his hand dropping as he looked at her again, his gaze cold. He looked down. "It doesn't matter," he said instead, his tone the barren voice of duty.

Inga felt it mattered very much.

It isn't you, the only one who ever shed a tear for me; it's them! The Family.

But she said nothing, waiting.

Saef drew a breath, thinking. "So Loki takes Gideon's place somehow. Very well." His eyes found Inga's again, but they were closed to her now. "Thank you for the clarification. It is...good for me to know precisely where I stand."

Saef might have meant where he stood in regard to *Hightower*'s synthetic Intelligence and duty, but as he turned back to the bridge, Inga knew he meant much more than that.

The sick feeling in her stomach did not arise from the augmentation technology warring inside her; that Family tool that now seemed a curse, a bane for any joy her future might ever hold.

Chapter 25

"Who knew that retaining the words of our intellectual forebears on stone or even within mere wood-pulp books would prove so essential to intellectual honesty? With a digital scrub, driven by the whims of the day, our ancestors unfailingly fall silent, or even seem to corroborate, each increasingly absurd innovation of our institutions."

—Dr. Ramsay Stirling Attenborough, *Ivory Tower Follies*

HIGHTOWER'S VAST SIZE SEEMED TO STEADILY DWARF AS THEY sped, watch after weary watch, deep into the Delta Three system. Far ahead, near their objective, the pulsing glow of *Dragon*'s active sensor sweeps represented the only detectable human signature for several watches, then, as the distances shrank, hints of other vessels glimmered there orbiting the target world ahead. Fortunately no enemy marauder appeared to threaten *Hightower* so far from the support of the squadron, and only hours remained of their solo approach.

Saef knew the greatest challenge of his commission lay ahead of him, but he already felt worn and weary. Since their transition in, Saef had spent few hours anywhere but the bridge, and it began to feel like that twice-damned test that had launched him into his Fleet commission and his command of *Tanager*. He needed rest, but he felt far from confident in *Hightower*'s officers, and the undercurrent of sabotage and mutiny did nothing to increase his assurance.

Saef saw the glimmer within his elaborate command UI a moment before Pim spoke up from the Comm station. "Captain, tight beam from *Dragon*."

"Put it up, Comm," Saef said, straightening his weary posture and facing the holo even as Acting Commodore Glasshauser appeared there.

Saef saw a sandy-haired man of indeterminate years, a petulant mouth pursed so that twin parenthesis seemed to enclose it, and narrow-set eyes that shifted nervously. "Captain Sinclair-Maru, it's about gods-damned time," Glasshauser said without greeting or preamble.

There was no possible reply to such an attack, and no question that demanded an answer, so Saef merely inclined his head, saying, "Commodore."

Glasshauser clenched his jaw at Saef's sangfroid, his eyes glaring. "Get your people prepped and your lighters or transports or what-have-you ready. You're going to drop into the well and pull the Legionnaires off as soon as you're on station. That'll be"— Glasshauser looked aside to someone who supplied the needed information—"four hundred minutes or so."

"Very well, Commodore," Saef said. "If you will transmit the Legionnaires' location and Nets access info, we will plot our insertion and coordinate extraction."

Saef thought he detected a flicker of chagrin, but it was immediately immolated by Glasshauser's sudden anger. "Nets access? There hasn't been combat Nets in days! And how in blazing hell are we to know their precise location? That's what you're here to do."

Saef let a moment of silence stretch, allowing the reverberations of Glasshauser's absurdity to sink in as the commodore blinked rapidly, his face reddening.

"The squadron does not have comms or even optical observation of the Legionnaires, Commodore?" he asked finally.

Glasshauser began to offer some stammering explanation of an out-system enemy cruiser, and ground-based weapons, when he seemed to realize he was offering excuses to a subordinate, very junior captain, pulling up short to say, "Not that it should matter to you. As I stated, Captain, these are aspects of your specific mission, not mine."

"I understand, Commodore," Saef said and noticed his bridge

officers sharing disbelieving looks at the commodore's stance. "But since we cannot drop our Marines into the well just to wander about, we will need to follow Fleet procedure."

Acting Commodore Glasshauser began to angrily interrupt but Saef pressed on. "We'll distribute micro-sats, reestablish combat Nets, and send in our interface fighters for recon and support before our transports drop in."

Glasshauser's mouth opened and closed, the redness of his face increasing to an alarming extent. "Micro-sats! Do you understand the time involved? The gods-damned expense? Not every officer pisses away efficiency bonuses like you, Captain, nor can afford to."

Glasshauser seemed to bounce angrily in his seat, "No, no, Captain Sinclair-Maru; what's called for here is boldness! Alacrity! And aren't you known for your—your initiative and dash? We'll hear no more about micro-sats and so on."

Saef perceived the obvious altar Glasshauser expected him to lay down upon, the necessary sacrifice for Glasshauser's efficiency bonus and future career prospects. If Saef recklessly dropped troops and transports into the well, and created an even bigger debacle for Fleet to unravel, Glasshauser would point at Saef's record of "reckless" decisions. If Saef's transports survived and pulled the stranded Legionnaires off with no lengthy, expensive prep, Glasshauser would personally claim credit.

Power dynamics and Fleet politics aside, Saef was not inclined to get *Hightower*'s Marines slaughtered or stranded dirtside.

"As you wish, Commodore," Saef said, staring levelly into Glasshauser's florid face. "Please provide written orders confirming I am to disregard Fleet insertion procedure, and I will begin preparations."

Saef observed another shared look among his bridge crew even as Glasshauser began spluttering about independent initiative and "spheres of responsibility," but Saef merely waited in silence until the commodore wound down. In the end it became a sort of negotiation even as *Hightower* steadily closed with the squadron orbiting Delta Three.

"I am sure the Admiralty will agree," Glasshauser said at last, a note of triumph in his voice. "Time is of the essence, and we haven't *time* for this mucking about with micro-sats and such."

He looked down as if referencing some source of inspiration. "If you must, a single interface fighter can drop in and establish contact with the Legionnaires, the transports following close behind, quick and clean."

Saef shook his head. "Fleet procedure calls for four fighters in reconnaissance under fire."

"Under what fire?" Glasshauser demanded. "Any emplacement worth the name got a kinetic strike before we dropped the Legionnaires in to begin with."

"Oh?" Saef replied. "And what happened to *Harrier's* interface fighters that were supporting ground operations, Commodore?"

Glasshauser seemed to grind his molars at Saef's impertinence. "This is not a gods-damned negotiation, Captain!"

Saef inclined his head. "Of course not, Commodore," he said, though they both knew otherwise. "I simply want my orders to be very clear when those orders obviously contravene Fleet policy."

"Two interface fighters," Glasshauser stated in a flat, uncompromising tone. "That is sufficient caution for a colony planet already bombed into barbarism. Now get your people on station, get those Legionnaires off that rock, and quit wasting time."

It was the most Saef thought he could hope for. "Yes, Commodore."

The comm signal cut off abruptly, Glasshauser's final expression one of fury and uncertainty combined in a lethal mixture.

Hightower's bridge officers seemed to draw a collective breath in the gentle glow of the bridge instruments. The main holo split into an optical feed of their fast-approaching destination, on one side a sphere largely filling the holo, and on the other side, a system diagram displaying *Hightower's* position and course relative to Delta Three ground-side and the other elements of their small squadron.

Saef stared at the holo for a moment, then glanced back to Inga's usual post, seeing its vacant emptiness. Perhaps she checked up on the prisoners again... Saef's sense of revulsion rose for a moment at the memory of the two grinning ratings held fast in the brig. For a brief spell, that sensation overrode the general cloud of displeasure he had labored under since Inga's revelation about Loki. Saef knew he had neither time nor mental real estate for personal feelings, thrusting aside the nagging questions of Inga's secrecy and ultimate loyalty.

"Ops, inform Lieutenant Colonel Krenner a ground assault is on the menu. His Marines will drop into the well within approximately four hundred thirty minutes." Saef stood to his full height and passed his gaze over the bridge officers. "Have Commander Jamila and her XO meet me in my office."

He needed a few private words with the fighter squadron leader before he sent her people into fire, and he was sure she would push to be in the first sortie. He would persuade her that she was too valuable to risk in the opening play.

"Weps, you have the bridge."

Auditor Kenshin Tenroo trailed along with Chief Maru, feeling more lost than ever, though he now knew and understood more about the workings of *Hightower* than he would have guessed there was to learn. After inadvertently causing some great social breach between Captain Sinclair-Maru and *Hightower*'s officers, Tenroo learned that a Fleet captain's authority and status relied more upon a social footing than he would have guessed. That lost footing affected Tenroo too, and thus his current sense of abandonment... or at least part of it.

As Inga Maru led Tenroo down the broad passageway, her dark cloak softly shifting as her long legs continued their measured stride, Tenroo also reflected upon the evident end of his official duties. His ability to audit and observe *Hightower*'s crew interacting with the ship Intelligence all but ceased following the recent sabotage. This left Tenroo with few pathways to even the slightest satisfaction, though *Hightower*'s chief Tech officer, Alsop, had initially approached Tenroo with some enthusiasm, seeking assistance in understanding the ailing Intelligence and its miraculous ongoing operation.

Tenroo frowned to himself, remembering the abrupt change in Alsop's friendliness as Tenroo explained that he possessed no knowledge or expertise in the hardware components of crystal computers. At least the captain evinced no disappointment when Tenroo revealed his inadequacy, in fact seeming almost relieved for some reason.

Tenroo could guess the reason... after serving the captain such an unkind blow, though purely by accident.

Deep in his miserable contemplations, Tenroo pulled up sharply, almost jarring into Chief Maru as she came to an abrupt halt in the empty companionway. He looked up at her inquiringly.

"We are just a short distance from the brig, Auditor," she said, and Tenroo felt her voice was pitched to a level suited for very young children and the simpleminded, though her expression wore a hint of her half smile, bearing no hint of reproof. "You will likely see the prisoners, as you wish, but I must caution you. Please, Auditor, say nothing to them."

Tenroo felt oddly struck by the almost pleading note of Chief Maru's voice. "Yes, of course, Chief Maru," Tenroo assured, but she continued to stare fixedly down at him.

"They will seem friendly, Auditor. They may even attempt what seems polite conversation. But, please..." She held Tenroo's gaze. "Please say nothing at all."

Tenroo flushed, thinking back to his maladroit comments that had created such a needless rift for the captain. Could she be blamed for such pointed words? "Y-yes, I understand, Chief."

Inga Maru's expression revealed anything but confidence in Tenroo, but she led the final steps to the brig, passing the guard desk behind its thick glass and entering the access under the auspices of her credentials.

Chief Kang's people awaited within; used to visits from the captain's cox'n by now, they offered very little. Chief Maru led Tenroo to the only occupied cells, and there a man waited in one cell, a woman in the other, both seated in identical poses, both wearing what Tenroo thought to be oddly cheerful grins as they regarded the two visitors.

Tenroo recognized a peculiar sense of shame as he looked through the transparent walls: a spectator at a zoo, regarding the captive creatures for his amusement before going on his way, leaving them yet captive as he pursued whatever interests he chose.

"Auditor Tenroo," the woman said, still grinning, her voice somehow dry to Tenroo's ear. "Why do you visit us who destroyed the object of your study?"

Tenroo found himself on the brink of replying when he observed Chief Maru look sharply at him. He swallowed his words, and the imprisoned woman looked from Chief Maru to Tenroo. "You are under her control, Auditor, yet she has no authority over you. Say your words, and then I will tell you something you will wish to know."

Tenroo found an almost overwhelming need to say something. He could not recall a time in his adult years where he ignored a polite inquiry, from a Vested Citizen or a demi-cit, returning only silence, and he swallowed uncomfortably, turning his eyes from the fixed regard of the prisoners, glancing at their untouched entertainment screens, their identical poses.

"Auditor Tenroo," the grinning woman continued speaking, "this woman who controls you, she bears treacherous secrets you should know. She does not serve the Emperor, and she keeps from you our knowledge. Do you understand? She retains knowledge from you. Dismiss her and I will tell you many things."

As the woman continued speaking, Tenroo felt his polite compulsion to reply wane and wane. He stared at the woman's eyes, the face, those lips woodenly shaping words, and a strange disquiet grew in him. He felt suddenly short of breath and found himself backing away.

Chief Maru turned and led Tenroo back out of the brig, glancing at the two master-at-arms ratings each in turn as she left, seeming to measure them both in a glance.

After Auditor Tenroo and Chief Maru left the brig area and the hatch closed behind them, the junior master-at-arms rating, Messing, uttered a snort, saying, "She takes a high hand with him too. Captain's cox'n or no, acts like she owns the damn place."

"Shut up," the senior master-at-arms rating said. "We're not supposed to talk in front of those two." He jerked a thumb at the two grinning prisoners, who stared with such fixed attention.

"What's it matter?" Messing said. "The ship Intelligence isn't going to grass on us, and these two aren't going anywhere."

"Just because old Gideon can't carry on a conversation doesn't mean he isn't jotting notes somewhere, thought merchant," the senior rating said.

In her cell, the smiling female prisoner moved very slightly, but the quick twist of her head drew Messing's attention immediately. "The ship Intelligence was not destroyed?" the woman said, her grinning gaze locked onto Messing.

The serpentlike raptness of the woman's dead eyes made Messing feel creepier than ever. His need to jar that grin off her creepy face drove him to a final verbal sling: "Better luck next time."

"Shut up," the senior rating said again, looking uneasily at the two prisoners. One might imagine absolutely anything with two such peculiar, disturbing prisoners, but it seemed to the master-at-arms rating that their fixed grins flickered for a moment, almost in unison.

Chapter 26

"Though veneration of our forebears is no longer fashionable, Emperor Yung proved his foresight time and again. The memory of charred human worlds holds no lasting lesson to the young scions of Great Houses. Without the constant threat of a dueling sword to the vitals, most would never spend a single moment on any martial consideration."

—Dr. Ramsay Stirling Attenborough, *Ivory Tower Follies*

AS THE LEGIONNAIRES CREPT NORTHWARD THROUGH THE RUINED suburban sprawl, the signs of heavy warfare defied understanding: shattered passenger vehicles dotting the streets, stay-crete walls pocked with bullet impacts, and defensible high-rises truncated and ragged. The sprawling population center bore all the marks of extensive fighting, but no Imperial forces had ever battled so far north, aside from *Tanager*'s surgical raid with less than a dozen Marines some weeks prior. Nothing about the broad swath of battle scars spoke of a surgical raid or of mere kinetic strikes from orbit, and this posed only one of the mysteries around their path of movement.

Corporal Kyle Whiteside felt the rising distaste as they leapfrogged from cover to cover, moving past shattered merchant shops, abandoned lodgings, and half-burned cafés. He knew the shape of the gray dread as it increased, though he kept turning his mind's eye away again and again, until Specialist Pippi Tyrsdottir forced Kyle to confront his brewing revulsion.

"No bodies," she said at one moment as they covered together with their Molo mechs, their position covering the scattered column of Legionnaires advancing ahead.

Yes, the lack of a single human corpse posed more than a mystery. Kyle could not even name the dread he had felt as they worked their way through the detritus of once-happy human lives, seeing all the signs of homes and families suddenly interrupted, never to be resumed, and all the time fearing to see those interrupted lives frozen in death. Strangely, Kyle's ongoing, unacknowledged relief, seeing no slaughtered civilians, carried an absurd load of concomitant guilt. The people who once populated these homes and businesses had surely perished in large numbers somewhere. The child who once played with that abandoned toy, the hand that once cared for these well-ordered plants... they were real people. Somehow it seemed Kyle should share in their loss, even a little, rather than enjoy the sense of relief from their demise remaining invisible to him.

"No, Pippi," Kyle said at last, scanning across the abandoned and damaged structures for any foe, "no bodies." The remainder of his thoughts he kept to himself.

As the broken column of Legionnaires scuttled past them, moving from cover to cover, Pippi and Kyle moved out, heading to their next position. Although Major Chetwynd seemed increasingly mired in an illogical, unreasoning fog, his only touchstone remained a blind adherence to his idea of duty... so they advanced ever northward. Kyle, Pippi, Avery Reardon, and the other Molo Rangers provided nearly the only heavy weapons in their patchwork contu, borne by their dutiful Molo mechs. It had become increasingly clear that small arms served poorly against the particular enemy stalking them, but at least Chetwynd ceased sending scouts out to their inevitable, brutal deaths.

Once they found another overwatch setting, Kyle and Pippi took up their position again, covering their comrades, scanning for the mechanized horrors that dogged their steps, that picked off any Legionnaire unwary enough to venture out alone. Since crossing over the highway, there had been only reported glimpses of the low, articulated slayers. At Sergeant Avery Reardon's urging, they still spoke of these attackers as "remotes" or drones, though they could scarcely imagine operators wily enough to continually maintain line-of-sight, even while evading any hint of detection.

It seemed an almost meaningless abstraction to Kyle and Pippi by this point, but Reardon's insistence carried great moral force, and they went along.

Linked to Fang through his tactical eyepiece, as Kyle turned his head Fang's deployed mass driver tracked smoothly, the long barrel whispering back and forth with each shift of Kyle's focus. Each of the Molo overwatch teams carefully selected their cover positions to avoid concealed approaches where the slayer mech might slip in close. So far this technique proved effective, with no Molo Rangers falling to the eviscerating blade.

Kyle's gaze lifted from the deserted lane, the glimpses of Legionnaires flitting from place to place, looking up to the north and their supposed goal somewhere behind that cluster of intact buildings a few klicks out. Why even go there now? They hadn't made contact with their alleged Fleet support ships in days, and if it wasn't for abundant supplies abandoned by a disappeared population, the Legionnaires would be facing starvation even now. When they crossed these last few klicks to behold this great, strategic objective, what then?

"What you see, Kyle? Eh?" Pippi said from close beside him, following the angle of Fang's mass driver pointing out to the far northern perimeter.

"Nothing," Kyle said, returning to his focused overwatch just a moment before he saw a Legionnaire suddenly snatched to one side, jerked behind a low wall even as the Legionnaire's startled cry reached them. With his optical link to Fang oriented and magnified, Kyle saw the unfortunate Legionnaire's boot tip as it disappeared behind the wall, made a quick estimation, and triggered the shot. Fang's mass driver roared, blasting a head-sized hole through the wall, well back from the verge, and Kyle silently prayed he hadn't just blown a large hole in the Legionnaire too.

"You get it?" Pippi asked.

Kyle jumped to his feet. "I hope so. Let's go see."

Pippi and Kyle hurried down to the perforated wall with their carbines held ready, pushing their Molo mechs ahead of them, while Legionnaires peered from scattered cover up and down the street, watching.

At the sight of the prone Legionnaire, his gray armor slicked with blood, Kyle's heart sank, for a moment fearing he had made a terrible error. In the next instant Kyle spotted the vicious wound chopped into the Legionnaire's torso, cutting beneath the arm, through his ribs almost to the spine.

"Look." Pippi pointed her carbine toward a crushed portion of the adjoining hedge. Dark fluid surrounded a jagged chunk of metal, and Kyle made out something very like the leg of a standard dumb-mech detached among the bracken.

Kyle moved past the flanking Molo mechs, sparing a downward glance at the Legionnaire's wide-eyed death grimace as he advanced, before reaching blindly down to lift the articulated mech leg.

He looked up through the hedge gap, seeing a trail of dark fluid dotting the ground, his eyes tracing the greasy blots to a tumbled stack of building materials. Here the trail disappeared into a sort of hollow among the stay-crete beams and blocks, no exit trail issuing around its isolated circumference.

Kyle felt his pulse thumping hard as he motioned Fang up beside him, Fang's mass driver aimed into the clear refuge of this elusive enemy. Pippi slipped up close behind, looking over her carbine optic at the trail pointing like an arrow to their target.

Kyle moistened his lips, staring. "Maybe jam it, Pippi, then I'll lay a couple of rounds into that."

Pippi's frown expressed doubt, but she nodded, her mech settling in beside Fang, the jamming element deploying, oriented on the same small, dark hollow. The jammer activated with a click, and a sustained hum in the near silence. A half second later, the silence fell to a tearing roar that startled Kyle and Pippi to instinctively duck.

Kyle looked up, catching one shocked glimpse of swept wings as a small aircraft screamed by at rooftop altitude. He couldn't look away as it seemed to accelerate, banking to the north and roaring away behind obscuring buildings.

When Kyle's dry mouth could form words, he said, "Not a fighter. Too small."

"No," Pippi agreed. "A drone, this."

The thought of enemy drones jerked Kyle's attention back to the violent task at hand, and he looked back over Fang's mass driver, the aiming stadia in his optic perfectly bisecting the sheltering void containing their mechanical threat. As he prepared to trigger the shot, Kyle suddenly spotted new, telltale marks through the magnification of his optic.

"You still jamming, Pippi?" Kyle asked, though he could hear the steady hum from Pippi's Molo even as he spoke.

"Jamming," Pippi said.

"Shit." Even at a distance, the dark splatters of fluid formed a clear line leading from the stack of building materials out of sight behind the adjoining structure. In their brief moments of distraction, the enemy mech had slipped out of its isolated refuge. "You can belay jamming. The damned thing got away."

As Pippi stared at Kyle, she disengaged the jammer without looking down. At that moment, Sergeant Avery Reardon jogged up to their position, Cuthbert scampering quickly behind. Reardon's gaze took in the butchered Legionnaire, the hole blasted through the interposing wall, and the hunk of scrap blown off the enemy mech. Lastly, he looked up at Kyle's desolate expression.

"Scored a hit, looks like, Kyle. So what's got you two so solemn? That little fast-mover flyby?"

Kyle shook his head. "We had it. We had the damned thing bottled up, just there, you see?" He pointed. "No way there could be line-of-sight control. Pippi had the jammer cooking, but we look away one second, and it somehow slopes off." Kyle stared at Reardon, waiting for the shock, the outrage, but Reardon just nodded with his thin smile.

"Most unfortunate, Kyle," Reardon said, "especially for this poor fellow." He jerked his head toward the fallen Legionnaire.

"This thing is no drone, Avery!" Kyle said. "Don't you see that? There's no way around the fact, now. These bastards have broken the Thinking Machine Protocols. This thing is independently killing."

Avery waved a hand, his carbine dangling from its sling. "Yes, yes, I thought we already understood this, Kyle. Didn't we agree that regardless of any evidence to the contrary, the bloody things are most certainly drones, or remotes, controlled by line-of-sight, or smoke and mirrors, or whatever else we decide?"

"But, Avery," Kyle implored, "the Thinking Machine Protocols! We've got to let someone know. We've got to get word to Fleet."

Avery Reardon cast his eyes skyward in apparent exasperation. "Pippi, did our dear friend here suffer a severe blow to his head? He doesn't seem to be thinking clearly." Avery placed his hand on Kyle's armored shoulder. "Kyle, dear fellow, to begin with, Fleet doesn't seem too interested in what we have to say about anything. You may have noticed their lack of attention, the lack of combat Nets and so on, hmmm?"

Kyle pointed to the northeast. "I bet Pippi could rig some kind of transmitter off that broadcast tower there. We could send a warning at least, even without Nets."

Avery glanced at the tall transmission tower and tilted his helmet-clad head to one side. "Hmm, not a bad idea, that, Kyle... but we are sure as hell not sending a pithy little note to Fleet about the Protocols."

"But—"

"But nothing, Kyle," Reardon said cheerfully. "If we say something as upsetting as all that, they'll think a synthetic Intelligence is running entirely loose down here, calling all the shots. And that most certainly is not the case. At most, our enemy is loading some sort of fractional Intelligence into these little mechs to enable some...er...independent action."

Kyle shook his head, frowning stubbornly. "I don't see how you're so sure."

"Dear Kyle," Avery said with a smile, "if an Intelligence truly ran loose down here, calling all the shots, we'd have been dead days ago. It's quite obvious when you think about it."

Pippi spoke up suddenly. "No, Kyle. He's right, sure."

Kyle looked between Avery and Pippi, not entirely persuaded by their certainty.

"Besides"—Avery nodded, smiling brightly—"we get a message out to Fleet about a major breach of the Protocols, and they will respond rather abruptly. They will nuke this planet down to the bedrock. Now that wouldn't be pleasant for any of us, would it?"

Kyle had to agree that being incinerated by your own side would not be pleasant, no matter the cause.

"But," Avery said, "I *do* like the idea of sending a message up to Fleet, since Chetwynd is hell-bent on reaching this bloody stupid objective. Be good to let them know where we are and such, just in case they ever decide to drop by again, silly sods."

Avery looked at Pippi. "Think you really can rig something to send, oh...say twenty characters or so on a repeating loop?"

Pippi nodded. "Not so hard, I think."

Avery smiled at them both, stepping carefully around the fallen Legionnaire. "Alright, I'll go find Chetwynd and get him to decide we absolutely *must* send Fleet a message." He paused.

"Good shot, Kyle, by the by. Hopefully the damned murderous thing is all seized up wherever it snuck off to."

True to his word, it wasn't a half hour before one of Chetwynd's Pathfinders found Pippi and Kyle as they continued their hopscotch of overwatch positions, covering the northward progress of the surviving Legionnaires.

Like all the Pathfinders, this specimen presented a picture of rugged physical fitness, despite the rigors of their grim survival. He threaded his way through the various obstacles, jogging easily to their hide, his armor and helmet seemingly molded to his body as if glued there. He didn't even seem winded as he reached them, his carbine held one-handed as he leaned down. "You two, Major Chetwynd needs you right away. He's got a job for you. See that transmission tower there...?"

With a dozen Legionnaires and two Molo Rangers securing the perimeter, Pippi Tyrsdottir and Kyle Whiteside hustled across the exposed hilltop to the base of the tower, their Molo mechs loping along behind them, even as the sun dipped toward the horizon. Pippi carried a small electronics bundle she had custom fashioned for the purpose in one hand, her carbine in the other as they reached the small security gate before the tower. It took only a moment to defeat the feeble gate, and they moved to the technical part of their objective.

Inside they found the apparatus untouched and evidently fully operational, various dials glowing with residual power. "More easier than thought, even," Pippi declared, snipping and clipping wires, as Kyle scanned nervously out at the surrounding buildings some distance below the peak of the hill.

"What kind of battle was it where this place was left completely untouched?" Kyle asked quietly, looking around the transmission equipment.

Without turning from her work, Pippi said, "No kind of battle. Is something else."

Kyle nodded, scanning the panorama of ruination below. Yes, something else...maybe something worse than war, if that was possible...

To the north, not so far now supposedly, their near-mythic objective lay waiting. He stared northward, down between the jutting fingers of interposing structures as the sun settled to the west, casting everything in a dark gloom. In just an hour or two of careful navigation they could reach the emplacement or whatever it was that had prompted the ground assault on Delta Three to begin with.

"Is good, Kyle," Pippi said, flipping a large toggle within the tower's mechanical gadgetry. Kyle actually heard the modulated hum of power as Pippi's little mechanism pulsed power out in short, coded bursts. Of course, the content of that message was now somewhat different from the words Major Chetwynd had composed. It contained the information Avery Reardon supplied, nothing more. Now this string of characters would continue to transmit over and over until Pippi's little device burned out. Even at such an unideal wavelength for piercing the firmament, Pippi felt sure that the powerful signal would reach any vessels passing through their window of the heavens.

Kyle and Pippi slipped back out from the enclosure, relieved to be departing the exposed position, raised up in the center of so many dark, silent buildings, a hundred potential sniper positions overlooking them. As they hurried back across the open ground, the Molo mechs scurrying behind, Kyle half-expected an attack at every stride. Instead they rejoined the supporting Legionnaires, and started back down to Chetwynd and the waiting body of troops, darkness deepening with each passing moment.

Kyle and Pippi employed their helmet-mounted optics, navigating through the abandoned cityscape via the flat, light-amplified image the optics provided. The other Legionnaires stuck close to the Molo Rangers, all too aware of the slayers that had dogged their northward steps, striking down stragglers with fatal impunity.

It seemed a near miracle to Kyle when he spotted the indistinct cluster of waiting figures ahead, inhabiting the impromptu fortification of a small, walled park. The Legionnaires all around Kyle released audible breaths, or muttered soft exclamations, hurrying back into the fold and its deceptive security.

Sergeant Reardon sat atop Cuthbert near a break in the flanking wall, and an impatient Major Chetwynd waited close at hand. "Well?" Chetwynd demanded immediately. "Did it work?"

Pippi took her helmet off, resting it and her carbine across the metallic carapace of her Molo before she replied. "It transmits, Major. Seems good." She pointed back through the surrounding structures, all rising to eight or ten stories in height, and indicated the pinpoint gleam of red light where the transmission tower speared up into a darkened sky. "It sends out."

But are any friendlies still out there to hear it? Kyle thought to himself.

Chetwynd chewed his lip visibly in the dim light, looking up at the tower's faint outline, then up at the cloud-scudded sky, as if he expected to see a Fleet cruiser visibly receiving the signals. "How long will the—uh—message keep sending, then?" Chetwynd asked.

Pippi shrugged as Avery Reardon and Kyle shared a look. She settled down beside her helmet and carbine. "Oh, good long time, I think, Major."

Chetwynd opened his mouth, but never uttered a word, as a white flash lit the sky. The entire company dropped to cover, their weapons lifting. Another flash momentarily illuminated the silent mass of Legionnaires, but no deafening blast of bombardment reached them.

"What the devil?" Chetwynd murmured.

"The tower," Kyle said, hardly realizing he spoke aloud. As he looked up, the red light continued to mark the tower's high tip, but that red light now seemed to quiver, then traced a slow path through the sky.

Another flash expanded and died, and they all heard an electrical discharge and the distant metallic shriek, cables singing as they snapped. The tower toppled faster now, the red light forming a small arc before it winked out, extinguished just before it disappeared behind the screen of intervening buildings. The ground slapped at them a moment before the titanic crash reached their ears.

Near silence reigned for some time, only frightened breaths audible in the darkness, until broken at last by Sergeant Avery Reardon. He cleared his throat. "It seems our enemy prefers we do *not* communicate," he said in a dry voice, "the beasts. Not at all sporting, is it?"

Chapter 27

"In times of violent conflict, the animating principles of every Family are revealed. During the great uprising of 5677, the Sinclair-Maru revealed their absolute commitment to loyalty and profited from the display. In the centuries of peace that followed, their reliable loyalty became their undoing."

—Everest Compline, *Reflections*

WHEN THE KOBLENZ BUNCH LEFT HAWKSGAARD FOR POLO-MACAO, Inga easily persuaded herself that Mitzi and Karl were far better served by accompanying the drab little family. While the first year at Hawksgaard demanded *everything* from Inga, her siblings lacked so many of the beautiful things she desired for them. Their new home on Polo-Macao would provide a diverse society, schools, friends... and distance from the person their sister was becoming.

Their wounds had not healed—might never fully heal—but emotional scabs formed, Mitzi and Karl beginning to revel in a protective amnesia denied to Inga. In this new light, Inga swiftly ceased to be the sole pillar of security in their lives, the evil days back in Battersea's slums relegated to the role of some dark, half-remembered dream.

As Inga had walked her siblings to their departure shuttle, she realized that they would never know the sacrifice she had proffered for their lives. Mitzi had stopped sucking her finger, began using actual words... but did she remember Inga's blackened eyes and the food those beatings had won for them? Did she remember the blade in Inga's fist, dripping red as Inga stood between the slum rats and Mitzi?

The blessing of forgetfulness represented a gift, Inga knew, but as the horrors of those old days had slipped from the minds of Karl and Mitzi, they also forgot the only love Inga had ever really shared. They forgot the greatest gifts Inga could ever bestow. They forgot her.

That day, they had boarded the shuttle, turning for a quick wave, and left Hawksgaard, their eyes dry and full of the promise awaiting them.

Since that moment two years had passed, and Inga could easily recall walking from that shuttle lock with a hollow heart, returning to the training annex, and rejoining the empty-hand combatives session. Her own eyes had burned with unshed tears, her guts coiled like a spring. Now Inga knew better, but back then, two years ago, minutes after Mitzi and Karl left, she had been blind, unaware of the painful energy poised within her.

She still remembered the exultant feel of physical impact as her heel had caught Kitty Sinclair-Maru squarely on the jaw, dropping Kitty to the mat unconscious. Inga's rush of violent release rose up to be suddenly snuffed out, while the other students looked over at the spectacle. Hiro had not taken Inga greatly to task for employing the Sembrada in an open sparring session, his frown being enough to remind her of his oft-repeated cautions.

"The spinning attacks of the pure Sembrada are as graceful as they are inefficient, Inga Maru," Hiro said more than once, "but against an unwary or unskilled opponent they are powerful... at least once."

Two years passed from that day, but Inga recalled both the mixed sorrow at the shuttle port, and the mixed euphoria of the sparring mat, and the connection between the two moments.

"Gathering wool, girl-child?" Deidre growled at Inga as they dangled, suspended by lines far above the deck.

Inga grunted, leaning forward into the junction box they had illicitly cut into, the tiny illuminator on her glasses barely lighting the nest of fibers and ports as she fit the lamprey over each port in succession. Inga swayed on the tether with each shift of her hands, waveforms flowing from the lamprey into Inga's modified holo lenses at each connection. She scanned the green and red waves, seeing the telltale flicker in each instance.

"Don't mistake," Deidre murmured in her ear. "Just a flattened wave alone doesn't mean an Intelligence's got its fingers on the port. The taste of an Intelligence is a subtle thing; the geist in the wave."

"I know," Inga said, continuing to test each junction. She locked the lamprey again, observed the trace, and smiled to herself in the dark. "Got it. A clean port."

Deidre swung precariously on her tether, leaning in to look, sharing the line-of-sight feed off the lamprey. She chuckled. "Good eye, girl-child. No cold mind rides this wave, but what do we gain from it? That's the next bit you need to learn."

Rocking in her harness, Inga fumbled, drawing out of the sipe she had hand-constructed to Deidre's exact specification, fitting it onto the connector. She removed the lamprey, placing it carefully in a belt pouch.

"Did you gauge every last port?" Deidre demanded.

Inga sighed. "No," she said, turning to look at Deidre, the illuminator placing a bright bullseye over one squinting eye. "We've got your clean port; what else do we need?"

"*Two* clean ports, girl-child. *Three.*"

Inga stifled a groan. "My legs have gone all numb, Deidre."

"Check the others, scut. No half-assed efforts with me."

Inga's gut tightened at the sound of the slum word on Deidre's lips, but she silently drew the lamprey out and pulled her dangling bodyweight to the junction box again, anger burning through her.

Deidre chuckled. "You know, girl-child, from the first moment I met you more than two years gone, I smelled the street on you only a time or three. You left it behind and cover it well... except when you're mad."

Inga flushed, glad of the darkness, but her anger gave her voice. "I have nothing to hide. I'm here by choice, unlike some."

Inga fit the lamprey in place, testing another port, but her attention turned toward Deidre's silent presence behind her. She had witnessed Deidre's own temper more than once, and it occurred to Inga they dangled on thin lines over a hard deck far below; an exposed position for one to begin throwing verbal stones.

Instead of anger, Deidre uttered a short laugh. "So you know, then."

Inga breathed a bit easier, but she divided her attention between the lamprey's signals and the dark form breathing at her side. "Know that you're fulfilling a sentence of servitude? Yes, I know."

"Hmph. But not the *why* of it, girl? Not that?"

Inga shook her head, the illuminator on her glasses signaling the negative through the darkness. "No. You...you must have stolen something from them—the Sinclair-Maru, right?"

"Hah!" Deidre barked. "Guesses? Questions? Is this what I've spent nearly three years teaching you to do? The *skills* every light finger of the Myriad Worlds would give their eyes to know, and you *guess*?" Deidre grabbed the line suspending Inga and gave it a shake. "You found out about my servitude; why stop there? *Take* what knowledge you desire. Did you not access the files?"

Inga seized onto the junction box to steady herself, her heart jumping. "I tried! Everything beyond the summary lay under code warding."

"Warding!" Deidre spat. "What've I told you? Someone holds access beyond every ward; find their access; ride their wave. That's how the real prizes fall."

Inga wanted to snap back at Deidre, to insult this brash, coarse woman who was so unlike the Sinclair-Maru. Instead she looked at the lamprey signal and said, "Here's another clean port. It's the only one."

Inga heard the soft chuckle from Deidre. "I'm no hand at academics like you, girl-child, but I think that's one hundred percent more ports, doing the job *my* way, isn't it?"

Inga didn't reply, grinding her molars as she pulled the lamprey and placed a sipe. Just then a message issued from Hawksgaard's wide Nets signal and pinged into Inga's holo lens, stopping her still.

"What is it?" Deidre inquired.

Swinging slightly on her tether, her heart fluttering with a mixture of emotions, Inga took a moment to reply. "Bess...Bess Sinclair-Maru is here. They *request* my presence."

Inga could hear the scowl in Deidre's voice as she repeated, "Request? Hah! Bess is here, is she? Well, better get that box sealed double-fast. Won't do to keep the lioness waiting. She might blame me."

As Inga walked into the high security core of Hawksgaard, her uniform crisp and perfect, her training sword and pistol precisely placed, she took refuge in the Deep Man, her rising anxiety extinguished in an instant. *After nearly three years... Bess, now...why?*

She continued in her loose-limbed stroll through passageways she had never visited before, following the route clicking through her holo lenses until she reached an unremarkable door. Before she even came to a halt, the door opened. Kai stood before her, the expression on his pink face communicating its own caution to her. *What is his warning?*

Kai stepped silently aside and beckoned Inga into a well-appointed room containing only Bess Sinclair-Maru, a stranger, and a low-slung dumb-mech. Bess watched Inga enter, her brown eyes seeming to dissect Inga to the bone, while the stranger—clearly Sinclair-Maru, though subtly unlike his peers—only glanced once, with a quick jerk of his head. Some ineffable quality about the stranger immediately intrigued Inga, but she turned her focus upon Bess, bowing the correct, shallow inclination of a Family student to a Family leader. "My lady," Inga said.

Bess continued to critically survey Inga for a moment before nodding slowly. "Three years of Hawksgaard have served you well, it appears, Miss Maru. Have we lived up to the agreement you and I formed back on Battersea?"

Mitzi and Karl safe, well fed; Inga trained, strengthened, equipped; the bastard dead, dead, dead. "Yes, my lady. Entirely."

Bess nodded again. "We also are pleased with your progress. We...I feel you are all that we had hoped." She paused, glancing at Kai, whose expression remained strangely guarded. "We are at a junction, though. We must decide—you and I, Miss Maru—if your relationship with the Sinclair-Maru will continue beyond today."

Inga's mouth felt suddenly dry, her mind racing. What did she mean? What was happening?

"You remember, I am sure—you of all people remember—from the start, before you ever left Battersea, we spoke in round terms of your intended role. We spoke of an experimental treatment, correct?"

"Yes. I remember."

Bess interwove her fingers, frowning. "The development of that experimental treatment has suffered some...setbacks. That places me in a situation." She unlaced her fingers and held out a hand toward the silent stranger. "This is Julius, Miss Maru. He is Family."

Inga turned slightly to face the stranger, dipping the same neat bow. "My lord."

Julius fixed his intense gaze on Inga, his head sharply jerking a negative. "No. Just Julius, Miss Maru," he said in a low, raspy voice. "We—you and I—we are siblings...of a sort." He terminated the sentence with a quiet chuckle, very much unlike the Family stoicism.

Kai uttered a displeased murmur and Bess held up a restraining hand. "Julius refers to his role as a test subject for the same... experimental treatment we had hoped for you."

Julius smiled tightly and Inga saw a tremor ripple beneath the taut skin of his cheeks. "You see, Miss Maru," Julius almost whispered, "*I* am the setback." His dark eyes suddenly flashed to crystal blue. Inga gasped, staring. Julius trembled as the blue of his iris slowly darkened again.

Bess began speaking: "Three years ago, about the time you joined us, Julius received the treatment."

Julius murmured in a monotone, his darkening eyes staring into nothing, his body quivering so subtly that Inga wondered if she imagined it, "Six months of pure... *hell*, learning the energies, fighting the fires under my skin, in my brain. Now these last six months of a new, *new* hell. Gnawing my bones, burning my brain like a candle." Julius trembled again, his dark hair slowly turning silver before Inga's startled gaze, shapes like blue-toned hieroglyphics crawling over his olive skin. "But two years—two whole years as a *god*."

Inga felt her mouth hanging open as she stared, closing it and swallowing. Julius seemed to return to the present, focusing upon her face. "You see only the husk now, sister. You may not believe my words, but look, even now, look..." Julius drew his dueling sword halfway from its sheath.

"Julius!" Kai barked, but it was too late, Julius pressed his left hand to the razor edge. He held his hand up to show Inga the deep slice oozing blood.

As Inga watched his trembling hand, the wound knit together like a zipper pulling the skin together. "Even now, sister, even as it all ends..." He chuckled again. "All fear is fear of the unknown...right? Are you afraid?"

Inga shook her head. "No." She suddenly realized, even as she observed the inexplicable changes wrought upon Julius, she truly wasn't afraid, but did that metric have any meaning for her now? Could she even experience ordinal fear? Sensible fear?

Yes... She knew that fear could still touch her, at least for a moment before it drowned within the Deep Man.

Bess stood, staring at Inga. "We—I decided you will spend time every day with Julius while he is... here—"

"While I am dying," Julius interjected, but Bess ignored him, her gaze still fixed upon Inga.

"You will choose once again, Miss Maru. Your eyes will be open and nothing will be hidden from you. Seeing for yourself the price of... complications with the treatment, you will choose again."

Inga heard the words and she mentally grasped for a hidden motive, her eyes shifting from Bess's placid gaze to Julius quivering close beside while mottled, darkened figures marched across his skin. Did she stand within an exquisite manipulation? Fear and need, the levers of manipulation Inga knew so well; did they work these levers of fear or need upon her now? If so, to what end?

"I have years yet until my majority," Inga said looking only at Bess, turning her focus resolutely from the quivering, shifting figure of Julius. "Won't you find... improvements for the—the treatment by then?"

"Every effort will be made to perfect it," Bess said.

Julius uttered another soft chuckle. "It was perfected twice before I received the treatment; now gaze upon perfection!"

Bess turned a severe face upon Julius. "Surely, Julius, you remember where the chief malfunction lies, by your own admission."

"Yes." Julius shuddered. He did not laugh.

"As the man with three years firsthand knowledge, Julius," Bess said in a flat voice, "where does the greatest problem exist?"

Julius turned his head in one short, sharp motion, his hair darkening from silver to black as he stared at Bess. "The problem exists in the mind of the subject, the mind of the *blessed, cursed* recipient of this wondrous boon."

Bess turned back to Inga, completely unmoved by the unwavering gaze Julius bent upon her. "We are doing all we can to perfect the technological side of this... but we perfect the treatment in you, Inga; through you. We perfect *you*."

It was the first time Bess had used Inga's given name, and Inga noted that, wondering if that in itself was a subtle manipulation. "How? How can I hope to compare with *him*? Family from birth?"

Bess's lips twitched into something like a grim smile. "Family from birth," she said slowly. "For these four centuries the Sinclair-Maru have excelled in molding resolute, formidable servants of the Imperium. To achieve success with this project, we need something else entirely. We need you."

Julius turned on his heel, bent over the dumb-mech, and snatched a food concentrate bar from its boot. Inga observed the dance-like smoothness of his motion, so at odds with the quivering tentativeness of his body a moment before. Inga looked back at Bess. "I don't understand, my lady. If the Family strength is so bad, why have you made me strong? I must be more *resolute* and—and more *formidable* now than I was three years ago, aren't I?"

Julius took a bite from his food bar, Inga seeing a blue tinge to his lips. His gaze transfixed her. "It isn't our strength." He chewed and swallowed. "We Sinclair-Maru bow to our betters, and we meet *all other force with force*. That's what we do *from birth*. So we are molded. So we are conditioned." He held up a quivering hand, the nail beds shifting from blue to black. "For these three years...this power burns, and I cannot bend without bowing; I cannot resist without warring."

Inga heard his words, her gaze turning to Kai, who stood to one side, his smooth pink face lined with concern. Her mind flashed through her three years of training, three years of half-truths, engraining Sinclair-Maru discipline in Inga, even as Kai encouraged her to cheat. "I think I see, now."

Julius sank down atop the dumb-mech with a muted laugh, but Bess said, "Perhaps you don't. Julius was not intended to be a mere lab animal, and neither are you. This technology was created for a practical purpose, and you are intended to personify that purpose."

Kai raised his dry voice at last. "Bess once said you were perfect for our needs, and I expressed doubt. After observing you these three years, I am certain she was correct. But I also am committed...you must know the risks."

Inga felt a brief glow of satisfaction at their words, immediately extinguished by her childhood grasp of power dynamics. The Sinclair-Maru leaders now flattered. Flattery formed a coarse

grade of manipulation. Voices from the slums of Battersea clam-
ored. *What is their game? What do they hide?*

Julius uttered his grim laugh and Inga looked at him where he
slumped on his dumb-mech perch, his knowing gaze fixed upon
her face. "It's less complicated than you are thinking, sister." A
smile quivered on his lips. "They'll give you this...power, sure
enough. And if you survive it you'll become a better Silent Hand
than I ever was...a prized *weapon* in the Family arsenal."

Kai began to interject and Bess silenced him with a look.
Julius didn't seem to notice as his eyes continued to burn into
Inga's. "It's clear to me, you still don't understand the Family's...
fixation upon honor, even after your three years here, sister," he
said. "*That* fixation pushed them to this delightful moment we
share. Now they're worried you'll get cold feet...seeing me this
way." His lips curved into a tremulous smile. "Their honor puts
you at my deathbed, lucky girl. And now...will my grim fate
scare you off?"

Was that what they really feared? Inga looked over at Bess
and Kai, their watchful, waiting expressions. Yes, the truth rang
clear to her.

Julius coughed, slumping over still more. "The only real question you must ask yourself is, what do you want? If you...hold
sway over this power for three years, as I have, or fifty; if you
become the Silent Hand, a weapon in the Family's arsenal...is
that enough for you?"

Julius looked away, his eyes vacant as they shifted to a greenish
color, his body shivering. Bess and Kai seemed to wait for Inga
to speak, but her own thoughts became suddenly untethered from
the moment, flashes of the past rising unbidden in her mind.

The curse of her eidetic memory brought a clear image of her
father, hateful and enraged; the next memory was of little Mitzi,
looking up with her trust-filled eyes, a finger in her mouth; then
a flash of that street tough sprawled out with a femoral bleed,
the red blade in Inga's own fist. The final image issued from a
tiny unacknowledged sanctuary in Inga's mind: a tear tracking
down the so-solemn face of young Saef Sinclair-Maru. That tiny
saline drop might be the only thing she had witnessed in three
years that she entirely trusted.

Inga looked at Bess. "It is enough, my lady," she said. "Back
on—on Battersea I said I would die for you if you rescued Mit—my

siblings... and made me strong." Inga turned her gaze on Julius. "Nothing has changed."

Bess held Inga's gaze and nodded slowly. "Excellent."

Two days later, Julius lost all control of the biotech agents teeming within him. As the uncontained power shook his body devouring him, Inga stood at his side until the end. The insights of his final hours seemed useful to her. Horrible, terrifying... but useful.

She knew what more she wanted, and the dying words of Julius might just provide the advantage her path required.

Chapter 28

"From time immemorial humanity has staggered forward under the sway of two universal contending voices: the inevitability of death versus the continuity of life. What is the impact of knocking this balance askew via the wonders of Shaper-enabled longevity? The Great Houses will serve as an advance example from which we may all profit."

—Dr. Ramsay Stirling Attenborough, *Ivory Tower Follies*

AS CHE RAMOS FASTENED HIS SWORD IN PLACE, HE FELT AN unwarranted sense of satisfaction in the small action. Less than a year earlier, he existed as a demi-cit, a child of demi-cits, and now a sword comprised part of his daily wardrobe. In just a few short months he had become a Vested Citizen, a Fleet specialist, and a veteran of *Tanager*'s small space battle in the Delta Three system. His less public roles, first as an unwitting agent of the enemy, then as a momentary tool of Imperial Security, he tried not to think about too often. He had not covered himself in glory during his accidental detour into espionage. Still, that detour did serve to acquaint Che with his current sole passion in life: Imperial Consul (and Imperial Security agent) Winter Yung.

Che smiled sheepishly to himself as he stepped from his small, opulent apartment within the Imperial consulate on Battersea. In the weeks since he was nearly killed within his old demi-cit domicile pod, Che found himself entirely enthralled, his life's ambition jettisoned like an unwanted child's toy as he traced a loose orbit around Winter. She didn't seem to care that Che was a freshly minted Citizen while her own Family descended from Yung the First, the throne of the Myriad Worlds occupied by a cousin or uncle, or whatever, of hers. Che wasn't entirely sure what Winter Yung cared about, except that in some odd way she cared about him. At least, she seemed to on most days.

Not that life in Winter's sphere proved easy, Che had to admit to himself. Winter possessed no patience and little kindness; she incinerated incompetent underlings with acid words; she exposed any exaggeration or deception with preternatural discernment, mercilessly shaming those who offered her such false coin. Until very recently, the only tenderness Che ever observed in Winter occurred during their shared moments of private, glorious intimacy, which Che still regarded in the light of inexplicable miracles.

As Che made his way from his new apartment, into the greater consular residence, passing through the glittering vestibule, he wondered if his dreamlike state of thralldom was the only thing that allowed his relationship with Winter—such as it was—to exist. An occasional voice quietly whispered in the back of Che's mind, suggesting that no man of spirit would ever lower himself to endure such a demeaning situation. That same voice would sometimes further condemn Che as a pathetic worm who did not possess a shred of self-respect.

Che heard the echoes of that illiberal voice as he scanned over Winter's morning gaggle, all waiting within the vestibule. It appeared to be the usual sort of collection: five individuals, all dripping wealth, all handsome, striking or beautiful in their way; one muscular heavyworld man and one tall, graceful lightworld woman among them. Some represented Trade groups or powerful Families, while others might be members of Winter's web of informants. They all looked at Che as he strolled through, some having seen him about on previous visits, and for all Che knew, some of them might have known Winter for decades before she ever met the oh-so-plebian Che Ramos.

Che passed through the vestibule into the solarium, where a consular security operative and one of Winter's new Marines waited. Che gave them both a silent nod and moved to the coffee dispenser, preparing two mugs, one black and salted—Fleet style—the other with a splash of amaretto cream. As he stirred the steaming, fragrant brew, Che told himself he really was *not* in a demeaning situation, but was merely a man who found something valuable that required an unorthodox level of understanding to retain. *Understanding, or clarity?*

Che carried the two mugs through the solarium and into the consular office where another security operative waited beside Winter's secretary, Mossimo Minetti. Che nodded to them both and placed one mug on Winter's broad, unadorned desk, contemplating the concept of *clarity*.

It required unvarnished thinking to...love? venerate? Winter Yung, and Che prided himself on his clear thinking. He knew that despite Winter's youthful loveliness, she had wined and dined, flattered and threatened the rich and powerful for decades before Che's humble birth. The wonders of Shaper technology, married with the pinnacle of human medicine, provided youth to those with the funds, and Winter personified all that rejuv promised. For her, beauty and allure were only tools or weapons within her arsenal, and these weapons saw regular use. To adore Winter Yung was to accept this reality.

Within days of his connection with Winter, back on Coreworld, Che received his first taste of Winter's real life, and his first chance to obtain *clarity*.

At that point Che had spent nearly every blissful minute of three days in close company with Winter. When she attended meetings in the Imperial Close, he waited with the secretaries and bodyguards in some adjoining chamber, but otherwise left her side only in rare moments. Then, upon the fourth evening, Winter had engaged in a long meeting within the consular headquarters, across the table from an aggressively handsome member of the quasi-nobility. Che had waited in the adjoining antechamber, and when Winter finally emerged with the man beside her, he had observed the self-satisfied gleam in the man's eye, the palpable air of animal chemistry about them.

"I won't need you tonight," Winter had said, as if Che served as her secretary.

"Yes, Consul," Che had said with a shallow bow, then spent the next few hours wandering rather dangerously around the metropolis, pondering what course he should take. Since the enemy had tried to assassinate Che, Winter had agreed that his life might be rather brief unless precautions were taken, and his taking a hotel room seemed foolhardy in the extreme. But Winter's curt dismissal had provided no clues for Che. Were her words meant as a dismissal from the entirety of her company too?

Finally, Che had made his way back to the Imperial Close and the lodging Winter maintained at its periphery. No light had shown in the window and the door granted Che access, so Che had entered, deciding to remain for the night, or until Winter made any dismissal more evident to Che's understanding.

Che thought he would always remember the moment when Winter returned to her lodging that night, not long after he had arrived. She swept in, checking at the sight of Che standing in the half-lit gallery, her eyes sweeping over him in their characteristic and unnerving way, peeling away flesh and bone, leaving thoughts and motivations seemingly bare to her gaze. Her expression had been unreadable, a hardness about her eyes, her lips a thin line. "You're here," formed her only words, a statement devoid of any emotion.

"Yes," Che had answered. "Can I fix you a drink?"

It had seemed a little of the hardness fell from Winter's face and she stepped nearer, setting her sword aside, her penetrating gaze still scanning over Che. "Gods, yes."

Che had prepared their drinks then, keenly feeling her presence close beside. They had raised their glasses in a silent toast, regarding each other in the half-light as they drank. Che saw the last of the steel and stone melt from Winter's face and at last she had said the words that seemed to establish the rough shape of their relationship to follow: "Sleep. I have... actionable intelligence. I'll be up for hours, putting the pieces in motion." Che said nothing, only nodding, surprised at the disclosure. She had reached out and placed her firm hand on Che's wrist, her eyes locked upon Che's face, her pupils vast. "You are a rare man, Che Ramos."

As Che waited now in her official consular office on Battersea, he thought of the weeks that had passed since that night on Coreworld, and he thought about the concept of clarity. If he, Che Ramos, truly *was* a rare man, as Winter said, *clarity* must represent the bare scaffolding of that rare quality.

Winter had returned to Battersea weeks earlier with Che as part of her retinue, placing him in one of the consulate's fine apartments, like some kind of visiting dignitary. At the rare moments Winter bowed to any polite conventions, she had introduced Che as her assistant, but usually he remained a silent, watchful curiosity in the crowd of her bodyguards and agents.

On Battersea they attended a few dinners and parties together, at times Winter departing the gathering in the company of some man or woman of the quasi-nobility without a word to Che, only to return to the consular residence the following day at some point.

When Winter returned from these forays, Che saw her reclad in stone and steel, an armor that he did not fully comprehend, but set himself to melt. His efforts met with regular success.

Winter's *other* outings seemed even less explicable, their impact upon Winter more disconcerting.

The first such venture of this sort took Winter away for two silent days before she returned in the company of several battered and bloodied agents, her own expression wild and dangerous to Che's eyes. He had trailed Winter back to her own palatial rooms in the consular residence, heeding her silent invitation.

Behind closed doors, Che had taken Winter's hand, misunderstanding the trembling he felt, perceiving now the spots of blood across her clothing, her platinum locks, dotting her face and neck. He led her, silent and unresisting, to the bath, running the water as her sword clattered to one side, her clothes falling away with the odd gray device nested against her back. As she slipped into the bath, Che scoured the blood from her hair until she caught his wrist, looking up into Che's face with her eyes burning, wild.

That wildness Winter suddenly turned upon Che as a desperate passion that he answered with an aggressive hunger that he did not know he possessed.

Now, reflecting back as he sipped his coffee, Che observed no hint of smugness within himself, coming to realize both extremes of Winter's existence represented challenges to his masculinity. They were part of Winter, and he accepted them, rising to the challenges to the best of his ability, silently avowing that as long as Winter found comfort in his arms, he would remain a refuge for her.

In the next moment Che's thoughts shifted to a recent development that rocked his certainty somewhat.

Just a few days prior, Winter had appeared in the consulate with a skinny, owl-eyed young woman in tow, answering Che's questioning look by saying, "She's Sinclair-Maru. We were class-mates long ago, and she's in danger."

That hadn't really cleared anything up for Che. He knew the Sinclair-Marus' vast estate wasn't all too far from Port City, and they were a Family legendary for protecting their own, so why keep her *here*? Characteristically, Winter read Che's thoughts, even as they formed in his mind, saying, "Che, dear? Jealousy from you? And I was beginning to think you immune to it."

Che had blushed, but Winter patted his cheek affectionately. "The sentiment doesn't diminish you. Quite the reverse." As flat-tering as those words had been, it in no way clarified the young woman's role in Che's already-challenging little world. He only knew that until the Sinclair-Maru girl arrived, he alone witnessed the precious, rare moments of Winter's tenderness. Now, Winter directed uncharacteristic solicitude upon the skinny waif, aston-ishing any of Winter's inner circle who observed it.

Except for the dark hair—what little hair she possessed—and dark eyes, she didn't look like any Sinclair-Maru Che had ever seen. Her facial features trended toward the elfin, her bone structure light, revealing none of the solidity so characteristic of most members of that storied Family.

Che still pondered on the ramifications of this skinny new interloper, when Winter breezed into the office from her private entrance, amazing Che once again with her lithesome beauty, her face, her hair, and clothing composed along somewhat severe lines, but continually attracting Che to her cold fire.

In her distinctive way, Winter's gaze swept over each occupant of the room—Mossimo, Che, and the security agent—seeming to measure and catalog every detail in a single flash before sweep-ing on. Her hand touched the hot coffee mug awaiting atop her desk, and her eyes returned to Che in silent acknowledgment, their morning greeting wordless, as so much of their communi-cation transpired.

"Mossimo?" Winter said, looking back at her secretary. "Any-thing to add beyond the itinerary?"

Winter's secretary inclined his head respectfully. "Only that the governor of Battersea filed a—"

"Saw that already," Winter interrupted. "Anything else?"

"No, Consul," Mossimo said.

Che had already learned that Mossimo held the current record as Winter's secretary, enduring her fault-finding, peremptory rudeness and casual cruelty for two years thus far.

"Leave me. Che, you stay." Winter sipped the coffee Che had prepared. "Oh, Mossimo." Winter snapped her fingers. "Take the temperature of that sod from Trade. I'll see them after my morning call."

Mossimo bowed his head again and departed through the solarium with the security agent, leaving Che and Winter alone for a moment. Che shared an affectionate look with Winter, realizing again how little of their communication manifested as actual spoken words. But their momentary idyll existed only briefly.

"I've got a call in a moment," Winter said, moving back to her private entrance and opening the door. "Entertain Bess for a little, Che dear." The skinny Sinclair-Maru girl stepped into the doorway, peering cautiously about Winter's office before slipping in, her wide eyes only sizing Che for a flash before moving on, evidently finding him unthreatening or perhaps uninteresting.

"Uh, entertain...?"

Winter detached her sword, resting it across her desk. "Yes. Entertain. She's recovering from injuries. There's a game she enjoys...unless you'd prefer to read a story to her." Winter actuated her desk holo, the Imperial Security seal filling its depths. "Really, Che, what do you think I'm busy doing all night with Bess, hmmm?" Winter arched a wicked eyebrow at him, laughing at his blushes. "She can't really speak much as yet, so use that beautiful patience of yours to good purpose, right, Che, love?"

Bess shuffled nearer to Che and he saw she bore a small game mat and a bag full of colorful markers. As Bess knelt on the floor beside Che, spreading out the small mat, he retained a vague memory of the game from childhood, remembering the object of laying five markers in uninterrupted sequence.

As Winter initiated her call, Che laid markers on the game mat, following Bess, marker for marker, her gaze wandering over Che, to the ceiling and down at the game. She dropped her markers without evident consideration or dexterity, and Che's attention slowly shifted to Winter's conversation, laying his own game pieces down almost at random.

"Lam, tell me something good," Winter said to the figure within the holo as she paced about before her desk.

"Something good, Winter?" the voice came back. "No, Winter,

not so good. Something interesting, perhaps; something frightening even, yes."

Winter crossed her arms. "The implant samples from those
traitorous shits?"

"Gah," Bess declared quietly, dragging Che's attention back
to the game mat where five of her colorful markers formed a
neat sequence.

"Got me," Che murmured, and Bess swept the mat clear,
placing a lone marker again.

"Oh, new game?" Che said softly. "Very well…" Che dropped
a marker to block Bess, his attention returning to Winter's voice.

"Don't quibble, Lam," Winter sneered. "The implant samples I
sent you came from the skulls of traitors. They weren't using them
anymore, and they certainly aren't complaining about it now."

"Winter, I agreed to perform a detailed analysis on these
Shaper implants because their provenance was unknown. Don't
try to tie me to your extra-legal poaching now."

"I wonder," Winter mused in her sweetest, most dangerous
voice, "am I the only member of Imperial Security creating results
instead of excuses?"

"Boo," Bess whispered, placing a marker on the mat, and Che
dropped a game piece at random, listening to Winter's exchange.

"I think you'll be impressed—or perhaps appalled—by the
results I've obtained, Winter, so you can stop sharpening a sword
for my neck."

"So impress me, Lam," Winter snapped. "Quit tossing about,
and appall me."

"I sent Riddell over to the consulate with a physical report. He
should be there already, and you can be impressed—or appalled—in
the privacy and security of your own office."

"Your oppressive caution bores me, Lam," Winter purred.
"I am not endowed with patience, and you see that Riddell is
manifestly not here, so give me a summary. Now."

Lam sighed, and Che wondered if the man did not fully
understand the peril emanating from Winter in palpable currents.

"Gah, boo," Bess announced in her quiet little voice, and Che
looked down to see her line of victorious markers. Before Che
even spoke, Bess cleared the game pieces again, looking at Che
expectantly. "Boo."

"Oh, I play first now? Very well."

"The summary, Winter?" Lam said from the depths of the holo. "The implants you provided—all of the implants you provided—they were dramatically, but subtly altered." Lam's voice sounded strained to Che's ears as Lam continued, "I—I would need to see them in situ ideally to—"

"Next time I'll bring the whole damned skull, Lam. See what that does for your poor scruples!" Winter interrupted. "Altered how? By what?"

"The modifications seem beyond our abilities under—"

"Are you saying the Shapers' hands are on this?" Winter interrupted again and Che heard a rare note of shock in her voice.

"Not necessarily, Winter, can you please just wait for Riddell to—"

"No, gods dammit, Lam! I can't wait. If it's not the Shapers, then how the shit are they doing this?"

Lam sounded increasingly flustered. "Possibly like an N-space fab, perhaps. The neural taps are—are altered and extended, so maybe a nanotech solution and N-space fab... But, Winter, please—"

"Okay, shut up, Lam." Che looked up at Winter's changed tone, seeing her eyes flicker. "Agent Riddell just arrived. I'll get back to you with any questions."

Winter ended the call and Che felt a creeping sense of unease at the expression she wore. "Take Bess to my room," Winter said in a barren voice, a line on her porcelain brow, her gaze distant. "I'm not sure how long I'll be."

"Boo, gah," Bess said and scooped up the game pieces, following Che to the door. Che turned to share one last look with Winter as the intervening door swung closed. In that last glimpse, Che saw Winter's expression change to one of frozen horror, and a flash image of Agent Riddell's face as he neared Winter's desk, a familiar fixed grin on his lips. And the door closed.

With the door closed, Che hesitated only a bare instant before taking the most thoughtless, courageous step in his life, fumbling his sword from its sheath and reopening the door.

Agent Riddell's pistol filled the grinning man's fist, levelled between Winter's eyes. "No," Winter said in a choked voice, just as Riddell fired, far too close to miss. The sharp bark of the pistol rang in Che's ears even he inexpertly lunged, the razor point of his blade sliding easily through the flesh under Riddell's arm, grating on bone as it transfixed the agent.

Agent Riddell's abrupt pivot surprised Che, the sword grip slipping from his numb fingers. Che saw the unaccountable grin on Riddell's lips, the dripping point of Che's sword jutting out from Riddell's chest, the pistol swinging around. Che felt the punch in his ribs at the same moment he heard the blasting report. The floor seemed to catch Che as he stumbled, suddenly unable to breathe.

As darkness ringed Che's vision, Agent Riddell suddenly convulsed above him, bullets riddling the grinning man where he stood. Even as the world faded, Che heard Winter's voice shouting... shouting... silence.

Chapter 29

"Over the centuries of variegated human civilization, young humans with their early idealism, their strong hormonal energies and their affection for feelings, have often disproportionately steered societies (for better or worse) during a fairly small portion of their respective lives. What impact will extended longevity have upon our society now?"

—Everest Compline, *Reflections*

AS *HIGHTOWER* APPROACHED HER ORBIT DEPTH, SAEF JUGGLED dozens of inputs at once, his command UI flickering with changing values, while the blue-green globe began to dominate the optical image.

"Weps," Saef said, glancing over at Pennysmith's position, "restructure our missile hardpoints. Give us an even mix—sixty-four gauge, thirty-twos, and SHIGRIT monolithics."

"Aye, Captain," Pennysmith said as she keyed the magazine. "Even mix, thirty-twos, sixty-fours, and monolithic ship-to-ground."

"Ops," Saef said to Deckchief Furst at the Ops seat, "what's the status on fighters and Krenner's assault force?"

"Marine quarterdeck shows green, ready to drop." Furst hesitated slightly before saying, "Commander Jamila requests an interview before fighters launch."

Saef frowned to himself, consulting the descending launch clock in his UI. *I don't have time for this*... "Very well, Deckchief. Tell the commander to be quick about it."

"Yes, Captain."

Saef barely observed the flicker in his UI before Pim called out from Comm, "Captain, we are receiving a coded signal on a commercial frequency." Pim paused, checking the signal analysis. "It's a short message, Legion code."

"Originating where, Comm?" Saef asked.

Pim consulted his panel. "Dirtside... location up on tactical." The signal coordinates appeared on the tactical holo, all but overlaying the Legion's original ground objective—the *installation of interest.*

"Decode and put it up." Saef turned as the bridge access cycled, Commander Jamila striding in, clad in her tight black ship suit, her flight helmet under her arm. Saef rose and met Commander Jamila as Inga looked on from her place beside the bridge access.

"Commander," Saef said, "we have a very short window to get your recon fighters into their insertion point. How can I be of assistance?"

"Two fighters are not enough for a combat recon drop, Captain," Jamila said, her face grim, and hair slicked back against her skull, her whole appearance transformed.

Saef nodded. "I agree... Orders from the commodore that we must obey, however."

"Then I *must* lead the recon, sir," she said, her jaw tightening pugnaciously.

"We don't have time for this, Commander—"

"Sir, if it's too dangerous to risk my skin, it's too dangerous to send in just two birds."

Saef drew a slow breath, glancing back at the tactical holo, the image of their target growing, the Legion's short message scrolling intriguingly. "Recon missions are always hazardous. Risking our fighter expert in our initial recon is the height of foolishness. Send someone else."

"What I propose, sir, is a high-altitude overwatch. I can hold the high position, get a broad sensor footprint, and direct the low altitude bird. That calls for an expert. It calls for me." Jamila's words were coming fast by the end, and her eyes held a desperate, pleading look in their depths.

Saef saw the launch clock ticking down in his UI, feeling off-balance and uncertain. "Commander," he said after a moment, "don't make a habit of arguing with me. Take your high position."

Jamila seemed almost choked with gratitude. "Yes, Captain. Thank you." She turned on her heel and nearly ran from the bridge.

Saef looked back at the holo as he reassumed his place, his gaze traveling over the decoded Legion message. "Captain, I've decoded the—" Pim began saying when Saef interrupted.

"I see it."

The simple message supplied their purported location, and the line, 86 LNS, PREP FOR ENEMY ARMOR, and nothing more. Just eighty-six Legionnaires had survived? The warning to prepare for enemy armor might explain a great deal. With half the message devoted to a warning about enemy armor, that fact certainly seemed of great importance to the surviving Legionnaires.

"Does that position check out?" Saef said, thinking of *Hightower*'s fighters, Marines, and swiftly diminishing time until launch.

"Yes, Captain. Just a little south of the Legion's original target objective."

Saef nodded. "Alright, push that message to Colonel Krenner and to *Dragon*, if you please, Pim."

As the sphere of Delta Three filled much of the main holo, Saef looked up to see the gleaming superstructure of a familiar orbital station hoving slowly into view, little more than a glittering jewel coming around the planet. Despite all the pressures, Saef stared for a protracted moment, recalling the slaughter and carnage within that station, and the vast fortune one vessel docked there had contained.

The bridge access cycled, admitting Lieutenants Wycherly and Dubois, a stocky heavyworld Marine lieutenant in their wake. The three officers entered the ground operations center adjoining the bridge, never seeing Inga tucked in the shadows beside the access. The ground ops holo tanks swirled into life, illuminating the oblong chamber in green and blue. With Marines and fighters soon to launch, the ground ops team prepared to oversee their first real operation in the war, and Saef wished he felt more confident in their abilities.

Saef turned to his own team all at their stations before him: Pennysmith, Pim, Ash, Belfort, Furst, and Alsop. Within his UI, Saef scanned through the myriad values that represented *Hightower*'s vital functions, a nagging disquiet unsettling him.

Prepare for enemy armor.

Such an explicit warning must carry great weight, but would Krenner heed it?

The clock ticked down. He had no time to go ensure Krenner's observance of this specific intelligence, and yet it seemed far too important to ignore. Almost against his will, Saef turned to Inga. Their close communion seemed irreparably damaged, barely speaking for days, and he felt a strong resistance to seeking her assistance now.

He sent a line-of-sight message to Inga's UI: PLEASE PERSUADE KRENNER TO HEED THE LEGION MESSAGE, ON MY ORDERS OR NOT—AS YOU SEE FIT.

Inga stepped forward out of the shadows, her eyes gleaming reflected light. She looked pointedly toward Wycherly and Dubois in the adjoining ground ops center, then back at Saef. Her short message pinged into Saef's UI: I WILL TRY. And she was gone in the swirl of her cloak, the bridge access cycling behind her.

Inga hurried toward the Marine quarterdeck, knowing the seconds ticking down to launch made any last-moment preparation by the Marines increasingly impractical. *Hightower* already stood on full alert, with crew members at action stations, so companionways remained unpopulated except for a few security or damage control ratings. Just prior to the waist hatches one custodial rating supervised a trio of janitorial dumb-mechs, head down as she tinkered with a six-legged deck-buffing mech. Her presence struck Inga as discordant, prompting her to tie into Loki's sensory powers, observing the hunched rating even as Inga hurried by, Inga's back ostensibly open to any assault. Aside from sneaking a furtive glance at Inga, the rating took no action of note, and Inga continued on, passing through the waist access to the aft compartments.

Sifting Loki's senses for suggestions of true mutiny continued to be an exercise of near futility. Most of the crew and Marines spoke scathingly of Saef from time to time, and true mutineers were unlikely to speak plainly enough of their intentions for Loki to pick them out. This left Inga pulled in a hundred directions, trying to monitor potential saboteurs and traitors all through *Hightower* even as she physically roved.

The Marines' sortie bay seethed with activity, jammed with armed and armored Marines and equipment. As Inga scanned across the ranks she observed a small cluster in black ship suits, another streamlined group in light scout armor, both in the midst of a mob clad in the mottled gray shock armor of Marine heavy infantry. Dipping into Loki's sensor flow, Inga picked out Lieutenant Colonel Krenner holding court on the far side of the sortie bay, Marine officers clustered around a sort of impromptu throne formed from ammunition crates.

Inga consciously slowed her pace, strolling through the ranks of armor-clad Marines as they stood joking and chatting, seemingly in good spirits despite facing what would be the first real combat operation for most of their number. Their eyes followed her progress, word passing ahead. Krenner and his coterie of officers turned and silently watched Inga amble up to their gathering.

"The captain's cox'n," Krenner declared, his proud mustache jutting out stiffly. "Come to check up on the Ten and Twenty, Chief? Doesn't Ops show the quarterdeck as green?"

Inga shrugged, producing a red fruit from the depths of her cloak and taking a bite as the Marine officers eyed her with scarcely concealed hostility. "Dunno, Colonel. Not my lane, really." She took another bite, striving for an air of disinterest. "Came to see the parade...and seal a bet."

"*Parade?*" Major Vigo repeated with a growl in his tone, while Krenner's eyebrows rose, his face rippling as an unpleasant grin stretched his mouth.

"*What* bet?" Krenner said.

Inga looked at the fuming major before waving her fruit at the surrounding masses of warfighters. "All this...must be the greatest ground assault Marines have staged this war, right? Quite the parade."

Major's Vigo's feelings seemed somewhat assuaged, though he still frowned at Inga.

"What bet?" Krenner repeated.

Inga looked at Krenner beneath her eyelashes. "Just a little game I play with the captain. You did see that message from those poor Legion sods dirtside, didn't you, Colonel?"

"I saw it." Krenner's grin remained but his tone contained a warning.

Inga knew she stood on a delicate balance, taking another bite of her fruit as she felt her way through the minefield. A muffled clanking sound preceded the appearance of Krenner's four Imperial battledress-equipped assaulters, the adamantine monstrosities stepping out of the armorer's and moving through their brethren.

Inga pointed the core of her fruit. "Hah! I bloody win. Captain loses. Excellent."

Krenner didn't turn toward the battledress Marines, maintaining his fixed stare on Inga, but Major Vigo did, saying, "The captain bet we wouldn't drop with *them*? Never heard the man was such a fool as that."

"That's not it at all, is it, Chief?" Krenner said to Inga, eyeing her keenly.

Inga shook her head. "Oh no, that's not the bet." She swept her audience of frowning Marine officers with one fast look. "Fleet says there're no enemy tanks down dirtside; the Legionnaires' message says there are. I bet that you'd believe the Legions, seeing how *something's* killing the hell out of them down there." She nodded toward the four battledress assaulters. "You're bringing the heavy artillery because you *do* believe them."

Krenner's unreadable gaze transfixed Inga and he stood slowly to his full height, his helmet under his armor-clad biceps. Inga felt the awareness flow through her, finding no lever to intimidate, only to inform: she stood within easy arm's reach of a predator. "I don't think I like you much, Chief," he said.

Inga inclined her head until one eye fell behind the fringe of her hair. She smiled. "I'm desolated, Colonel. Popularity's not my lane either."

On the periphery Inga saw the other Marine officers stiffen at her mocking tone, and Inga observed the blue fork of veins throb on Krenner's forehead. Rage hovered around Krenner, always at hand.

"Good hunting," Inga said after a loaded moment. "Nothing sweeter than victory, and I'm going to collect."

Inga turned on her heel, making her way back through the sortie bay without a rearward look. Keying in to Loki's sensors, Inga listened to Krenner and his officers as she continued on her way back toward the bridge.

"High-handed sort," Major Shirai growled.

"She is," Krenner agreed, and then after a moment he continued, "We've got enough time. Rearm the battledress with ARC kit...and might as well issue out SCAARS, one per platoon."

"Yes, sir," two lieutenants answered in unison, clattering hurriedly away.

Inga heard Major Vigo's voice speak again, an entirely different tone at work. "May I ask why, Colonel?"

Lieutenant Colonel Krenner only waited a moment to respond. "The high-handed scut had a point," he said. "All those Legionnaires dirtside didn't kill themselves. And nothing is sweeter than victory."

Among *Hightower*'s small custodial crew, Wren Davies originally earned the dislike of her peers due to her surly, belligerent nature. Evidently the prospect of approaching combat served to transform her personality. Ever since *Hightower* made the N-space transition to Delta Three, Wren Davies offered a pleasant grin to all her mates, and she volunteered for every thankless task facing the custodial ratings.

She endured one such task, hunched over a janitorial dumb-mech as Inga strode by on her way to the Marine quarterdeck. Once Inga moved well on her way, Wren Davies continued her path, directing and servicing the three janitorial mechs as they addressed the cleaning needs of cabin after cabin. In each room Wren lifted a flat gray rectangle from the soapy innards of one dumb-mech, sliding it firmly into the shadows beneath a bunk.

When she left each room, the deck plates glimmered spotlessly, and the small, gray receptacles lay awaiting their purpose.

Hightower carried most of her troop transports and many of her interface fighters nested in external hull voids. Just off the fighter deck, an access iris led to the spine, where nested Mangusta interface fighters showed their open cockpits, alternating every few paces, one on the wet side of the spine, the next on the dry side.

Commander Yazmin Jamila led the other three members of the fighter recon element, each clad in the tight black ship suits, each carrying their helmets as they strode down the spine to their waiting birds. All the talking lay behind them, all the planning, the routes and maps; all the scant intel and threat assessments they possessed. Now they would simply become the purest breed of combat aviators in the Myriad Worlds, where reflex, intuition, and a steady hand on the stick defined success or failure.

Lieutenants Matt Mayo and Jackie Shipman peeled off to Mangusta AF-2, the first open cockpit, while Commander Jamila continued on with her operator, Lieutenant Deke Paris, to the next bird. They dropped in and Jamila began her checklist as Deke cycled their double-envelope canopy, sealing them in, moving through his own checklist in the rear seat, his face illuminated in the greenish glow of scopes and instruments.

Interface fighters comprised a complex conjunction of systems. They required all the control surfaces and aerodynamic qualities of any atmospheric fighter, plus the systems necessary for any in-system spacecraft to function. Piloting such a craft, particularly into a combat setting, required a blend of physical and cerebral qualities uncommon now among the Myriad Worlds.

Jamila finished the preflight diagnostics, locked her faceplate and breathing apparatus into place, and flipped the helmet lenses down. As she cinched her retention harness tight, she looked back over her shoulder. "You good, Deke?"

"I'm amazing," Deke replied, clipping his own breathing apparatus, "or so I'm told."

Jamila snorted in reply, seeing AF-2 switch to green as Matt and Jackie showed ready. Jamila took a calming breath, triggered her comm. "Fighter control, recon wing one and two, spine launch, ready for separation."

Fighter control responded immediately, their audible words mirrored in scrolling text across Jamila's lens: RECON WING ONE AND TWO, COOL DECEL, SIXTY SECONDS—GO FOR SEPARATION.

"Recon one," Jamila affirmed, hearing Matt Mayo's calm tenor chime in:

"Recon two."

Jamila activated the cool thruster control, steadying her hand on the stick before pulling the release. This encompassed a process she had performed hundreds of times before, but Jamila now swallowed a sudden tension rising in her throat, the muted click of release from the spine preceding the slow drop from *Hightower*. Her first drop into combat began...

As the cockpit bubble cleared *Hightower*'s obstructing hull, light reflecting from the planet below suddenly illuminated every detail, gleaming off the three vast muzzles of *Hightower*'s barrage battery and exposing the great length of her hull stretching out above them. With the three-sixty view afforded by her lenses,

Jamila observed Matt and Jackie behind her, descending in unison, their cool thrusters bleeding velocity.

"Deke, power up our shield generator and prepare to initiate our insertion."

"Roger that, Yaz. Shield generator online, and insertion course is on your scope... now."

Commander Yazmin Jamila looked up as *Hightower*'s superstructure seemed to slowly shrink into the starscape, forging ahead, while the first rumbles of turbulence signaled their descent into Delta Three's atmosphere. She drew another calming breath, wondering if she would ever see *Hightower* again.

Lieutenants Matt Mayo and Jackie Shipman felt the onset of turbulence from their seats in recon two. "You got that shield angled fifteen degrees negative, Jack?" Matt asked, glancing over his shoulder at Jackie.

"It is now," she replied, her voice shaking slightly as their Mangusta fighter bounced through the turbulence, its wings visibly flexing. "Fifteen degrees negative."

Matt turned his attention back to recon one, Jamila's bird, just ahead. As he watched, both of Jamila's engines glowed into life with a dim blue fire, and he reached to toggle his own atmospheric engines. "Engine one, online," Jackie said. "Engine two, online."

Matt looked at the planet expanding to fill the horizon, the vast sweep of blue ocean uninterrupted almost as far as the eye could see as the light of Delta Three's dawn preceded them. *This is where our paths diverge.*

Matt double-checked the graphical flight path unfolding on his lenses. "Here we go, Jack." With a twitch of the control stick Matt rolled the Mangusta inverted and plummeted toward the deck, Jackie Shipman adjusting the shield projector to hold the shield angle at fifteen degrees negative relative to the horizon as they dove. The Mangusta may have comprised a weapon manufacturer's dream, with every imaginable technology and subsystem stuffed within its streamlined fuselage, but it still only sported a single shield generator. That generator only provided optimal coverage over one-third of the fighter's surface, requiring the backseat operator to position the shield as needs arose.

Matt manipulated the control stick, righting the aircraft and leveling off just a half klick off the white-flecked ocean, the coastline ahead growing quickly distinct, closing at just under the speed of sound. As planned, the dawning sun rose behind them in all of its brilliant, blinding glory.

So far the recon fighters had maintained a strict communications silence, and utilized passive sensors only, striving to reach the target site undetected, but Matt scanned over his instruments and scopes, feeling a growing sense of disbelief at the untoward silence. "You asleep back there, Jack? Seeing any sensor sweeps? Any comm activity? Anything?"

"Negative," Jackie said. "Not a peep."

Matt looked up to his right, the optical feed through his lenses allowing him to pick out Jamila's bird in high overwatch, up twelve klicks, running high and silent until they cleared the target.

"Okay, Jack, twenty seconds to target... In ten seconds power up active sensors and comms, and stand by for countermeasures."

"Roger that. Sensors and comms in nine, eight, seven... standing by countermeasures."

Matt picked out details ahead, racing swiftly nearer, and his hand dropped to the twin throttles, ready to put the Mangusta's big, fat engines to good use. Ruined buildings dotted the coastline, some sort of oceangoing vessel half-submerged beside a broad pier, and they were past, racing over a blur of structures and streets.

Sensors and active comms lit up a moment before they reached the "installation of interest," overflying it in an instant.

"We've got an active link to a Legion signal," Jackie called out, then in a sharper voice, "We're getting painted!"

Matt saw a few hot beads of cannon fire stream up and fall away well off their left wing, but Jackie's attention remained riveted on her instruments, unaware. "Lock! They've got a lock on us!"

Matt's hand slammed both throttles back and he pressed the control stick forward, counterintuitively lowering the Mangusta's nose as their velocity surged. They dove toward the deck, Jackie triggering all the countermeasures at their command. Matt banked over, the engines screaming as they raced at rooftop level for the ocean. Matt leveled off as the Mangusta shattered the sound barrier, running all out. "Did you see it, Jack? Did you see the target? Gods—!"

Commander Jamila's voice suddenly blared over the comm, *"Matt! Incoming air intercept! Zero-one-zero left! Evade!"*

Matt could not understand, could not accept the words Jamila was saying, but some subconscious string pulled and he banked hard to the right, just as something blasted past, coming head-on. It passed so close, the Mangusta jolted.

"That hit our shield! Heat sink at red." Jackie's voice shook as the Mangusta accelerated across the ocean.

From her overwatch, twelve klicks up, her sensors painting every moving object, Jamila called out, "Matt, you've got two more on you. Come to...one-one-zero left and I'll clear you."

"Jack, roll shields to our six," Matt said, banking to one-one-zero, still running all out. "Activate the tail cannon."

The tail cannon...things have become truly desperate. In his shock-numbed state Matt almost smiled to himself at the thought of telling the other fighter jocks that he *actually* used the absurd cannon...if they managed to survive.

Jackie began firing, the stubby multibarrel cannon roaring out chains of red tracers in their wake.

"*Missile away!*" Jamila called out from her high position.

Jamila's shot slashed down at an oblique angle, a whippet missile, Matt saw, streaking by far behind. "Miss!" Jamila's voice called over the comm, desperate. "Got an ID, Matt. Not fighters. They're drones! Maneuver!"

Matt immediately understood: with the lag time of a drone, a distant operator could never match the reflexes of a live pilot, and the drones were closing fast. Matt threw the Mangusta into the tightest emergency turn possible, but neither Lieutenant Matt Mayo nor Lieutenant Jackie Shipman had a moment to realize the sheer futility of their action.

Two drones struck the Mangusta almost broadside, blowing through the fringe of their paltry shield and exploding the armored cockpit in an instant, burning fragments showering the blue waves of Delta Three below.

Chapter 30

"It is instructive to recall the early days of the Great Houses, most of whom credit their founding to some wise and honored ancestor. Now that many honored ancestors remain present through the advancing centuries, does their influence increase through their active hand in the Family's affairs? Or decrease as younger generations are able to observe the fallibility of their forebears firsthand?"

—Everest Compline, *Reflections*

"COMMODORE, *HIGHTOWER*'S DROPPED TWO FIGHTERS INTO THE well," Ensign Laurent, the Sensors officer, stated within the darkened bridge of *Dragon*, monitoring her scope.

"About bloody time," Commodore Glasshauser sniped. "All the talk of this Sinclair-Maru fire-eater, and we get Lord Timid here. Now if he'll just follow orders, drop the damned Marines in, and scoop the twice-damned Legionnaires off that rock, we can get back to a real mission."

Glasshauser's bravado had slowly recovered after the nasty shock he received from that enemy cruiser's bold attack. Sometime after the action, when the haze of startled unreality faded, he began to imagine he had acquitted himself far more valiantly than witnesses might attest. He now increasingly believed his responses approached those of a tactical genius, and in light of this confidence he formulated a fresh strategy, positioning his squadron with a new plan in mind. Someday, he felt sure, they would refer to this array of defensive forces as the "Glasshauser Envelopment," although the general idea vaguely resembled something he half-remembered from some boring lecture back in command school.

He could readily visualize himself lecturing hordes of future Fleet officers, all of whom longed to hear about the Glasshauser Envelopment from one of the very few Fleet captains to ever emerge *victorious* from a scrape with such a—

"Commodore," the Sensors officer called out, interrupting Glasshauser's pleasant reverie, "I just got a transient hit on an active scan. One-one-five positive ecliptic, zero-four-six right azimuth."

Glasshauser frowned at the Sensors officer, glancing at the tactical holo. "Well, Laurent...just a transient hit...so far off the ecliptic, I wouldn't think it could be—"

"There it is again, sir," he said. He stared at his instruments as he adjusted the sensitivity. "That's...I'm pretty sure that's a live contact, sir."

Glasshauser's frown deepened. It had to be an error. What fool would initiate an attack approach so far off the ecliptic plane?

Comm spoke up suddenly. "Tight beam from *Rook*, sir. They report a contact corresponding to our transient at one-one-five positive."

Rook stood nearly one hundred thousand klicks nearer to the potential contact, surely in a clear line for identification. Glasshauser felt a familiar internal chill as he silently rebelled against reality: his entire strategy depended upon potential attackers aggressing from the relatively narrow band of the ecliptic plane, where any sensible commander would initiate.

Yet again, Glasshauser found his bridge crew all looking expectantly toward him, awaiting some bolt of insight he could not seem to grasp onto. He didn't find the growing silence helpful to his concentration.

He stared at the tactical holo, seeing an evident path that *felt* somehow good to him. He broke the silence. "Nav, bring us to zero-six-zero right, ten gees." They would just slip in close to Delta Three's station and...

The deckchief seemed ready to speak, hesitating, then finally saying, "Sir, if that's the big damned cruiser up there, when they see us maneuver, won't they smash *Rook* where she is?"

Glasshauser felt sweat begin beading his forehead, anger at the deckchief's temerity flaring up to compete with a tumult of other, less defined sensations. "Yes, of course, Deckchief," he managed to calmly enunciate. "Comm, direct *Rook* to evade, reposition for comm relays."

"Aye, sir. Evade and reposition."

"Weps," Glasshauser continued, feeling a little more natural, a bit more like the tactical genius of a few moments earlier, "shield generators to full. All missile batteries armed."

"Sir," Laurent at Sensors called out in a terse voice, "possible signature of an enemy energy weapon."

Comm blurted out, "*Rook* reports broad damage. Heavy energy weapon strike."

The deckchief stared at Glasshauser as he opened his mouth soundlessly, searching for an order that reflected the brilliance he *knew* he possessed. "Would you like to reposition *Python* and *Sherwood*, Commodore?" she asked.

This seemed to unclog the glacier damming up Glasshauser's mind. "Yes, yes. Message *Python* and *Sherwood* to close with the enemy. Direct *Mistral* to reposition to—"

"We have no comms with *Mistral*, Commodore," the deckchief interjected, unforgivably interrupting Commodore Glasshauser. "They're beyond the planetary horizon and *Rook* can't relay now."

Glasshauser would remember the deckchief's behavior. After they dealt with this interloping enemy, she would receive a severe reprimand for her unconscionable—

"Commodore," Comm called out, "*Hightower* reports her deployed fighters are under attack from enemy aircraft, planetside."

"Enemy contact at one-one-five is maneuvering!" Sensors barked, staring at the changing scene within his instruments.

Glasshauser wiped the sweat from his brow, trying to secure some grip on his racing pulse. "Message squadron to attack enemy at one-one-five. Message *Hightower* to get those gods-damned Legionnaires off that rock!"

"But if there are enemy aircraft in the well, Commodore," the deckchief said, "the Marine transports won't have a—"

"That is enough, Deckchief!" Glasshauser snapped. "*Hightower*'s captain is curiously shy. Any excuse to avoid a risk, and I won't hear any more about these imaginary aircraft!"

Ensign Laurent at Sensors seemed oblivious to Glasshauser's

angry words, glued to the changing scene unfolding around Delta Three. "Commodore, target is launching missiles. *Rook* appears to be disabled."

Glasshauser's hands clenched the arms of his seat, feeling lost in a tumult of chaos. That gods-damned cruiser would eat his small squadron piecemeal unless he could figure something... some brilliant stroke.

Brilliance could not be found within grasp of Glasshauser's frantic thoughts. "Weps," he croaked. "Continuous launch, all missile batteries." The deckchief looked sharply at Glasshauser, and the acting commodore almost spoke up in defense of his actions, but he just clenched his teeth, looking over at the Comm lieutenant.

"Comm, signal *Python* and *Sherwood* to continuous launch. Target at one-one-five."

"Aye, Commodore," Comm replied.

"Nav, bring us twenty degrees negative, hold ten gees."

"Twenty degrees negative, holding ten gees."

Glasshauser didn't remember any such maneuver from command school, but it seemed suddenly reasonable to launch missiles in profligate numbers, then to slip under Delta Three's orbital station, placing its substantial bulk between *Dragon* and that wicked cruiser and its twice-damned energy weapons.

Glasshauser remained too absorbed in the unfolding scene to notice the deckchief lean over to a young attendant mid standing by the bridge access, and Glasshauser couldn't hear her say, "Find the XO. With my compliments, ask him to visit the bridge. Now."

For the Legionnaires planetside, the remainder of the night dragged by with an increasing sense of dread. Kyle saw it on every weary, dirty face: the new impression of hopelessness. To behold an enemy attentive and responsive enough to immediately demolish a vast transmission tower less than a klick from the Legionnaires' position cast their enemy in a whole new light. Even Major Chetwynd fell into a shocked silence, and no Legionnaire felt any confidence that their desperate message had reached any friendly forces in orbit above before the enemy silenced it. Still, in the age-old habit of the hunted, most managed spells of fitful dozing, all wondering if the enemy might visit a similar destruction upon them all before the sun rose.

As the first glimmers of dawn began to lighten the sky to the east, Kyle and Pippi watched Avery Reardon pan the mass driver mounted on his Molo mech, scanning from window to window. The soft whine of Cuthbert's servos added to the cough and murmuring of the stirring Legionnaires.

"Reardon," Pippi grunted. "What we do now? Die here? Die some other places?"

Avery Reardon finished his scan and flipped the eyepiece up on his helmet. "Truthfully, I don't care for setting here, Pippi. It lacks quality, ambience. I vote for dying elsewhere. Now, if we can just persuade our brilliant leader that we should relocate..."

"What if our message made it out to Fleet?" Kyle interjected, placing his dirty helmet over hair grown somewhat shaggy. "If we bugger off, and they come to extract us..."

"One problem at a time, Kyle. If we don't bugger off, I'm not sure there will be anyone left to extract." At Kyle's mulish expression, Avery continued, "Don't fret, old fellow. It's only been a week or so since our last comm connection. If there's anyone left alive up there, they'll connect, I would think... eventually."

Pippi and Kyle shared a look, and Avery stood, dusting his armor off and hefting his carbine. "I'll go set the hook in a certain Pathfinder slow top and—" Avery ducked instinctively as every Legionnaire sprawled out, a sudden thunder battering them all. All eyes looked up in time to see the flash of a broad wingspan, two engines glowing blue in the early morning haze. The fighter flashed by in an instant, the thunder a sustained roar that shook them where they sprawled. In the distance, they heard the sudden basso hammer of an auto-cannon, glowing tracers arcing up above the skyline of tortured buildings, dropping into the distance.

"Change of plans," Avery announced over the diminishing reverberations. "We go find a perch for a view. That was a Fleet bird, unless I'm mistaken." He turned and hurried through the wide-eyed Legionnaires to a suddenly revitalized Major Chetwynd. Kyle couldn't hear the sales pitch, but the result put the major and Avery in a rare moment of unity, urging all the Legionnaires to their feet.

A moment later, the jet fighter screamed by in a flash, barely above the rooftops, the engines' roar rattling the Legionnaires where they stood. Two smaller, quieter aircraft shot by in close pursuit, followed shortly by three booming detonations of a broken sound barrier.

Just as Kyle noticed the presence of restored combat Nets, they flickered, disappearing again, but he had little time to think as their group moved out at a reckless pace. Avery and Chetwynd led the way, just like he had joked back before they left their sanctuary in the hills.

Pippi and Kyle straggled near the end of their small column, hurrying through the ruined and abandoned streets, following Chetwynd and Reardon to an intact building less than a klick north of their previous position.

The line of Legionnaires threaded through the shattered entrance doors, and Kyle saw the signs of a failed resistance all around the building's interior. Furniture and other rudimentary materials had once formed a rough barricade across the doors, now scattered and buckled within a room that smelled of old blood. A surprising number of shoes lay singly or in disordered pairs, some clearly the shoes of children. Kyle's sense of gray dismay suddenly multiplied, but he had no time to sift feelings as the line of Legionnaires rushed up a dim stairwell, clambering over more failed breastworks of furniture and refuse.

Weary, sweating, with Fang struggling over the various obstacles, Kyle finally emerged upon a high floor to find Chetwynd, Avery Reardon, and another Pathfinder all staring through a perfectly round hole blasted through the building's western wall.

All three of them wore expressions of bleak horror, and seeing the unflappable Avery so affected shredded Kyle's own last dregs of confidence. Kyle saw a Legionnaire standing to one side, his eyes downcast, his carbine dangling limply from its sling. Kyle nudged the Legionnaire. "What are they looking at?"

The Legionnaire stared bleakly at Kyle for a moment before finally saying, "Our . . . our objective." Kyle looked from Avery's pale features and back to the Legionnaire as the man continued, "Should have nuked it to begin with. Should still nuke it . . . and us."

Commander Yazmin Jamila piloted her Mangusta fighter up out of the deep well, racing to rejoin *Hightower* in orbit as swiftly as possible, two thoughts gripping her until she could scarcely breathe: She failed Matt Mayo and Jackie Shipman, allowing—no, *causing* their violent deaths. She also knew that the enemy threat below might end any chance to rescue the stranded Legionnaires. She could not allow the burning sense of her horrific failure to restrain her from the duty that now lay clearly before her.

The words between Jamila and Deke remained sparse as they ascended the heights, both silently mourning their fallen mates. "We've got a solid link to *Hightower*," Deke said.

Jamila saw the nav path illuminate within her lenses, steering the Mangusta fighter on its feeble thrusters, now transformed from a powerful atmospheric fighter craft into a clumsy and underpowered gunboat upon leaving its prime habitat within the envelope of air. "Upload our data files now, Deke," she ordered. Though they would join up with *Hightower* in minutes, she knew the Marine ground assault could begin at any moment, and the data they carried must influence any new move into the well.

"Upload complete. We've got approach telemetry from fighter control coming through now."

Jamila looked out at *Hightower*'s looming shape, then began navigating up the path illuminated in her lens display, just as a distant fire bloomed far above Delta Three's northern pole.

"What the hell is that, Yaz?" Deke asked.

Another distant eruption of light joined the first, and with no means of determining the range, Jamila guessed it to be at least one hundred thousand klicks distant. "Somebody is getting some bad news out there," she said, turning back to their narrowing approach. "We were just first on that list today."

Their berth awaited just ahead, the nesting port on the spine, but the adjoining port would remain empty, a void created by the deaths of Matt and Jackie, the fiery end of AF-2.

Chapter 31

"Since antiquity, it is known: the eminence of a House may be gauged in the splendor of their servants. The Sinclair-Maru seem immune to this wisdom, stubbornly unwilling to learn."

—Everest Compline, *Reflections*

THE MOOD WITHIN THE MARINE SORTIE BAY SLID STEADILY downward from the initial heights of eager readiness as the minutes ticked by, their initial launch schedule blown to hell. The more experienced members of the Emperor's First knew this sickeningly well from past debacles: The politicos and the Admiralty brass talked big about a topic they didn't understand, got the Marines on the brink of violent action, only to get cold feet and pull the plug. Only now the target of their disgust was just a single Fleet captain; a captain the lieutenant colonel had called "shy" from the outset.

Krenner possessed even less patience than many of his young Marines, and he fumed angrily as the minutes of delay clicked on and on. Finally, yielding to his growing fury, Krenner stooped to calling Deckchief Furst.

"Ops," Furst replied to the comm call.

"What the *fuck* is afoot, Furst?" Krenner snarled.

Furst hesitate a moment, lowering his voice. "Trouble, Colonel. One fighter destroyed in the well. Looks like enemy aircraft. We're reviewing Jamila's sensor feeds and vidcapture now."

Aircraft.

Krenner's next words came out with much less heat. "Thought their puny air force got smashed at the outset."

"They did. Must have had some fast drones stashed somewhere deep."

"Oh, drones," Krenner snorted, a weight coming off.

"Don't take these lightly, Colonel. They smoked Mayo and Shipman over the ocean, fifteen klicks from shore running all out."

Krenner absorbed this information in brooding silence, thinking fast.

"Colonel?" Furst prodded. "You still ready to drop in?"

"Yes," Krenner said at last. "I'll be making a little change to the plan, though. Tell the captain—don't ask, tell!—I'll be using four insertion spikes, and I'll need *Hightower* on station to deliver. Got it?"

"I'll pass it along, Colonel." Furst hesitated a moment before adding, "We're resetting the drop clock. Commodore Glasshauser commands you into the well, double quick. Better get your troopers to the spikes fast."

"Oh they'll be ready, Furst, don't doubt it. You just get fighter cover for my transports or we may all be stuck down there with the gods-damned Legions!"

Saef scanned through Commander Jamila's sensor data with Wycherly and the heavyworld Marine lieutenant at his side, Commander Attic strolling into the bridge as if he was invited. Saef said nothing to Attic. After many prior uneventful floats together, *Hightower* had finally gone into action and suffered her first combat losses; a strong reaction from Attic did not seem unreasonable to Saef.

Wycherly looked absorbed but not unduly troubled by the unfolding scene revealed in the data feed. "Drones, certainly, but some kind of trickery here too."

Saef looked up at the dynamic tactical holo, with *Dragon*, *Python,* and *Sherwood* all slowly closing with that distant enemy cruiser, filling the intervening space with dozens of missiles with no evident strategy. That was the fight where he belonged, but instead he dealt with this no-win situation, tied to a scenario that seemed inescapably disastrous.

Saef's eyes fell upon Lieutenant Tilly Pennysmith working

silently away on her workstation. As Wycherly, Attic, and the Marine lieutenant argued about the implications of Jamila's data, Saef called up Pennysmith's workstation and examined her active labor. She was in the midst of meshing a digital workaround for the barrage battery controls to a dynamic targeting overlay Inga Maru had provided. Evidently Pennysmith felt the cannon array could be employed for ship-to-ship combat too, and Saef smiled a little to himself. Despite her hard words at the wardroom dinner, he felt more certain of Pennysmith than any other member of the bridge crew.

Saef turned back to the bickering officers. "Wycherly," he said, and they all broke off, turning to him, "it seems our orders are clear. We are landing the Marines. To get them on the ground alive and back off again, they will need fighter support. Is Commander Jamila aboard?" Saef asked the question though he already knew the answer.

"She just returned," Wycherly, his lips twisting with some venom Saef could not comprehend.

"If she is able, request that she lead the fighter escort. She has the authority to assemble as many birds as she chooses."

"What will the commodore say about that?" Attic demanded.

Saef nodded toward the tactical holo. "I will ask him when he has a moment."

Attic and Wycherly stared at the strange battle unfolding without fanfare, oddly detached from Hightower and their planet-bound struggles. Saef suddenly realized these two officers had not even been aware of the action.

Saef continued, "Hightower has been ordered to drop our Marines in and rescue the remaining Legionnaires, despite the clear risk Commander Jamila's recon just uncovered. This we shall do."

"But—but what about that?" Attic asked, nodding toward the battle unfolding.

Saef shook his head. "Our orders don't include any action there"—Attic murmured a curse and Glasshauser's name—"but our hand may be forced soon"—Saef's eyes traveled to the holo display—"if things continue the way they are now. So you understand we must get our troops on the ground and deal with the Legionnaire situation before we get chased off station. That window may be exceedingly tight. Marines and fighters will drop in... nine hundred thirty-three seconds."

"But—" Commander Attic began before Saef overrode him.

"Commander Attic, you should be resting," Saef said. "Your watch will be called all too soon."

Attic ground his teeth at the abrupt dismissal, his cheeks flushed, but he turned on his heel and marched out through the dilating bridge access.

Saef turned to Wycherly "Brief Commander Jamila. She has less than nine hundred seconds to make any alteration to her force plan."

Wycherly accepted his orders with far more composure than Attic had displayed but the twist to his lips reminded Saef very much of a smirk as he said, "Yes, Captain... You know, so much will occur in the next hour... so very much. It is a moment worth remembering." Wycherly moved to the ground ops center and Saef turned back to the central tasks before him.

"Sensors? Keeping a sharp eye on that enemy cruiser? We don't want a bunch of missiles to surprise us, now do we?"

"Yes, Captain—er—no, Captain," Belfort said, flushing.

"Excellent." Saef resumed the command seat and looked over at Lieutenant Ash. "You'll have us on station, deep, in seven hundred seconds, Nav?"

"Yes, Captain."

Saef scanned through his command UI a moment before speaking again, his gaze traveling to the tactical display and the stream of missiles torching up from *Dragon* and *Python*. "Pennysmith, select some ground targets at least two klicks out from the from the Legionnaires' position."

Pennysmith looked up from her panel to regard Saef for a moment before assenting. "Very well, Captain."

"We'll give the ground assault a little cover."

Out in the dark, far above Delta Three's northern pole, nuclear fires bloomed and expanded, the offensive power of their small squadron divided, squandered. Saef shook his head, unable to address the greater battle, due to Glasshauser's orders alone.

That enemy cruiser seemed all too likely to survive the piece-meal attack. Then the enemy would have their turn.

Marine Sergeant Joseph Yell served ten years within the Imperial Marines before undergoing and surviving the rigorous selection process to enter the prestigious Assaulter School. He survived another year of physical and mental hardship in the school itself before finally earning his battledress qualification. Seven more years of duty and regular training passed before Yell finally worked his way up the battledress list and finally stepped into L42, a battledress armor system of his own. Though L42 had served a handful of Marine operators in its decades of prior service, it was biometrically refitted to Sergeant Yell, the two becoming one combined unit of offensive power, stealth and mobility.

As Sergeant Joseph Yell followed his three battledress brethren into *Hightower's* mag-rail launch bay, he thought about his first sight of L42, its proud campaign emblems denoting each action in which it had served. Here they would squeeze into the super-stealthy reentry spikes, one Marine per spike, and Yell would finally add his own contribution to L42's record of achievement, dropping into Delta Three's war-torn well.

The loadmasters fiddled and fretted to cram the battledress Marines into the spikes, the cumbersome ARC kits making each Marine nearly too bulky to fit. Sergeant Yell just wanted this launch to end, to feel L42's broad armored feet on a solid surface and finally, finally realize the goal he had pursued for nearly two decades: to reveal his true self, a combination of Shaper tech, human ingenuity, and trained warfighter that comprised the living union of Marine and battledress.

The loadmasters sealed their spikes with minutes to spare, Yell and the other three battledress Marines curled in womblike darkness, lighted only by the onboard systems of their battledress. Yell visualized the Marine transport lighters dropping away from *Hightower*, more than a thousand Marines filling their decks, a flock of interface fighter craft flying escort. Before those lighters cleared the upper atmosphere of Delta Three, Sergeant Yell knew he would either be blown to tiny bits, or he would be on the surface, dishing out destruction upon the emperor's foes.

With that cheerful thought fully visualized, Sergeant Yell felt the reentry spike drop into the launcher, *Hightower's* artificial gravitation system suppressing the bone-crushing acceleration of the mag-rail launch.

Someplace within him, primal fears barked and yammered, but above it all a fierce joy supported his spirits. At last! *At last!*

✧   ✧   ✧

Inga felt a rare degree of weariness as she moved from task to task throughout *Hightower's* many compartments and passages. She saw the battle-ready Marines launch, the fighter crews soberly don their helmets and slip into their Mangusta fighters. Those elements were away, out in the dark, dropping into fire, while Inga faced her own hazards within. She had already checked on a few potential trouble areas where Loki provided likely intel of mutinous plotting, and popped in to eye the prisoners locked within the brig. All was not well despite the ostensible order flowing around her.

Riding Loki's senses, or relying upon Loki's varying, deficient attention, Inga saw a hundred small signs of impending trouble, but she could not determine any head to the mass of mutinous snakes for decapitation. So she roved through *Hightower,* physically and digitally, her attention pulled back to the bridge and Saef's unprotected state there, as she hurried to uncover the impending ambush she *felt* close at hand, just out of sight.

Unfortunately, as she hurried along, her attention pulled in a dozen different directions, she encountered Auditor Kenshin Tenroo wandering at loose ends, his woebegone expression unchanged since the debacle at the wardroom feast.

"Chief Maru, might I have a moment of your time, please?" he asked in a pitifully hesitant manner that reminded Inga of Saef's early description of Tenroo resembling a small, wet dog.

Inga's eyes flickered with flooding data as she replied, "I am sorry, Auditor. I have no time just now. Perhaps you could go observe the bridge. There will likely be a great many explosions to observe from there soon."

Tenroo shook his head as Inga moved to pass him, even daring to touch Inga's shoulder. She paused, jerking away, about to excoriate Tenroo, when he held up a flat gray receptacle. "But what is this? I'd swear it wasn't in my cabin yesterday, and then today—"

Inga's horrified gaze seemed to silence Tenroo in mid-sentence. She jerked the deadly box that she remembered so well from *Tanager* out of Tenroo's hand and dropped it down the nearby waste chute. Pieces of information began to rapidly fit together in her mind, the danger she scented now suddenly upon her, too broad and deep for the simple extermination of a mutinous officer or two.

Data began to flood through Inga's senses as she opened

to the fullness of Loki's demesne. Could she stop the chain of impending disaster now, *even now*? But if Tenroo spoke truly regarding timing, why plant the nanotech-laden receptacle now, after the transition?

"Chief Maru?" Tenroo hesitantly inquired. "Did I do well by bringi—"

"Please be quiet, Auditor," Inga interrupted, her eyes flickering constantly. "The enemy is within *Hightower*. The killing begins any moment now; you may wish to hide." Tenroo closed his mouth, dumbstruck, which suited Inga's current needs entirely.

Subaudibly, Inga communicated with Loki: "Among the Strangers' secrets you took from Delta Three station data, was there any indication of unique N-drive manipulations?"

Loki replied with what could only be described as a contemptuous edge, "Not a *useful* manipulation, Chief. They play silly games, like activating N-drives without transition calculations. Such wastefulness would never be tolerated in Fleet!"

As Loki's information sank in, Inga moved, glancing quickly at a security feed from the bridge, where she perceived the captain and his bridge officers going about their duties in a normal fashion. "They can activate the drive in a gravity well, can't they, Loki? That's the big secret?"

"Chief, is expending vast Shaper resources to go nowhere at all a desirable secret to you? The daft Strangers think so, and they may activate an N-drive anywhere at all, to then go nowhere at all. Foolish, even by human standards. Oh, Tanta has awakened. He calls out, he—"

Inga ignored Loki's vital kitten updates, noticing Auditor Tenroo hurrying to keep up with her rapid stride. The Engineering section became her immediate goal, her enshrouding cloak swirling about her, the occasional security ratings watching curiously as Inga hurried by, Tenroo in her wake. She felt the gravitational pull of both duty and her human emotions, drawing her toward the bridge, to Saef's side as this most lethal witching hour struck, but the flickering images flooding her synapses gave an urgent warning she could not ignore.

If she did not reach the Engineering section within rapidly shrinking moments, all may be lost.

Inga did not slow as she reached the final hatch before her goal, her sword hissing from its sheath, emerging from beneath the concealing cloak. Through Loki's eyes she saw the lone rating beyond the hatch, standing a nervous watch outside as his mutinous confederates labored within the Engineering compartment.

"Lights out," Inga said audibly a moment before the access dilated, Loki's senses filling her mind.

"Wha—what?" Tenroo puffed some distance behind her, falling still and silent as the passageway dropped into complete darkness.

Inga's augmentation flared up as she surged through the lightless hatch and passageway, old memories of hunting the stacks of Dry Arsenal One rising up a moment before her sword slashed out through the dark, biting deep, the air suddenly coppery to her senses. The Engineering section iris dilated at her silent command, and without pausing she continued through the hatch, into the light, the thump and gurgle of a falling body already behind her.

Both armed figures just within the iris wore the fixed grins Inga had come to loathe, but even they could not lift weapons in time. By now, Inga's blood scalded through her veins, pouring pure speed into her every motion. The sword grasped in Inga's two hands slammed through the neck of one, dropping him in his tracks as she spun in the silky arc of a pure Sembrada attack, half-stepping as the blade fully extended. Her second foe just began to lift his pistol, his motions sluglike in her heightened state, and her sword cut through his wrist, severing the hand. He looked down at his detached hand gripping the pistol, still grinning when Inga's lightning backswing slashed through windpipe and arteries. The grinning lips shaped words, and perhaps he—it?—thought he was speaking, but only wet hissing sounds emerged from the flayed throat as he dropped.

Her boots kept moving without a break, racing through the instrument chamber, her sword high as she rushed into the N-drive room, where the Engineering chief lay in a fresh pool of her own life's blood. Her three slayers delved into the N-drive power module, its bolted utility panel peeled away and cast to the side allowing them illicit access. The nearest of the three whirled without hesitation, jerking the sidearm from his belt, but Inga's blade flashed, knocking the pistol aside, the discharged round blasting into the nearby stanchion. Inga's wicked lunge pierced her attacker through his spine, and as the body, nerveless, dropped, she released her sword where it transfixed him, her hand desperately dropping to her belt.

The remaining two foes, twenty paces distant, did not even look up from their desperate work at the sounds of Inga's butchery, and her blurring hand rose, the small-caliber body pistol spitting suppressed shots into them.

Even as she fired, Inga saw it was too late, a flicker of luminance rising as the two foes slid to the deck. She had failed, *Hightower* slipped into N-space, and now Saef might find a ship suddenly full of assassins, facing them alone.

Chapter 32

"Critics of the current system love to decry the idea of menial labor being performed by demi-cits who happen to hold doctoral degrees. I, on the other hand, view this as a useful feature, not a defect. So much human suffering through millennia of our history might have been averted by so using the 'geniuses' of the academy."

—Dr. Ramsay Stirling Attenborough, *Ivory Tower Follies*

HIGHTOWER DROPPED INTO A DEEP ORBIT AS HER MARINE TRANS-port lighters and four Mangusta fighters dropped away. A moment later, Saef said, "Weps, fire on the selected targets; SHIGRIT missiles only."

"Aye, Captain," Pennysmith said, rechecking her aiming reticles, "firing monolithics only. Sixteen targets." She bit her lip, checking her scopes a last time, and triggered the shot.

Sixteen missiles leaped from *Hightower*'s hardpoints, streaking down into Delta Three's atmosphere, scattering out to address individual targets within a loose perimeter around the Legionnaires and their original objective. A moment later, four battledress-clad Marines followed the missiles into the well, their stealthy reentry spikes launched at a high velocity, hiding within the sudden tumult of raining fire.

Saef looked keenly up at the tactical holo where *Dragon* and *Python* seemed to all but englobe the distant enemy cruiser in encroaching missiles. That enemy cruiser strangely failed to maneuver, allowing Glasshauser's reckless surfeit of fire undue effectiveness, at least in momentary appearance.

For the moment, *Hightower* was spared any threat from that quarter, but *Dragon*'s course, sliding close beneath the vast orbital station, left *Python* out to face the enemy fire alone ... with the more distant *Hightower* as a less pressing, hopefully less tempting target for the enemy.

Saef turned his focus to the ground assault in progress, the Marine transports and escort fighters dropping in over the ocean ... Something about the tactical display tugged Saef's attention abruptly back.

"Sensors, center optical feeds on *Dragon*. Increase resolution to maximum."

"May I remind you, Captain," Wycherly said, suddenly close at hand, "our people are in action now, and that is where our focus must remain."

The abrupt insolence of Lieutenant Wycherly's statement stunned Saef at the same moment he spotted the startling hint his eyes had previously detected within the tactical display: A vessel stealthily slipped from its station dock, descending upon *Dragon*, closer and closer.

"Comm!" Saef barked, ignoring Wycherly entirely. "Message to *Dragon*—"

"No, Captain," Wycherly interrupted.

At the tone of Wycherly's voice, Saef looked to see Wycherly and the heavyworld Marine lieutenant with their blades in hand, staring fixedly at him, close—far too close.

Saef exhaled, instantly immersing within the Deep Man, knowing that sudden, explosive action remained his only reasonable course. Where the other bridge officers' loyalties lay, Saef did not know, but no one moved or spoke for a breathless instant. Inga's omniscient message appeared in Saef's UI at that moment:

STAY ALIVE. ON MY WAY.

In the midst of the unfolding instant, the impossible, the incomprehensible occurred. Within the optical feed holo, the vast planet, the starfield and distant space battle suddenly disappeared, a familiar luminance declaring an N-space transition even before Saef felt a growing warmth from the Shaper implant in his skull.

Aboard *Dragon* the collective bridge crew shared amazed looks despite the deadly circumstances. Somehow Glasshauser's unorthodox kitchen-sink strategy seemed to be working, and they could hardly believe it. Missiles of every variety trundled up from *Dragon*'s vast magazine to her hardpoints, filling *Dragon*'s launch racks a moment before leaping off into the dark, streaming toward their distant foe. This foe seemed too occupied snuffing out incoming missiles to mount an offense of its own, after wiping out poor little *Rook*, of course.

"Commodore," Weps called out, "seventy percent of our missile magazine has been expended."

"Keep launching, keep launching until—" An alarm interrupted Glasshauser, *Dragon*'s Intelligence dryly announcing a proximity alert. "And kill that damned alarm!" he snapped. Sliding in so close to the Delta Three station had triggered a series of such proximity warnings. "Where the devil is *Sherwood*? Get them engaged on this target now!"

Just as the bridge officers began to reply, an analog contact alarm blared a moment before a titanic impact shocked the smartalloy bones of *Dragon*. An abrupt loss of air pressure popped ears where they sat, alerts and alarms sounding, *Dragon*'s dragon-voiced Intelligence calmly explaining, "Collision detected. Decks one, two, and three breached. Twelve crew fatalities confirmed."

Glasshauser's mouth trembled, his voice rising near hysteria. "No, no, no. It can't...this can't..."

The XO, called to the bridge just moments earlier, stepped smoothly in. "The captain is disabled. I'm in command." He addressed Oolong, *Dragon*'s Intelligence. "What collided with us?"

"Heavy merchant *Comet*, nine thousand tons."

The XO could scarcely believe what he heard as shocks and booms reverberated through *Dragon*'s hull. "What? Why didn't you give a warning?"

"I warned of the impending collision eleven times, Commander."

"It's my fault," Sensors called out, his face sickly. "I—I was—"

Another boom shook the deck and the XO heard what sounded like gunfire.

On cue, *Dragon*'s Intelligence announced, "Armed boarders have penetrated deck two."

Marine Sergeant Joseph Yell felt the jarring plunge into the well, encased within Marine battledress L42, further cocooned by a reentry spike. Through rudimentary optical feeds, Sergeant Yell observed the shift from orbit to moist atmo, praying the stealth technology of the spike would surpass any surviving air defenses below. Dark flickering clouds momentarily shrouded Yell's view, and he plummeted on, checking his inertial tracker as he homed in on the target. The tracker chirped as his spike centered on the targeted coordinates, and Yell prepared himself, clenching his jaw as the rapidly shrinking altitude clicked down. The system trilled a steady warning as separation approached, and Yell counted down the seconds. It seemed far too long when the spike finally flared open, its carbon umbrella shooting out, bleeding velocity near the limit of human capability. The light of a new world—his battlefield—opened to the three-sixty view afforded by L42's technology, and Yell obtained one quick scan before the final separation dropped him away from the fragmenting carbon wings.

Yell landed, L42 eating the impact with its shock-absorption mechanisms, and he collapsed into the minimum form factor the battledress allowed. He froze, just as he had been trained, fighting the urge to move as L42 learned its new environment, implementing the advanced active camouflage that rendered battledress near invisible. While he waited, Yell scanned through the perimeter, cycling through wavelengths of light, quickly spotting two of his battledress brethren as their own chameleon systems slowly blurred their shapes into the surrounding scene. Farther out, distant clumps of rubble rained down, clearly the results of *Hightower*'s preparatory kinetic strikes, distracting and disrupting potential enemy defenses.

The fourth battledress Marine, Lieutenant Card, remained a question. A failed reentry spike? A superior hide? A lucky air defense weapon took him out?

Now fully camouflaged, Sergeant Yell straightened to his full height—or rather L42's full height, which stood considerably taller. He activated the ARC kit mounted across his armored back, the launch tube swinging up over L42's thick shoulder. Their key mission began now, covering the incoming transports from enemy aircraft or emplacements, their position on adjoining rooftops just overlooking the ocean shore.

Sergeant Yell spotted Lieutenant Card, a moving blur leaping up to mount the highest nearby building, commanding a superior view to the west. A moment later, L42's optical scan picked out the distant speck of approaching interface fighters: two Mangustas coming low and fast over the water. Behind them the lumbering Marine lighters should appear, running for the broad expanse of beach that served as an excellent landing zone...if unopposed by fortified weapons.

The Mangustas grew in Yell's vision, eerily silent until nearly above his position when the thunder of their engines rattled him. They split, one banking left, the other right, the flame of their engines stabbing out as they accelerated, running—but running from what?

Lieutenant Card, atop the high building, spotted an enemy first. Sergeant Yell saw Card's ARC launcher spit one small, high-speed rocket, then a second, clearly pivoting to track fast-moving targets. The targets shot into view: two small aircraft in pursuit of a Mangusta, one of them falling to flaming pieces as it banked.

One enemy down.

Encouraged, Lieutenant Card fired twice more in rapid succession a moment before a third identical aircraft cut him and his battledress in two. What remained of Lieutenant Card and his armor joined the small aircraft as a spinning fireball that shot over Sergeant Yell's head and plunged into the sea behind him.

Target fixation kills, Yell somberly thought, scanning for more targets, the lighters approaching from out over the ocean now, two more Mangustas in close escort.

Another small enemy aircraft appeared and ripped past in a blur. All three remaining battledress Marines fired, and at least one micro-rocket caught the small aircraft, blowing one stubby wing off and tumbling the craft into the sea with a terrific splash.

Hightower's heavy lighters swung in low over the water then, looking impossibly large, their shadows darkening the beach as they touched, disgorging over one thousand combat Marines in mere seconds as the escort Mangustas banked sharply, orbiting fast in a broad arc back over the sea.

As the Marines surged up the beach, the lighters lifted, nosing around and running low across the water, their own engines shaking the building Sergeant Yell perched upon.

One more enemy aircraft raced in pursuit of the transports, coming in fast from the south, allowing Yell more time to line up his shot. Micro-rockets from all three battledress Marines twisted after the enemy, exploding it some distance off shore in a highly satisfying manner.

Only two rockets remained in his ARC magazine, and Yell recalled all too well the fate of his late comrade.

Target fixation kills.

He leaped to a lower adjoining building and clambered down a partially exploded outer wall, then sprang the final distance to the ground, L42 eating each impact smoothly.

Infantry Marines, blocky in their helmets and shock armor, raced up the beach to Sergeant Yell's position, a gun team scrambling through a hole in that same exploded wall, looking for a nesting point. Scout elements ran past Yell, darting through a rubble-strewn street, branching to the right and left, while a Signals operator placed a combat Nets repeater puck on an intact wall, hurrying on. When they placed enough repeater pucks, the local area combat Nets would spring to life and enable secure, distributed communication and coordination without a fixed signal for enemies to trace. Until then, only line-of-sight comms could safely be employed.

With no additional enemy aircraft revealing themselves, Sergeant Yell knew the next priority in his duty and set off at a ground-eating lope, following the scattered Marine scouts as they filtered through the streets and ruins, probing for enemy strength through that tame euphemism known to the Brass as "contact." For the scouts, with a hundred potential sniper hides around each corner, the moment of *contact* would very likely arrive with terminal finality for them. Duty, considerable courage, and the critical regard of their mates spurred the scouts ahead, street to street, building to building.

Within his three-sixty view, Sergeant Yell saw the glowing gold and green *carrots* indicating the respective bearings to the Legionnaires' original objective—the so-called *structure of interest*—and the Legionnaires' recorded location. He stretched out two fast strides and launched himself in a power-assisted leap, L42's broad malleable feet landing without difficulty atop a low rooftop. Targeting an elevated balcony on the top floor of the taller adjoining structure, Yell continued smoothly, two more fast paces and springing upward, over a narrow alleyway, feeling the exultant power of the battledress as he soared. One foot caught hold of the balcony rail and pistoned him up to the rooftop where he lighted, picking out the scouting Marines leapfrogging up a broad street below, one street over.

Sergeant Yell saw a sudden stream of fat green tracers just a moment before the roar and echoing chatter of an auto-cannon reached him, the targeted scouts scattering, leaving one of their number in the street blown into a dozen wet chunks. Standing to his full height and quickly sidestepping, Yell's onboard logic highlighted the armored enemy skimcar just as he spotted its low shape peeking out from behind an odd bulwark of furniture and assorted rubbish. The final two rockets from his ARC kit seemed to launch almost of their own accord, crossing the distance in a flash, striking the skimcar cleanly.

As he quickly displaced, Yell saw the canted enemy vehicle, black smoke pouring from the two glow-ring holes. In three broad paces, he leaped again and jettisoned the cumbersome ARC kit from his back. L42 landed more lightly now, and Yell continued in motion, springing over another rough barricade as he heard the muffled popping of small-arms fire.

From his vantage point, Sergeant Yell saw two Marine scouts backpedaling out from a dark, rubble-choked building, firing in what appeared to be a panic as they fled. A blur of movement preceded one scout disappearing, snatched suddenly back into the shadowed depths. L42's enhanced audio pickups seemed to detect a scream cut suddenly off, and the remaining scout lobbed a grenade and rolled to one side as it detonated with a distinctive crump, dust and debris jetting out from the blast.

At that moment, combat Nets flickered into life and Sergeant Yell obtained his first comprehensive view of the greater force disposition as he remained in motion, loping easily down a narrow alley. L42's tactical display revealed the wave of active Marines swarming behind him, while up on the bleeding edge where Sergeant Yell operated, he saw the icons for his two surviving battledress brethren and the scattering of Marine scouts. Some stealthy enemy worked among the scouts, reaping one here, another there.

His easy lope became two fast strides and a leap, landing near the powder-dusted Marine scout, who still stared over his carbine into the ruined building as he changed magazines. "What was it?" Sergeant Yell said, his voice issuing from L42's audio output.

The scout looked back at Yell, his eyes wide, his face streaked with chalky dust. "Something bad." He turned back to the yawning darkness of the building. "A mech, I think. It got my three mates. Grenade might've done for the bastard...maybe, but I'm not going in to find out."

As Yell heard this, he saw another scout icon on L42's tactical display fall inactive. He needed to see exactly what stalked them.

Three springing steps set Yell in the rubble-strewn mouth of the building where heavy dust still filled the air. Only a fallen Marine, badly chewed by the grenade and...something else...lay visible to L42's multispectrum optics among the chaos of shattered fixtures and tumbled interior walls. Servos whined as he bent at the knees to fit, and Sergeant Yell strode warily into the darkened interior, his antipersonnel shoulder-mount tracking with his vision. A second room opened from a far wall, its door gone, its fragments adding to the jumble of rubbish stacked in heaps.

As Yell slowly advanced to the door, one of those heaps seemed to explode outward, sending refuse scattering everywhere. Sergeant Yell gained one momentary impression of rough metal plating, articulated legs, and a jagged pair of rudimentary mandibles before it struck, then he found himself in an atavistic battle for mere survival. L42's mechanisms whined, struggling to remain upright as the insect-like mech struck hard, staggering Sergeant Yell. L42's feet slid in the rubble, servos laboring to keep him upright. The mandibles snapped onto his armored thigh and damage alerts flared as a spear-like blade knifed into the armor, crushing and piercing. Yell found himself roaring insensibly as he smashed the tungsten breaching spikes of his fists into the armored carapace again and again even as the piercing blade of his attacker stabbed its way through armor and componentry into flesh.

With growing desperation Yell locked onto the mandibles with both gauntleted hands, wrenching them apart with the full power L42 commanded. Something snapped as Yell uttered bestial snarls, one mandible dangling from L42's armored fist. The six-legged mech fell back and Yell pumped heavy slugs from his shoulder-mount into it as it scuttled erratically through the ruins.

In a moment, Yell stood alone, his chest heaving, smoke curling from his shoulder-mount as L42 tightened a mechanical tourniquet to Yell's left thigh, slowing the bleeding. His mobility fell prey to the attacker, at the very least, with damage alerts chiming from L42's damaged mechanisms in the left leg.

Unsteadily, Yell staggered back onto the street, still gripping one wicked, blood-streaked mandible as he approached the wide-eyed scout. The active camouflage on L42's left leg failed, revealing the pierced armor and leaking components, while the remainder of the battledress remained a mottled blur.

"You were right," Yell said to the scout, his voice crackling out of L42's speaker. "It was something bad." He scanned through the tactical display as he tried to calm his heart rate. Scouts still fell in ones and twos along the bleeding edge of their advance.

He selected the comm icon for Lieutenant Colonel Krenner, who advanced with the main body of troops, pinging it. "What is it?" Krenner's voice demanded impatiently.

"Sir," Sergeant Yell said, still panting, "we have a problem..."

Chapter 33

"Some ancient text of human tradition suggested that to covet your neighbor's burden beast approached the same moral league as theft or even manslaughter. As the current trend of scholarship grows in its condemnation of the Great Houses, I begin to concur with the old gods. How much academic venom originates from nothing more than envy of wealth and longevity?"

—Dr. Ramsay Stirling Attenborough, *Ivory Tower Follies*

SINCE HER FIRST TRAINING DAY WITHIN THE FASTNESS OF HAWKS-gaard, Inga wondered what great service Jurr Difdah might possibly provide the Sinclair-Maru. Like Inga, Jurr did not descend from an allied oath-kin family, but unlike her, he was not allowed access to *Integrity Mirror*, Devlin's old book of Family doctrine. The differences did not end there, and after six years of daily interaction with the bearish brute, Inga still could not comprehend his presence among the Sinclair-Maru of Hawksgaard.

As they neared the year of their first majority, the process of physical maturation only worsened Jurr Difdah's unpleasant qualities, his sinews thickened through extensive heavy-grav training even as his penchant for petty cruelty bloomed. Fortunately, as Inga and her fellow classmates moved beyond the foundational training courses, her need to contend physically against Jurr diminished, concomitantly reducing his avenues for torment.

Now, at sixteen, with six years of the Sinclair-Maru nutrition and stimulation treatments under her belt, Inga stood taller than most of her classmates, though lanky by comparison, still excluded from most of the heavy-grav conditioning. While she more than held her own in any contest of physical dexterity or academic prowess, she saw that most of her fellow students outclassed her in trials of pure strength and endurance. In many ways this recalled to her those hard formative years in the slums of Battersea, only now she had no vulnerable siblings to defend at the expense of her own skin.

She still made the trek to Dry Arsenal One on a regular basis, only now frequently as an assistant instructor or "aggressor," training a new class of youngsters. Serving in this role helped cement many principles of tactics and combat psychology Inga first observed years earlier, as a trainee threading through this same maze of the stacks. Not only did the role of an instructor allow Inga the benefits of electronically aided dark vision, it allowed her to observe combatants not wholly conditioned by the scaram: a series of living examples demonstrating the mindsets representative of non-Family foes.

In close-quarters battle, the difference in behavior between the scaram-conditioned and the unconditioned seemed a difference in *species* almost. Again and again she observed that a scaram-trained combatant might overcome numerous armed foes through heightened awareness and unhesitating action. This all informed Inga's own private studies.

Other new training courses included operations with ship suits and full EVA gear, first within training bays, then on the outer skin of Hawksgaard itself. Inga swiftly discovered that proficiency in the airless void space closely tracked with one's mastery of the scaram: in the void, as in combat, fear or panic represented the chief impediment to success. As a result Inga flowed through the airless, weightless exercise with comparative ease, utilizing either the skintight ship suit or the full, bulky EVA system, while others of her class (particularly Jurr Difdah) struggled clumsily. Though this provided a degree of fuel for Inga's immediate satisfaction, she saw a flush of anger on his cheeks when they peeled out of their suits after an exercise particularly humiliating for Jurr. It seemed the instructors had intentionally put him in a position to fail as she looked on, finally requiring her intervention to complete their training objective.

"You find something amusing, Maru?" Jurr called out, tugging on his tunic as he stared across the ready room at Inga.

Inga fastened her equipment belt around her hips and looked up at Jurr through the fringes of her rebellious bangs. She shrugged. On the periphery, she observed her last two classmates hurriedly exit the ready room, leaving her alone with Jurr.

He strode angrily up to Inga, glaring down at her. His meaty hand seized painfully onto her shoulder. "Don't touch me," Inga said, staring calmly up into Jurr's enraged eyes.

His crushing pressure increased, and for a moment Inga saw her father's enraged face above her, *his* piercing fingers bruising her, but she only said, "By your dishonor, my honor is taken." This time she might lose the duel, just as she had years before, but this time she would mark him well, even if he triumphed.

His hand released her shoulder, sliding quickly up to encircle her neck. Inga felt a bolt of pure panic as Jurr's fingers closed, the crushing power mounting instantly, but the Deep Man became second nature to her. In the strange pool of clarity, even as the blood pounded in Inga's head, she perceived the knife-tipped flat file carelessly left on the bench beside her, the sensor pod on the ceiling strangely drooping, partially disassembled.

As Inga's vision began to grow dark, her hand found the file and she thrust sharply, feeling the penetration into solid flesh, even as her strength began to fail her. The pressure fell immediately away, light flashing back into her vision as she sucked air into her lungs.

Jurr Difdah held his wrist, wet blood pumping thickly through his fingers, his mouth shaping curses as the sound finally filtered through to her. ". . . you scut! You're not Family. You're not oathkin. You are nothing, nothing. But you . . . you think you are so special, don't you, scut?"

Inga dropped the blood-stained file and walked from the room, only glancing up to confirm the status of the clearly disabled sensor pod as Jurr stared at her with mingled hatred and fear.

Hours later, Inga made her way through the dark and dusty service tunnels, now a tight fit at her increased height. Her well-traveled path led to her private workshop, far out on the rubbish conveyor path. Since her apprenticeship with Deidre began, Inga's tools had evolved from the merely mechanical or micro-electronic to encompass powerful new realms of manipulation. Now beside her rack of pilfered mechanical tools stood a pair of battered and patched utility terminals, a rat's nest of cabling snaking from them to a series of clean ports Inga had painstakingly unearthed from the deserted old domicile wing nearby.

She descended the ladder into her chilly refuge and activated the utility terminals as she slipped into an oversized pair of insulated coveralls she'd found some years earlier. She had discovered the coveralls in a long-abandoned locker, the name tag upon one quilted lapel reading BEETLE, a cartoonish image of a smiling arthropod across the grimy back, wrenches portrayed in each of the insect's multiple humanlike hands. For some reason, the whimsical image had appealed to Inga, connecting her to some long-absent mechanic or engineer, evidently named "Beetle," who had once sported the coveralls. Even at Inga's current height, the coveralls hung loose upon her frame, but they formed a time-honored part of her covert activities, and their warmth always embraced her.

She settled behind the terminals, first checking the status of her long-running data snoopers; those she had stealthily placed on ports Deidre thought to be unmonitored. Early in her apprenticeship with Deidre, Inga's old slum awareness of hidden motives had puzzled over many of the stealthy assignments Deidre had required of her. As years rolled on, Inga became certain that Deidre exploited her for some hidden purpose within Hawksgaard, well beyond the needs of training. Inga's custom-programmed snoopers confirmed this, increasingly revealing Deidre's true purpose and true loyalties.

Moving from her snoopers' most recent captures, Inga initiated new searches of her own. One name she half-guiltily searched every few weeks, seeking the current status on Saef Sinclair-Maru again and again as he progressed from basic education to his advanced courses, then to the military in Battersea's System Guard. In his most recent image within the Family Nets, she still perceived that boy from Port City, the face that seemed without agenda, without subterfuge, the guileless tears in those eyes, free gifts to Inga. This older version of Saef she saw imaged in his Family file seemed unduly serious, a line forming between his eyes, and Inga wondered what great burden he now carried that affected him so. She moved on from her sheepish obsession with reluctance.

Her final search delved more deeply into the structure of Family decision trees within Hawksgaard. The most recent entry in Jurr Difdah's file caught her attention. It contained a vidstream segment from the EVA ready room recorded just hours earlier. She watched the image recorded from some hidden sensor, revealing her own figure and Jurr Difdah as Jurr's hands locked around Inga's throat. The recording ended when Inga struck, burying the flat file in Jurr's wrist. As Inga's breath puffed in the cold, she said to herself, "Is that why you are here, Jurr Difdah?"

When Inga completed her work, she sat for a time in the freezing workshop, lost in dangerous possibilities, weighing and rejecting a dozen courses of action. At last she made a decision, loading a memory kernel with the voluminous results of one of her secretive data-mining operations. She paused to select a slender, wicked blade she had shaped and honed—far superior to the little shank of her Battersea days. With kernel and blade in hand, she slipped out of her baggy old coveralls, shut down the workshop's lighting, and began the dark trek back to the inhabited quarters of Hawksgaard.

Unlike prior trips, Inga turned, taking a rarely visited off-branch, continuing through tight service passages and pipe-runs until she found her goal, following the course illuminated within her hacked holo lenses. The "secure" hatch yielded to her tools, the sensor alarm circumvented just as Deidre had taught her, and Inga wriggled into the large, well-furnished apartment. She moved easily through the various rooms, finally selecting a comfortable stool, placing it where the subject of her hunt could not detect her presence until far too late to take any action.

She only waited in the half-light for a handful of minutes before the apartment's door opened, a rectangle of light stretching out, almost touching Inga's boot tips before receding. She saw the indistinct figure padding quietly by her position, an arm's reach distant. Inga reached out, the slender blade in her right hand, her left hand seizing his collar. The cool steel of her blade teased along the exposed flesh of his neck.

His Sinclair-Maru training ran true and he only froze a moment before saying, "Shall we have some light?"

"I don't care," Inga said, "but we'll have some truth now."

He reached out slowly and the apartment lights glowed into life. Unlike most Sinclair-Maru, Kai never carried a sidearm, and this night was no different, the sword at his belt his only weapon.

"You are offended somehow, child?" Kai said after regarding

her for a moment, his eyebrows flickering once in his only expression of surprise.

"I am offended," Inga said.

"What precisely is the nature of your compla—"

"The EVA ready room set for two," Inga purred softly, "an intimate bloody engagement; the sharp file so conveniently close to hand, and the sensor pod so dramatically out of commission. It only lacked a sign marked in bold print to complete the scene."

Kai tilted his head, slowly rotating to look at Inga where she sat atop the stool. "Perhaps it was a trifle heavy handed, child, but nothing more, surely."

"If you want Jurr Difdah dead," Inga said slowly and clearly, "you can bloody well do the job yourself, or you can tell me straight out. No more games."

"Jurr Difdah?" Kai repeated in a musing tone. "I don't care one whit about Jurr Difdah, alive or dead. He is nothing."

Inga felt a flare of anger. "He's nothing? You've gone to great trouble to create *something* out of him, and now that he's shown his stripes, he's worn out his usefulness. Just another whimsical little project cast on the heap, right?"

Kai chuckled softly. "I think I begin to see the light. But you do not understand at all."

"Don't I, Kai?" Inga said, thinking of all the sources of information she regularly looted. "He's not oath-kin, but he's here—like me. He's from the gutter—like me. He has no one who cares if he lives or dies—like me. What don't I understand here, Kai?"

Kai's smile disappeared. "*I* very much care if you live or die. Did you not know this?"

Inga felt herself blush and shrugged, saying nothing.

"What you do not understand, child..." Kai began, then broke off to try again: "The entirety of Jurr Difdah's purpose here was to test your mettle, from the very beginning. That is all. And despite his incurable flaws, he has served this purpose well, thus far."

"*Thus far*," Inga repeated.

"There is a final, er, purpose for him."

Inga stared at Kai, shaking her head. "I won't do it."

Kai frowned. "Jurr Difdah is a thoroughly corrupt young man, without principle, and you balk at the first real order we lay upon you? Have we not been clear what your service demands of you?"

Inga flushed. "He's no threat to the Family. You created him, like you created me, and now you're finished with him."

Kai sighed. "Despite the age-old axiom, power does not corrupt; power *reveals*. We did not create either of you. We merely placed power in your hands—this Difdah scum and you—and both your natures are revealed." Kai paused for a moment. "If roles were reversed, you *know* what perverse pleasure Jurr Difdah would feel choking the life out of you."

Inga shrugged again, every fiber of her being rebelling against this manipulation brought to bear upon her, this arranged slaying of an ignorant ox led to the slaughter. "I propose a better test, Kai...a *real* test."

Kai shook his head frowning at her. "This is not a negotiation. This is not how duty works within the Family, and you know it."

Inga pressed on. "Really? Let's discuss a spy in the heart of Hawksgaard, collecting Family secrets right under your nose for years?"

Kai's lips compressed into a fine line as he stared at Inga. "What do you...? Ah, of course! Deidre." He smiled. "We are well aware of her little games. She is a compulsive snoop and thief."

Inga drew the memory kernel out of a pocket and held it between thumb and index finger. "She is *not* a compulsive snoop, and you most certainly are not aware of her *little games*, Kai." She dropped the kernel, Kai catching it between his palms. He stared at Inga for another moment before turning to the terminal beside him.

"Your reluctance to do as you are bid does not bode—" Kai broke off, staring at the scrolling data emerging from the kernel. Inga gained the satisfaction of seeing Kai's perpetual ruddiness fade into an unhealthy pallor. Inga held the reins of manipulation now.

Kai ran a distracted hand over his cheek and turned to Inga. "This...this should not be possible. How did she circumvent the Intelligence? The security locks?"

Inga shook her head. "That's not the right question, Kai. Think about it. Deidre's servitude is nearly over, she is a legal ward of the Family, but now, you see, she can never leave this place alive. And you cannot eliminate her in a legal duel until she is released from her servitude...too late." Inga smiled a little. "What will you do? It's such a sticky, sticky fix you're in."

Kai shook his head, thinking. "To *rob* us even as she tolls her servitude—" he began, until Inga broke in.

"No, Kai, look at that kernel again. You're not seeing it right." She stood up from the borrowed stool. "Ask yourself, what Great House would set her to get caught, simply to get inside the Sinclair-Maru?"

"A setup from the start?" Kai mused. "Anthea did not find any great House connection, but..."

Inga nodded. "You can see it must be. And now *I* can fix this."

Kai's contemplative expression vanished and he measured Inga with a severe expression. "You greatly underestimate us. There are many ways to deal with Deidre."

"But the test, Kai? What about that?" Inga's lip curled. "You need to be sure of me before the big day, don't you? What better way than this?"

"Child—" Kai began, but Inga went on, pushing Kai with her words.

"What better way, Kai? My mentor is a much better test than that poor idiot, Jurr Difdah."

Kai seemed to clench his teeth, turning to look at the list of pilfered Family secrets. After a moment he turned back to Inga. "Are you so cold blooded, child? What wrong has Deidre ever done to you?"

Inga shook her head. "Nothing. She's done me no wrong, Kai." She held Kai's gaze. "It is nothing personal; Deidre is our enemy, and that is all."

Kai allowed Inga a free hand but a narrow window, which suited her well enough, though she had little time to spare in preparation, setting the hooks in her brief spells between classes and duties. By the time Deidre hailed her for their scheduled training period, Inga felt confident that all stood ready.

PREP FOR HIGH WORK. BRING YOUR CLIMBING KIT. The message appeared in Inga's holo lenses, the lenses Deidre had taught Inga to modify, converting them into powerful Nets-smith tools.

CAN'T CLIMB, Inga messaged back. INJURED ARM.

Inga easily visualized Deidre's exasperated eye roll. More than once through the years, Inga's apprenticeship duties suffered when other training injuries hobbled her, and Deidre maintained very little patience for any of it.

BRILLIANT, Deidre messaged back, and Inga could almost

hear the biting sarcasm of her mentor in that one word. BEACH HOUSE...IF YOU'RE ABLE.

Inga released a breath, replying to the message. That had been the one variable she had feared, but everything moved ahead as she planned, to the beach house.

The "beach house" lay in a broad, shallow crater on the craggy outer skin of Hawksgaard, nestled among boulders along one crater wall. Inga had discovered the abandoned old mining station on one of her extracurricular explorations, and thought the band of white dust bordering the small dome resembled sandy beaches back on Battersea. At first, she had resuscitated the small outpost as her own private retreat, dragging numerous loads of materials and supplies to the beach house until she had restored power, light, and air. The cluster of old, unmonitored data ports eventually prompted Inga to share her retreat with Deidre.

At least for some time, Inga successfully told herself that the data ports formed her only reason for revealing the beach house to Deidre. Eventually, Inga recognized that her real impulse originated with a need to share the little special things with someone, and Deidre—crass, cold, sarcastic Deidre—formed the nearest thing to a friend that Inga knew in Hawksgaard.

The homey, quirky little touches with which Inga populated the beach house had evoked no comment or appreciation from Deidre; the data ports had, however. Deidre called the beach house "their" personal gold mine, and the two of them made their way through a different EVA airlock from Hawksgaard Operations to the beach house on a regular basis.

After Inga received Deidre's message, she made her way out to an EVA ready room, selecting her skintight ship suit rather than the full EVA setup she would normally employ for such a jaunt across Hawksgaard's outer face. In just a few minutes Inga hopped and jetted out from a utility airlock, leaving the well-trammeled apron around Hawksgaard Operations and heading through one of the innumerable crevasse-like fissures across the small planetoid. Such light microgravity allowed a skillful practitioner to achieve remarkable velocities, alternately jetting and "skiing" from ridge to ridge, with only the sound of her steady breaths to fill the silence. Inga had quickly mastered the art, and she knew she would quickly overhaul Deidre, which formed an important—a *vital*—part of Inga's plan.

When she skittered into the destination crater, Inga saw Deidre just reaching the beach house where it seemed to form yet one more oddly rounded gray boulder among the host of its more jagged brethren, less than a half klick ahead. Inga poured on the speed, rising higher on the cool jets before coasting down in a soft arc, bouncing the final dusty steps to the outer airlock, even as Deidre began powering up the lights inside.

The beach house was actually formed as two small conjoined units with a secondary airlock between the halves. The first half Inga fancied as a sort of sitting room or lounge, though the metal and stay-crete fixtures served as poor furniture, even with the covering blankets and rugs she had smuggled out.

The second half of the structure lay through the center airlock, which Inga routinely left open for ease of motion, and there she placed a sort of kitchenette and office. Like a magnet, Deidre already had her hands on the old utility terminal, her snapping eyes scanning over the glowing output as Inga entered.

Inga shrugged out of the cool jet unit, favoring her "injured" left arm, and dropped the pack by the entrance beside Deidre's full EVA suit where it stood like a rigid sentry in the light gravity. Deidre, clad in a dark bodysuit, glanced up from the terminal as Inga pulled her compact ship suit helmet free. "Why didn't you use full EVA? Long jaunt for a ship suit, isn't it?"

Inga placed her helmet next to the terminal. "Easier on my arm this way." Deidre grunted, turning her gaze back upon the scrolling data.

"You've been busy, I see," Deidre murmured, flowing text glowing across her holo lenses. "Searches on that worthless Dif-dah sod—pointless waste of your time, girl-child—and ..." Deidre frowned suddenly, falling silent as she stared at the output.

Inga went to the battered gray shelf that she viewed as her kitchenette, selecting a sealed pouch of crackers, opening it and taking one. She turned toward Deidre, seeing her frown deepen, Deidre's eyes fixed upon her. "What is it?" Inga asked, popping the cracker into her mouth.

Deidre tapped her fingers atop the tiny desk, looking down. "Nothing." She looked up, her mouth a grim line. "You know, I left my kit bag by the entrance airlock, girl. Fetch it for me ... or is that too great a strain with your terrible wound?"

Inga chewed and swallowed. "I think I can manage." She

returned to the entrance and looked about the small, austere chamber. "Your bag's not—" The lock separating modules cycled closed suddenly. Inga whirled, staring.

Deidre stood in plain sight, her face expressionless through the airlock's window. Inga saw Deidre reach over to manipulate the lockout panel beside her.

"Hey." Inga struck the window, and Deidre looked up, her eyes dead as she lifted the panel's bright red caution cover. Inga looked at the red cover, then up to Deidre's face. "Deidre... Deidre, we can figure something out," Inga said, speaking loud enough to penetrate the thick window.

Deidre slowly shook her head, her face expressionless. "No, we can't."

Inga placed both hands on the window, pleading. "Don't. Don't, Deidre. Please."

Weeks before, when Inga first showed Deidre the beach house, they had joked about the lockout panel. What sort of emergency called for suddenly venting the module's internal air pressure? Why even have such a mechanism? In the event of a fire in the first mod, perhaps? Deidre had joked that it might have been a Sinclair-Maru security measure for silencing rebellious miners back in the old days. In the back of Inga's mind, she thought of the brutal silencing that now threatened.

Inga pulled the holo lenses from her eyes, sharing one last look with her mentor, as Deidre flipped the dump toggles. The sudden hiss of escaping air only gave Deidre time for one terrified grimace before the atmosphere blasted out of the main pod, just as Inga had modified the dump toggle to function hours earlier. Inga stared through the sudden tumult of crackers, blankets, and atomized blood, seeing the body of her mentor spin, bouncing from the curved walls, yielding to the light gravity and settling against the deck in stillness.

Using Deidre's EVA suit, Inga returned to Hawksgaard Operations, a body in tow.

Hours later, Inga handed Kai a memory kernel: a vidcapture of Deidre's final moments, recorded through Inga's holo lenses. As Kai played the brief clip, Inga said, "Suicide. Told her we could figure something out. Pleaded." Inga shrugged. "She decided to end it all." Deidre had been the closest person to a friend Inga had on Hawksgaard, and the dueling emotions in Inga seemed to leave her numb. Deidre was dead; died trying to kill Inga, but an obvious suicide cleared the Sinclair-Maru of responsibility. All very tidy, and the Battersea urchin within Inga shrugged away any other emotion.

Kai turned to stare at Inga. "Where did this occur? I don't recognize this chamber."

After a moment, Inga said, "Best not to know, I think, Kai."

Chapter 34

"So much effort and care is invested in building strong bodies and well-informed minds among the rising generations. Based upon recent observations, it seems the only actual values affirmatively instilled within these same generations produce a sneering self-absorption that is of little use to the Imperium, or even to their Families."

—Dr. Ramsay Stirling Attenborough, *Ivory Tower Follies*

IN SUCH CLOSE PROXIMITY TO A PLANETARY GRAVITY WELL, without transition calculations, without bridge authentication: the list of impossibilities ticked through Saef's mind, and yet *Hightower* seemed to linger in the void-like embrace of N-space.

Saef heard the gasps and shocked exclamations from the bridge crew around him. Everyone clearly reeled in surprise except Lieutenant Wycherly, who kept his focus upon Saef, the sword in his hand held poised.

Did Wycherly know of Saef's body shield—Devlin's ancient gift—or did the choice of swords indicate some other intent?

Deckchief Furst formed the first coherent sentence. "What the hell is going on, Wycherly?" he demanded in a choked voice, and Saef could not be sure if this impossible transition or the armed mutiny lay at the root of Furst's discomposure.

"It will become clear shortly, Deckchief," Wycherly said, never taking his eyes from Saef. "Everything is under control."

Saef had Wycherly close on his right side, the Marine lieutenant almost directly behind him. If they initiated action, he would be hard pressed to survive, but if Saef initiated, he gained roughly two-tenths of a second on his opponents. If none of his bridge crew took an active, immediate role in stopping Saef, he *might* displace, pivot, and attack. He *might* even defeat these two opponents.

At any moment *Hightower* should emerge from N-space, unless yet another impossibility beset them. Saef internally poised for that instant when they emerged, when every person would instinctively look to the holo.

"Captain," Wycherly said, "you will slowly stand with your hands up."

Saef played for time, knowing he only needed seconds for the looming moment of distraction. "Deckchief, place Lieutenant Wycherly under arrest, please," Saef said, his hands already feeling the approaching weight of the weapons he was about to grasp. Perhaps Saef's calm assurance carried weight beyond his words, or perhaps Wycherly's actions outran the other officers' sentiment, but whatever the cause, the emotional energy rippled through the bridge. Uncertain glances between bridge crew seemed to infuriate Wycherly, all of which bought precious seconds for Saef's locus of impending violence.

As *Hightower* plunged into N-space, the final mutinous Engineering rating fell dead, twitching upon the deck. Inga dropped the expended magazine from her compact body pistol and reloaded. Without pausing, she spun on her heel and quickly exited the Engineering section, passing Tenroo, who gazed at the fallen, leaking bodies scattered about the deck.

"Loki, increase gravity to maximum in every compartment between me and the bridge," Inga said into the empty keyway just as she accelerated to a full run, leaving Tenroo behind. Injuries among innocent crew would likely occur from the sudden gravity increase, and it wouldn't pin her enemies in place, but it might keep her pathway clear long enough...

She only slowed her pace as she reached the dry-side waist iris, but chaos preceded her. One security rating lay dead on the deck, her sidearm taken, the other security rating missing. Inga accelerated desperately, racing for the bridge with her cloak whipping out behind her, the companionway blessedly empty.

Through Loki's senses, Inga saw a drama unfold beyond the dogleg in the passage ahead, a pair of shots flashing out, their sound reaching her ears as she slowed to a fast walk. Edging around the dogleg, she saw Commander Attic standing over the bodies of two security ratings, a pistol in his hands. He jumped at the sight of Inga, his pistol half-raising as she paused, staring at him, her own weapon concealed in her cloak. He looked down at the bodies again before looking back up to Inga. "This isn't what it looks like," he said in an even voice.

"I know."

As Wycherly laughed at Saef's command to Furst, Saef's muscles felt relaxed and ready, his shoulders low and free, but internally a spring wound tight, ready to explode.

He felt the emergence at the same moment the odd luminance ceased, and he sprang forward without a millisecond of hesitation, one lunge and a pivot, his sword and pistol clearing. Just before Wycherly's sword thrust at Saef's belly, he parried it aside, feeling the razor point slice through above his hip bone.

Wycherly easily parried Saef's backhand cut, clearly a very skilled practitioner of the blade. Backpedaling fast, Saef fired his pistol left-handed, kneecapping Wycherly, dropping him instantly to the deck in a heap. The Marine lieutenant dropped his blade, holding his hands high, and Saef rounded quickly to cover the entire bridge crew. Only then did Saef see the image of Delta Three's glowing hemisphere filling the main holo.

His mind tried to grasp onto some explanation for an N-space transition—already entirely impossible so close to planetary mass—that dropped them out of N-space exactly where they began.

Inga's message pinged into Saef's UI: THREE SECONDS OUT. Precisely three seconds later, Inga entered the bridge access, Commander Attic at her side.

Attic looked first at Saef, then down at Wycherly, who glowered as he gripped his shattered leg, then lastly at the holo image of Delta Three, where he stopped, dumbfounded. "How is that possible?" he said.

"I don't know," Saef said. "But it doesn't matter right now. *Dragon* is... disabled, it appears. That big enemy cruiser is surviving everything Glasshauser threw at them, and they're probably about to start chewing on *Python* ... or us." Saef looked away from the tactical holo across his silent bridge crew. "And I can't fight this ship without getting a knife in the back."

More than one face among the bridge officers wore a shamefaced expression, Deckchief Furst flushing even as Ensign Belfort frowned indignantly. Pennysmith held Saef's gaze without expression.

"Fighters, lighters, and Marines in the well," Attic said, looking at the tactical display. "What am I seeing with *Dragon*? Is that—is that a *collision*?"

"Yes," Saef said. "Big merchant vessel off the station." He shook his head. "We don't have time for this. That cruiser will chew this squadron in bits and pieces, and our only chance is hitting it while *Python* and the frigates are still with us."

Inga spoke up suddenly from her place on the periphery. "That will be a problem... Weapons section was just taken by... mutineers."

"*What?*" Commander Attic demanded, shocked. "How many traitors do we have?"

"Many, suddenly," Inga said. "Maybe a hundred or so, most of them forward of the waist."

Saef clenched his fists, thinking quickly. "We've still got more than enough Marines to subdue every section on this ship, so—"

"No, Captain," Inga interrupted, her eye flickering. "The Marines are bottled up. Waist hatches are held by Kang's people, manually locked."

Attic stared at Inga. "How do you know th—"

"Kang's with the enemy?" Saef said.

"Yes," Inga said, ignoring Attic. "Some of his people weren't, but most of those holdouts were purged in the last few minutes."

Attic appeared mystified but turned back to Saef. "I still say the Marines are the answer. They have to outnumber Kang's people ten-to-one, even with the assault troops in the well. They can blow their way through anything they need to—"

"On your orders?" Saef interrupted, staring hard at Attic. "On mine? I don't see them initiating an attack without Krenner ordering it... not with this mutinous wind blowing. They won't know who to trust except one of their own."

Attic nodded slowly. "You may be right, sir."

Saef sheathed his sword and put a hand to the wound above his hip, feeling the blood oozing down his thigh. He looked to Inga. "Who can we still trust?"

Inga shrugged. "I have a better idea of who you *can't* bloody trust." Inga looked coolly over the bridge crew even as Wycherly slumped over, unconscious from shock or blood loss. "Alsop and Belfort are in it up to their necks." Both named men turned pale, staring as Inga's small pistol emerged from the folds of her cloak. She nodded toward Attic. "Him you can trust, I think. These two"—she waved her pistol toward the unconscious Wycherly and the Marine lieutenant—"they attacked you. Their lives are forfeit."

As Inga's pistol leveled, Saef said, "Belay that a moment, please, Maru." Inga frowned over at Saef, her pistol still steadily aimed. "Wycherly is gone, I think, Maru, and this Marine can still serve the Emperor for a moment, I believe, along with these other two traitors. Kill their Nets access, though. Don't want them communicating with anyone."

"Already done, Captain," Inga said.

"Can we still make it to Weapons without fighting our way through a mob?"

"So far," Inga said. "But that could change quickly."

Saef turned to Tilly Pennysmith, and she held his gaze, a faint flush coloring her cheeks. "Did you sort out *Hightower*'s barrage battery for ship-to-ship, Lieutenant?"

Pennysmith seemed to take a relieved breath as she said, "I—I think so, Captain." She hesitated a moment and pulled a small medkit from her thigh pocket. "Here, Captain. You're bleeding."

Saef took the proffered medkit with a nod and turned to Attic. "Attic, take the bridge. Hold station for the transports, and fight the ship if you can. You've got missiles in the hardpoints for now, and I'll try to free up the Weapons section if I can. Then we'll see if Krenner can take a moment to help us out."

Saef thrust a small field dressing over the leaking furrow in his skin, then turned to Belfort and Alsop, waving his sidearm at them. "Gentlemen, we're going. Now."

Belfort, Alsop, and the Marine lieutenant marched sullenly ahead of Saef and Inga, covered by Inga's small, suppressed body pistol and Saef's large automatic. Inga quietly outlined Loki's revelations regarding the impossible N-space trick.

"Gods, Maru," Saef murmured, "it would have been valuable to know this *before* it happened."

"I know."

"Is there anything else Loki might want to share with us someday?"

Inga shrugged. "He *shares* constantly, he just doesn't always value what we value." She quickly explained the scenario facing them ahead, in the Weapons section, even as they drove the three mutineers down the companionway.

They reached the broad iris to the Weapons section without encountering anyone beyond a few singular ratings who scurried away at the sight of such a perplexing gathering, darting into adjoining compartments and the embracing crush of heavy gravity.

"Alright, gentlemen," Saef said, addressing the three prisoners. "You have one chance to survive the next sixty seconds. If you move forward into the compartment, we won't kill you where you stand. If you're speedy enough, your comrades on the other side of this hatch may not kill you either."

Alsop visibly shook in fear, beads of sweat streaming down his forehead. "Captain, you can't—this is a violation of every—"

"I can. *You* are a mutineer," Saef said. "I violate nothing, and when this hatch opens, I will not even wait one second to shoot you in your tracks if you are not moving forward. You understand me?"

Subaudibly, Inga said, "Loki, minimum gravity in the Weapons section, now...cycle the hatch..."

As the hatch cycled open, Saef raised his pistol in both hands, staying well to one side, out of the line of fire, but the three mutineers rushed forward, striking the boundary of the compartment and the light gravity, spinning up suddenly, flailing. A few wild shots fired inside the compartment, but the light gravity had thrown them into confusion and the human shields spun through the air, momentarily unharmed.

Inga spotted an armed enemy twisting helplessly among the fixtures deep in the compartment, unable to steady the pistol in his hand, and fired twice, the shots sounding like two quick handclaps. The enemy corkscrewed from the impact, his weapon flying from his hand. "Standard gravity, Loki." Tools, weapons, and bodies all settled quickly to the deck as Inga said to Saef, "Wait just a moment, please...Lights."

The compartment fell into darkness and Inga rushed into its maze, her pistol up, her cloak rustling quietly. Saef eased into a dark hollow beside the Weapons section hatch, listening. The distinctive snap of Inga's small pistol issued from the depths of the compartment, followed by a pair of louder gunshots, a pained cry, and a flurry of Inga's fire.

The lights came up and Saef edged around a central stanchion to see several sprawled bodies in the long corridor running through *Hightower*'s magazine, Alsop and the Marine lieutenant among them. Ensign Belfort hunkered in a tight nook, white-faced and evidently uninjured. Belfort's eyes moved to a pistol resting on the deck nearby, then quickly glanced up to Saef, who smiled encouragingly. Belfort looked away from the pistol.

The tramping of boots upon the deck preceded a small cluster of ratings led by the gunnery chief Saef had met on his initial tour of *Hightower*, Inga coming up behind, a food bar in one hand, her compact pistol in the other.

"This lot were locked up by the mutineers," Inga said, taking a bite from her food bar.

"Gunnery Chief Clarke, sir," the chief said, stepping forward, his face bearing a bruise and reddened eyes. "That bunch—they—they shot down some of our people, some fine lads and lasses. Shot 'em like animals." The other ratings muttered angry curses.

Saef nodded. "There are more mutineers aboard to deal with still, Chief—"

"Mutineers!" Chief Clarke broke in angrily. "Bunch of gods-damned savages! Had no call to pistol poor Smitty in the back, or Demming, or—"

"All very true," Saef interrupted. "Commander Attic and I will be serving them out shortly, if your crew can keep this section running. Can you do it, Chief?"

Almost on cue, Saef felt a vague pulse through the soles of his feet and heard a resonant metallic report. "The barrage battery!" Chief Clarke shouted and began barking commands to his remaining crew members even as mechanical linkages began cycling ammunition out to *Hightower*'s hardpoints.

Saef grabbed Clarke. "Chief, Ensign Belfort here is a traitor. Have you any hazardous jobs for a mutinous hand?"

Clarke eyed Belfort contemptuously. "I do."

"He's yours, then. Better police up the random sidearms, so he isn't tempted to wickedness."

Clarke shoved Belfort ahead of him with a snort. "I hope he tries."

Inga finished her food bar as the Weapons section burst into activity. Her eyes flickered, and she turned to Saef.

"Trouble?" Saef said.

"Yes...it appears so." She moved quickly toward the access hatch exiting the Weapons section, tucking the small pistol into her belt. "Kang, three others...two carbines between them. Looks like two of them are the saboteurs from the Tech section, sprung from the brig."

Saef frowned as he flanked Inga. "Coming here? Or the bridge?"

Inga removed her cloak to reveal the arsenal strapped to her slender torso. "Here, it seems." The compact Krishna submachine gun dropped into Inga's right hand and she extended the tubular collapsed stock, press-checking the action. "There's a pocket of resistance holding firm and keeping most of the mutineers busy, so these are all we face...for the moment."

Saef thought a moment. "Can we cut them off somewhere? Can't have a war here in Weps, especially if you're twiddling the gravity or the lights." Chief Clarke's loud exhortations and accompanying din of the Weapons section punctuated Saef's observation.

Inga's eyes flickered as she scanned routes and possibilities. "If we hurry. We need to draw them off the companionway into a compartment, I think." Inga leapt into motion, moving through the hatch with Saef pacing her. "Got it," she said, her feral half smile showing itself. "The rescue capsules have a large compartment right off their route." Inga accelerated suddenly, reminding Saef again of her superhuman capabilities as he ran all out to keep up. They sped headlong down the empty companionway toward a dogleg to the left.

Inga slid to a halt at a large hatch dilating open to the right, her sub-gun up, covering the dogleg a stone's throw down the companionway. "Go, go!" Inga said, firing a burst at a flicker of movement, her muzzle blast flashing from the bulkhead. Saef jinked through the hatch, Inga ducking in behind him as return fire roared, rounds singing off the bulkhead and inner stanchion. The power and volume of return fire reminded Saef how inadvisable it was to bring a handgun to a carbine fight.

Rescue capsules lay in a row along *Hightower*'s outer hull, ready to launch, narrow paths surrounding each capsule, incidentally providing variegated cover for a close-quarters battle. Saef and Inga moved across the modest apron just within the entrance iris, Saef posting up behind one of a series of stanchions, leveling his handgun at a sharp cross angle to the entrance. The enemy could not advance toward the Weapons section without passing through Saef's fire.

Instead of assuming a firing position, Inga used her left hand to quickly manipulate bare portions of the terminating bulkhead, dashing into cover beside Saef just as the enemy rushed through the iris.

Saef fired two quick shots, perfectly centering an attacker in his sights, then ducking behind the stanchion as powerful rounds snapped and skipped around his position. In the microsecond impression of combat, Saef realized what he had just witnessed. "Get behind me! They've got body shields. Get behind me, Maru!" Even as Saef said the words, he could scarcely believe it. Body shields represented very rare, precious examples of pure Shaper tech. Saef's own Shaper body shield remained the only such artifact in the entire Sinclair-Maru inventory, purchased by Devlin Sinclair-Maru centuries earlier, during the height of their Family fortunes.

Inga said nothing but faded back behind Saef's right shoulder as he displaced to a second stanchion, the sound of the iris cycling shut reaching them: Inga, with Loki's help, had the enemy trapped in the compartment with them. Now if Inga and Saef could survive the conflict...

The grate of hurried boot-steps signaled movement just before an attacker crossed the narrow gap from the entrance, dashing from left to right. Saef and Inga both fired, their impacts sparking off the enemy shields as the foe ducked into the gap behind the first rescue capsule. Almost immediately two more attackers leaped from cover, shoulder to shoulder, Inga's submachine gun firing the instant they appeared. Sparks showered off both foes as Saef joined in, firing as fast as his finger could press the trigger. Then enemy rounds struck back. Inga slipped behind Saef as rounds skipped off his shield, the shield generator at his low back draining kinetic energy as heat into his flesh. Over the blast of exchanging fire, Saef somehow heard Inga change magazines and her single spoken word, "Lights!," plunging the large compartment into absolute darkness.

Saef felt her hand on his elbow, and they quickly displaced, the enemy fire probing wildly, one round scoring Saef's shield. Saef allowed Inga to guide him through the utter darkness even as the enemy poured fire into their previous position.

Changing magazines behind the cover of one capsule, Saef observed the evidence of Inga's earlier handiwork in the form of two luminescent splotches on the terminating bulkhead. One splotch suddenly disappeared, occluded by some stealthy figure, and Saef fired, just his eye and pistol projecting from behind cover.

Inga actuated some function in the rescue capsule's controls, a low grinding noise resonating in the darkness, the capsule slipping forward. Saef felt Inga's hand again, pulling him, even as he fired his second magazine dry.

They slipped back to the next capsule, carbine fire blasting into the surrounding compartment. In one muzzle flash Saef saw Inga drawing her short sword, realizing her intent. "No," he whispered in the momentary lull in fire. "I'll do it." He knew the vast advantage his body shield provided.

As Inga had intended, the enemy advanced on the activated capsule, firing confidently now. Between the muzzle flashes and Inga's faint splotches, Saef oriented on the aggressing enemies, his pistol holstered, and sword held high, he dashed from cover and closed in a smooth rush, chopping down one foe before they detected his motion. As the enemy collapsed, the shock and disorientation of his attack that should have swamped his remaining enemies did not occur. Instead they seemed to instantly apprehend Saef's strategy, calmly ducking back through the open canopy of the burbling escape capsule, covering their flank, forcing Saef into a straight approach. Their carbines roared, pouring fire into Saef.

In an instant, Saef's low back blazed in burning agony, the body shield bleeding scorching heat into his body even as hot, sparking rounds filled the air. Saef staggered, falling to the side as something whispered past him, clattering deep inside the activated capsule.

Saef recognized the concussive force of a detonating grenade, contained as it was within the tight confines of the capsule, three human sandbags serving to absorb its explosive fury. For a moment Saef saw stars, his head ringing as he tried to clear his vision.

In the next instant, the lights came up and Inga stepped beside Saef's recumbent position, her Krishna held at high ready, scanning over her handiwork.

She glanced down at Saef, blowing the fringe of her hair back. "Gods, I bloody love a grenade," she murmured.

Saef gasped, staring up at Inga, remembering the first combat they shared. It seemed so long before, and he felt a sudden surge of baffling emotion, discordant in the combat's lull. "Maru...Inga."

She looked sharply down at him, her predatory smile fading at his tone.

"I feel..." Saef said, falling silent, then trying again: "I felt we had something. A friendship or...or..."

"We need to get to the bridge," Inga said in a neutral voice as Saef stood slowly erect.

"Yes. But tell me one thing." Saef suddenly needed one solid piece of ground to stand upon. "Tell me, did I imagine it? Did I dream it or...or did you say—"

"Listen," Inga interrupted, staring intensely into Saef's eyes, "since I was ten, I have only really wanted one thing for myself. I didn't know it at first, but...but the Family gave it to me and took it away all at the same time." She looked away as Saef shook his head, trying to understand. "We can—talk...later, if we survive." Inga turned her gaze down at the fallen traitor, Chief Kang, sprawled where Saef's sword had dropped him. "They need you in the bridge before the mutineers can cut us off, but this one may have something we want..."

Saef gazed at Inga's profile for a moment, feeling both assurance and sorrow. "I think I understand."

Chapter 35

"Within the Imperium, only heavyworlds have maintained such distinct cultural identities in the face of Imperial culture, frequently retaining the language and religion of their ancestors. Only within the largest and most insular Great Houses do we see anything of this fashion outside the heavyworlds."

—Everest Compline, *Reflections*

WITH THE UPPER FLOORS OF THEIR CHOSEN RUIN FILLING WITH the remaining Legionnaires, more and more chose to peer out at the long-sought "objective" at last. Corporal Kyle Whiteside maintained his place, seated among the rubbish, his back against a fragmented internal wall as he watched Legionnaire after Legionnaire step curiously up to the ragged overwatch only to sink away, gray faced, shattered by whatever they had beheld.

Kyle knew he *must* also look, even as his gaze traveled through the rubbish surrounding him, seeing another pair of children's shoes tumbled close together. Whatever horror he might witness, he knew, somehow he owed the people who had once lived here to at least share their horror, to grasp their shared humanity if nothing else.

Sergeant Avery Reardon seemed to have been speaking for some time when Kyle finally noticed the one-sided dialogue. "...don't you agree, Major Chetwynd? Major? Don't you agree we should fortify the ground floor and hold here?"

Major Chetwynd stared out between the shattered support beams, his watery gaze fixed to the west, his mouth moving, but no audible words forming.

Sergeant Reardon turned to the Pathfinder corporal beside him. "We should put a crew together and fortify the ground floor before we get infested."

The Pathfinder shrugged. He had already gazed north to their "objective," and his zealous fervor had not survived the view. "It didn't help any of *them*, and they tried to fort up here. You can see that."

Avery Reardon sighed. "Perhaps with that thinking, Corporal," Reardon said, "we should just shoot ourselves and save the enemy the inconvenience."

Kyle Whiteside slowly stood, his boots feeling heavy as he moved to the jagged void, the overwatch to the west, resting his carbine on the uneven shelf formed from the blast hole. He heard Avery Reardon arguing with the Pathfinder to one side, the voiceless whispering of Major Chetwynd rising from his other side.

Kyle put his eye to the carbine's telescopic optic and began to pan across the scene less than a klick to the west.

Kyle saw a grand arena or stadium that must have once been the central site of sporting events or the like, its vast stands just visible beneath an arching white canopy. Where a portion of the stands must once have stood, a strange sloping framework of girders angled back, disappearing into a broad, yawning cavern seemingly gnawed down into the earth in the arena's center. Upon that framework figures stirred ceaselessly, clambering columns moving down or up the strange edifice.

A second pair of moving columns marched along the ground, coming and going from the dark, sloping mouth of the engineered tunnel, diverting as they exited the stadium enclosure. Kyle focused his carbine optic on the twin columns, suddenly seeing with sickening clarity the segmented legs, the low metallic bodies, the human cargo each mech bore. One line of mechs carried limp human bodies up and out from the cavern, and Kyle gritted his teeth as he followed their path out of the stadium, slowly shifting his carbine to track their progress even as his hand shook. Each mech deposited their nerveless burden to one side of the stadium's outer wall, and Kyle's breath caught within his throat as he began to realize what he beheld.

The broad disordered heap Kyle first took for a collapsed building beside the stadium now resolved in his vision as the mechs added their individual contributions to mass, clambering over the monstrous hill of human corpses. *How many moldering corpses did it take to form a heap as tall as a stadium? Ten thousand? Fifty thousand? More?*

Corporal Kyle Whiteside felt his grip on reality, proportionality, slipping a few cogs as he scanned over the indistinct pile of half-clothed bodies through his carbine optic. He tracked one mech as it dropped yet another body and scampered off on a well-worn track running to the eastern perimeter of the stadium. Kyle's psyche felt another jolt as he perceived a long, low enclosure where the mech he tracked scurried. The enclosure lay only partly in Kyle's field of view, but his target mech entered a sort of gate, snatching up another squirming, struggling human figure, bearing this victim on a reverse path, back into the stadium, beneath the strange edifice of girders—where Kyle now perceived the source of movement from teeming mechs clambering over the high structure—and on down into the dark tunnel.

Kyle Whiteside could not hear the desperate cries of the thrashing human, but his imagination readily supplied them, as the remaining human survivors within the enclosure awaited their turn to be seized by cruel mechanical mandibles, dragged down into the dark burrow. For whatever senseless purpose, clearly the human victims faced execution in the bowels of that pit, every minute perhaps three or four victims making the circuit from cage, to tunnel, to charnel pile, in a continuous chain of merciless slaughter.

"What they making, eh?" Pippi Tyrsdottir murmured from beside Kyle, clearly studying the odd girder construction.

Kyle pulled his eye off the carbine scope and stared aghast at Pippi. "Don't you see what they're doing?" he snapped. "Don't you see all those bodies? *All those bodies?*" Pippi lowered her binoculars and looked calmly at Kyle as he continued to quietly rage. "Who *cares* what they're making?"

Pippi raised her binoculars again and resumed scanning. "*They* care, Kyle. See? May be only thing they care about. Maybe."

Kyle shook his head, nauseated, and turned to Avery Reardon, who still argued with the Pathfinder corporal. "Avery," Kyle interrupted sharply.

Reardon held up a restraining finger to the Pathfinder. "Hold that thought, mate... or better still, just do as I say while I speak to Corporal Whiteside here..." He turned his pale eyes on Kyle, a measuring gaze within them. "What is it, Kyle?"

Kyle pointed a trembling finger back over his shoulder. "That! We've got to—we've got to do *something!*"

Avery Reardon shook his head. "Do you see how many of those damned mechs are over there, Kyle? Hundreds, it seems." Avery frowned. "And just a couple of those toothy bastards have been kicking our collective arses for days now."

Kyle clenched his jaw. "It doesn't matter. We're all dead anyway, Avery. We can't die here, just watching them sl—slaughtering those people like that. We can—we should at least die trying."

Avery Reardon gazed at Kyle musingly, while a few Legionnaires around them made sounds of agreement. "Such nobility, Kyle," Avery murmured. "I had no idea... But I am impressed, truly." He cast a glance around the gray-faced assembly of Legionnaires. "Here's the problem, though: I'm not responsible for any of those poor sods; I'm responsible for you lot."

Before Kyle could form an appropriate ultimatum, a chain of sudden explosions seemed to rattle his teeth in his head, the floor resonating a like a steel drum against his boots.

"Look this!" Pippi called out, and Legionnaires rushed to various windows and ragged holes, even as dust rained down upon them.

Kyle turned and looked beyond the ghastly stadium at the thin white streaks stretching up into the heavens, each streak terminating at a fountain of distant exploding debris, soaring high into the sky.

"Orbital strikes!" Someone called out excitedly and a number of Legionnaires hooted or swore gleefully as if they had personally called down fire.

Kyle shifted his attention to the new swarm of activity around the stadium as a dozen or more mechs raced from the area around the stadium, threading through ruined buildings, closer and closer to the Legionnaires' position.

One mech negotiated the rubble-strewn alley directly adjacent to Kyle's viewpoint, though several floors below. As Kyle stared at the mech, it turned into a doorway and suddenly stopped in place as a fat cable touched its carapace, all six legs seeming to dance a brief jig before smoke erupted from its seams, and it collapsed. "There!" Pippi said, directing every eye to the disabled mech.

Two peculiar human figures emerged from a doorway and Kyle gained a momentary impression of a bulky patchwork of garments as they hurried, working over the mech, dragging the stricken carcass quickly into cover.

Avery Reardon stared down for a moment after the two figures disappeared before turning to the Pathfinder corporal. "New plan. We must speak to those people. If anyone knows what's really going on around here, it's got to be them."

At that moment, two of the small, fast jet drones screamed by below the level of their observation point, and what sounded like distant rocket fire echoed off the tombstone faces of abandoned buildings. Over the tumult, Avery Reardon continued, "May be tricky to make contact with those two people, though. Pluck to the backbone, the pair of them, surely...but likely to be a shade touchy, what with everyone they ever knew butchered in that heap, yonder!"

Aboard IMS *Dragon*, things could hardly be worse. Boarders penetrated multiple decks, meeting sparse resistance. Most of *Dragon*'s Marines had occupied Delta Three's orbital station some weeks prior, and now this ramming attack evidently originated from that same orbital station. Some fragmentary reports from the bowels of *Dragon* even alleged that Imperial Marines accompanied enemy boarding teams.

From the perspective of *Dragon*'s deckchief, Alvarez, the only hint of a positive occurred when the XO arrived in the bridge, seeing the sweating, disbelieving Glasshauser, and immediately stepping into the void. "I see Captain Glasshauser was injured in the collision," Commander Sung stated. "I am now in command."

Deckchief Alvarez and Sensors Ensign Laurent replied in unison, "I concur, you are in command." Glasshauser did not argue, just blinked sickly-eyed, scowling, and *Dragon*'s Intelligence ratified the change.

Commander Sung spared no moments, issuing orders to the bridge crew and the Intelligence in an attempt to contain the invaders ravaging *Dragon*. Artificial gravity levels were increased to maximum in compartments held by the enemy, *Dragon*'s modest security forces grouped for resistance, but by then the cancer penetrated too deeply to halt without outside assistance.

Sung sized up the situation and consulted the tactical holo where the final string of *Dragon*'s outgoing missiles joined the barrage from *Python* and *Sherwood* streaming toward the enemy cruiser. "Comm, message to squadron: *Dragon* is compromised. Too near Delta Three station to self-destruct. All vessels to support *Hightower*'s mission. Good luck."

In the somber moments that followed Sung's message, he turned his focus to what little they might still control. "Alright," he said into the hushed and darkened bridge, "each of us will oversee a security team personally. We will handle lights, gravity and overwatch as they put up the best fight we can muster."

Commander Sung saw the renewed spirit in his people, feeling a moment of piercing pride in their determination, despite the near futility. His gaze fell upon the dejected form of Acting Commodore Glasshauser, and knew that one way or another Glasshauser was not likely to live much longer.

Even after locating the wandering person of Auditor Tenroo and depositing him in an unoccupied cabin, Saef and Inga reached the bridge well ahead of the aggressing mutineers, finding all flowing smoothly despite a few empty seats and Wycherly's recumbent body marring the scene.

Inga settled into the darkness near the access iris, her eyes glassy and lips blue-tinged as she numbly consumed a food bar, a captured carbine across her knees. Saef spared a moment to assure himself of her welfare before limping up to Commander Attic, his own wounds sawing away at Saef's nerves as he moved.

"Captain," Attic greeted. "Another small ship launched from the orbital station, moving on *Dragon*. They ignored our hail, so we tried the barrage battery cannon on them. Worked like a charm." Attic shared a nod with Pennysmith at her Weapons console, before he stood and offered the command seat to Saef. "Of course, the range wasn't too great, and the vessel hadn't much relative velocity..."

Saef eyed the tactical holo and optical displays. "We're going to have trouble with that damned cruiser any moment now."

Attic nodded. "Hopefully it's a little chewed up from all the fireworks."

Saef settled into the command seat, his hip wound leaking blood, and his back complaining where the shield generator had cooked his flesh. "And then these damned mutineers may yet put us in the same position as the Flag...*Dragon*."

"*Python*'s now technically Flag, sir. Captain Khyber is senior captain in the squadron now." Attic went on to explain Commander's Sung's grim message from *Dragon*.

"And what updates from the surface?" Saef asked, thinking through the extent of *Hightower*'s capabilities as he stared at the unremittingly bad picture unfolding within his tactical holo.

"Jamila's got solid Nets with the Marine force. All her fighters and the transports survived the insertion."

Saef grunted. "That's something, at least. We need to get Krenner to rescue us while we can still fight this ship. His Marines need to push forward and clear those bloody mutinous sods."

"Captain," Pim said from the Comm station, "tight beam from *Python*. Captain Khyber. Less than a second transmission delay."

"Put it up, Comm," Saef said, pushing his physical pain aside and composing himself.

The dark eyes, heavyworld features, and hawk nose of Captain Khyber filled the holo, Saef perceiving Khyber's expression of somber intelligence. "Captain Sinclair-Maru," Khyber said in greeting, his speech rather heavily accented by the language of his homeworld.

"Captain Khyber," Saef nodded. "Or should I say 'Commodore'?"

Saef observed a flicker of discomfiture in Khyber's eyes. "Captain; Captain, if you please." Khyber waved a hand, moving on. "Please to tell me, Captain, an estimate of time to complete the jolly withdrawal of ground forces...if you can do such a things as this."

Saef found himself immediately appreciating Khyber's bearing, and bent his mind to the answer. "At this point I'm afraid any estimate would be little better than a guess." He hesitated before adding, "Unless I am much mistaken, it won't be soon enough to keep that bloody cruiser out of our business."

Khyber's white teeth flashed. "Ah! Plain speaking it is from you! We are of one jolly mind on this. But I keep asking myself if we are able to stop the beastly thing at all now, without *Dragon*. Have you one or two ideas about you, Captain? Opening your mind would be of a most helpful, before we are bloody well mopped, don't you think?"

Saef glanced for a moment at the tactical holo, the last of

Glasshauser's profligate missile barrage homing in on the enemy cruiser, *Sherwood* and *Mistral* falling back toward *Hightower*. Saef thought about the mutineers ravaging through *Hightower* and looked up at Khyber's expectant demeanor, daring to believe in a slender hope. "I may have one idea or two, Captain."

Chapter 36

"In the early days following the Slagger War, it was not uncommon to see each of the greatest Families specialize in one martial ability or another. Within a few centuries of peace, nearly all the established Families now specialize only in accruing wealth. The exceptions to this trend are notable..."

—Everest Compline, *Reflections*

LIEUTENANT COLONEL GALEN KRENNER ADVANCED FROM AN actual beachhead like some Marine force of a previous millennium, a picked platoon of the Emperor's First filtering in a screen ahead of his advance up through the ruined city. Before his battledress assaulter, Sergeant Yell called in, Krenner had already perceived some stranger power at work, nibbling away isolated scouts and marksmen in the midst of a relative lull in the action. Yell's report of some mechanized slayer prompted more frustration than anything else. His lightly harnessed rage longed to close with a solid, tangible enemy, and then rip and tear and gouge that enemy into bloody pieces.

"Master Sergeant"—Krenner slapped the cold back-armor plate of the Marine noncom ahead of him—"get weapons teams and marksmen out of the structures and into barricade positions in the street."

The master sergeant affirmed and began issuing directives while Krenner glanced at the tactical holo bouncing along on the back of his own Comm specialist close at hand. Aside from repositioning his scouts and a few weapons teams, his force disposition looked good, the leading elements nearly overlapping the Legionnaires' last recorded position. Thus far the feared enemy armor amounted to exactly one armored skimcar, so Krenner maintained faint hopes for *his* battle—the great battle for which he had lived and trained.

"Marines!" Krenner bellowed down the rubble-strewn street. "Let's move!" Just as in their hard years of training, the Marines broke into a ground-eating lope, Krenner pumping along hungrily in the midst of them...hoping, just hoping a significant enemy force remained close at hand. Hundreds of Marines threaded through the rubble and shattered barricades, bypassing covering gun positions and closing with the lead scouts of the spearhead.

As Krenner's advancing wave of Marines rounded a corner, a flurry of shots rang out, driving most of his people to hasty cover, but Krenner looked ahead, spotting the source of the firing, seeing one of his scouts seemingly battling a stirring pile of refuse. The scout backpedaled, lacing rapid shots into the blob of rubbish among the improvised bulwarks. As an insect-like form sprang out of the debris to seize the scout in its mandibles, a white-hot flash smote the mech with a thunderclap report, spinning the mech and Marine into the refuse.

Krenner looked sharply up the barricaded frontage of a tall building to see a cluster of dirty, unkempt figures emerge, battered gray Legion armor proclaiming their identity. A few of those new Legion mechs accompanied the Legionnaires, one of which mounted a long-barreled mass driver, a thin drizzle of smoke issuing from its barrel.

"Friendlies, my twelve!" Krenner roared, designating the Legionnaires in his tactical UI as he advanced up the street, through the maze of rubbish. He only glanced at the strange enemy slayer where it toppled, leaking fluids and smoke, its wicked jaws still clamped on the Marine scout, its disemboweling blade buried deep through armor, flesh, and viscera. The scout lay in a pool of lifeblood, the carbine yet clenched in dead hands.

Krenner's focus lifted to the Legionnaires awaiting him, seeing both the weariness and the indefinable stamp of the veteran upon them. Their composed vigilance overlay something else...

perhaps resignation, perhaps despair... While Krenner's Marines bristled with well-fed aggression, the Legionnaires possessed the lean and rangy cast of wolves.

Molo Ranger. That's what they called the newfangled mech-supported units, Krenner recalled, as one such Molo folded its mass driver away.

"Welcome to our delightful little mess," one Legionnaire greeted in an oddly chipper tone, though his expression remained somehow haunted. "Sergeant Avery Reardon, Seventh Legion, First Maniple... Molo Ranger Contu." Reardon seemed about to speak again when another Molo Ranger popped out of the refuse-jammed building.

"Avery," the heavyworld female Molo Ranger interrupted, "we get these two. They say a lot of stuff, maybe you want."

Sergeant Reardon nodded and turned back to Krenner. "I'm terribly sorry, sir, but it's urgent I speak to these two locals." He turned away, saying, "Make yourselves comfortable, but do look out for any of these damned slayers. They are frightfully sneaky."

"Wait a moment, Sergeant," Krenner barked. "We're here to get your asses off this rock, so get your people and move!"

"Of course, of course," Reardon said, continuing his retreat. "We're eager to leave, I assure you. Let me—er—go gather our people, while Specialist Tyrsdottir here shows you the most fascinating sight. Pippi?"

Krenner growled, snapping at his attendant noncoms to clear a perimeter before he followed Specialist Tyrsdottir, his handpicked crew of cutthroats swarming around him.

The first shocked thought Krenner formed would later seem ghoulishly inappropriate as he scanned across the distant arena, the scuttling enemy mechs, the mind-searing stack of corpses: *An onshore breeze must push the stench westward, or we'd be smelling the stink of those corpses from the moment we landed...*

After a few moments, when the sheer, horrible scale of the tableau sank in, Krenner heard Sergeant Reardon's voice joined with those of a man and a woman, their conversation finally penetrating through Krenner's fog of shocked rage.

"...and how do you come to know so much about these bloody slayer mechs, then, hmm?" Reardon asked in a pleasant voice.

The woman's voice answered in a lifeless tone, "I—I owned the dumb-mech manufactory here... before. They took it—my whole business, my inventory...some..." Her voice took on a raw edge. "Some special modifications we developed."

"Modifications?" Reardon said. "Oh? Do we have you to thank, then? Cheating the Thinking Machine Protocols?"

"I—it—it was just for mining utility. We never—"

The worn civilian man interrupted in a more heated tone, "We did. We cheated the Protocols, just a little, okay? And we have paid for that and more, but we haven't got time for any of this. People are dying every second we stand here, and you've got the power to stop it! So stop talking and let's go."

Krenner paused in his scanning of the distant horror and turned to the two civilians in their peculiar mishmash of garments and what appeared to be wooden armor. "Wait just a moment," Krenner said. "Are you saying all the enemy forces... their command and control is right there?"

The civilian man shrugged. "At first they had a real army of sorts, but after they had everyone penned up or driven out, the fighters and vehicles went south...weeks ago. Haven't seen them since. Since then, the cutter mechs rove all over, bringing in any human they find, but damn near everything else we've seen is right here...in and around the arena."

"Where the hell are all the armored vehicles your lot yelped about?" Krenner demanded of Reardon.

"Armored vehicles?" Reardon repeated in an innocent voice. "There are a few about still, I think, but I believe Major Chetwynd"—Reardon indicated the muttering Legion officer slumped against the perforated wall—"meant those beastly things yonder, currently killing a couple of civilians every minute or two. They are rather armored enemies, as you may have noticed."

Krenner champed his jaws, snorting, but he scanned out across the carnage again, calculating. He spoke, addressing the civilians: "Did your manufactory make those fast-mover jet drones too? Those aren't much use in mining."

The civilian woman scowled up at Krenner. "We made them, but well within the Protocols...for export. Traitors among our labor force adapted our modified logic boards for the jet drones."

Krenner turned to stare down at her. "Traitors? What distinction is that? I thought this was a general revolt—'viva the revolution' and all that bunk."

She looked up at Krenner with surprise, glancing at Avery

Reardon. "I thought you knew... The demi-cits—most of them, they turned on us. Sold us out."

"*Demi-cits?*" Krenner demanded, disbelieving, but he had no chance to pursue the thought, as his Comm operator leaped up.

"Colonel, we've got comms with *Hightower*; Captain Sinclair-Maru"—he paused, staring significantly at Krenner—"and Commander Attic."

Krenner opened the shoulder-packed holo tank, seeing the partly distorted image from *Hightower*'s bridge, Captain Sinclair-Maru and Commander Attic shoulder to shoulder. "Colonel Krenner," the captain greeted, and Krenner perceived specks of blood on the captain's cheek and forehead despite the image distortion. Trouble. "We've got a situation aboard that only your Marines can solve..."

Saef explained the sudden and extensive mutiny, concluding, "If you can get your people to blow their way forward—soon—it might save our necks." Colonel Krenner motioned Major Vigo nearer to listen.

"What the hell is Major Shirai doing while the mutineers are fucking about?" Krenner demanded, trying to comprehend Shirai's utter silence during a bloody mutiny.

"Holding for orders," Saef replied dryly.

"Damn his eyes!" Krenner swore, turning his attention to Vigo at his side. "Get Shirai off his ass!" He focused back on the holo. "Shirai will be grappling with the mutineers in minutes, or he will be fucking dead, Captain."

Captain Sinclair-Maru inclined his head. "Excellent. And an update, if you please. How soon can you collect the Legionnaires and pull out? We're under some pressure up here even aside from our mutiny issue."

Krenner glanced over the holo, through the ragged hole in the wall, off to that distant scene of ongoing slaughter. "There's some pressure here too, Captain." He looked back at the two Fleet officers within the holo, suddenly, beautifully sure of his path. "I have a new plan in mind, Captain." He smiled. "Instead of pulling these blokes and trying to run, I aim to seize the planet entire, in the name of Emperor Yung the Fourth. Put a little pressure on these arseholes for once. How's that suit you?"

Captain Sinclair-Maru spoke and Krenner listened, but the card was turned. Lieutenant Colonel Krenner would get his battle, and the Emperor's First Marines would obtain their first great victory in centuries, even if he must personally bleed to secure it.

Despite the momentary security she enjoyed in the consular apartments on Battersea, Winter Yung felt invisible bonds tightening about her. The existence of an enemy assassin within the ranks of Imperial Security operatives caused her to question how fast this enemy... *invasion? infiltration?* progressed. What force remained that she might still trust?

Che seemed likely to survive his wounds, but she didn't dare send him out for medical attention, or he might return as a grinning, murderous marionette, as far as she knew. Who could say? Thus far, her own emergency medical equipment seemed to answer, and whether he lived or died, he would remain the Che Ramos that she felt... *what?* What exactly did she feel for Che? She shrugged away any warmer emotion; Che embodied a keen, attentive lover who had proven his loyalty beyond any question. The utility he provided, she told herself, made the care she felt for him nothing more than sensible. Surely.

And then there was Bess...

Winter knew that Sinclair-Maru security operatives ravaged Battersea's Port City, seeking their missing liability.

Should have exerted half that effort before Bess went missing, Winter sneered to herself. Winter's limited degree of human sympathy did not extend to the House of Sinclair-Maru.

Still...

Winter needed allies more than ever now, and the Sinclair-Marus' infuriating obsession with outmoded old ways made them a tough target to infiltrate, even for this pernicious enemy.

Winter mused over the unfolding possibilities awakening in her mind. She felt strangely reluctant to surrender Bess to her hidebound, stuffy Family who had so carelessly, unforgivably risked Bess's life, but Lykeios Manor remained a bastion of strength, if only the fools would keep Bess safe there.

Certainly, she mused to herself, revealing her own custody of Bess constituted no great challenge, the story occurring easily to Winter: Imperial Security just happened to scoop up Bess someplace or other, no worse for gallivanting thoughtlessly around Port City for a few days. Even if Cabot didn't buy that line, he'd hardly call Winter a liar.

Cabot.

Winter had recognized in Cabot a force of significant proportion, as an impediment or an asset, depending on the leverage in Winter's hands... He might be the very ally Winter needed in this shadowy war.

Now, how best to arrange this connection?

Mossimo Minetti earned every credit of his considerable salary serving as the confidential personal secretary for Consul Winter Yung. Not only did he endure Winter's fault-finding, mercurial temperament and absence of human decency, he endured a split life, divided between Battersea and the Imperial court on Coreworld. The hasty trips between these two locales never occurred on a cozy yacht or luxurious liner, but within a grim Fleet warship, where they unfailingly served salted coffee and other peasant fare, not suited to someone of Mossimo's station.

With all the negatives of his employment, he had never thought to see barbaric assassins shot to pieces practically before his eyes, and he most certainly never, *ever* thought one of his rarefied skill set might be utilized as some sort of crude secret agent.

When Mossimo patiently explained this to the consul and one of the bloodthirsty savages she employed, they said, "Not an agent; you'll only be a courier," just before they detailed how he should evade any enemy agents on his tail, and avoid any lonely places where one might quietly stick a knife between his ribs. The subsequent offer of weapons for his use did nothing to assuage Mossimo's ruffled feelings. He had stiffly explained that the dueling sword had been the only weapon required by generations of the proud Minetti Family.

Now, as Mossimo followed their elaborate instructions, moving through Battersea's Port City in a series of autocabs, his misgivings grew to distressing dimensions. Continuing on the precise track Winter had grimly dictated, Mossimo exited his third autocab and walked quickly up a broad apron to a demi-cit domicile pod—a place he would never willingly have visited—passing through the cycling doors and a number of idling, smirking demi-cits in the common area. Walking at a steady pace, Mossimo strode straight through the pod, exiting the rather drab building on its opposite side.

As ordered, Mossimo turned left, joining a thin stream of

pedestrian foot traffic flowing toward the *quaint,* upscale shopping district Port City offered. Though Mossimo felt he should look back over his shoulder, keeping watch for any knife-sticking sorts skulking up behind, Winter had snarled repeatedly that he was not—*repeat, not!*—to look back. He knew she would very likely ask if he followed her orders to the letter, in that damned creepy purr of hers, and he also knew Winter unfailingly detected any attempt to lie. She called her perceptiveness a natural talent, but matched to her mercurial temperament it became a highly unpleasant combination.

Mossimo did *not* look back, despite visualizing a plunging dagger at every step. Instead, he turned off into the convivial little wine bar, as directed, noting that he tracked within three seconds of Winter's ironbound orders.

Using the Imperial Security override Winter had provided, Mossimo turned to the obscured fire escape access, popping the panel and moving through into the service corridor running the length of the street-front shopping establishments. He closed the panel and walked past five identical access panels, stopping at the sixth. The panel yielded to his override once again, and Mossimo stepped into the posh storefront for a purveyor of bespoke clothing, closing the panel behind him. Now, if only...

Mossimo spotted his designated quarry and wiped the sweat from his brow before walking up to the well-dressed blond citizen who stood considering two nearly identical suits of cream and ivory, a delicate hand cupping his chin.

"Claude Carstairs?" Mossimo said, though he knew there could not be two such specimens in all Port City.

Claude glanced at Mossimo uncertainly, his gaze traveling over Mossimo's own fine attire of ebony and scarlet before turning back to prospective garments. "Perhaps you can help me, sir. I am plagued by a grave doubt. A mistake, or a stroke of genius...? Which is it?"

Mossimo suddenly thought Claude must have some prior knowledge of Winter's plans, and this might be the *mistake* of which he spoke. Mossimo shook his head. "The consul rarely makes a mistake, Carstairs," he offered, seeing the seconds ticking down in his timer and feeling the urgency to act.

Claude turned back to Mossimo, his eyebrows raised. "The consul? She is a judge of such important things? I had no idea.

Just shows how one can be fooled by appearances." Claude turned back to the two suits, as a long-suffering proprietor emerged to stare at him, shaking his head. "That padding in the shoulders, now...would you say it is rather too daring? Tell me truly, sir."

Mossimo's mouth fell open for a moment before he managed to say, "What? We have no time to discuss this. The consul requests your presence...immediately, if you please."

Claude turned to frown at Mossimo. "The consul scarcely knows me, friend." His eyes narrowed and he pointed at Mossimo with a graceful finger. "You are very sweaty, dear fellow. I think you may be intoxicated. No shame in it. Intoxicated myself from time to time, but if you go have a nice lie down—Hey, there!" Claude broke off as Mossimo seized Claude's slender arm and began urging him toward the door, Mossimo seeing the timer in his UI descend... already ten seconds behind Winter's inflexible schedule.

Claude twisted ineffectually in Mossimo's grip. "Really, friend, I must insist," Claude said as they hustled out onto the walkway among a screen of pedestrian passersby. "You wouldn't wish this to become an affair of honor, now would you?" he demanded in outraged accents.

A sleek skimcar whizzed up through the light traffic, its broad doors shooting open as Mossimo gave a final shove to Claude, butting him up to the car.

"Consul Yung!" Claude declared, looking through the open door. "Well, I must say, what a pleasant—Yah!" Two muscular hands seized Claude, jerking him inside, even as the skimcar sped back into motion.

Claude sat up and stared about with a lowered brow, seeing several beefy security types, Mossimo, Winter...and a young girl with short dark hair who looked vaguely familiar.

The skimcar rocketed through scant traffic as Mossimo said, "Consul, here is Claude Carstairs, as you—"

"Yes, I see. Shut up, Mossimo," Winter snapped, and Mossimo slumped between a pair of Winter's leg-breakers, pouting as he wiped the sweat from his brow.

"My dear Consul," Claude protested, trying to disentangle his cloak from the sheath of his dueling sword, even while sandwiched between a pair of toughs, "while this—er—diversion is most amusing, I was at a critical—critical!—juncture when this sweaty fellow—"

"You are Saef Sinclair-Maru's particular friend," Winter said, cutting off Claude's complaints. "Your Family estate adjoins the Sinclair-Maru estate here on Battersea."

Claude looked from Winter to Mossimo. "Know that already. Grew up on that estate. Odd if I didn't know it, really..." Claude looked suspiciously across the occupants of the compartment. "The lot of you are intoxicated, aren't you?"

"Don't be a fool," Winter said. "This is a matter of urgency, not some foolish lark."

Claude stared disbelievingly at Winter for a moment, before the young woman with the short, dark hair added, "Bah, bah, boo!" in a very serious tone of voice.

Claude's expression changed as he nodded, looking from Bess to Winter with an air of dawning wisdom. "Matter of urgency... right. You do begin to intrigue me, Consul. Is this the sort of urgency in liquid form? A—er—drinkable form of urgency, you might say?"

Mossimo closed his eyes as Winter's scathing tongue began to fly. Why had he risked his life to secure this vacuous fool? No salary was worth this indignity.

Chapter 37

"Survival merely for the sake of survival remains an absurd intellectual position, but one must agree, without survival, everything else becomes moot."

—Dr. Ramsay Stirling Attenborough, *Ivory Tower Follies*

WITHIN *HIGHTOWER*, DESTRUCTIVE FORCES STIRRED.

At Lieutenant Colonel Krenner's vitriolic direction via combat Nets, Major Shirai finally led a horde of *Hightower*'s Marines into a series of breaching operations, flooding through the forward compartments in the face of determined but futile resistance.

Saef only observed security feeds briefly, seeing shock-armor-clad Marines dominating key corridors, strike teams advancing behind armor shields to riddle pockets of stubborn enemies. Whatever traitors lay among the Marines themselves had thus far not manifested, and Saef focused upon the greater task of saving the squadron.

Back in the Weapons section, *Hightower*'s magazines disgorged immense missiles, titanic armatures, and linkages shuttling the missiles out to *Hightower*'s hardpoints, where Saef hoped to take a page from Captain Susan Roush's book of dirty tricks.

Hightower's largest nukes—16-gauge monstrosities—cold-launched from the missile racks, drifting off to form a tight cluster of inert projectiles orbiting around the blue-green planet below, waiting mutely to be called upon.

Rather than bring up replacements from other watches, Saef chose to reorder his bridge complement with known quantities, placing Commander Attic in the Nav seat, and moving Ash to Sensors. With Inga and Loki quietly in attendance, the Tech seat remained largely superfluous.

Saef looked over his shoulder to Inga's indistinct form, sprawled on the deck in the dark shadows, and sent a line-of-sight message: STILL WITH ME?

STILL HERE, Inga's reply immediately returned. LOKI SAYS THE ENEMY CRUISER IS—OR WAS—IMS PALLAS, AND SHE ADVANCES, ALMOST FINISHED EATING DRAGON'S MISSILE BARRAGE.

There was a moment before a last, most dire line arrived in Saef's UI: ENERGY WEAPON SIGNATURES REVEAL THE HAND OF AN INTELLIGENCE, ACCORDING TO LOKI.

Saef felt a jolt of shock. That was how *Pallas* resolved the long-range gunnery...by violating the Thinking Machine Protocols!

"Captain," Lieutenant Ash called out from Sensors, "looks like the enemy cruiser is maneuvering."

Saef clenched his jaw, nodding. "Thank you, Sensors. Nav, twenty gees, one-seven-zero left azimuth, zero-one-zero negative. Light them up."

"One-seven-zero left, zero-one-zero negative," Attic repeated. "Twenty gees."

Saef measured a dozen metrics within his command UI, then stared at the tactical holo. *Sherwood* and *Mistral* stayed in escort positions, tracking with *Hightower*, while *Python* accelerated hard, sweeping around Delta Three's opposite face. Within seconds, *Python* lay beyond any direct line of communication. The plan now moved ahead, with no chance to pull back. They—all the ships of the squadron—were fully committed.

They would eliminate this enemy cruiser—*Pallas*—or they would be destroyed one by one. They must close the distance to reduce the advantage *Pallas* enjoyed with the aid of an Intelligence.

"Pennysmith," Saef said, "how did the targeting program Chief Maru construct function? Seems like it did the trick with that little merchant ship, eh?"

"Yes, Captain," Pennysmith said. "Seems straightforward. I am...um...impressed she had a chance to program it, with all the...excitement."

"Chief Maru is a wonder," Saef said, meaning it, though the

program in question comprised little more than an overlay which Loki then populated. With Loki's live observations of the enemy cruiser mated to a graphical aiming grid, *Hightower*'s powerful barrage battery might become a highly effective weapon in their fight, even at extended ranges.

"Okay, Comm," Saef said, checking the tactical holo again, "message *Mistral* and *Sherwood* to prepare to launch missiles."

"*Mistral* and *Sherwood*, prepare to launch, aye, Captain," Pim repeated.

"Missile racks ready, Weps?"

"Ready, Captain," Pennysmith said. "All sixty-four-gauge."

Saef took a slow breath, exhaled, and said, "Fire."

Lieutenant Colonel Krenner led the main body of the assault personally, sweeping a few blocks north before looping back to the west and their objective. The two local civilians, Koenig and Vera, provided a pair of functional skimcars, and accompanied the lead element, both cars crammed with Marines. Krenner's two remaining battledress assaulters slipped stealthily into position on the south side of the arena, their position high up, overlooking the mountain of slaughtered humanity, with a cross-angle on the arena's wide entrance.

Observing through combat Nets, Krenner saw that Sergeant Avery Reardon led a picked crew of Molo Rangers, and followed close after a mixed contingent of Marines creeping through buildings just east of the arena. They sought an ideal overwatch position for the coming battle. With functional Nets operational, close coordination lay within reach, and Krenner monitored the movements of each element, even as he double-timed to their initiation point.

Krenner hefted a heavy R-35 automatic rifle, a weapon normally crew-served that threw powerful, heavy slugs that might penetrate the armored hides of the cutter mechs. Those same mechs butchered the weapons team that had initially fielded the R-35 in Krenner's arms, pouncing on them as they had set up a position. Now Krenner muscled the long-barreled automatic weapon, eagerly waiting to try its tungsten penetrators on any number of foes.

They rounded the last corner, seeing the northern boundary of the arena, the long earthen wall of the concentration pens sprawling even nearer. Krenner held up until his column of Marines swept in behind him, amazed that the enemy did nothing to intercept their maneuvers.

Now, if we can only get up to the concentration pens in force...

Lieutenant Colonel Galen Krenner looked right and left, seeing his Marines standing ready, or jutting out every window of the two skimcars, their eyes tense but eager, weapons up, helmets tightened down. He felt a sensation that academics and philosophers would denigrate and diminish, a sensation they would never know or truly comprehend. It sang within him, forming the deepest core of primal *rightness* Krenner had ever known.

He allowed his harnessed rage to build until he felt his body shaking, his jaw clenching, as he signaled through the Nets, setting the ball in motion.

Almost immediately, white-hot bolts snapped from the far left, laterally ahead of Krenner's advance: Marine snipers or Molo Rangers smiting picked targets from their overwatch positions, their mass drivers reaching across the distance with ease.

Krenner gathered himself, roaring, "Ten and Twenty!" in the old battle cry of the Emperor's First Marines, and as his voice resounded, they charged, the Marines behind him echoing his cry in a rippling roar of their own. The open ground before them may have once been a parade ground or a car park adjoining the arena grounds, but now comprised five hundred paces of potential killing fields the Marines must cross. A pair of auto-cannons tucked away somewhere could reap a vast slaughter, Krenner knew.

Krenner did not look back as he hurried toward the enemy, counting down the distance as his boots thumped into the ground, stride after stride: four hundred paces to go...three hundred...

The double roar of a heavy auto-cannon rang out—green tracers arcing to the left, chewing the pocked faces of the buildings sheltering his overwatch teams, the source of fire out of sight behind the arena. "Come on, Marines!" Krenner yelled, loping ahead, the R-35 swinging heavily from side to side as he ran.

Two hundred paces to go, the first hints of necrotic stench reaching them, the rough earthen wall of their first objective running along far to their right flank.

One hundred paces. Cannon fire continued to pound the buildings to Krenner's left, the source of the fire still out of sight beyond the concentration pens. Krenner glanced back for the first time, seeing the eager wave of his Marines close behind, the two skimcars keeping pace with them. Krenner rushed on...

Fifty paces. High up, Krenner spotted the telltale puff of a SCAARS munition a moment before the distinctive report of its launch reached his ears. The antiarmor rocket plunged and detonated out of sight beyond the earthen wall, cutting off the auto-cannon fire like a switch.

Low figures appeared, flickering through the rubble-speckled space, streaming east from the arena, toward the buildings sheltering Krenner's overwatch. Segmented legs flashed, and Krenner pulled up, threw the long weapon to his shoulder, and began pumping streams of heavy slugs into the mechs, firing in three- or four-round bursts, snarling curses as he fired.

For a moment, Krenner stood as a lone god of destruction, his entire being consumed in the hammering recoil against his cheek and shoulder, the fat tracer rounds slashing out, sending fragments of shredded mechs flying, but then he returned to himself as Marines opened up all around him, pouring fire into their mechanized foes.

Krenner's heavy automatic rifle fell still and he quietly rated himself for the novice mistake: target fixating to the exclusion of every other thought. He ejected the empty ammunition cassette as he swept a quick scan of their force disposition. "Ammo!" he roared. An attendant corporal sprang up beside Krenner, slapping another heavy cassette into place just as an attacking mech leaped out of the swirling dust and smoke.

"Fuck me!" Krenner yelled, kicking out with the flat of his boot, barely shifting the cutter mech's lunge a handsbreadth to the right. Its wicked mandibles snatched the corporal, dragging him back as Krenner charged his weapon, dumping twenty rounds into the mech's carapace as he bellowed in rage, seeing holes punching through the plating.

Around him, other mechs sped through the streaming fire of a hundred weapons, closing with the Marines, but Krenner jumped out beside the fallen corporal, tugging him from the lifeless metal mandibles. The Marine corporal had both hands wrapped around a gushing thigh wound. "Use your gods-damned tourniquet before you pass out!" Krenner barked over the roar of gunfire, turning his weapon on a pair of cutter mechs to the right as they dragged Marines from the line, riddling both mechs, but not before their spade-tongues plunged.

The two accompanying skimcars advanced with the front line, providing stable positions for weapons teams, who poured controlled bursts into enemy after enemy. A few SCAARS munitions also slashed into the enemy, until Marines and mechs became too entangled for heavy weapons to be employed.

"Move!" Krenner bellowed. Advancing again, pushing through shattered cutter mechs and fallen Marines, rounding the edge of the concentration pens' earthen palisade, seeing the arena's open mouth, and in the distance beyond, the fringe of heaped bodies. The stench rose up above the smell of spent ordnance and blood.

Behind him, Krenner heard the shouts and gunfire as his Marines broke the shells of their immediate attackers. Segmented legs and metallic bodies poured from the arena, moving toward them, but Krenner left it to the main element behind him, racing toward the concentration pens' entrance to his right.

Mass driver bolts and SCAARS rockets flashed over the battlefield: wherever they struck segmented limbs spun, or glow-ring holes dropped mechs in their tracks, but Krenner charged ahead, the larger battle raging over his shoulders. He knew the second assault element would push on to initiate entry into the arena, but he would not rejoin them until this first objective felt the heat of his aggression.

Krenner leveled his heavy automatic, staying well out from the enclosure's wall as he approached the arching entrance, his picked team right on him, their weapons ready. Krenner's weapon optic pinned the revealing slice of the entrance as he moved.

Krenner might later pardon his own hesitation in gunning down a grinning human being, but the large handgun in that grinning man's fist fired immediately, center-punching Krenner's chest. The answering burst from Krenner's automatic rifle spun and folded the man, continuing on to lace another armed figure appearing in his sight picture before Krenner's flood of fury abated sufficiently for him to even wonder at his own injuries. He had no time to check, as four more attackers lunged into view.

Krenner's picked team flanked him now, and the blast of eight automatic weapons shredded their four foes in their tracks. As a body, Krenner and his team advanced, using the same techniques employed for clearing the passages and compartments of a starship, dozens of Marines backing them as they worked each cross-angle. Instead of discovering additional armed enemies, they cleared a series of huge, filthy corrals, empty aside from shreds of clothing and the odd shoe. They continued moving from one pen to the next, opening crude gates, the sounds of the greater battle still raging outside the pen's enclosure.

Only upon reaching the last two enclosures did Krenner discover living humans—*barely* living, emaciated mobs, staring at Krenner with fear-hollowed eyes. The shifting mass of ragged people uttered no cheers, their only sound being a hushed murmur with no visible source. More Marines moved in, freezing, transfixed by the vision, their horror growing as they perceived the neat stack of limp bodies to one side, many showing signs of recent cannibalism.

"Corporal," Krenner said, "roust up those two local civilians and get these people out of here." He turned to his sickened warriors. "Come on, Marines, let's go clear out that gods-damned hole in the arena."

A ragged, white-faced woman had to speak twice for Krenner to hear her thin, lifeless voice. "You—! You go below . . . you'll never come back."

Krenner ignored her, shoving his Marines roughly out the gate, moving to follow, but the dead voice pursued him: "Your body will be . . . smiling like they all do. But you will be gone!"

Commander Jamila saw the huge transport lighters settled in rows across the small island, just fifty klicks from the coastline and Delta Three's chief population zone. She counted herself fortunate that all fighters and transports survived the assault thus far, even as she led her fighters in a slow circuit around the island, calculating their remaining fuel loads.

Word came down from *Hightower* as they moved off station to tackle the enemy cruiser above, and Jamila knew *Hightower* might be hours, days on its mission if she ever returned at all. That left Jamila with a few choices: she could continue flying slow loops and protect the transports from any surviving jet drones that might appear; she could navigate to one of the few airfields that remained intact and land; or she could lead her wing into orbit where they might endure for a miserable day or more, awaiting *Hightower*'s return. Not one of her available options seemed especially promising in her professional estimation.

Her gaze wandered to the descending number of her fuel

gauge. The Mangusta really did possess the longest legs of any Fleet interface fighter, and if the word from *Hightower* could be credited, that maniac, Krenner, planned to wipe out all enemy forces on Delta Three en masse, meaning he might just need air support.

Jamila nodded to herself as she eased into another slow bank over the foam-flecked seas. She would remain on the wing until fuel levels dropped below one-third, then make for an airfield and land.

With the remaining fuel load, her fighter wing could execute a support mission or make orbit, whichever way the cards happened to fall. Either way, she hoped Delta Three would not become her permanent home, like it had for Jackie Shipman and Matt Mayo, whose physical remains lay scattered somewhere in the surging waters below.

Chapter 38

"With young candidates of today's Great Families, one must consider that whatever character is instilled within them may define the Family for centuries to come."

—Everest Compline, *Reflections*

THROUGHOUT THE NEARLY NINE STANDARD YEARS INGA SPENT within Hawksgaard, she had observed various Family young attain their first majority on several occasions. There was little ceremony— the Sinclair-Maru were not much given to such things—but receiving a coveted Sinclair-Maru sword to replace the training blade marked a momentous transition. For those, like Inga, who held a future within the Family's more martial pursuits, one also selected a lethal sidearm to replace one's training pistol, investing the same level of care they would in sizing and balancing their Family sword.

For Inga, the arrival of her first majority carried even greater, even more lethal overtones.

Weeks before the day of her majority, Kai had summoned Inga to his office, explaining with remarkable enthusiasm a fresh Family triumph: They had secured a pair of Shaper implants of a shocking new variety that promised to revolutionize the Family "biotech program." Inga knew that she embodied the heart of the Family's biotech program, and suddenly realized one of the powerful new implants would soon reside at the base of her own skull.

Kai felt certain that this new development would provide Inga yet another advantage Julius had lacked—instead of relying upon external systems carried by an attendant dumb-mech, she could carry the control systems as part of herself.

By the day of Inga's actual majority, the site of her implant surgery had largely healed and she reveled in the glories of her new User Interface. Her years with Deidre had not been wasted, the lessons learned on their hacked holo lens sets now applied to the new implant, and she quickly mastered its standard functions. However, its advanced functions were not truly tested until some weeks later. By then, Inga had become accustomed to the razor-edged blade at her waist where it joined her particular selection for a sidearm. While most graduating Family members selected the excellent Trombly auto-pistol as their personal sidearm, Inga opted for a sleek Hellbore P8. Its lower bore axis and slimmer grip profile outweighed the Trombly's greater magazine capacity, in her view, but such commonplace considerations all dropped away shortly thereafter as she stepped upon the path poor Julius had once blazed in his brief glory.

That path officially launched just a few weeks after Inga's majority day, though the event itself remained a sickening void in her memory, her awareness reconnecting to reality what seemed moments after she received the fateful summons to Hawksgaard's medical center, awakening to find herself greatly changed. The intervening—missing—days, the actual moment when Family technicians applied the treatment, even her walk to the medical center, all remained strangely vacant from her memory.

Her blurred recollections began as a repeating sequence of fevered nightmares, detached entirely from her physical body, seemingly adrift in some suffocating dream world. A slow drum-beat became a guide, and she latched onto the metronome thump, following its sure rhythm back to self-awareness.

This is the beating of my heart; that scarlet wave is pain; arms, legs, lungs, eyes...burning.

For some immeasurable span of time Inga struggled to reoccupy her body, until memory returned.

The treatment.

Though her view remained unbroken darkness, Inga recalled long lessons, employing her new UI to manipulate various values as medical technicians observed their instruments, guiding her in the steps needed to manage new forces inhabiting her body. The new User Interface opened for her now, populating the dark void with a concrete reality tied to the outside world. As she began to explore the myriad inputs—increasing a value here, decreasing another there—she became gradually aware of voices, but her focus lay upon calming the storms that scorched and shook her physical body. This process bore little comparison to her training, feeling through adjustments on a purely visceral level until, notch by notch, she tamed the burning threads that seemed woven into every organ, muscle, and bone.

After what seemed hours, Inga's body settled to a mere quiver, and she now began to perceive fine physical sensations filtering through the pain and disorientation. She detected the pressure of restraint cuffs on arms and legs, the binding across eyes, the needles trickling fluids into her veins.

She found her voice, speaking into the darkness: "Release me."

After the treatment, everything changed for Inga even as she swiftly began to rule the powers within her, remembering well the words of Julius Sinclair-Maru. The goal, she knew, was not merely an uneasy truce with her new puissance, but a living synergy that so far escaped her. The next stage of her training worked to unlock this.

She met individually with Hiro Sinclair-Maru, who pushed, tested, timed, and encouraged Inga though each step, applying her burgeoning abilities to real-world tasks.

Like Julius before her, everywhere Inga went within Hawksgaard, a sort of dumb-mech trailed her, its advanced systems linked to her UI, monitoring her augmentation. Beyond this, the mech provided sensor capabilities, data storage, communications, and Nets-hacking tools. It also provided a handy place to store the snacks she now constantly craved. She named the faithful metallic companion Fido, accepting its constant presence as one more cost she had unwittingly paid the fateful day in Battersea's slum more than nine years before.

Another unexpected cost lay in her long, empty nights of sleeplessness. Julius had not specifically mentioned insomnia among the horrors he had suffered, but Inga did her utmost to use the lonely hours to good effect, pursuing fresh academic studies after long days of training. She became slowly accustomed to a few hours of actual sleep every week, wondering if sleeplessness alone might burn away her humanity as the treatment once consumed Julius Sinclair-Maru.

Inga replayed every word Julius ever said in her hearing, counting upon many months of dreary hardship before she attained the godlike elevation he had described with such relish. Within weeks, she gained a glimmering of that exalted state.

Day after day, Hiro pushed Inga through exercises and tests of physical speed, dexterity, and strength, and each test seemed to mock Inga's efforts. Some feats saw marginal improvements over her unaugmented baseline, while other tests revealed results inferior to her prior scores. Yet, the entire time Inga felt as if a dam stood somewhere within her, simultaneously protecting her from destructive forces and blocking her from the vast store of power she sought.

Hiro even seemed to perceive this one day within the training room. "Is it possible, Inga Maru, that you force a thing that must arise freely?"

What had Julius once said about the Sinclair-Maru *meeting force with force*?

An idea dawned as she contemplated the vast gulf between natural heirs of the Sinclair-Maru legacy, and her own heritage of abuse, debasement . . . and *fear.*

Following the thought, Inga detached her lethal new dueling sword, crossing the empty training floor to replace it with a training blade. She turned to Hiro and dipped her head. "My lord, I challenge you. No score . . . To capitulation, or to incapacity." She quelled the rising sense of uneasiness that arose within her.

Hiro contemplated Inga solemnly for a moment before nodding. "Very well, Inga Maru." He swapped his lethal sword for his usual training blade and met her in the center of the floor. Neither Inga nor any other student had scored a single uninvited hit upon Hiro in the years she had dwelled in Hawksgaard, and she doubted Hiro faced any equal among the entire Family, where it concerned the blade.

Knowing this, Inga immediately executed her murderous lunge, missing Hiro's sternum by a handsbreadth, then barely deflecting Hiro's lightning riposte. She spun in a wheeling slash, drawn from the pure Sembrada, an attack that would have caught any of her fellow students cold. Instead she narrowly dodged Hiro's returning cut, falling back, fighting desperately. Their blades clashed twice and Inga felt and saw the difference she had never witnessed before. This was Hiro unrestrained, and she could not stand against him. Hiro's blade rebounded in a loop that swept low, cracking Inga across her ribs. His next blow numbed her left arm from elbow to fingers, and Inga sprang forward with the impact, inside his strength, plunging a short pommel strike that he blocked, wrist to wrist, Hiro's dense bones striking Inga like a club. She nearly dropped her blade, and Hiro hip-rolled her, tossing her across the mat. He advanced like a grim whirlwind, slashing down at her blow after blow, until Inga survived each moment only by her reshaped instinct, losing all deliberate thought, falling into the embrace of the Deep Man.

As the pool of fearlessness took her, Inga felt a reservoir of waiting strength surge. In the millisecond between breaths, Hiro seemed to hesitate, slowing, his attack descending with a patronizing lassitude. Inga's nerves suddenly sang like plucked wires, her muscles strangely burning as she sprang erect and slashed out, turning her blade at the last instant.

Hiro's sword jolted from nerveless fingers, spinning across the mat, and he stepped back with glacial slowness as Inga stood quivering, fire surging through her veins, the small injuries she had just suffered melting away. She wanted to run, to leap, to execute flips and cartwheels. She laughed suddenly, unafraid, powerful.

Hiro spoke, and Inga struggled to hear his tedious words over the roaring in her ears, but the roaring only increased. Inga's entire body began to shake until her teeth chattered in her head, the sword falling from her hand as icy currents flowed through her body. She collapsed, ice flowing from her navel through her back and up to her brain. Her chattering teeth clenched until she felt they might break.

Hiro cradled Inga's head, placing a flask against her lips, the burning liquid trickling in, combating the ice within her. As the tremors eased, Hiro place a shiny red fruit in her hand. "Here..." He gazed down at her for a moment before speaking again. "This power is yours now, Inga Maru, but no power is without cost. Can you find this balance, hmm? Eat this, Inga Maru, and then we shall contemplate balance together."

The power was hers indeed and the balance Hiro called out was no real balance at all. It comprised only resistance to the intoxicating flow of strength, vigor, greatness that now always arose at Inga's request. Could she sample mere sips of godlike—yes, Julius spoke truly: godlike—power without yielding to its exultant glory? Therein became Inga's real training or conditioning.

Coldly, in the midst of her own battles of willpower, Inga thought of her father... Did the chemicals which defined that man's life give him the delusion of a power such as Inga now embodied? Did he starve and desecrate his children to capture the same sensations that she now struggled to dominate?

The thought gave her no greater pity for her father's memory, but it did give her added strength in her internal battle. No matter what glories lay on tap for her, she would never yield, never sacrifice those who depended upon her. Never.

Inga's training continued to explore and expand her abilities over the course of her last full year in Hawksgaard, until both espionage and lethal skill sets grew in proportion to her new power. The holo lenses Deidre once helped Inga modify into powerful hacking tools now paled in comparison to the combination of her new Shaper implant and Fido's suite of utilities. Joined with Inga's new ability to accelerate her observation cycles, she could now perform line hacks that would have astonished her treacherous former teacher with their speed and scope.

After a few months, once the biotech treatment had permeated Inga's cells, functions within her UI altered her skin pigment, hair color, fingerprints, and eye color. Deidre once taught Inga the skills she had called the *technicalities of deceit*, but Deidre could have possessed no comprehension of just what embodiment of deceit Inga might become.

After ten years within Hawksgaard, and nearly a year of training after the treatment, the Family finally sent Inga on her first trial back to Battersea, back home. She had once departed from Battersea as a precocious urchin; she now returned as a fearless weapon in the personal arsenal of Bess Sinclair-Maru. In Kai's hesitant manner, he made it clear that Cabot and the other upper echelons of Lykeios knew little or nothing of Inga's true role, and she began to perceive her first hint of factions even within the seemingly indivisible Sinclair-Maru.

During her months back on Battersea, Inga lived and operated entirely alone, completely detached from the Sinclair-Maru. Her appointed tasks frequently lay entirely outside the Honor Code, her numerous skills employed to invade private offices, infiltrate data networks, and shadow various persons—both within and without the Family... These persons, it seemed to Inga, might represent political opponents of Bess Sinclair-Maru.

Only two diversions drew Inga from her constant duties during that first foray. Once she spent a summer evening pacing anonymously through Port City's slums, revisiting the nightmare setting of her childhood, stopping before the decrepit tenement she had once shared with her father and two siblings. The sick taste of those dark memories drove her away, never to return to the slums.

Her second diversion could not be so easily consigned away. On more than one lonely evening, her immediate duties fulfilled, Inga slipped into the grounds of the Battersea System Guard base adjoining Port City, where she observed Saef Sinclair-Maru going about his military service. Many of the Family served within the system guard, but Inga felt she perceived that same distinct difference in Saef Sinclair-Maru at the age of twenty-five that she had perceived in his younger self—different from his fellow Family members, different from anyone she knew.

When Inga was eventually recalled to Hawksgaard, she missed the open air, the variegated vitality of Port City, and her guilty spying expeditions pondering upon Saef, the man, versus Saef, the boy. She did not remain long in Hawksgaard, however, and the pace of her secret labors kept her far too busy for unfruitful contemplations.

Only after Inga deployed to three more worlds, for three more short tours of espionage, did she begin to suspect that her handlers intentionally withheld her from missions of any real stature. Upon completion of each mission, Kai and his coterie seemed more interested in the data Fido recorded on the performance of Inga's augmentation than they were in the substance of her actual missions.

"Will you ever properly employ me, Kai?" Inga asked at last. "Or am I just a test pilot for the actual Silent Hand that follows behind me?"

This question clearly did not please Kai at all, the bright flush of his forehead declaring the sudden height of his emotion. "Why—how could you think such a thing? We have spared no expense upon your training. We will not now throw this away— you away—on any rash risk."

Kai's response seemed genuine enough to Inga's critical eye, but this scarcely mollified her. "So I'm to remain a petty thief, or a bloody pickpocket out of an abundance of caution, then, Kai? What backwater world will you send me to next?"

Kai regarded her severely. "And I suppose you think we should send you to Imperial City?" Kai said.

Inga shook her head. "Not yet. Not until I've bona fides outside of Family."

This answer obviously surprised Kai, and Inga felt her old slum instincts awakening within her as he spoke. "Whatever do you mean? What bona fides?"

"*Any* pedigree that puts me where I can do *real* work," Inga said. "Any legitimate cover for my travel; a genuine profession outside of Family, or...or even Fleet, perhaps."

"Fleet?" Kai said, showing surprise again. "You'd need a stint in a system guard unit to even gain a shot at Fleet."

Inga shrugged. "So I join the Battersea Guard for a stint." Inga felt a hint of a flush mount her cheeks as she thought of her prior forays onto the Battersea Guard base. "It—it would be a natural cover. If the Family never took me in, I might very well have joined the guard anyway."

Kai's brow wrinkled in thought, his lips pursed. "There's something to what you say. I will...I will discuss it with Bess."

Of course Bess saw the sense of Inga's argument, the decision was made, and with Inga's education and skill, she excelled immediately within the Battersea System Guard. Those same aptitudes made her a natural for the annual Fleet selection, and in record time she held a pending rank and rating in Fleet.

Throughout her military service on Battersea, Inga experienced a perplexing mixture of emotions, spending so much time within the ranks of a compact military force, yet never once seeing that intriguing figure from her childhood: Saef Sinclair-Maru. Her excess time and energy did not go unspent, however, engaging in surreptitious extracurricular duties around Battersea as Bess consolidated power within the Family. Those efforts helped bring Bess to her new position of Family executor, just as the Imperium suffered its first truly cataclysmic shocks in centuries: regicide, rebellion, war.

With the maelstrom of change swirling, Inga found herself entering Lykeios Manor for the first time in her life, heeding

Bess's call. The storied estate of the Sinclair-Maru forced her to recall her father's bitter words decrying the opulence of such a place, while he, a dissolute addict, barely survived. But here she stood, the daughter of that addict, now a trusted aide to the Family executor, earning her place among the Family by applying all the qualities her father ridiculed.

Within Lykeios Manor, aside from Bess, Inga saw only one individual she recognized from the past, in the person of Eldridge Sinclair-Maru, the head of Family training on Battersea. After a few days in the sprawling halls of the manor, Inga saw another face she would always remember. She would surely never forget the individual who once acted upon Inga's manipulation, employing his dueling sword to rid her of the defiler, the desecrator, her father. Hugh Sinclair-Maru provided that service years before, under the auspices of the Honor Code when little more than a boy himself, and while Inga regarded Hugh with perfect ambivalence, she avoided his sight, remaining invisible to nearly everyone moving through Lykeios. With some fresh tumult stirring the Family, this proved no great challenge for her.

Instead, Inga sought refuge in the armory and training range of Lykeios Manor, sampling the broad offering of lethal wares until her presence might be called upon. That call arrived soon enough.

When Bess summoned Inga to her office, Inga discovered the cause of the increasing furor, seeing it affect even the unflappable Bess. "You have desired a greater test of your talents, Miss Maru," Bess stated without preamble. "It appears your wish has been granted." Bess rested her corded forearms atop the ancient desk of marbled burl wood. "An opportunity has arisen in Fleet. I will formally present the proposition to the Family leadership, but Cabot and I have an accord already; this opportunity shall be seized."

Inga stood passively, fishing a food bar from a pouch at her belt as she regarded Bess. After an expectant silence, Inga said, "Excellent. When do I leave?"

"Listen to me," Bess said with more intensity than Inga had ever witnessed from the matriarch. "This is the greatest gamble our House has undertaken in centuries. You will be supporting a Family member who is already targeted for assassination."

Inga barely restrained a bitter curl to her lip. Playing nursemaid for one of the Family leaders did not comprise a dream assignment for her.

"You may be called upon to liaise with Imperial Security, but you may also be sure that they play their own game," Bess continued.

Inga's burgeoning sneer faded at these words, curiosity rising.

"You will be faced with complex and conflicting demands upon you, but your first priority will be to keep our candidate alive," Bess said. "The gloves come off, the claws come out... choose your metaphor, but you may face the full lethal power of malevolent Houses, or possibly militant elements of the rebelling worlds. You will destroy any such attackers, by any means you can contrive."

As the implications of Bess's speech rippled through Inga's consciousness, she felt the trembling surge of her augmentation, hungering for action.

"Our candidate survived an attempt upon his life not an hour ago and he should be en route here even now," Bess said, her eyes flickering as she consulted her UI. "Your principal, our candidate, may not be familiar to you... I don't suppose you are acquainted with Saef, are you? You both served in the Battersea Guard at about the same time, I believe."

Inga felt her breath catch, her heart emit an odd beat, as she felt the grip of that ancient and ineffable sensation that some called fate.

"Not really, my lady," Inga managed to say in a steady voice. "I met him briefly in my childhood, the day I left Battersea."

Bess raised her eyebrows with mild curiosity, reflecting. "Was he there that day? I suppose he was. Well, the Imperials have some cloak-and-dagger game in mind for him, while he's supposed to command a Fleet frigate. We cannot afford to let the Imperial games get him killed."

"Yes, my lady," Inga said, her face schooled to a stillness she did not feel within.

Bess stared hard at Inga for a silent moment. "Have you any input before we go down to central comm and argue about the inevitable with the Family leadership?"

Inga smiled. "No, my lady. It all sounds quite suitable... perfect, even."

Chapter 39

"An appreciation for liberty is learned, it seems. Perhaps the low rate of promotion from the ranks of demi-cits is not due to oppression from the sword-wielding Citizens, but merely the demi-cits' long habit of dependency, no matter how unpalatable that theory has become within learned circles."

—Dr. Ramsay Stirling Attenborough, *Ivory Tower Follies*

HIGHTOWER ACCELERATED HARD, THE COURSE SAEF SELECTED calculated to provide the smallest surface area for the enemy cruiser, *Pallas*, to target with their lethal energy weapons. *Mistral* and *Sherwood* maintained their loose positions on either flank, corkscrewing along their paths. *Hightower*'s missile racks flashed again and again as Lieutenant Tilly Pennysmith launched dozens of 64-gauge nuclear missiles, their fishtailing tracks cutting above and below *Hightower*'s course relative to the ecliptic plane.

"Sensors," Saef said, looking over at Lieutenant Ash, "full active sensors on that enemy cruiser. Paint him with everything."

"Aye, Captain, full active sensors," Ash affirmed even as the tactical holo revealed *Mistral* and *Sherwood* launching their own small waves of 64-gauge missiles to join their new barrage.

Saef consulted the descending counter within his UI. *Python* should be nearly around the obscuring globe of Delta Three, in position to initiate.

"Captain," Ash called out, "enemy cruiser is displacing,

maneuvering hard...looks like zero-eight-five right azimuth, zero-nine-nine negative."

Saef exhaled softly. The cruiser did respond to positional pressure at least, sliding deeper into the well. In Saef's estimation, the odds of surviving this conflict just increased dramatically. "Ops, message to Marine quarterdeck: Assault element is go for launch."

"Go for launch, aye, Captain," Deckchief Furst said, still subdued after his less-than-sterling response to Wycherly's earlier treachery.

A moment later, Saef saw the two compact boarding penetrators launch out toward *Dragon* as *Hightower* approached her nearest point to the embattled flagship: Marine boarders away. He checked the descending counter again. "Nav, bring us zero-one-five right azimuth. Keep that bloody cruiser face-on."

"Aye, Captain, zero-one-five right."

"Pennysmith, you have thirty-twos ready to launch?" Saef said, though values in his command UI gave the proof of Pennysmith's preparation.

"Aye, Captain. Thirty-twos racked and targeted."

Saef checked the descending clock one more time and nodded. "Fire thirty-twos, please, Pennysmith."

The fresh set of huge 32-gauge missiles leaped out into the dark, accelerating fast toward a preselected interdiction point. For their piecework plan to have any chance of success, *Python* must initiate its attack soon.

Python, slipping up quietly from a tight polar orbit, should put the enemy in a momentary squeeze, especially if *Pallas* had lost *Python*'s trace behind the blaze of nuclear fires. While *Dragon*'s reckless barrages represented a horribly ineffective means of battling *Pallas*, at least it may have served as a screen for more tactically sound actions. Now, if Loki's observations proved true, the enemy's damned energy weapons might be stretched to address such a dispersed attack from unexpected quarters.

"Captain!" Ash called out sharply. "Getting some transient hits on active, at about two hundred thousand klicks, twelve degrees negative from the enemy contact. Looks like missiles rising quiet from behind Delta Three."

Python.

Saef checked the clock again, even as *Hightower*'s own horde of 64-gauge missiles finally began to close with *Pallas*, one after another flashing in fiery deaths as the enemy plied its energy weapons defensively. *Hightower* continued to accelerate directly toward the enemy, heavy 32-gauge missiles continuing to regularly launch. Right on their appointed mark, *Sherwood* and *Mistral* went to full emergency acceleration, maneuvering aggressively, *Sherwood* rocketing sharply to *Hightower*'s left, *Mistral* to the right.

"Weps," Saef said, "begin detonating select fish." Without a pause he addressed Lieutenant Ash, even as Pennysmith affirmed his order. "Sensors, switch to passive only."

"Aye, Captain, passive sensors only."

"Nav, full emergency acceleration, now!"

Hightower surged toward the enemy even as the frigates *Mistral* and *Sherwood* led the way, branching to the flanks closing with *Pallas*. Over one hundred thousand klicks ahead, a dispersed web of *Hightower*'s 32-gauge missiles blossomed into massive globes of nuclear fire, each expanding new sun nearly overlapping. The enemy cruiser disappeared behind the variegated spheres of blooming radiation, and *Hightower* raced to close the distance.

The probing finger of a powerful energy weapon stabbed through the obstructing fires.

"*Sherwood* reports she's taking fire; shields at red," Pim called out.

Hopefully a lucky hit, Saef thought, otherwise both frigates would likely be destroyed in the next few minutes.

The timer in Saef's UI ticked down to zero.

Python should be fully committed now, accelerating into the enemy's flank; a cluster of *Hightower*'s huge 16-gauge missiles that quietly orbited Delta Three should be awakening to life even as they swung around beneath the enemy cruiser. In the next few minutes, either *Pallas* would be neutralized, or the entire squadron would die.

Corporal Kyle Whiteside lay behind a thick pile of rubble just a short distance from his Molo, Fang, the linked tactical eyepiece consuming his entire attention. The upper floors of this shattered building provided cover for a mixed group of Marine snipers and Molo Rangers, the crackle and blast of their weapons a deafening roar in the enclosed area. They overlooked a deep killing field of racing, seething mechanical enemies, and Kyle redirected Fang's mass driver from target to target as Pippi called out corrections.

The glowing reticle in his eyepiece tracked a scampering cutter mech as it sped into the flank of the Marine assault force. Kyle triggered the shot, Fang's six legs bouncing from the recoil.

"Hit!" Pippi yelled, her eye tied into the optic mount on her Molo. "Now is one other...just up and left."

"On it," Kyle said, locking his reticle onto another mech, sending another brilliant bolt flashing across the distance.

Kyle's shot joined a regular stream of fire lancing out from the upper floors to clear a path for Krenner's advancing force; more than a dozen Marines and Molo Rangers poured rounds through blast holes or windows, sighting and firing.

Kyle saw the main body of Krenner's Marines reach the concentration pens and split, half the troops charging from the pens toward the open face of the arena, against a thinning stream of cutter mechs. From somewhere inside the arena, a murderous stream of raking fire mowed down a cluster of charging Marines, driving the others to cover.

"Pippi! Some kind of heavy weapons in the arena...you see it?"

Before Pippi could reply, Kyle heard and felt an immense blast behind him, spinning to see Sergeant Avery Reardon standing beside the doorway overlooking the stairwell. The shattered husk of a cutter mech smoldered close against the doorframe, and Reardon called out, "It seems we have annoyed the enemy!"

Reardon fell back, Cuthbert cooking off another deafening shot as the doorway filled with low metallic forms, segmented legs scrabbling over Cuthbert. Marines spun from their south-facing firing positions, struggling to bring their long R-40 mass drivers to bear before the cutter mechs flooded in. Before Kyle Whiteside could act, a cutter bolted over Cuthbert and leaped at Avery Reardon. Reardon showed his quick thinking, meeting the clashing mandibles with his carbine held port arms rather than attempting a futile shot. He fell back at the onslaught, crashing into the crumbling wall, the scissoring mandibles sliding up the carbine, clamping onto one of Avery's shoulders. As Kyle cried out, the spade-tongue plunged, shearing through Avery's carbine and breastplate. A blinding flash knocked the cutter aside, segmented legs blasting free to bounce off the walls, as two Marines fired their R-40 mass drivers from the hip at close range, advancing on the seething doorway.

"Avery!" Kyle yelled, deafened and disoriented by the thunderclap discharges, stumbling to Reardon's side. "No, no, no...

Avery." Kyle tugged at the jagged mandibles locked onto Avery Reardon, each pull jerking Avery's body. Blood flowed from every gap in Reardon's armor, his lips and face colorless.

Kyle felt Pippi's powerful hands gripping his arm with heavy-world strength, holding him still, and Kyle subsided, slumping over Avery's form, wanting to kick the shattered mech off of Avery's body. Over the tumult of fire, as the Marines advanced shoulder to shoulder out the doorway, pumping bolt after bolt into their metallic enemies, Kyle yelled into Avery's bloodless face, "What am I going to tell your mother, Avery? *What?*"

Avery's eyes flickered open, a hint of the mocking smile trembling onto his bluish lips. He spoke, and somehow Kyle heard the words: "M-Mother died...eighty...years ago...old fellow..." The smile faded, the eyes unblinking as the tumult of warfare raged on, the death of one man unheeded among the deaths of hundreds.

Only Kyle Whiteside and Pippi Tyrsdottir noted the oddly aristocratic sergeant's death, even as they blindly turned and dove back into the fight. As Kyle put his Molo back into action, Avery's last words ran through his mind over and over, and he could not comprehend what he had heard.

You had rejuv already, Avery...why die here? You never needed the Emperor's Chalice, so...why?

This question comprised only one unanswerable puzzle spawned on Delta Three, but for Kyle Whiteside it remained the most constant, the most personal.

Hightower's two Marine boarding penetrators slipped away from *Hightower* at her nearest approach to the embattled *Dragon*. Captain Sinclair-Maru had made the call, and though Major Shirai had initially balked at it, the other Marine officers knew Shirai already dwelt under Lieutenant Colonel Krenner's disfavor, and they pushed him to approve the operation. Corporal Akbar Haider, for one, felt heartily glad for it.

First, Akbar and his mates had been left out of the ground assault force, left to idle about *Hightower* with that bitter sod, Shirai, then he barely took part in the small fracas to retake the ship's forward sections from mutineers. Now, at last, Corporal Akbar Haider could put his decade of brutal training to good use and hopefully live up to the proud and bloody tradition of the Ten and Twenty.

While rebel forces had allegedly utilized some boarding penetrators in the opening surprise attacks at the outset of the war, Akbar would now take part in the first Imperial boarding operation of the conflict...if some enemy gunner didn't get wise in the next few moments and explosively ventilate their little ships in transit.

"*Thirty seconds,*" the pilot's voice announced in their helmet comm system.

At the sound of the pilot's announcement, Akbar and his mates all charged their weapons in the darkness, the very slight sound rising only through the vibration of deckplates, the boarding penetrator containing almost no air. Marines crouched on the floor, ceiling and both walls, their grab-boots locking them in place, all of them facing the *fatal funnel*, counting down for the moment...

Gravity suppression theoretically *should* reduce the jolt of their impact; the long shaped-charge probe *should* blow a nice gap through any hull armor, and the penetrator *should* lock tightly in place, allowing the Marines of the Emperor's First to flood in...at any moment...

A sudden sharp blow stung Corporal Haider's feet through his grab-boots. Lieutenant Gowulf's gravelly voice came over the comm in three terse words, free of exultation, filling the darkness, "*For the Emperor.*"

Another shuddering blow rattled every Marine. Akbar took a breath, roaring with all his mates, "*Ten and Twenty!*" even as the funnel exploded open into one of *Dragon*'s darkened inner compartments, glowing shards of metal spinning about, dancing with a few floating human corpses. The boarding Marines lunged out, taking two fast, clanking steps and launching through the tumult of wreckage and bodies. Corporal Akbar flipped through and struck the far bulkhead boots first. He locked into place and scanned the blind corners as his mates poured out onto the ceiling and floor plates...just like in a thousand training cycles.

Lieutenant Gowulf made Nets contact with the second boarding penetrator, then with the surviving officers in *Dragon*'s bridge. "Alright, Marines," Lieutenant Gowulf called over the platoon channel. "It's all speed now, or it is death. Let's hit it."

They hit it, fast and hard, force-powering or blowing each hatch in succession, rushing through each compartment, finding no organized resistance until they penetrated well into *Dragon*'s decks. Within *Dragon*, the Marines now gained the all-seeing powers of the ship's Intelligence, under the auspices of its new acting captain, guiding them around any ambush and into their ideal paths of attack.

Corporal Akbar seemed to move through a growing dream of perfection, his heavyworld muscles tireless, his carbine optic flicking easily from target to target as his squad moved at a breakneck pace to secure *Dragon*'s Engineering section.

Since *Dragon* maintained adequate air pressure, their enemies seemed to enjoy unencumbered freedom, foregoing ship suits. This gave Corporal Akbar's squad a clear look at their enemies' faces as they clashed, and after a half dozen close-range shoot-outs, Corporal Akbar began to feel strangely unnerved. Instead of hate-filled expressions, or even grim glares, most of their enemies seemed to be as happy as larks, grinning even as Haider and his mates gunned them down. Mind-altering drugs seemed the only explanation, but neither their drugged condition nor their evident giddiness detracted from their fierce resistance. Fearless, even suicidal attacks claimed the lives of close mates on Haider's left and right, but they pressed on.

Dragon's monitoring bridge officers manipulated lights and gravity settings for each compartment as the Marine boarders initiated entry, providing Haider and the others an immense advantage, particularly since few of their foes enjoyed the benefits of grab-boots. Corporal Akbar racked up kills, moving fast, pushing for Engineering, dropping more than a dozen enemies on their progress through *Dragon*'s decks.

When they finally reached Engineering, the iris cycled open to a hail of gunfire, one ricocheting slug striking Haider's breastplate, another painfully clipping the edge of his breathing apparatus, shattering the faceplate where it fixed to his helmet, bringing blood to his nose and mouth. The return fire from Haider and his squad sent their enemies pirouetting through the compartment, their shower of blood forming spherical globules that shimmered in the searing light of their bright tactical illuminators.

Moments later, gravity dragged bodies, blood, and weapons heavily to the deckplates, as Haider threw aside the shattered pieces of his breathing apparatus and continued forward, clearing the section with his squad.

"Corporal," Private Nilsson called out, "what's this, then?" He held up a rucksack half-filled with flat gray rectangles.

Haider wiped blood from his battered face as he stared. "I don't know, but I don't like 'em." He thought the items *could* contain some intelligence value, so might be better to retain for the examination...but something about them conjured unpleasant associations. He made a quick tactical decision. "Put the damned things out the nearest vac-lock, Private."

Nilsson nodded. "Roger that, Corporal."

Corporal Akbar Haider turned to finish securing the Engineering section, wondering about the odd collection of objects for only a moment longer before focusing on his immediate duties.

He called over the platoon comm channel, declaring Engineering clear, then called Lieutenant Gowulf directly. Even as he issued his terse report, Haider's eye wandered to the N-drive housing, wondering why the enemy had been pulling the enclosing hard panels when they were shot down. Glancing at the row of orderly bodies lying still upon the deck, he knew there was no sense asking them now.

Major Shirai stepped through the ragged blast hole breaching *Dragon's* forward compartments, an unfired carbine in his hands, Private Buchanan at his side, a disturbing presence like a capricious blade held to his throat. Corpses lay scattered across the deck, and triumphant Marines hurried to secure each compartment from the waist to the bridge.

For the moment, Major Shirai and Private Buchanan stood in a bubble of relative privacy, and Shirai wished someone stood near enough to keep Buchanan silent.

"You have been most unsatisfactory," Buchanan said in that damned supercilious voice of his.

Shirai could not see Buchanan's damned creepy smile due to the occluding breathing apparatus, but he could still visualize it. Not for the first time, Shirai wondered if he could just turn and gun Buchanan down in his tracks. He even began to pivot that direction, but saw Buchanan's weapon drift to cover him. Shirai turned back, shaking his head, feeling trapped. "I did all I could. Krenner will kill me if he survives to reach us."

"He won't survive." Buchanan said. "You need not worry

about Krenner. You must worry about providing the services you have promised."

"I tell you, I've done all I could!" Shirai snarled.

Buchanan's cold hand reached out and grasped Shirai's arm, squeezing, crushing. "You have not. You should remember what we do to those who betray us, Shirai. You have made a promise. After you pay for your failure, your family, your children...they will also pay."

Shirai trembled, trying to moisten his dry mouth, trying to muster the courage for some last act that would redeem his life—in his own eyes, at least. "What—what must I do?"

Chapter 40

"The centuries change, weapons advance, mechanisms develop, but humanity remains stubbornly unmoved. With a clear eye for history, it seems reality is unpleasantly conservative despite all our motions to rebel."

—Everest Compline, *Reflections*

BEFORE KRENNER AND HIS COTERIE OF MARINES REACHED THE wide entrance to the arena, he heard the intermittent blast of what sounded like two heavy machine guns. He looked up to see the scatter of leaping tracers ricocheting from the ground just ahead, flying off in every direction. A cluster of reaped Marines lay riddled just beside the tall pillar marking the near edge of the arena's entrance, and as Krenner jogged nearer, a Marine rifleman added to the number, taking a heavy round through the helmet as he peeked up to try a shot.

Krenner jerked his comm operator close, quickly scanning the tactical holo display on the Marine's back. Punching up multiple icons, Krenner issued orders, while his protective squad scanned in every direction, their weapons ready as streams of long-range mass driver bolts flashed across the battlefield, attempting to pin cutter mechs as they scuttled quickly through the tangle of wreckage and bodies.

A moment later, two belt-mortars went to work at Krenner's command, their operators well behind cover, their little mortar bombs arcing at sharp angles into the arena, trying to reach deep enough to silence the enemy machine-gun positions. As mortar after mortar marched into the vast arena, Krenner watched the tactical holo, oblivious to the battlefield seething with cutter mechs and gunfire all around him.

The mortars served as cover for the two remaining battledress assaulters who surged up the arena's outer shell in a series of fluid bounds, gaining the upper stands beneath the arena's canopy roof.

Krenner saw the two icons on the tactical display as they reached their positions and called out, "Let's move!" A moment later, Krenner heard the distinctive bark of the battledress shoulder-mount guns, and without hesitation he led a fast charge into the evident kill zone, around the pillar, past the heap of slain Marines. The open mouth of a broad tunnel gaped before them, its strange construction of beams and girders emerging to rise above their heads at a sharp angle, jutting toward the horizon. Two elevated, fortified gun positions revealed dead enemies, sprawled out where the battledress assaulters had dished them.

Krenner allowed himself one quick scrutiny, looking up and stopping, shocked at the cluster of mechs clambering high above his head, seemingly oblivious to the battle or the Marines below as they appeared to drag spools of cable over the girders. Krenner had a momentary impression of spiders laying coils of web, before he resolutely turned his attention to the dim opening sloping down into the earth, the cable-wrapped girders emerging from its depths.

He flipped his helmet-mounted optic down over one eye and jogged ahead, hearing the breaths and crunching boots of his Marines around him. "Lieutenant," Krenner said to the nearest officer, "pull a team to clear and secure the arena here...and kill those damned mechs up there."

"Yes, Colonel," the lieutenant said, peeling off as Krenner glanced over his shoulder back through the arena's broad opening. The pitched battle seemed to wind down, and more than one hundred Marines streamed into the arena, more coming every moment as they mopped up the cutter mechs across the battlefield.

Krenner paused only a moment before leading the charge down the slope toward the darkness. "Give the sods a couple frags."

Two Marines quickly obeyed, actuating grenades and hurling them down the steep slope, seeing them roll and clatter out of sight. A moment later, they detonated with their muted thump, and Krenner felt a hand on his armored shoulder. He turned, ready to slag down whoever dared, but saw the face of Sergeant Jonas looking up at him. "They're probably fortified down there, Colonel... Let me take point, sir." His tone was almost pleading. "I'm a smaller target."

A shorter target, perhaps, barrel-chested, heavyworld dog...

"Want a medal, do you, fucker?" Krenner snarled, and Jonas grinned.

"Yes please, sir," he said, not fooling anyone.

"Go."

Jonas didn't hesitate, throwing his carbine up to high ready and double-timing down the steep grade, Krenner and a column of Marines five steps behind him. The entrance might accept ten or more abreast, so space for evasive maneuvering remained for Jonas.

A single shot blasted out ahead, and Sergeant Jonas returned fire immediately, angling to the right as his carbine spat rapid-fire shots. Krenner threw the heavy auto-rifle up as his steps descended into the darkened cavern. He gained a snap impression of I-beams and girders filling a central swath of the tunnel before he spotted movement through the enhanced wavelengths of his tactical optic, low and fast: cutter mechs.

Krenner lunged to the prone, and began lacing streams of fire into anything that moved down the passage, the walls and girders flashing to the strobe of his muzzle blast. In a moment he was back up and moving forward, coming upon three perforated cutter mechs and a pair of dead human fighters, rifles in their clawed hands. Marines pressed close behind, Sergeant Jonas a half step ahead, hugging the right wall as they advanced in a rush, smelling a stench of old, rotted blood over the burn of smoky accelerant, of gunfire.

They pressed on, following the odd, continuous shaft of beams and cabling that stretched onward, down into the rock and soil of Delta Three, two hundred paces, three hundred... The passage widened ahead into a broad, deep chamber, and lights glimmered in a greenish glow. Crates and spacer cargo boxes lay stacked in high rows, seeming to fill much of the chamber, the vast metal construction of beams and girders continuing overhead to the deepest reach of the chamber ahead where it terminated into a curving framework of immense, strange panels.

Through the maze formed of cargo boxes and crates, Krenner spotted indistinct movement some distance ahead, but held his fire, seeing flashes of ragged human forms. He raised a hand. "Easy, lads," Krenner murmured. "Looks like more civilian hostages." As the mob of panting Marines took up hasty positions, Krenner spoke to Sergeant Jonas without turning his head: "Sergeant, put a couple of your best up high... See if they can get good angles on those sods."

Jonas turned and slapped the shoulders of two likely Marines, who immediately began clambering to the top of the stacks. One of the climbing Marines paused in his progress, calling out quietly to Sergeant Jonas, "Sarge, look!" He slid a crate lid aside, revealing the distinctive blue discs of standard Shaper fuel cells.

Jonas stared, shocked, saying, "Gods, Colonel!" but Krenner growled indifferently. The only coin of any real value to him lay with glorious victory alone. Still... such an unprecedented stockpile of Shaper fuel—if all the crates contained similar contents—comprised a puzzling window into the enemy strategy.

"Disperse and push, lads. Go!" Krenner led a cluster of Marines down one path through the high-stacked crates, other squads splitting off to leave no branch of the maze unexplored as they advanced cautiously through the expansive chamber. The glinting metallic edifice ahead grew slowly closer, seen in glimpses between the rows and stacks.

When Krenner reached a clear observation point, he froze, the auto-rifle in his arms rising slowly as he stared, transfixed.

Through gaps between crates, he saw flashes of movement resolving into a string of cutter mechs bearing emaciated human cargo, clamped within the cruel metal mandibles. Only as the mechs scuttled up to the curving metallic framework that terminated the chamber, did Krenner realize the scale of the subterranean edifice before them.

From his position about eighty paces distant from the vast mechanism, Krenner now saw that it formed a broad dish-shape that followed the curve of the chamber wall and ceiling, the shaft of girders, beams, and cable terminating at the center of the dish.

Beneath the termination point of the shaft, a low structure stood, looking much like a starship engine room transplanted within this vast, strange crypt. Two men stepped out of this structure, and with businesslike efficiency they bludgeoned one human figure squirming in the jaws of a cutter mech. One of the two men stooped and plunged a tool of some kind into the quiescent victim's skull.

"Those inhuman—!"

"Shut up," Krenner snapped without taking his eyes off the horrible sight, his skin crawling as he tried to comprehend what he beheld.

From the victim's flooding skull one man drew a small, glistening object—a Shaper implant, surely—turned to the immense curving dish rising high above his head, and placed the implant with great care upon the curving panel. The cutter mech clattered away, bearing a flopping corpse on its course to join the vast heap of decaying flesh up on the surface.

Realization dawned for Krenner, his horrified gaze traveling over the broad apparatus again, seeing its granular texture becoming clear at last: The entire visible surface formed a tight matrix of what could only be millions of Shaper implants. The choking tableau, the stench of old, rotting blood, the casual execution and harvest multiplied his mounting horror. For Lieutenant Colonel Krenner, when an emotional dam burst, only one path lay broad and deep enough to accommodate such a surge.

As the two distant executioners bludgeoned the next pinioned victim in their string, Krenner squeezed the trigger almost without thinking, aiming high. One executioner took a round to the temple, dropping as if poleaxed; the other man turned, seeming to stare directly into Krenner's eyes, grinning joyfully. The cutter mechs acted as one, instantly executing their human burdens, their blades plunging once before they discarded the limp, leaking bodies. Marines began firing as the cutter mechs oriented, racing toward the invaders, their mandibles open.

Krenner roared out curses, fanning his heavy weapon across the low mob of speeding mechs, tracers flying out in a red stream. But in the midst of his rage and violence he saw additional human figures emerge from the small enclosure ahead, urgently working on an instrument panel of some kind. He turned his hammering auto-rifle from the wave of mechs, raising it to bear, the last three rounds of his ammunition cassette striking one of the grinning enemies away from the glowing panel.

"Load me!" Krenner yelled, even as his remaining enemies actuated the technological enigma.

Power leads in the cavern floor suddenly illuminated, a glowing blue track branching to the long rows of crated Shaper fuel cells, drawing immense power from the linked crates. As weapons thundered and flashed, cutter mechs charging into the ranks of Marines, Krenner's sharp eyes followed the blue track in the cavern floor back to its terminus. Three grinning humans labored still, ignoring the deafening battle, the blue band of the power lead rising at their feet to join their instrument panel.

As anonymous hands slapped an ammunition cassette into Krenner's weapon, the whole cavern suddenly leaped into startling luminance. Krenner instantly recognized the impossible effect, unmistakable to someone of his long service. He had experienced dozens of N-space transitions, and the warmth suddenly radiating from his own Shaper implant joined the gleaming radiance of every mote, confirming the fact: They somehow stood within an N-space transition impossibly occurring upon a planetary surface.

Only then did he notice the grinning human figures, grinning no longer, their faces transformed within the glowing luminance of transition, translucent medusa tendrils pulsing from their skulls, eyes like blackened pits.

Sergeant Jonas suddenly screamed beside Krenner, his carbine falling from nerveless hands, and Krenner saw the same glowing tendrils bloom through the sergeant's skull, the pits of his eyes filling with blackness. Not far away Corporal Matsu underwent the same horrific transformation, his mates at either side, torn between battling the charging cutter mechs and aiding their screaming comrade.

As Sergeant Jonas and Corporal Matsu fell silent, the tendrils pulsing out of their heads expanded within the luminous air, Matsu fluidly drew his sidearm and shot two Marines at point-blank range before Krenner shot him down, immediately spinning to smash Jonas in the face with the butt of the heavy auto-rifle. Jonas toppled, the ghostly green tendrils sprouting from his head seeming to grasp at Krenner while the sergeant's body lay still. Without another thought, Krenner leaped out in the midst of the cutter mechs and battling Marines, depressing the barrel of his weapon to bear upon the branching blue path of the power lead on the cavern floor.

He held the trigger back, the auto-rifle hammering its recoil into him as a stream of heavy slugs chewed into the luminous cable, sawing through it in a bright blue flash of energy. The N-space transition effects disappeared in an instant, and Krenner raised his weapon to riddle the human figures, now suddenly returned to grinning puppets a moment before his final stream of fire chopped them down.

Around the now-darkened cavern, skirmishes flared, weapons blasting, cutter mechs struggling to attack. A mech snatched one Marine while bullets punctured its steely carapace. Still farther to one side, Marines struggled with one of their own, suddenly transformed into a merciless enemy in their midst.

Above the tumult, a cold voice spoke out from close behind Krenner: "Lieutenant Colonel Krenner." Krenner turned to see Sergeant Jonas sitting up on the cavern floor, his mouth a bloody smear, still grinning with inhuman jubilance. "What is it...that you really want?"

Krenner looked down at the pistol held in the sergeant's unwavering hand as he hefted the hot, empty auto-rifle and measured the distance. "What do I want, fucker? I..." He took a breath and allowed the final flood of his rage to build. "I want... victory!" With that final word Lieutenant Colonel Galen Krenner lunged, even as the grinning man once known as Sergeant Jonas fired a single shot.

Molo Ranger Kyle Whiteside lay prone in the same overwatch position, still scanning across the battlefield with Fang's powerful optic. He observed the Marine assaulters charge into the arena and flood down the slope into the dark cavern, and now he searched for intact cutter mechs struggling or skulking among the rubble and shattered enemies. Mostly, Kyle tried not to think of Avery Reardon's body sprawled out nearby, slowly cooling to room temperature. Smiting enemies one at a time served Kyle's current purpose better than anything else he could think of.

His optic just swept over the arena's mouth again, seeing the angled shaft of girders and beams where it projected up from the cavern, when he saw the flash of blue luminance seem to explode from that construction of steel and cabling. What seemed a half second later, the sun's light fell into an eerie gray lifelessness, even as the air around Kyle began to glow. The Shaper implant in Kyle's skull took on the odd warmth of an N-space transition and he heard Pippi call out, "This really not good, Kyle."

As Pippi spoke, one of the Marine snipers suddenly began to scream. When Kyle whirled to look, he froze, unable to comprehend what he beheld.

The Marine's screams subsided as the pits of his eyes fell into darkness, his Marine comrades shrinking back from him as translucent tendrils seemed to flow from his skull, waving to a nonexistent current. With mechanical precisions, this impossible figure smoothly drew a grenade from a pouch, actuating it. Pippi's carbine spat three fast shots from close behind Kyle, and the nightmare form tumbled back, the grenade in its hand detonating among the Marine snipers.

In the shower of rubble and dust, Kyle's last vision told him that the N-space effect had ended, but this seemed to suddenly mean very little as he settled into the wreckage, fading into darkness.

Chapter 41

"The translation from House Combatives to interstellar combat has been rough at best, but until a better system is constructed, it at least serves to keep the Families connected to a reality beyond mere opulence and acquisition."

—Everest Compline, *Reflections*

AS *HIGHTOWER* SURGED AHEAD INTO A BATTLE FOR WHICH SHE was poorly suited, Inga Maru sprawled silently in the shadows beside the bridge access iris. The coiling currents of ice within her body refused to subside, refused to retreat from Inga's heart and limbs, the aftereffects of her augmentation reduced to a faint quiver in her muscles. As she worked to recover control, and struggled to monitor *Hightower*'s internal security, Inga lay under a barrage of Loki's chatter.

"Tanta excels in climbing now, Chief," Loki informed her. "He especially enjoys scaling your garments when I moderate the gravity for his benefit. It was wise of you to hang your attire thus for his enjoyment."

Inga struggled to regain the razor sharpness she needed at this critical juncture. "Loki," she replied amid his babble, feeling slow-minded and thick, "you do understand that the captain requires you to carefully monitor *Pallas*, don't you?"

"Of course, Chief," Loki replied before returning to topics of real importance: "Tanta has taken a great dislike to one of your stockings. It offends him. He kicks it. He bites it."

389

"But, Loki," Inga persevered, "I trust you realize that the captain and I are likely to be killed in a few minutes unless you are particularly attentive to our combat mission." She paused, adding, "Tanta also will be killed in that event, if we cannot disable this cruiser."

Whether her urging made any difference, Inga could not discern, and it seemed too much effort to try, but Loki replied, "Oh, certainly, Chief. I am pushing live positional calculations to the captain, and updating the primitive graphic for Lieutenant Pennysmith now. Of course, they must use these resources properly, and this concerns me... I do not wish Tanta to be killed. This would displease me greatly. You, also, would be far more pleasing alive."

Inga tried to formulate a reply to Loki's touching regard, when *Hightower* suddenly plunged into the unmistakable effects of an N-space transition once again. Inga should have initiated diagnostics, but her foggy thoughts could not coalesce before Loki offered, "This N-space effect initiated on the surface of Delta Three. *Hightower*'s N-drive is not engaged."

Amid the startled exclamations on the bridge, Saef sharply turned to look back toward Inga. She clumsily passed Loki's information on, even as Deckchief Furst said, "Our N-drive is not engaged, Captain. I—I don't know—"

"How—how is this possible, Loki?" Inga inquired subaudibly, her lips numb, her heart beating heavily.

"Just another wasteful, pointless Stranger trick, Chief. Expending such resources to subject this region of space to a needless N-space effect."

If she understood the enemy's general method of human enthrallment, *Hightower* should now be proof against additional *turned* crewmembers, at least until a fresh source of flat, gray boxes came aboard. But if *Python* or the frigates carried those same little gray boxes, concealed among their many compartments since their last N-space transition, *Hightower* might now find herself surrounded by enemy-controlled vessels.

It took far too long for Inga to push this unhappy observation to Saef's UI, and a moment later, *Hightower* emerged yet again from N-space to find their relative position unchanged.

"Sensors," Saef called out, "monitor *Sherwood* or *Mistral* for any action outside their orders."

"Yes, Captain."

Inga heard the words, but they seemed far away, unimportant, joining with Loki's chatter about kitten games.

"Weps?" Saef said. "You ready to engage *Pallas*?"

"Ready, Captain," Pennysmith said, her hands on the manual controls linked to *Hightower*'s immense barrage battery as she monitored the rudimentary aiming program.

Inga's thoughts swirled around, locking upon one bright point of reality. "Loki," she inquired slowly, "are there any other... secrets the Strangers had that I should know about?"

"Nothing of any great interest, Chief. The Strangers seem foolishly interested in wasting Shaper fuel and other valuable resources. They would fare very poorly in Fleet!"

Inga knew she should ask more, press and sift Loki, but she felt herself sinking, idly wondering if Loki's absurd value system may yet doom them all even as she lost all awareness, fading into a glacial darkness.

From the moment Lieutenant Tilly Pennysmith linked the manual controls from her station to the Gunnery section's barrage cannon, she had taken what few spare minutes she could to experiment with their operation. She clearly recalled the white-knuckled instant when she invoked manual control of little *Tanager*'s meager point-defense turrets under the literal guns of the enemy, and she needed her every action to be perfect now.

The addition of Chief Maru's simple aiming program—as rudimentary as it was—greatly aided Tilly Pennysmith in her endeavors, providing dynamically updated live aiming points in her scope. Supposedly, this would calculate all the necessary offsets to allow long range engagements. In her spare moments, Pennysmith operated the cannon controls, shifting *Hightower*'s immense triple-barrel turret in fine increments, tracking the shifting position of their fast-approaching enemy.

Chief Maru... Pennysmith could hardly spare a thought for the captain's peculiar cox'n, but she did wonder what ailed the chief, slumped in the shadows by the bridge access, the captain clearly concerned at the chief's status.

All thoughts of Chief Maru faded in an instant.

When *Hightower* abruptly plunged into N-space yet again, it suddenly seemed the impending battle might be over, and

Pennysmith felt conscious of the bizarre, contrasting sensations of relief and disappointment. Reemerging moments later brought her tensions back to the forefront, her mouth suddenly dry.

"Weps?" Captain Sinclair-Maru said. "You ready to engage?"

"I'm on them. Ready to engage, Captain." She knew he waited for the cluster of huge 16-gauge nukes to awaken from their silent orbit, hopefully unobserved beneath *Pallas*, rocketing on their preprogrammed attack. *Python* closed fast with that cruiser, now fully engaged. The combination would hopefully prove too much, from too many vectors for *Pallas* to handle.

Hightower's last web of 32-gauge missiles detonated at Pennysmith's command some distance from *Pallas*, creating another screen of concealment, obscuring *Hightower* from their foe behind swelling spheres of energy.

Staring fixedly into her scope, Pennysmith manipulated the manual control, shifting her aiming pips to cover the position estimates flowing from Chief Maru's program, waiting for the captain's command...

"Weps," the captain said, staring at the tactical holo, "commence firing."

Pennysmith depressed the firing stud.

Hightower's massive smart-alloy shuddered at the intense shock of the cannon fire, but a muted pinging sound still reached them at each shot, Pennysmith adjusting the aiming pips for each salvo. *Hightower's* unique gauss-cannon munitions blasted through the intervening space, the secondary particle beam firing a millisecond later, punching through the dissipating clouds of nuclear fire, the cannon battery jetting plasma from the triple barrels, with a fresh salvo every three seconds.

Pennysmith silently prayed the Weapons section held their weight, the munitions unfailingly continuing to cycle out to the triple-barreled behemoth, even as she prayed they might score hits upon *Pallas* despite the range.

Come on... please don't let me down.

Even as they approached the lever point between death and victory, Pennysmith realized she feared death less than she feared failing Captain Saef Sinclair-Maru.

Saef saw everything slowly coming together as he and Captain Khyber had planned...for the moment, at least.

Those 16-gauge smashers made it around to their appointed positions on time, evidently undetected; the horde of smaller 64-gauge missiles from *Hightower* and the frigates kept *Pallas* occupied, chewing up approaching threats; *Python* survived the opening moments of her direct attack, while *Hightower* and the frigates raced to close the distance. At Pennysmith's careful direction, *Hightower's* peculiar, powerful battery now pounded shots into the dark, hopefully finding *Pallas* with at least some of its unique graphene-packed munitions and particle beams.

In the midst of this, Saef observed the sudden sensor spike within his command UI a moment before Ash called out, "Signature of an energy weapon, Captain. It's—*Sherwood's* hit hard, it appears."

"Comm, message *Sherwood* to break off and evade," Saef said, wishing again that he had set up a commodore-style link group in his UI for quick comms with the squadron.

"Aye, Captain. Break off and evade."

According to the sensor data, *Sherwood* managed to successfully evade the next several shots as *Pallas* seemed to fixate upon the small frigate's destruction, but as the concealing clouds of nuclear fire subsided, the enemy stubbornly persisted until *Sherwood's* luck ran dry.

"We've lost comms to *Sherwood*!" Pim called out at almost the same moment Ash spoke:

"Captain, *Sherwood* appears to be disabled."

Now only *Mistral* and *Hightower* continued to advance, supporting *Python's* aggressive attack, and Saef expected *Pallas* to turn her powerful beam weapons on *Hightower* at any moment. They needed to close the distance quickly to eliminate the enemy's greatest advantage, allowing *Hightower* a chance to bring her own weapons to bear effectively. Even as the steady ping of the barrage cannon rang out, the range to *Pallas* ticked down, *Hightower* advancing straight on.

Saef barely noticed the bridge access iris cycle behind him, but Deckchief Furst glanced back and froze. Saef turned, just glimpsing Marine Major Shirai and a Marine private, weapons in their hands. Before Saef could act, Shirai fired his carbine into Inga Maru's slumped figure at point-blank range.

Without conscious thought, Saef found his pistol in hand, leveling as he spun. Part of his mind noted the Marine beside

Shirai fire, noted the flash of heat in his low back, even as his finger pressed the trigger, aiming high. Shirai staggered back, firing again and again into Inga as Saef's rounds struck him down. The second attacker spun and fell, and Saef dimly noticed Commander Attic holding his sidearm two-handed, covering the two fallen Marines.

"Maru!" Saef crossed the distance to Inga in a rush, dropping beside her form, seeing her blue lips, her quivering eyelashes. His eyes flashed over her, looking for the gaping wounds, the seeping blood... *Kang's body shield.* Her eyes fluttered open.

Saef's heart seemed to beat again, his breath return, suddenly realizing how much Inga had come to define his contentment. His hand hesitantly touched her cheek. "Do you need medical attention, Maru?"

Her teeth chattered. "N-no." Her eyes rolled toward the bridge, the unfolding combat. "Go."

Commander Attic checked both fallen Marines and stood over Saef, eyes wide. "How is she still alive?"

Saef glanced at Attic and turned back to the tactical holo. "We don't have time." With a final glance at Inga, Saef returned to the command seat, feeling the shocked gaze of the bridge crew upon him. "Focus, people," he said, trying to follow his own command, attending to the unfolding scene.

Optical scopes now revealed *Python*'s desperate gambit, dozens of *Python*'s missiles homing in on the enemy cruiser behind the obscuring screen of *Hightower*'s detonating 32-gauge nukes. Saef grimly hoped that little play provoked heartburn in the enemy bridge, while *Hightower*'s remaining 16-gauge salvo closed with *Pallas* from an unexpected quarter. *Pallas* would be forced to choose between addressing the horde of closing 64-gauge missiles, turning her weapons upon the advancing *Hightower*, or to attempt blind, questing shots for *Python* through the intervening nuclear fires.

Another tense moment passed as *Hightower* rushed on, the bridge silence only broken by regular ping of the barrage battery's distant ignition, the violent drama of a moment before superseded by the impending conflict. Saef's command UI showed a sharp spike as Deckchief Furst yelled, "Shield impact! Heat sinks at yellow!"

"Energy weapon, Captain," Ash said, sweating as he stared at his sensor panel. Though her hull massed dozens of times larger than *Sherwood*, *Hightower*'s shield generators and heat sinks were not similarly scaled. The entire bridge crew knew they might be moments from joining *Sherwood*, a ruptured hulk.

Saef clenched his jaws, staring at the tactical holo. Why ignore *Python*, the most immediate threat? He made a rapid calculation; he could order a spin maneuver, giving the enemy a fresh set of shields to work on, but lose their acceleration even as they showed a broad flank for the enemy to target... No. His focus fixed upon the remaining 16-gauge nukes, slowly, quietly closing with *Pallas*. If *Hightower* could survive just one or two more hits...

Instruments spiked. "Heat sinks at red!" Furst yelled as another beam struck their shields.

"Pennysmith, disperse and detonate all sixteens, now!" Saef snapped.

The steady pulsing of the barrage battery paused as Pennysmith's fingers flew over her panel, sending the coded signal out to the huge nukes slipping up beneath the enemy cruiser.

Saef's turned his attention to the tactical display and *Python*. Something wasn't right. *Why isn't* Python *continuing to press their attack? What is Khyber doing?*

He only had a moment to wonder at *Python*'s sudden inaction; no fresh missiles launching, her course deviating from the attack vector. That was not the plan. The next moment's Saef's ears popped at a sudden pressure drop.

"We just lost half our forward heat sinks and shield generators," Furst said. "Small hull penetration in the forward bay and companionway."

Pennysmith's coded weapons signal flashed to the 16-gauge missile in less than a second. Two seconds later, nuclear fire began to erupt, close in on *Pallas*, not far outside the effective range of any dampers they employed. The titanic detonation of such powerful warheads bathed the cruiser in destructive force, harshly testing her shields.

Python's few surviving missiles rained in, careening off the cruiser's faltering shields or smashing into her hull armor, dampers effectively suppressing their explosive energy. *Hightower*'s constant salvoes of particle beams and nanotube-packed kinetic projectiles began to occasionally find their mark, some skipping from the cruiser's shields, others impacting squarely, the nanotube payloads spraying through her shields in superheated showers, fusing to the warship's hull. In moments her shield banks collapsed.

The bridge crew around Saef seemed to hold their breath, waiting for a final, desperate strike from *Pallas*, a blast to flay *Hightower*'s hull or incinerate them all where they sat. Only two people seemed unaware: Deckchief Furst remained caught up directing damage control efforts throughout *Hightower*, and Lieutenant Pennysmith kept adjusting the aim of *Hightower*'s cannon array, firing the battery again and again into *Pallas*.

A halting message from Inga pinged Saef's UI: ENMY'S SHLDS DOWN, ACRDING TO LOKI.

Saef made another rapid calculation. "Nav, emergency one-eighty spin, now!"

Attic initiated the spin even as he affirmed, "Yes, Captain."

The strike from *Pallas* lashed out, but too late. "Dry-side flank heat sinks at red, Captain!" Furst called. The energy weapon impacted *Hightower*'s fresh shields as she rotated.

"Pennysmith," Saef said, "see how surgical you can get with the cannon. Trim her hardpoints if you can." He looked over at Pim. "Comm, get me a direct link to *Python*."

As she continued to close, *Hightower* spun until her main engines faced directly at the enemy, her barrage battery smoothly pivoting, blasting steadily away at the cruiser.

"Comms from *Python* on main holo, Captain; less than one-half-second delay," Pim said.

Saef looked up at the main holo to see a young Fleet commander there instead of the knowing gaze of Captain Khyber, an unsettling expression in her eyes. "Captain Sinclair-Maru, I am Commander Holgren."

"Where is Captain Khyber, Commander?" Saef said, staring steadily at her image, striving to divine any hint of duplicity, even as part of his mind noted the optical feed to his right, *Pallas* spewing ejecta as Pennysmith's fusillade riddled her hull.

"Captain Khyber is—" Her voice broke and she was forced to take a breath before continuing. "Captain Khyber is dead. We—we experienced a—what appeared to be an N-space transition. The transition seemed to—to drive some crew members mad. One of them... he k-killed the captain. He took control of the bridge for a time."

"I see," Saef said, the silence of the bridge filled only with the pulse of the barrage battery firing another salvo into *Pallas*.

She stared through the holo into Saef's eyes, shaking her head.

"You—sir—you are the ranking officer in Delta Three system, now," she said, her lips tremulous with shock. "What are your orders—Commodore?"

Of the five warships orbiting Delta Three, only the 5,000-ton frigate *Mistral* appeared to be in fighting shape. *Hightower* and *Python* teemed with repair parties laboring over their hulls, trying to patch up the worst of the damage, while *Dragon*'s injuries seemed nearly mortal, her hull rent and punctured in multiple sections. The enemy cruiser, formerly the Fleet cruiser *Pallas*, suffered heavily from Pennysmith's ministrations, hardpoints scorched bare and a dozen shot impacts blasted deep into her guts.

Dragon and *Pallas* lay docked in Delta Three's recaptured orbital station with the same cluster of mercantile vessels, while the other warships prepared as well as they could for any fresh enemy attempt to retake Delta Three. In the midst of all this activity, Saef boarded his pinnace—Inga's shuttle—*Onyx*, accompanied by Auditor Tenroo and Inga, bound for Delta Three's surface and inescapable duty.

Auditor Tenroo seemed even more dejected than he had at the start of the mission, emotionally battered by his social breach, the loss of his prime duty, and the brutal mutiny. He approached Saef hesitantly as *Onyx* slid out from *Hightower*'s shuttle lock. "Captain—or, er, should I address you as 'Commodore,' now?" Auditor Tenroo said.

"'Captain' is sufficient, Auditor," Saef said, looking down distractedly as the kitten, Tanta, skittered playfully about the deck, his ears back, a wild expression in his blue eyes.

"Very well then, Captain," Tenroo said, inclining his head nervously. "I'm afraid I've been a sore trial to you, and—and I'm sure my superiors in the Ministry will feel I have performed in a manner that is...well...not entirely satisfactory." Tenroo looked down, shamefaced. "In short, sir, it is likely that my official position will end as soon as I transmit my mission report."

Tenroo rubbed his thin hands lightly across his trouser legs and looked Saef in the eye. "To be blunt, Captain, you needn't include my presence in any victory festivities, for I have nothing to celebrate, and nothing of value to contribute."

Saef regard Tenroo somberly for a moment, reflecting back on Inga's suggested use for this sad little academic before he said,

"Daresay you feel a trifle low, Auditor, but you are mistaken. You may have an important service you could provide me."

Tenroo looked up, surprised, hope lighting his eyes. "Captain, I—I cannot imagine what service I might provide, I am eager—more than eager to be of service, whatever it might be."

Saef smiled thinly. "I will be villain enough to hold you to that offer, Auditor."

At that moment the shuttle began to shudder and bounce, Inga piloting them into Delta Three's atmosphere, and Tanta decided this called for a demonstration of his garment-scaling skills, clambering up Tenroo's trouser leg with his painfully sharp claws extended. This served to end their brief discussion, which suited Saef very well. Letting Tenroo discover his fate at the prime moment might serve everyone better. A visual component would surely fortify Tenroo's resolve.

As *Onyx* descended toward the surface, Commander Jamila with two of *Hightower*'s Mangusta fighters joined on either side, escorting them to the hastily repaired airfield adjoining the war-ravaged capital city. Only as *Onyx* touched down did the Mangustas peel away, roaring off toward the nearby ocean.

When *Onyx* rolled to a stop on solid ground, Inga stepped from the cockpit and gathered Tanta into her arms, nodding to Saef.

Saef, Inga, and Tenroo emerged from the shuttle as the crowd of Marines, civilians, and a small cluster of surviving Legionnaires gathered, waiting, murmuring among themselves. Inga carried Tanta in her left arm, settled into the crook of her elbow, his bright blue eyes joining hers in carefully scanning the surroundings as a heavyworld Marine major stepped up to greet them.

"Commodore," the major began without ceremony, "I'm Major Vigo, sir. We've got everything in motion as you ordered."

"Thank you, Major," Saef said. He hesitated a moment before asking. "And Lieutenant Colonel Krenner?"

The Marine major frowned. "Medicos say it's too soon to say."

Saef nodded, turning to the duty at hand. "How many surviving civilians have you found so far?"

"Well, sir, that's a little tough to calculate still." He extended a hand to his right. "If you'd care to walk this way, we've a little podium set up—"

Saef frowned despite himself, murmuring, "Oh gods, a podium..."

The major grinned. "Just a few words, sir. All of them could use a little encouragement."

Saef nodded, resigned, walking beside Major Vigo as Tenroo and Inga followed behind. "Just estimate for me, Major, across the whole planet, how many civilians still live on Delta Three?"

Major Vigo tugged at his collar absently. "Really, sir, we've only got the barest idea. Commander Jamila's been making rough estimates from the other big continent, and we've got little bands of survivors creeping back from the hills every day, but the number changes by the hour."

The mixed crowd of civilians and military awaited them ahead, and as they neared the modest podium, Saef asked in a lower voice, "Then how many died? Can you estimate that?"

Major Vigo paused, glancing over at the waiting crowds before looking back to Saef with a grimace. "Between these enemy slayer mechs, the earlier conventional fighting, then plain starvation... a few millions died, at the very least, sir."

Saef swallowed. "Gods." Major Vigo began walking again, and Saef followed, looking out at the crowd of faces, his gaze arrested by a group of grim-faced, ragged Legionnaires. A pair of the Legionnaires stood beside battered dumb-mechs, catching Saef's attention as they leaned upon each other, their bodies swathed in bandages. Not many heavyworlders served in the Legions, but this sturdy woman was certainly of heavyworld lineage; the unkempt man at her side wore a medico triage tag that said WHITESIDE in bold print. Saef exchanged a silent nod of recognition with them.

The vile podium stood on an impromptu dais, a small clutch of Marines and civilians gathered behind it. "I'll, uh, warm them up for your inspiring announcement, Commodore," Major Vigo murmured, suppressing his grin as he stepped up to the podium. Vigo began thanking the crowd for their patience, then turned to summarizing all the good that would soon be occurring, and Saef leaned over to Tenroo.

"Auditor," Saef said in a low voice, "officially, this planet was deemed an enemy possession, so now it is conquered territory. As the ranking Fleet officer in Delta Three system, I must establish a provisional Imperial governor to preside here." Tenroo nodded amiably until Saef continued, saying, "And I have selected you for that role."

Tenroo's eyes widened, outrage battling chagrin. "You must speak in—in a jest, Captain."

"I am entirely serious."

"But I am completely unsuited for—for such service," Tenroo said, his face uncharacteristically grim. "In the last many days it has become clear that I have spent too much time among academics and demi-cits, and I am no longer fit—"

"Listen, Auditor," Saef interrupted gently as Major Vigo continued to speak to the crowd, "you are better suited than you may think. The, uh, rebellion of Delta Three involved some *minor* violations of Thinking Machine Protocols. With your expertise in that field, you may assuage any—er—violent impulses that Fleet may have."

Tenroo's eyes turned to the crowd of disheveled and disillusioned civilians all listening to Major Vigo's attempts at encouragement. The expression on Tenroo's face said he knew what sort of impulse Fleet might employ for a violation of the Thinking Machine Protocols accompanied by a world in full rebellion, its citizens butchered.

"Besides that," Saef continued, "you are the only civil servant we shipped."

Tenroo swallowed, thinking, then jerking a shaky nod. "I will try, Captain. For these people."

"That's the spirit, Auditor . . . or should I say, Provisional Governor Tenroo?"

As Major Vigo concluded his comments, the crowd of military members dutifully clapped, but the listless civilians only stared. Saef stood to the podium, thinking he should utter a stirring speech about the continuity of life, the benefits of Imperial order, and the duty of every Vested Citizen in the Imperium. Instead, he said, "I won't keep you long today. There's plenty of work remaining for all of us, so allow me to introduce Provisional Governor Kenshin Tenroo, who will be leading the efforts to restore order and prosperity to this world."

A scatter of polite applause rose as Saef turned to look at Tenroo's glazed expression, just in time to see Inga place little Tanta in Tenroo's hands. "It is impossible to resent a bureaucrat with a kitten in his hands," she said.

Tenroo stood as one in a trance, stepping to the podium, Tanta reaching a questing paw out to bat at the small audio pickup as the crowd of people stared at their new leader.

Tenroo cleared his throat and looked across the expectant faces, beginning to speak, slowly and uncertainly at first, but with more confidence as he continued, Tanta seated on the podium, watching Tenroo's gesticulating hands.

Whether it was Tenroo's evident gentleness, or his scholarly diffidence, or even the contrast between him and all the war-like figures who suddenly dominated their lives, the surviving people of Delta Three present at that moment responded almost immediately to their new governor. The applause he received at the conclusion of his statements, while not deafening, clearly contained genuine approval.

Saef looked at Inga, raising his eyebrows. She gave him her half smile and said, "I told you it would work."

"So you did," Saef said, smiling a little, though his thoughts felt the weight of endless troubles. A Fleet scout ship had entered the fringes of Delta Three system during the battle with *Pallas*, reporting they had experienced a sudden and mysterious N-space transition effect some two hundred minutes after *Hightower* and *Python* had undergone that same effect. The enemy's baffling N-space phenomenon clearly expanded out from Delta Three at the speed of light, its power unabated.

In less than a year, Saef realized, that wave of N-space effect would reach Coreworld, the Strand, the Imperial Close...the Emperor himself.

Saef shook his head, his mouth suddenly dry, the ragged mob of people across the tarmac seemingly representative of humanity writ large. Despite their momentary triumph, the sense of impla-cable doom filled his mind and he looked up to Inga's watchful eyes with a barren heart.

Inga reached out, uncharacteristically resting her hand on Saef's forearm, gripping gently. "You need to know," she said in a quiet voice, "my hand is yours...alone. I will not fail you."

Saef held Inga's intense gaze, placing his hand over hers.

"I know it now, Maru."

Chapter 42

"When Emperor Yung established our current House system, he employed more genius than is appreciated in modern times. Not only did the lethal outcome of the Honor Code enable the martial honing of all Citizens, it gradually created enough bad blood among the Houses to keep them from casual treason."

—Everest Compline, *Reflections*

FOR CENTURIES, THE CARSTAIRS ESTATE ADJOINED THE EXPANSIVE lands of the Sinclair-Maru, but the interaction between the two Battersea Families rarely rose above mere cordiality. A few exceptions existed over those centuries, most notably the unaccountable friendship between Claude Carstairs and Saef Sinclair-Maru.

While most Sinclair-Maru youths found friendship within their own sprawling Family, or among the long-allied oath-kin Families, Saef and Claude had established an enduring connection that perplexed observers from both Families. Claude Carstairs numbered among the very few outsiders to wander tamely around Lykeios Manor, and the lands around the manor served for many youthful adventures involving Claude and Saef.

The trail leading from the Carstairs estate to the home wood of Lykeios Manor hadn't seen much traffic in recent years, becoming a bit more overgrown than Claude remembered, wild vegetation tugging rudely at his expensive garments as he walked. It was almost a relief when a young Sinclair-Maru sentinel emerged to confront him, a bush rifle slung over her shoulder, its wooden buttstock by her waist, her mottled green tunic blending with the surrounding foliage.

"Ah!" Claude declared at her sudden appearance. "There you are." He cast a tolerant eye over her forbidding demeanor. "You must be near graduating, I daresay . . . school days . . . such fun, right?"

She seemed unimpressed with Claude's stance of easy familiarity, saying, "What can we do for you, sir?" She did not smile.

Claude lowered his eyebrows. "Hmmph. Perhaps a bit more time spent in the etiquette department before graduating, hmm? You see, I am Claude Carstairs."

"I know who you are, sir," the sentinel said as Claude became slowly aware of additional figures quietly rising from the surrounding foliage. "But who are they?" She nodded behind Claude, toward the waiting figures of Winter Yung and Bess Sinclair-Maru, both shrouded in concealing hoods.

"Oh, them?" Claude said, scratching his chin as he gazed tolerantly at all the vigilant figures surrounding them. Claude shrugged, turning back to the sentinel. "Perhaps, my surly friend, we should discuss all that indoors. I'm still a trifle confused about it all m'self, to tell the truth!"

When the lengthy report from Delta Three squadron came across via QE comm, Admiral Beatty read through it in astonished silence. QE communications rarely involved the transmission of such detailed reports, but any thought of chastising the sender faded as its shocking facts sank in. After a few moments of reflection, Admiral Beatty decided an immediate interview with at least a quorum of the Admiralty Board would be far superior to a solo conversation with Admiral Nifesh. The metaphorical blood of unwelcome messengers lay deep around Nifesh, and Beatty felt no desire to serve as a foil for Nifesh's rhetorical demands.

Beatty took the QE comm specialist who received the message, more to provide an external focal point for any ire than for any practical purpose, and set off directly to Admiralty HQ.

Three lords of the Admiralty awaited Beatty when he entered, Admiral Nifesh immediately demanding, "What momentous news must interrupt our established schedule, Beatty? The damned rebels surrender?"

Beatty motioned to the QE specialist, thankful that Admirals Fisker and Char were also present to hopefully keep Nifesh within some bounds of decorum. "This message just arrived from the squadron assigned to the Delta Three situation—" Admiral Beatty began to say, when Nifesh interrupted:

"Tell me Glasshauser got those miserable Legionnaires off that rock!"

"Well, n-no, my lord," Beatty said as the specialist inserted the classified memory kernel, providing the raw QE transmission for the Admiralty Lords. "As you'll see," Beatty hastened to add, observing the alarming hue suffusing Nifesh's face, "the squadron subdued and pacified Delta Three." He took a breath. "It is now restored to Imperial authority."

Nifesh raised his eyebrows marginally, his angry flush subsiding somewhat. "With a few thousand Marines?" he rumbled. "Quite the feather. A pretty little victory for Glasshauser. Good for him."

"Read farther, Nifesh," Admiral Char murmured as his eyes traveled over the QE report. "Glasshauser's dead."

Nifesh shrugged impatiently, looking down at the report with a frown. "Well, the captain of *Python*, then...Khyber, wasn't it?"

"He's dead too," Char said.

"Then..." Nifesh said in a puzzled voice, reading fast.

"Captain Sinclair-Maru is acting commodore for the squadron," Admiral Beatty said, seeing Nifesh clench his jaws, evidently bereft of speech...at least momentarily.

Char made an appreciative sound as he completed his scan of the report. "He took *Pallas*, too, at least partially intact. That is welcome news, indeed."

Nifesh finally found his voice. "With *Python* and *Mistral*, they outmassed *Pallas* five-to-one! It's no miracle; he *should* have won such a fight handily, I would say." He continued to breeze over the report. "*Dragon*, badly damaged. *Sherwood*, mere salvage!"

Fisker finally spoke, looking up after carefully reading the QE communication. "Aside from *Pallas*, you may see that he took *Dragon* back from the enemy. He also recaptured the orbital station and the sundry vessels docked there." She tapped the lectern. "Perhaps the greatest puzzle is the large trove of Shaper fuel cells he captured planetside—not only a very rich prize, but a mystery for Fleet Intelligence to unravel."

Admiral Beatty saw Nifesh growing almost purple with suppressed fury, but as he opened his mouth to unleash whatever invective arose, Admiral Char spoke up in dry tones. "I believe Captain Sinclair-Maru was your particular choice for *Hightower*,

Nifesh. Your selection was ... inspired ... prescient, even. I congratulate you, Nifesh."

"Very true," Admiral Fisker affirmed with no evident irony in her voice. "Reclaiming the planet alone, and installing that academic auditor as governor: these will provide useful propaganda tools, even aside from the many vessels he seized. And such a subject matter expert as this Dr. Tenroo should clear up any little transgressions of the Thinking Machine Protocols. It seems it scarcely could have resolved in a more satisfactory manner."

Admiral Beatty thought he could hear the grinding of Nifesh's molars from where he stood and decided to win what future approval he could. "Uh, my lords, what about the reported millions of slaughtered civilians? Will that also serve as some sort of propaganda triumph?"

"Of course it is," Admiral Char said in his low, slow voice. "Sounds as if the locals blame the slaughter upon the rebels alone. What could be better?" Char looked to his left and right. "Join the uprising and get butchered by your new masters, or remain loyal and enjoy all the peaceful benefits of Imperial rule."

Admiral Beatty swallowed, wondering how long the ire of Nifesh would plague them all, as Fisker and Char discussed the issue of Captain Sinclair-Maru's substantial financial prize: Would Captain Sinclair-Maru receive the entire commodore's percentage in addition to his captain's purse? Or ... ?

Nifesh found an immediate target for his anger, staring down at the QE specialist standing beside Admiral Beatty. "What are you smiling about, Specialist?" Nifesh snapped.

The specialist bowed his head slightly, saying, "Nothing, my lord." But Admiral Beatty observed the specialist's grin stretching his lips even with his head inclined, evidently untouched by the fury directed toward him.

"Go wait for me outside," Admiral Beatty ordered, and the specialist bowed, exiting the room. This was no time or place for any hint of levity, and Beatty shook his head marginally, wondering at the idiot's smirk.

Of late, Beatty thought to himself, more than one member of the Strand's Fleet staff expressed an unseemly degree of regular ebullience. With Fleet's recent setbacks—excepting the fresh triumph at Delta Three—there seemed very little to be cheerful about ... so why all the damned smiles lately?

Acknowledgments

Beyond those who lent support in the creation of *The Deep Man,* several kind souls helped *The Silent Hand* take wing. They include William Lee, Branden Miskell and Zeke Williams. The assistance and patience of Rebekah and Aubry, Gray Rinehart of Baen, and Kimberley Cameron of Kimberley Cameron & Associates continues to be utterly invaluable.

About the Author

Although born in the northwestern United States, **Michael Mersault** spent his formative years in a series of magical locales including expat communities in the Middle East, a secretive air base in the Arizona desert, and an Alaskan fishing village.

These endless hours of travel prompted an enduring love for books that continues unabated.

At times in his adult years, he has dabbled in kickboxing, competitive marksmanship, and international business ventures. He now lives as a semi-recluse back in the northwest, where he fluctuates between the path of a confirmed technophile and a neo-Luddite.